T0359198

HISTORICAL

Your romantic escape to the past.

A Wager To Win The Debutante
Eva Shepherd

The Lady's Proposal For the Laird
Jeanine Englert

MILLS & BOON

A WAGER TO WIN THE DEBUTANTE
© 2024 by Eva Shepherd
Philippine Copyright 2024
Australian Copyright 2024
New Zealand Copyright 2024

First Published 2024
First Australian Paperback Edition 2024
ISBN 978 1 038 92180 2

THE LADY PROPOSAL FOR THE LAIRD
© 2024 by Jeanie Englert
Philippine Copyright 2024
Australian Copyright 2024
New Zealand Copyright 2024

First Published 2024
First Australian Paperback Edition 2024
ISBN 978 1 038 92180 2

Published by
Harlequin Mills & Boon
An imprint of Harlequin Enterprises (Australia) Pty Limited
(ABN 47 001 180 918), a subsidiary of HarperCollins
Publishers Australia Pty Limited
(ABN 36 009 913 517)
Level 19, 201 Elizabeth Street
SYDNEY NSW 2000 AUSTRALIA

MIX
Paper | Supporting
responsible forestry
FSC
www.fsc.org   FSC® C001695

A Wager To Win The Debutante

Eva Shepherd

MILLS & BOON

After graduating with degrees in history and political science, **Eva Shepherd** worked in journalism and as an advertising copywriter. She began writing historical romances because it combined her love of a happy ending with her passion for history. She lives in Christchurch, New Zealand, but spends her days immersed in the world of late Victorian England. Eva loves hearing from readers and can be reached via her website, evashepherd.com, and her Facebook page, Facebook.com/evashepherdromancewriter.

Visit the Author Profile page
at millsandboon.com.au.

Author Note

A Wager to Win the Debutante is the first book in the Rakes, Rebels and Rogues series and features Thomas Hayward.

Thomas made an appearance in *Miss Georgina's Marriage Dilemma*. He was so contemptuous of his sister's reasons for marrying that I thought he deserved to fall prey to love himself and be forced to deal with its turmoil and unexpected consequences.

When complete cynic Thomas meets dreamy, sentimental Grace Lowerby, he finds himself fighting off an unwanted desire to protect her. But he soon discovers there is more to this debutante than meets the eye, and she is more than a match for the jaded businessman.

Thomas's friends from school, Sebastian Kingsley and Isaac Redcliff, make up the trio of rakes, rebels and rogues, and their own love stories will be coming soon.

I hope you enjoy reading *A Wager to Win the Debutante*. I love to hear from readers. You can reach me via my Facebook page, Facebook.com/evashepherdromancewriter, or through my website, evashepherd.com.

DEDICATION

To the staff at South Library Christchurch.
Thank you for supporting the Word X Word
writing group and tolerating the sometimes
noisy discussions, the raucous laughter and the
occasional silent periods of intense writing.

Chapter One

Like most little girls, as a child Grace Lowerby loved fairy tales. When her nanny had read her those enchanting stories, she would disappear into a fantasy world, one where she was swept into the arms of a handsome prince and danced the night away at a magical ball. She would picture him pledging his undying love and taking her away from harsh reality. With him by her side, no one would ever criticise her again and her grandmother would finally find it in her heart to truly love her only grandchild and everything would be right with the world.

Once she was old enough to read for herself, she did not stop indulging in her love of fairy tales, or imagining herself as a princess, loved by all for her beauty and majestic elegance. It was *The Princess and the Pea* that most captured her imagination. She simply adored the story of the ordinary girl who was revealed to be a princess. One day she, too, would be transformed. The world would no longer see her as the daughter of a woman who had shamed her family by marrying a man beneath her, but as a beautiful princess worthy of admiration.

When she reached the age of eighteen and was presented to Queen Victoria, along with all the other debutantes, she was certain her fairy tale was about to become a reality. She was not a child any more and was no longer so silly as to think she actually was a princess, or that she would marry a prince. Such things did not happen in real life, but she was certain she would have her dream Season and had her heart set on marrying a handsome duke and making her grandmother proud.

And she knew exactly which duke would be her husband: Algernon Huntingdon-Smythe, the Duke of Hardgraves. He was by far the most eligible man available and, despite never having met the Duke, she knew for certain that by the end of the Season they would be man and wife.

In preparation for finding the best possible husband, her grandmother had described every eligible man, their background, their interests, their achievements and admirable features. This was to ensure she could engage in captivating conversation sprinkled with fitting compliments sure to pique their interest.

Of all the men discussed it was the Duke of Hardgraves who had the highest number of achievements and the longest list of admirable features. He was noble, from an illustrious family noted for its chivalry. In other words, he was perfect in every way.

The arrival of an invitation to attend the Duke's ball, the very first ball of the Season, hosted at his Kensington address was all the proof she needed that she was about to embark on an enchanted Season.

Every time she looked at the crisp white invitation emblazoned in gold with the Duke's crest, excitement fluttered through her. She saw it as a private message from the Duke to herself, telling her that he, too, was waiting for their romance to begin.

* * *

On the night of the ball, as she stood in front of her grand-mother dressed in her flowing ivory silk gown embroidered with tiny pink roses, her nervous anticipation grew with each passing minute. She placed her hand on her chest and stom-ach to try to calm her pounding heart and rolling stomach.

'Stand up straight, for goodness' sake,' her grandmother commanded, eyeing her up and down. 'And turn around slowly so I can see how you look from every angle.'

Grace moved in a slow circle, loving the feel of the cool, soft fabric draped against her legs and the way it caught the light and appeared to shimmer as she moved. She really did feel every inch like a princess ready to meet her prince, or, to be more accurate, a future duchess ready to meet her handsome duke.

'Yes, you are certainly pretty enough,' her grandmother said, more as a statement of fact than a compliment.

The fluttering of her heart increased. Her grandmother had never called her pretty before. She never made idle compliments. In fact, Grace had never received a compli-ment from her before, so it must be true. She was pretty.

'Stop that twirling and listen to me.'

Grace did as she was told, delighted by the way the long silky train of her gown continued to elegantly swirl around her feet after she had come to a halt.

'Tonight, you must remember at all times that you are descended from a noble family. Your grandfather was an earl. I am a countess. You can trace your family back to the time of Queen Anne when she created the first Earl of Ashbridge.'

'Yes, Grandmama,' Grace responded in answer to the familiar speech.

'You must forget all about the shame your mother brought on this family.'

Grace could say it would be easier to forget about it if her grandmother did not keep reminding her, but she would never question anything her grandmother said. To even think of doing such a thing merely showed what an ungrateful child she was, one who should know better.

'Yes, Grandmama,' she said instead.

'Now you have the opportunity to redeem the family name and make a good marriage.'

'Yes, Grandmama,' she repeated as the speech continued in its usual vein. 'That is what I hope to do.'

'Hmm,' her grandmother said, which was as close as she ever came to approving anything Grace did or said.

'I intend to marry the Duke of Hardgraves.' Grace's heart seemingly jumped into her mouth. It was the first time she had expressed this ambition out loud and she waited in dread for her grandmother's response.

Her grandmother's eyes grew wide in surprise, causing Grace's heart to thump louder. Then she narrowed them in thought.

'A duke in the family,' her grandmother mused, tapping her chin with her forefinger. She lowered her finger and smiled. A rare event, one that caused Grace to smile in response.

'And why not? Our family is as esteemed as any that will be present tonight, more so than many. You are a pretty little thing and your dowry is certainly generous, very generous indeed.' She nodded her head, looking Grace up and down as if weighing up her ability to perform this task.

'You have to marry a titled man, so why not reach for the highest position available? Yes, I believe, if you do everything right, there is no reason why you can't marry a duke.'

Grace's heart soared with pleasure at her grandmother's approval. This had to be a good sign that all her dreams were about to come true.

'Remember all you have been taught. At all times your focus must be entirely on the Duke as if he is the most fascinating man in the room, which of course he will be. Smile at him, laugh at anything amusing he says, but not too loudly.' She frowned at Grace in admonition as if she had already broken that rule.

'No, Grandmama,' she said, expressing her shock that she would ever do something so gauche.

'You will have to make a good impression immediately and stand out from the other debutantes, so join his circle as soon as we are introduced. And the moment you do get his attention, all your conversation must be about him. Ask him questions about himself, especially ones that allow him to show himself off in the best light. Compliment him when appropriate and, if he asks you about yourself, keep your answers brief and your eyes lowered, so he can see you will be an obedient and compliant wife.'

'Yes, Grandmama,' she said, lowering her eyes in the appropriate manner.

'Good.'

Her grandmother performed one last inspection, handed Grace her fan and they briskly left the house, climbed into the carriage and set off across London to the Duke's home.

Grace was rarely allowed out in the evenings, it being inappropriate for a young lady to do so before her coming out, and she so wanted to see all the sights that were unfolding before her. But she saw little of the bustling London streets outside the carriage window. She was too consumed with a mixture of excitement and trepidation.

This was it. Just like Cinderella, she was off to the ball and tonight was the night her life would change for ever.

Their carriage joined the throng lining up to drop off the guests outside the Duke's elegant, three-storey town-house, which shone out like a beacon in the tree-lined street. Warm yellow lights glowed at every window, music flowed out through the open doors and already a large crowd of elegantly dressed men and women were making their way up the steps, laid with a deep red carpet to protect the la-dies' evening slippers.

Grace's hand moved to her heart to calm its jittering, and she smiled at the magical sight.

'Didn't you hear a word I just said?' her grandmother snapped.

Grace immediately focused on her scowling grand-mother. She was right. Grace had not been listening. That was so remiss of her.

'Stop smiling like that. A lady does not show her teeth when she smiles. It makes her look like a horse.'

Grace's beaming smile disappeared. 'Sorry, Grandmama,' she said and adopted the correct demure smile.

'That's better,' she said, eyeing Grace carefully. 'You won't disgrace me tonight, will you?'

'No, Grandmama. Of course not.'

'I hope you realise that good looks alone are not enough. Your mother was also pretty and could have had the pick of any man. But she was disobedient and stubborn. She threw all her advantages away and ruined everything. You won't be like that, will you?'

'No, of course not, Grandmama.' Grace was shocked her grandmother thought she even needed to ask such a thing.

'Your mother married beneath her. You won't do that, will you?'

She shook her head, then smiled slightly. 'I will make you proud of me, Grandmama, and become a duchess.'

'Good girl.' She smiled, and warmth radiated through Grace at the unfamiliar sign of approval.

'It's such a shame your dear grandfather won't be here to see it,' she said, touching the edge of her eye to wipe away a non-existent tear. 'Your mother's disobedience broke the Earl's heart, but you will be the one to make things right.'

'Yes, Grandmama,' Grace repeated.

The slow-moving carriage came to a halt directly outside the Duke's home and the footman opened the door.

'Right, chin up, shoulders back,' her grandmother commanded.

Grace assumed the correct posture, took the footman's hand, stepped down from the carriage and, keeping her head high, walked up the path and into the Duke's home.

They made their way to the crowded ballroom and paused at the top of the stairs while they waited to be announced. Grace smiled with genuine joy and, despite her excitement, ensured her smile remained the requisite level of demure.

The ballroom was even more magnificent than she had imagined. The row of silver chandeliers suspended from the high, gilded ceiling were all adorned with countless candles that sent shimmering light over the room. Ferns and enormous bouquets of flowers lined the walls, providing a delightful floral scent, and the music from the orchestra seated on the minstrel gallery above the dance floor filled the air.

Her gaze moved to the fashionably attired guests circulating the room and her smile died. This was something she had chosen not to think about. When she was presented to the Queen at Kensington Palace, there had been many other attractive girls present. She should have realised they, too, would be attending the same balls as her. The room appeared packed with young ladies, many of whom were much prettier than Grace. They were all dressed in beautiful gowns equally as elegant as Grace's and, she had to admit, they all appeared much more confident than she ever could.

'Chin up,' her grandmother snapped out the corner of her mouth, while still smiling politely.

Grace immediately lifted her chin and adopted her own polite smile.

The steward announced them. Controlling her nerves as best she could, Grace walked down the marble stairs, in what she hoped could be described as an elegant and sweeping manner. The Duke was waiting at the bottom, and Grace found it all but impossible to look into the eyes of the man she was to marry.

With as much composure as she could muster, she performed a low curtsy and, summoning up every ounce of courage she possessed, she willed her eyes to rise and meet his, desperate to see how he would react to the sight of his future bride.

His gaze moved slowly up and down her, an assessing expression on his face, one she had often seen on the face of the family's estate steward when he was considering the purchase of livestock. Then, to Grace's horror, he looked away at the next young lady lined up.

Something was very wrong. This was not how their first meeting should go.

Why hadn't there been an immediate spark of recognition between them? Why hadn't he looked at her with interest, affection and even dawning love? And why hadn't her heart taken flight at the first sight of the man she was to wed?

Had she been dismissed as unworthy before the night had barely begun? That could not be.

Her grandmother took her arm and led her away.

'That did not go as well as expected,' she whispered discreetly so only Grace could hear. 'But you've been introduced now. All you have to do is get his attention so that he asks you to dance.'

Grace's forced smile quivered. It was wonderful her grandmother still had such faith in her, but after that first meeting Grace suspected it was misplaced.

The attraction between them was supposed to be immediate, just like in the fairy tales. It shouldn't be something Grace had to orchestrate.

How on earth was she expected to attract the Duke's attention? How was she to get him to ask her to dance? And how was she to become his fairy-tale bride if she couldn't hold his attention even during their introduction?

For the first time since she had decided she was going to marry the Duke, she wondered about the wisdom of her plan.

Thomas Hayward avoided society balls like the plague. When he did attend, it was always under sufferance. And attending a ball hosted by Algernon Huntingdon-Smythe, the Duke of Hardgraves, caused him to suffer even more than usual. There was only one thing that would drag Thomas to the Duke's home and find him standing at the edge of the dance floor, stifling a yawn.

It wasn't for the debutantes, all lined up in their pastel colours, like pretty unpicked flowers. It certainly wasn't for the conversation, which made a wet weekend with his maiden aunts seem amusing and scintillating in comparison. And it wasn't to mix with the aristocracy. He'd experienced enough of his so-called betters at the prestigious and ridiculously expensive school his father had enrolled him in to last him a lifetime.

No, he was here for one reason only, to get the Duke of Hardgraves to sign the documents he'd had in his possession for over a month now and surrender large tracts of his Cornwall estate over to Thomas's family firm.

He shook his head in disbelief as he watched the Duke, surrounded by those pretty, pastel debutantes and their equally ambitious mamas. They were drawn to the unmarried Duke like proverbial moths to a flame. If they could see the state of his finances, Thomas wondered if they'd still be as enamoured by the imbecile.

Probably, Thomas admitted with despondency. He'd learnt the hard way at school that a title counts for more than intelligence, skill, wit, or any other quality one could name, and was certainly more important than something as uncouth as a healthy bank balance.

He pulled his fob watch out of his jacket pocket and flicked open the cover. It was still only ten o'clock. It was painfully obvious what the Duke was doing. He was hoping to make Thomas suffer, just as he had attempted to do at school. Nothing gave the Duke more pleasure than to put the son of a wealthy industrialist in his place. The Duke had failed to do so at school, again and again, but apparently that did not stop him from continuing to try.

They had been rivals from the moment Thomas had arrived at boarding school, a sad and lonely seven-year-old missing his family dreadfully. On his first day, the Duke had tried to give Thomas, 'that no-account upstart', what the Duke called 'a hiding he would never forget'.

Neither of them did forget that fight, but not for the reasons the Duke had expected. But that resounding defeat had taught the Duke nothing. Throughout their school years, he had continued in his fruitless quest to beat Thomas at games, at lessons, at everything, anything, something. And he never did learn that one simple lesson: being born an aristocrat was not enough. Winning took skill, skills that did not come automatically with a title.

Now he was prevaricating in another futile attempt to put *the no-account upstart* in his place. And once again the Duke would fail. Thomas knew the Duke's precarious financial situation. He would have no choice but to sell the land and Thomas was offering more than a fair price.

He looked around the ballroom and wondered if anyone else had noticed the empty sconces missing precious artifacts or the gaps on the walls where paintings had once hung, all sold off to fund the Duke's gambling and extravagant lifestyle. And if he continued to host lavish events such as tonight's ball, his finances were going to become ever more perilous, particularly if he followed his usual course of action and retired to the card room as soon as possible, where he would undoubtably lose more of the money he didn't have.

Thomas shook his head slowly in amazement at the folly of men such as Huntingdon-Smythe. They still thought they lived in a world that no longer existed. They had not adapted to the modern world and believed owning vast amounts of land and a large country home was enough to ensure you remained a wealthy man. Like their ancestors before them, they thought all they had to do was sit back and let the money created by other people's labour roll in.

He took another look at his watch. This was becoming beyond tedious. He'd wait another half an hour, then the deal would be off. There was other land that would serve his needs, even if it was the Duke's land he really wanted.

It perhaps did not make good business sense to offer so much more than the rival railway companies for the Duke's land, but, after all the Duke had put him through at school, taking his land was going to give him so much satisfaction it was worth spending the extra pounds.

He released the yawn he'd been trying to suppress and looked around the room. The group of fluttering debutantes surrounding the Duke continued to grow, the band continued to play and time continued to slowly tick by.

He could, he supposed, pass some time dancing. There were certainly plenty of attractive females in the offing. But really, what would be the point? Despite the elegance of the ornate ballroom, despite the expensive gowns and the murmur of polite conversation, this was little more than an auction room, where everyone was attempting to get the best marriage offer available.

All those young women were in search of husbands and he was most certainly not in need of a wife, and, if he was, he would not find one among this privileged, self-entitled lot.

While several of the attractive young things had sent glances in his direction to express their interest, they had been quickly called to order by their ambitious mamas. They were after a man with a title for their daughters and that excluded him from the ranks of desirable husbands.

Only those whose families were desperate for money would be pushed in his direction and the last thing he wanted in a wife was a vacuous ninny who was prepared to lower herself by marrying a member of the nouveau riche to save an aristocratic family from the horror of having to earn a living.

He watched in sardonic amusement as yet another debutante attempted to join the coterie swirling around the

Duke. From across the room an elderly woman was urging her on with the flicking of her hands and angry glares. As pretty as the debutante was, with her artfully styled blonde hair and big blue eyes, she looked far too sweet and uncertain to enter that particular fray.

The huddle of debutantes compacted closer together, like a rugger scrum around the ball, blocking in the Duke and preventing the newcomer access.

The poor thing looked so out of her depth. Despite his disdain for the aristocracy, Thomas couldn't help but have pity for her. She flicked another look in the older woman's direction, then lifted her chin, squared her shoulders and smiled coquettishly. It did her no good. She remained on the outskirts of the circle, blocked by an impenetrable row of silk and satin backs.

A small gap opened behind the Duke and the little blonde moved quickly to fill it. Thomas had to give the newcomer points for her fast movement. Like a good tactician she had seen a weakness in the opposing side and had not let that opportunity pass her by.

She was in, for all the good it was doing her. The Duke's back was to her. She was all but invisible to her quarry. Thomas considered what her next move might be. Whatever she tried, it was not going to be easy. She was either going to have to somehow manoeuvre the entire pack of young ladies so they circled around the Duke, placing her in the front, or get the Duke to turn around. Both were tricky strategies requiring a level of dexterity he suspected was beyond this obvious novice.

Thomas once again glanced down at his watch and saw that the Duke's time was up. He looked over at the trapped debutante and wished her every success with whatever ploy she chose. He did not particularly care if the Duke noticed her or not, but he was grateful that for a few moments she had provided him with some much-needed entertaining diversion.

The Duke looked up from his harem, but it was not Thomas who had caught his eye. The Earl of Sundervale was summoning the Duke from the other side of the ball-room and pointing towards the card room.

Thomas gritted his teeth. That did it. He would not wait a minute longer, not while the Duke gambled away what little money he still had with his cronies.

Not bothering to say a word of explanation to the twittering debutantes, the Duke turned and pushed his way out of the throng. In doing so, he somehow brushed up against the little debutante. Thomas heard her small squeal as she skittered on the highly polished parquet floor on her satin slippers.

Her hands flew up into the air, circling as if looking for something, anything to hold on to as she fought to steady herself. Thomas winced as she hit the floor with an unseemly thud, landing in a pile of lace and embroidered silk.

Oblivious to the mayhem, or not caring, the Duke strode off, while the throng of debutantes erupted into giggling, their mockery barely disguised by their fluttering fans.

It seemed upstarts such as himself were not the only ones who could be made victims of a pack of aristocrats after blood. When the opportunity arose, they'd also turn on their own.

Ignoring the retreating Duke, Thomas strode across the floor, placed himself between the fallen young lady and the giggling pack and offered his hand to the blushing debutante.

Her head remained lowered as she placed her hand in his.

'Thank you,' she murmured, her face so red he could almost feel the heat radiating off it as she rose to her feet.

Thomas rarely danced at society balls, but for this poor creature he would make an exception. He hated bullying, having experienced such cruelty at school, and it was something he would never countenance. He needed to get this young lady away from those mocking debutantes and try to redeem her dignity or they would make the rest of her Season a living hell.

'If your dance card is not full, I would be honoured if you would grant me this waltz,' he said, bowing his head as if her embarrassing fall had never happened.

The giggling halted, but the debutantes continued to stare at them over their fans, their looks gleeful, as if anticipating more entertainment.

She gave a small nod, not meeting his eye, and he led her away from the pack.

'I thought you said her name was Grace Lowerby,' he heard one debutante say. 'More like Graceless Lower-Born,' she added, causing giggling to erupt again.

'Ignore them,' he said. 'Lift up your head and pretend nothing they are saying can possibly affect you.'

She gave a small gasp that sounded like a suppressed sob. He hoped and prayed she would not start crying. To do so would give those bullies their victory and only have them baying for more.

He placed his hand on her slim waist, lifted her limp hand and placed it on his shoulder, and looked over her still lowered head as he waited for the waltz to begin. From the far side of the room, he caught the eye of Algernon Huntingdon-Smythe, watching them with studied interest.

Thomas knew that look well. The Duke was nothing if not predictable. Like a spoilt child, for whom a toy only became interesting when another was playing with it, the Duke now wanted the young woman in his arms.

He pulled her in slightly tighter, wrapped his arm further around her waist, and smiled down at her as if she was all he desired in a woman. He had no doubt what would happen next. The Duke would pursue her, determined to have what he thought Thomas wanted. She would get her revenge on those merciless debutantes and there was nothing Thomas enjoyed more than getting the better of bullies.

Chapter Two

It was all over before it had even started. After such a display, Grace knew she would never win the heart of the Duke, or any other man. From now onwards she would be known as the gauche woman who had taken a humiliating fall and no one would want to be associated with her.

Graceless Lower-Born.

Lady Octavia's words echoed in her ears. It was exactly what she was, graceless and lower born, and her dreams were now completely shredded. And worse than that, her grandmother was going to be furious. It was up to Grace to restore the family to its rightful place in society. She *had* to marry well. She *had* to have children who were titled. And now that would never happen.

Any vitriol that came her way from her grandmother would be well deserved after such a shameful performance from *Graceless Lower-Born.*

If only this man hadn't made things so much worse by asking her to dance. She would much rather have fled the ballroom, found somewhere quiet and private to cry out all the tears she was holding back and brace herself for the onslaught of her grandmother's disapproval and disappointment.

Instead, here she was, in the middle of the ballroom, where everyone could see her and laugh at her disgrace.

Her cheeks continued to burn as she stared at the buttons on her dance partner's waistcoat. Lift your head up high, he had advised her. Grace doubted she would ever lift up her head again, certainly not in public.

As soon as this dance was over, she would run away, maybe join a convent or sail off to some far-flung country where nobody knew her. She wasn't entirely certain what course of action she would take, but one thing she knew for certain: she would never, ever attend another ball.

She just had to get this dance over with first. Still staring at the buttons on her partner's maroon waistcoat, she focused on the tiny stitches of the silver embroidery and the delicate buttons. How she had ended up in this stranger's arms she had no idea. Her mind was a blank from when she had hit the floor until she was moving around the dance floor.

Had he asked her to dance? He must have. But who was he? She ventured a look at his face, gasped and once again stared back at his waistcoat buttons. The sight of him did nothing to assuage her discomfort and her cheeks did the seemingly impossible and burned even hotter.

She was in the arms of the most handsome man she had ever seen. Dare she admit it, even more handsome than the Duke, whom she had considered the epitome of the dashing, fairy-tale prince.

She flicked another quick look upwards, then just as quickly looked down. While the Duke was blond with blue eyes, this man had black hair, deep brown eyes and what some would consider unfashionably olive skin. And there was something else about him, something almost wild, that was decidedly attractive, albeit also decidedly unsettling. She dared yet another peek.

He was no dashing prince from a fairy tale, but she

could picture him in a tale of pirates on the high seas, the wind blowing through that coal-dark hair, or one of high-waymen holding up passengers with his pistols raised. She could see him causing maidens to swoon as he ripped the jewels from around their necks, because he was certainly causing her to become light-headed.

This devilishly handsome creature had seen her fall and, instead of laughing, ignoring her, or dismissing her as being too graceless and low-born to bother with, he had actually asked her to dance. She hoped he was a duke, a viscount or an earl. Then he would be perfect. This would be perfect. He could be the man of her dreams. The one who had saved her and would now sweep her away into her very own fairy tale.

She slowly lifted her head again and this time attempted to smile. She gave up on that immediately, her quivering lips making it an impossibility.

'Allow me to introduce myself,' he said, his deep voice decidedly piratical, causing a little shiver to run up and down Grace's spine. 'I am Thomas Hayward, at your service.'

She waited for him to continue, to inform her of his title. He said nothing. Did that mean he possessed no title? Her grandmother had made her read and reread *Debrett's* until she had committed to memory every member of the British peerage and their lineage, but she could not recall the name Hayward.

All her hopes deflated. He had no title. It was nice that he had rescued her, but it was to no end. Her grandmother would be further incensed. Not only had she made a complete fool of herself, but then she had gone on to waste her time dancing with a man she could never wed.

But there was nothing for it now. She *was* dancing with

him and the least she could do was be gracious to a man who was kind enough to dance with an ungainly bumbler such as her.

'I'm pleased to meet you,' she said. 'I'm Miss Grace Lowerby.' She nibbled on her top lip, then remembered that was yet another uncouth action her grandmother had warned her she was prone to and immediately released it.

'I'm the granddaughter of the Earl of Ashbridge,' she added, so he would know she wasn't entirely Lower-Born, even if she had proven herself to be Graceless.

'I'm pleased to make your acquaintance, Miss Lowerby,' he said as he swept her around the floor. He really was a rather sublime dancer. This was the first time she had actually been in a man's arms, the dancing instructor at her finishing school excluded. And it did feel rather nice. There was something safe about being held by him and, as he was an untitled man, she had no need to impress him. That was some consolation, she supposed. She could just relax and enjoy the dance before she had to face the inevitable wrath of her grandmother.

'Are you a friend of the Duke?' she asked, clinging on to the last vestige of hope.

Maybe that was the role he would play in her quest to capture the Duke's heart. He would be the friend who helped her grow close to the man who would soon be her husband. Maybe, just maybe, all was not yet lost.

He laughed as if she had made a joke, which she most certainly had not.

'Friend might be an exaggeration,' came his unexpected reply.

Grace tried not to be too disappointed. While he might not be the Duke's closest friend as hoped, they were surely associated in some way. After all, he had been invited to this ball. And even an associate could play a role in a fairy tale, couldn't he?

They continued to dance in silence for a moment until Grace remembered her manners. 'Oh, and thank you for, you know, for...' Her voice trailed off as her cheeks burned a hotter shade of red.

He shrugged as if her complete mortification was something easily forgotten. 'I'm sure no one apart from me and those debutantes noticed.'

'And the Duke of Hardgraves,' she added quietly.

'No, I don't believe he saw what happened.'

'How could he have not noticed?' she blurted out, her voice affronted. 'He had inadvertently caused me to fall and had been right beside me when I'...when I...' She shrugged, something else her grandmother told her never to do, but in the circumstances, it was surely the better option than once again restating her humiliation.

'I believe the Duke was more interested in departing to the card room.'

She frowned. That couldn't be true. The Duke was a noble man, both from birth and breeding. He came from a long line of aristocratic men who were noted for their chivalry and courtly manners. Her grandmother had regaled her with tales of how his family were once knights of yore, fighting in battle beside their King. Surely if the Duke knew what he had done he would have been conciliatory and charming and she would now be dancing with him instead of Mr Hayward.

'I suppose you're right. If he had seen what happened, he would not have just walked away.' Yes, that explained it. A noble man would always help a lady in distress, even one who has shown herself to be a clumsy dolt. This was good. The Duke hadn't seen. All was not lost.

'Perhaps,' he replied somewhat ambiguously.

'But you saw?'

'Yes.'

'So if you saw, everyone else in the ballroom must have seen as well,' she said, cringing inside. 'Even if the Duke did not.'

'No, I saw what happened because I was watching you.'

Heat once again rushed to her cheeks and this time consumed her body, but it was heat of a different order. It wasn't embarrassment. She wasn't sure what it was, but knew it was in reaction to the realisation that this sublimely attractive man had been watching her.

'So why were you trying to get the Duke to notice you?' he asked.

Surprise replaced her unfamiliar reaction to the thought of him watching her. How could he even ask such a question?

'He's a duke,' she said, stating the obvious. 'The only Duke present here tonight. Well, I mean, the only unmarried Duke.' It would horrify her grandmother to hear her say such a thing so boldly, but as Mr Hayward would never be a marriage prospect Grace could see no reason for going against all her etiquette lessons, just this once. And he did ask. It would surely be impolite not to answer.

'And do you know the man?'

'No, I was introduced to him for the first time tonight, but my grandmother does and she says he is a man of impeccable character. He can trace his family back to Tudor times, you know?'

'Yes, so he has told me, many, many times.'

'So you *are* friends with the Duke,' she exclaimed. She was right. He *would* be the close friend who would act as the go-between and bring her and the Duke together, although she suspected go-betweens were not supposed to be so handsome that their good looks were somewhat of a distraction.

'We went to school together,' he replied, the tense look on his face not quite as effusive as she would have expected from her future go-between. 'It was the Duke who gave me a lifelong abhorrence of bullies such as those debutantes and taught me how to deal with them.'

She smiled at him. A genuine, satisfied smile. The Duke had helped him. That was just how her grandmother described him, as someone gallant, honourable and admirable.

'And one of the things he taught me was you can never show fear in front of a bully,' he continued. 'They feed on it. With those debutantes, you need to ignore everything they say to you, no matter how painful. If they think they have hurt you, it will only make their behaviour towards you even worse. If they believe you are unaffected, they will lose interest.'

She looked over at the group of debutantes, watching her from the side of the ballroom and her body tensed at the thought of the cruel things they were no doubt saying.

Graceless Lower-Born, dancing with an untitled man, is that the best she can do?

'Relax,' Mr Hayward said. 'Lift your head proudly and I'd recommend laughing now as if you are having a glorious time.'

She looked up at him, into those deep brown eyes. Despite everything, she *was* having rather a pleasant time. It was nice being in his arms, very nice indeed. And while he did not have a title, he was undeniably the best-looking man in the room. That was sure to be something those debutantes would not have missed.

She did as he suggested and gave a little laugh, then the ludicrousness of her false laugh struck her and her laugh became genuine. She was laughing at herself for laughing and at the absurdity of her situation.

'That's better,' he said. 'And the debutantes are not the only ones watching you.'

She bit her bottom lip in an attempt to stop herself laughing. Such behaviour would not have been missed by her grandmother. As she well knew, a young lady should never laugh loudly in public. She had already committed so many unforgivable faux pas tonight. She did not need to add to the growing list her grandmother was no doubt tallying up.

The thought of that lecture brought the laughter to a complete halt as dread gripped her.

Once this dance finished, Grace could see herself being dragged out of the ballroom, driven home immediately and, once home, made to stand in silence in front of her grandmother as she was regaled with a list of criticisms and recriminations, of how she was such a disappointment, how she was no better than her mother, how she had proven tonight she was the daughter of a man who was a no-account nobody. Maybe her grandmother would give up on her entirely and she would be cast out and made to fend for herself.

She closed her eyes and prayed that she would not start crying and further humiliate herself.

'There is no need to look so upset, Miss Lowerby. You have now achieved your goal and have the undivided attention of the Duke.'

Her eyes sprang open and she stared at him. He must be jesting and it was a cruel jest she would not have expected from a man she had taken to be kind and considerate.

'I suggest you don't make it too obvious, but if you look towards the French doors under the minstrel gallery you will see he is watching you.'

She flicked a hasty glance in that direction and nearly tripped over her feet once again. Mr Hayward's arm immediately moved further around her waist, holding her steady. She was unsure whether it was Mr Hayward's touch or the sight of the Duke watching her, but she was suddenly decidedly dazed and bewildered.

'I believe you are about to make those debutantes very jealous indeed and get the revenge you deserve,' Mr Hayward said as the waltz came to an end and he led her off the dance floor.

Her heart thudding hard in her chest, she sent another furtive look in the Duke's direction. He was crossing the dance floor and coming straight towards her. She covered her mouth with her gloved hand to suppress a gasp.

'Thank you for that dance, Miss Lowerby,' he said as she continued to stare in the direction of the Duke, her disbelief mounting with every step he took towards her. 'You are about to get what you *think* you want. I just hope it is what you *really* do want,' he added somewhat cryptically just as the Duke reached them.

The Duke bowed low. 'Hayward, are you going to introduce me to your lovely companion?' he said, his eyes firmly on Grace. She had to be dreaming, but if she was, she hoped she never woke up.

'Miss Lowerby, may I present Algernon Huntingdon-Smythe, the Duke of Hardgraves,' Mr Hayward said, his voice decidedly laconic, as if being presented once more to such a man was not the greatest honour possible for Grace.

She gave her lowest, most elegant curtsy, similar to the one she had performed when presented to Queen Victoria, and she had to admit, this was even more exciting than that auspicious occasion.

'May I have the honour of this dance, Miss Lowerby?'

the Duke said, taking her arm before she had the chance to reply. Not that he needed to wait for her answer. She was hardly likely to say no or claim to have promised the next dance to another, not when her future husband had made such a request.

'We need to talk,' Mr Hayward said, his voice moving from laconic to stern.

'Not now, Hayward, I'm about to dance with the enchanting Miss Lowerby. Come to my house party this weekend. We can talk then.'

Enchanting. He had called her lovely and now enchanting. Could this evening get any better?

'I'll be inviting Miss Lowerby and her grandmother as well. I do hope the two of you will be able to make it.'

Grace was hardly able to answer, she was so breathless with excitement. 'I'd be honoured,' she finally gasped out.

'Good, I will see you then, Hayward,' the Duke said and led her out on to the dance floor.

They lined up for the polka and when the Duke placed his hand on her waist she looked over at the teasing debutantes. As expected, they were all staring at her, scowls on their otherwise pretty faces. If one actually could turn green with envy, she was sure they would all now be resembling a row of moss-covered trees.

She almost felt sorry for them. Almost. How could they not be jealous of her success? The Duke had danced with no other young lady tonight, but he was dancing with her.

The music started and they moved off in time with the jaunty tune. This was it. This was the start of her magical future. She was in the arms of a duke. All her dreams were coming true.

Chapter Three

Thomas watched the Duke lead Miss Lowerby around the dance floor. The young lady was smiling fit to burst and the Duke wore that familiar, smirking expression. They both looked as if they had just won a great victory—the Duke because he believed he had bested Thomas by taking the object of his affections off him, Miss Lowerby because she was dancing with the most sought-after man in the room.

She was such a sweet young thing and he wished her every happiness, although whether she would get it with the Duke remained to be seen. And whether the Duke's interest would continue once he discovered Thomas was not pursuing her also remained to be seen.

He cast a look in the direction of the debutantes who had teased her so unmercifully and smiled to himself. They, too, were watching the Duke and Miss Lowerby as they moved around the floor and it was easy to read their thoughts.

Good. Nothing gave Thomas more satisfaction than seeing bullies get their just deserts.

His gaze was drawn back to the dancing couple. He should leave now. The Duke had made it clear he had no intention of signing those papers tonight. Instead, he'd have to attend a damn weekend party. He was tempted to tell the Duke to keep his land, but it would give him far too much satisfaction to watch the man put his signature at the bottom of the document and sign over land that had been in his family for generations to a man he considered a no-account upstart.

And as much as he loathed the idea of spending any more time in the company of vacuous aristocrats talking about the weather or the latest social scandal, Miss Lowerby would be there and he was not averse to her company.

He watched her smiling at the Duke and an image of a gambolling lamb being led happily to the slaughter entered his mind, before he pushed it away. She was not his responsibility. It was not up to him to protect her, especially from something she wanted so badly.

But she was an innocent. He shook his head slowly as he remembered those blushing cheeks. He doubted he had ever seen a young woman turn such a bright shade of red. When he'd first taken her in his arms, she had been unable to even look at him and her body had been rigid with mortification.

But then she had relaxed and he had to admit dancing with her had been rather pleasant. There was something soft and soothing about her. Perhaps she'd even be capable of smoothing the harsh edges off Hardgraves, although he suspected it would take even more than Miss Lowerby's gentle nature to do that.

And there was no denying she was pretty. When that flawless complexion wasn't blushing a shade of bright red it was like fine porcelain and when her petite body wasn't stiff with embarrassment it was delightfully curvaceous. Only a blind man would fail to miss those full, cherry-red lips that appeared to be almost pouting.

It must have been her beauty that had drawn his gaze

to her in the first place, even if he had been unaware of it at the time.

If she wasn't a debutante, he'd be interested, very interested indeed. But she was a debutante, an innocent young woman destined to remain innocent until she made a suitable marriage.

He cringed at the thought that it might be the Duke who tasted those sweet lips for the first time, who was able to explore the curves of her delightful body, who had the right to take her to his bed and make her his own.

Again, none of his business.

He looked towards the beckoning door. He should leave Miss Lowerby to her quest of finding a husband and adjourn to one of his usual haunts, where the women were just as attractive and had no interest in becoming anyone's wife, or were already married and seeking some pleasurable diversions with men such as himself.

His gaze returned to Miss Lowerby and the Duke. Yes, he should go. He had already done enough for that sweet young thing. He'd got her out of an embarrassing situation. He'd captured the Duke's attention for her, which had led to him dancing with the young lady and given those bullying debutantes their comeuppance.

Yes, all and all, he'd done more than enough for Miss Lowerby.

The Duke smirked in Thomas's direction as his hand slid further around Miss Lowerby's waist.

A tightness gripped his chest. He drew in a deep breath and consciously released his hands, which had unaccountably curled into fists.

This was ridiculous. It was time to leave. It was obvious the Duke would not be signing those papers tonight and it was obvious he thought he was taunting Thomas by being overly familiar with Miss Lowerby.

Instead of watching this ludicrous display, he could retire to one of the many gentlemen's clubs of which he was a member. Instead of standing on the side of the dance floor, he could be savouring a glass of brandy and enjoying the charms of a beautiful woman who was far from innocent and chaste. Yes, that was where he should be, in the company of a woman who did not indulge in absurd mating rituals like the ones on display in this ballroom, a woman who wanted no more from a man than to give and receive pleasure. In other words, exactly the type of woman he was attracted to and whose company he enjoyed.

There was nothing keeping him at this ball now, yet he stayed, unable to look away from the dancing couple.

Keep your smiles demure and dignified, Grace reminded herself, a ruling that would be easier to abide by if she wasn't so gloriously happy.

Tonight was now beyond magical. She was in the arms of the Duke of Hardgraves, being whirled around his magnificent ballroom. It was almost impossible to believe that after her humiliating tumble that such a thing could happen. She had danced with the most handsome man in the room, now she was dancing with the most eligible. It was a shame they were not the same person, but to expect that would surely be being far too greedy.

The Duke spun her in a circle. He wasn't quite as skilful a dancer as Mr Hayward, but he was a duke—what did it matter whether he was a superb dancer or not?

She looked towards Mr Hayward and smiled in thanks. He did not smile back. Her own smile faltered slightly. No. It mattered not what Mr Hayward thought, all that mattered was that she was more joyous than she would have thought possible.

She looked towards her grandmother, whose smile was even brighter than Grace's. This was all so marvellous. There would be no lectures, no recriminations, she was a success and would be rewarded with her grandmother's approval.

Her gaze took in the cluster of debutantes, standing near the spot she had fallen. They were still glaring at her and she did exactly what Mr Hayward had suggested, raised her chin in an act of defiance and let them know that nothing they could do or say could possibly hurt her.

Then she turned her full focus back to the Duke and sent him her best smile, the one she had been forced to practise until it was the perfect coquettish smile of an available young debutante. Unfortunately, it was wasted as he was not looking at her, but staring over her shoulder.

Panic gripped her stomach. Was his interest waning already? Had another debutante caught his eye? This could not happen. He had said she was lovely, enchanting. He could not have tired of her already. If she was to keep him interested, she had to continue to amuse him and make him see that she was his perfect duchess. But how was she to do that?

The pain gripping her stomach intensified as the lessons she had learnt in finishing school whirled through her mind. How was she supposed to keep a gentleman's interest? She could remember nothing of those lessons the tutors had drummed into their students. Her grandmother's words of wisdom, imparted before the ball, came thankfully to mind.

Compliment him. Focus all conversation on him. Flatter him and keep smiling. The last one would not prove difficult. Now she had to put the others into action.

'The ballroom looks simply divine.'

The Duke made no response.

'It's like being in a fairy tale.'

'Hmm,' was the disappointing response the Duke finally gave. 'I saw you dancing with Hayward,' he added.

'Yes,' she said, there being no other answer to that statement of fact.

'Hmm,' he repeated.

'I believe you and Mr Hayward know each other from schooldays,' she said, fighting to keep the conversation going. That was surely in line with the rules of polite conversation. Her grandmother had said it was important to encourage the man to talk about himself and to remain interested in everything he had to say. The Duke had raised the topic of Mr Hayward and she was also interested in hearing more about him and his friendship with the Duke. Not that it mattered what Grace was interested in, but talking of Mr Hayward would certainly make conversation easier.

'We attended the same school, but we hardly mixed in the same circles,' the Duke said with a slight sniff. 'He's not one of us, you know.'

'I see,' Grace said, not entirely sure what that meant. Was he referring to Mr Hayward's lack of title? And if that was the case, would the Duke consider Grace to be not *one of us* either? Or was he including her in his circle? In which case, he had paid her a compliment.

'His family's new money, you know,' the Duke continued. 'Grandfather or something was a baker, or maybe a butcher or a candlestick maker.' He gave a bark of laughter at his own joke.

She forced herself to keep smiling and even managed the required titter at the Duke's witticism, trying not to wince at the implication of his words. Did the Duke know that her father had been a piano teacher and was that more amusing than a butcher, baker, or candlestick maker?

'It's wrong, so wrong that a man like that should have attended such a prestigious school,' the Duke went on, almost as if talking to himself. 'It should be reserved for the sons of the very cream of society, not the riff-raff.' He gave a derisive laugh.

He looked down at Grace and she made her practised smile, pleased he was talking to her, even if the conversation was making her uncomfortable.

'But you can rest assured we put him in his place quick smart,' the Duke added. 'We let him know, no matter how much money his father had, he would never be good enough for us.'

The tightness gripping Grace's stomach moved up to include her chest and shoulders. Hadn't Mr Hayward said the Duke taught him how to deal with bullies? The Duke could not be a bully, could he? Her grandmother had said he was admirable, honourable and a man worthy of his position in society. No, he could not possibly be a bully. She must have misunderstood. And he had invited Mr Hayward to this ball and to his house for the weekend. He wouldn't do that if there was any animosity between the two men.

'Did you enjoy dancing with him?' The Duke's piercing look suggested this was no innocent question and Grace was unsure how to answer.

'He's a very accomplished dancer,' she said tentatively.

The Duke sniffed. 'I suppose even a tradesman can dance.'

Grace did not know what response was required. She had never danced with a tradesman so did not know. All she knew was she had enjoyed every minute she had been in his arms. Nor had she had to worry so much about every word she said the way she was with the Duke.

'I'm so looking forward to the weekend party at your estate,' she said, changing the subject on to a less confusing one, one about which she could be completely truthful. 'I hear your estate in Cornwall is one of the finest in the country.'

The Duke thrust out his chest and smiled at her. She smiled back, knowing she had said the right thing.

'It's one of the largest in the county, with more than ten thousand acres, and has been in the family since the fifteenth century, since the time of the first Duke of Hardgraves.' He barked another laugh, but this time did not sound amused. 'The Haywards' estate might be bigger, but they bought it, you know, furniture and all, from some aristocrat or other who had fallen on hard times.'

Grace suppressed a sigh. She had failed to turn the conversation away from Mr Hayward and now she was once again unsure what she was supposed to say. So she took the safest option and just smiled.

'They're absolute scavengers, you know. Can't be trusted.'

Grace continued smiling, although the smile was becoming somewhat strained.

'I so love the polka, don't you?' she said in desperation.

'Hmm,' came his dismissive response. 'Oh, look,' the Duke added, his voice once again animated. 'The cad has finally turned tail and run.' He barked out another laugh while looking over her shoulders.

He spun her around so she could see what he was talking about. Mr Hayward was walking towards the door. He was leaving. A peculiar sense of abandonment washed through Grace. Why she should feel that way she did not know. She hardly knew Mr Hayward and she was now dancing with the man she hoped one day to marry. That was all that should be concerning her. And hopefully, with Mr Hayward's departure, the Duke might speak of other things.

'He had been watching us the whole time, you know,' the Duke said with an air of satisfaction.

'No, I didn't realise,' Grace said as her heart gave a strange jolt. Mr Hayward had been watching her dance with the Duke, just as he had been watching her when she took her unfortunate tumble. All that time, she had been under the gaze of those dark brown eyes.

'The bounder knows when he's beaten, what,' the Duke said, his voice triumphant.

Grace had no idea what he meant, but assumed a smile was required, so that was what she gave him.

The dance came to an end. The Duke led her off the dance floor to where her beaming grandmother was waiting.

'Your Grace,' her grandmother said with a low curtsy.

The Duke gave a small bow of his head. 'If you'll excuse me, ladies, I believe the card room is calling.' With that, he turned and strode away.

His curt goodbye did not dampen her grandmother's excitement.

'Oh, my dear, dear girl,' she said, causing Grace's heart to swell. Her grandmother never used such terms of affection. Such approval was so reassuring and wiped away any remaining confusion caused by her conversation with the Duke or the thought that Mr Hayward had been watching her.

Her grandmother lightly brushed a curl beside Grace's cheek, her face becoming serious. 'You have done so well tonight and redeemed yourself admirably from that early unfortunate incident. That…' she swept her hand towards the site where Grace had taken her tumble '…is something we will never mention again. Nor will we talk about you dancing with that Hayward fellow.' Her grandmother's smile returned. 'Because tonight you are a triumph. The Duke has danced with no other this evening. Only my granddaughter.'

'And he is to invite us to a house party next weekend.'

Her grandmother's eyes grew enormous, as did her smile, which revealed both sets of teeth, a behaviour Grace had repeatedly been told never, ever to do.

'No young lady does that...not unless she wants to look like a horse.'

Should she remind her grandmother of her words? No, of course not—to do so would require a great deal more courage than Grace possessed.

'My dear girl, I could hug you right now.'

Grace's smile grew so large she was in danger of doing her own horse impersonation.

Her grandmother had never hugged her. Well, she still hadn't, but had said she wanted to. Throughout her lonely childhood she had longed for her grandmother to take her in her arms and show her some affection. Maybe, just maybe, she would do so on her wedding day when she became a duchess.

'And Mr Hayward has also—'

'I said we do not speak of that man,' her grandmother said sharply.

'No, Grandmama.'

Grace had merely been going to inform her grandmother that Mr Hayward had also been invited to the weekend party, but she would do as her grandmother instructed and not speak of that man again.

That did not, however, mean she would not continue to think about him.

Chapter Four

From the moment the invitation to the Duke's estate arrived, the entire Ashbridge household was dedicated to preparation for the weekend to come.

Grace was made to stand in front of her grandmother for hours on end as she tried on every gown in her wardrobe, along with her day dresses and tea gowns, so only the most flattering could be packed. Her lady's maid was instructed to work on Grace's hair, creating several different fashionable styles, and made to do so again and again, so her technique was perfected.

Each piece of jewellery was taken out of her jewellery box, assessed for its worth and how much it would add to Grace's attractiveness and status.

Clothing for every possible occasion was also packed so Grace would be ready for all eventualities, including horse riding, tennis, croquet and walks in the countryside. No matter what the Duke wanted to do, whether it was planned or spontaneous, Grace would be prepared.

The servants who were to accompany them were given strict instructions that they were to conduct themselves at all times as if they were already from the household of a duchess. Their uniforms were inspected and reinspected, so that no thread, button, pleat or trouser crease was out of place.

Her grandmother had even contemplated taking their carriages so they would arrive in vehicles bearing the Ashbridge crest, reminding the Duke that Grace had a titled background and came from one of the best families in England.

It was only the thought of several uncomfortable days in a jolting carriage that made her change her mind and opt for a more convenient trip by train.

As the days had ticked off and the weekend drew closer, Grace's dread of what was to come increased until, by the time Friday arrived, any possible joy had been stripped away. The weekend had turned into an ordeal that had to be endured with as much fortitude as possible.

Finally, she found herself seated across from her grandmother while the train rocked them through the countryside. Grace tried to keep her apprehension covered by a joyful expression and polite smile. And it seemed to be working, as her behaviour was yet to receive any criticism.

'This is rather exciting,' she said in her most buoyant manner.

'Hmm, I still think it would have been better to arrive in our own carriages,' her grandmother said, looking disapprovingly at the rich upholstery and polished wooden panelling of their first-class compartment. 'But needs must,' she added, as if sitting in these luxurious surroundings was a great hardship.

'Your grandfather would be so proud of you.' She touched the edge of her eye with a lace handkerchief as if to wipe away an imaginary tear, something she always did when she mentioned her late husband. 'Your mother's marriage drove that poor man to an early grave, but this weekend you can undo all the damage she did.' She smiled at Grace. 'I am so proud of you.'

Despite her nerves, Grace forced herself to smile back. She so wanted to make her grandmother proud, but she wasn't married to the Duke yet and so many things could still go wrong. Throughout the week Grace had envisaged the disastrous scenario of being completely ignored by the Duke, or, worse, him courting another. Her grandmother would be livid and Grace knew she would be blamed entirely. Then she would have to face the shameful train ride home listening obediently while her grandmother recounted everything Grace had done and said that had made the Duke reject her.

The thought that Mr Hayward would be present was some consolation and went some way to preventing her rumbling turbulence from becoming unbearable.

Why she felt so comfortable in his company she could not fathom. She would expect a man as handsome as him to unnerve her as much, if not more, than the Duke. Perhaps it was simply because he had no title and was therefore not a man she needed to impress. She could be herself, not worry about saying the right thing, smiling in the correct manner, or behaving with the expected level of demureness. Something she rarely, if ever, had the opportunity to do.

While her grandmother read her book, Grace attempted to soothe her nerves by watching the scenery pass by outside the window, taking in the farms, villages and the busy country stations.

After several hours they arrived at the small station closest to the Duke's home and disembarked on to the busy platform. Porters rushed hither and thither, collecting their trunks and loading them on to the waiting carriages. The driver helped Grace and her grandmother into one, while the servants rode in another with the luggage.

'It's such a shame we have to use public carriages and not our own,' her grandmother said, sniffing in disapproval as she looked at the leather seat, on which people whom she did not know had sat.

As the carriage took them closer and closer to the Duke's home, the tension in Grace's body increased. She would soon have to put on the most important performance of her life and she was unsure whether she was up to the task.

They turned off the country road and drove through the large black-and-gold wrought-iron gates signalling the entrance to the Duke's estate. Then the wheels crunched on the gravel as they travelled up the long drive, under a canopy of oak trees.

'Magnificent, simply magnificent,' her grandmother declared, as the house came into view.

Magnificent was no exaggeration. The three-storey ochre-coloured stone home stood beside a lake and appeared to float on the shimmering water. The countless windows glinted in the early-evening light and large Corinthian columns stood proud beside a portico in front of the grand entrance.

It was a house designed to make a statement. And it was doing just that. Her grandmother's Suffolk estate was so large that as a child Grace had often got lost as she wandered alone through its warren of corridors, but the Duke's home made the Ashbridge estate look small and insignificant.

'And if you do everything right this could all be yours,' her grandmother said, smiling at Grace.

She swallowed down a lump in her throat and attempted to smile back. It had been nerve-racking enough trying to gain and keep the Duke's interest during the ball at his townhouse. To do so when surrounded by this grandeur was going to demand a level of confidence she was certain she did not possess.

'Never forget, you are the granddaughter of an earl,' her grandmother said, sensing Grace's trepidation. 'Your family harks back to the days of Queen Anne. There is absolutely no reason why you cannot become a duchess and all this cannot be yours.' She patted Grace's hand. 'Right, put on your prettiest smile, keep your chin up, your eyes lowered and your shoulders back.'

Grace did as commanded as she stepped down from the carriage. But it was all for nought. The Duke was not there to welcome them.

She lifted her gaze to her grandmother who was far from pleased. The Duke's absence was not a good sign. Did it mean he did not consider them important enough to greet in person?

A servant bowed to them as they entered the great hall and, while he was discussing the arrangements for their bedchambers with her grandmother, Grace took the opportunity to take in the grandeur of the room.

Like the house itself, it was designed to impress. Light shone through the large glass dome two storeys above her head. The cream walls edged in gold and the marble floor gave an opulence to the large space, while the columns added an extra touch of elegance.

The only note of discord in the otherwise harmoniously designed room were the spaces on the walls where paintings had presumably once hung and the empty sconces in the walls that Grace assumed had once housed works of art.

They must have been taken to be cleaned or repaired, Grace assumed.

She followed her grandmother up the sweeping staircase and along the corridor that led to her bedchamber.

'We're late,' her grandmother said to Grace's lady's maid as if it was somehow her fault. 'We should have taken an earlier train.'

'Yes, my lady,' Molly said apologetically, as if she had been the one to decide the timetable, not her mistress.

'Make haste in dressing my granddaughter,' her grandmother continued. 'But ensure she looks more beautiful and elegant than she ever has before.'

Grace and Molly exchanged looks, both wondering how they were to achieve the impossible, but both knowing somehow they would have to do so.

As soon as the door closed behind them, Molly set to work. Grace was bathed and scented, her hair styled to perfection, her corset pulled in so tight she wondered if she'd be able to breathe and the Ashbridge family jewels of diamonds and sapphires draped around her neck, hung from her ears and even placed so they would adorn her hair.

When Grace was ready for inspection, her grandmother was summoned.

While her grandmother looked on critically, Grace turned in a small circle, hoping the pale gold gown embroidered with tiny butterflies in silver thread, with matching elbow-length gold gloves, would get the nod of approval and she would not have to go through the process of undressing and dressing in another of the myriad gowns that had been packed.

'Yes, perfect,' she finally declared, and Grace and Molly both released their held breaths.

'I believe our late arrival might be for the best,' her grandmother said as she hurried Grace out of her bedchamber. 'You'll be able to make an entrance and the Duke will have to notice you. Now, remember, don't talk too much.'

That was an instruction Grace was sure she would be able to follow, the constriction of her throat making the idea of trying to form words seem an impossibility.

They reached the door of the drawing room. Her grandmother stopped and grabbed Grace's arm, her brow furrowed. 'Tonight is the most important night of your life. Under no circumstances are you to appear anything other than a refined young lady of good breeding. Do you understand?'

'Yes, Grandmama,' Grace said, wishing she had the courage to pick up her long swirling train and run as far away as possible.

'Do not, I repeat, do not do anything unrefined. You won't get away with embarrassing yourself a second time.'

'No, Grandmama.' Grace knew she was referring to that incident that was to be never mentioned again, and colour flooded her cheeks at the memory of just how humiliating that had been.

'And if you must blush, do it prettily to show that you are coy and chaste. Do not under any circumstances turn into something resembling a beetroot the way you did at the Duke's ball.'

'Yes, Grandmama. I mean, no, Grandmama.' Grace was unsure what she meant, she just wished her cheeks and stomach would settle down and this awful trial would be over.

'Right. Let's go and capture the heart of the Duke,' her grandmother said and nodded to the footman to open the door.

They entered the drawing room and Grace fought to do as she was instructed. She continued smiling while her stomach churned, tried to look dignified while her heart pounded fiercely against the wall of her chest and fought to stop her cheeks from blushing and turning her into that forbidden beetroot.

'There he is,' her grandmother said quietly while still smiling.

Grace looked in the direction her grandmother indicated and saw the Duke standing beside the mantelpiece, a crystal glass in his hand, surrounded by a ring of talking and laughing gentleman along with several young women, all adopting the same well-practised smile as Grace.

She was presented with exactly the same challenge that had confronted her at the Duke's ball. Her grandmother would expect her to somehow join that group, to dazzle and shine, and, of course, to remain firmly on her feet at all times. It was all too much.

Her gaze flittered around the room, searching for somewhere, anywhere, she could hide. Her wandering gaze halted at Mr Hayward. He was watching her. Her nerves stilled slightly. If only she could rush across the room and take refuge in his strong arms.

He nodded his head in greeting and her forced smile became genuine. It was truly delightful that he was here tonight. It was as if she had a friend, someone who would not be judging her, not putting demands on her, someone who would rescue her rather than condemn her if she failed to behave with the requisite level of elegance demanded of a debutante.

He excused himself from the group of men with whom he had been talking and crossed the room towards her. Her anxiety turned to anticipation and excitement, even though the fluttering in her stomach and warmth flushing her cheeks and body remained the same.

She had been thinking of his dark good looks constantly over the time they had been apart, but it was now apparent her memory did him a disservice. He was more handsome than she had remembered. He was dressed in the same style of black swallow-tailed evening suit as every other man in the room, but on him it looked so much better. Despite the formality, he still bore the appearance of a man who would be more at home on the prow of a pirate ship and his crisp white shirt and cravat added to this image, contrasting with his olive complexion that suggested a life spent outside and not in the confines of drawing rooms.

'Miss Lowerby,' he said with a bow. 'Lady Ashbridge,' he added as he bowed to her grandmother.

'Mr Hayward,' her grandmother said in a distracted voice, still looking towards the Duke. 'I am surprised to see you here this weekend. What brings you to the Duke's estate?'

'I have business with Huntingdon-Smythe.'

Her grandmother turned to frown at Mr Hayward. Grace did not know whether it was the shameless mention of business or calling the Duke by his given name that had caused such offence, but her grandmother was doing nothing to hide a look of distaste.

Mr Hayward smiled as if offending her grandmother was an enjoyable pastime. 'I intend to buy a substantial amount of the Duke's land to extend my family's railway lines to this part of Cornwall.'

Her grandmother's eyes grew larger in shock, before she once again smiled. 'That's very progressive of the Duke to want to open up this area to such modern means of transport. Very progressive indeed.'

Mr Hayward laughed. 'That's one way of looking at it, I suppose.'

'Well, please don't let us keep you,' her grandmother continued. 'I'm sure you have…' she paused, her nostrils flaring '…business to conduct with other guests.'

Mr Hayward bowed and departed. Grace's heart sank. She did not want him to abandon her. Now she was all alone, alone and expected to perform some sort of illusive magic trick and make the Duke fall under her spell.

'All the time that Mr Hayward was speaking to us the Duke was watching you,' her grandmother whispered through smiling lips. 'I had to get rid of that man as quickly as possible. It would not do for the Duke to think we consort with such types.'

Grace took a furtive look in the Duke's direction. If he had been looking at her, he was not doing so now. He was watching Mr Hayward and, like her grandmother, it was with a look of disapproval.

'Keep smiling, Grace,' her grandmother whispered. 'I'm sure he'll approach you soon.'

Grace did as she was told, feeling somewhat silly that she was smiling at nothing.

The Duke did not approach. He remained the centre of a group of fluttering debutantes, many of whom she recognised from the ball. Grace kept smiling, her jaw starting to ache. Nothing continued to happen.

'I don't think he's coming,' she said quietly to her grandmother, still forcing herself to maintain that smile.

'No, I believe you're right. But his focus had been intent on you while we were talking to Mr Hayward.' Her grandmother looked over at Mr Hayward, who was in conversation with a man Grace did not recognise.

'Come with me.' Her grandmother took her by the arm and the nerves flittering in Grace's stomach burst into manic flight. She was about to be thrust on the Duke. Last time she had done that she had ended up slipping over on the ballroom floor and landing in an undignified heap. That could not happen again. It simply could not happen.

She fought to remember her instructions. Smile. Don't laugh loudly. Don't show any teeth. Compliment when appropriate. And do not, under any circumstances, do anything awkward and clumsy like falling over in front of these elegant, sophisticated people.

But they did not head in the direction of the Duke but towards Mr Hayward.

What on earth was her grandmother up to?

Mr Hayward turned to face them. One questioning eyebrow briefly rose as if he was wondering the same thing. Then, as etiquette demanded, he introduced Grace and her grandmother to his companion, who, after a brief exchange of polite conversation, excused himself.

'I was fascinated to hear about your business dealings,' her grandmother said, surprising Grace and, by the look on Mr Hayward's face, surprising him as well.

'And what is it about the railways that particularly interests you, Lady Ashbridge?'

'Oh, all of it,' she replied, not looking at Mr Hayward, but to where the Duke was standing.

'Would you like to hear about the problems with different-sized gauges? Or perhaps you are more interested in the various methods for the transportation of goods. Or maybe you would be excited to hear how the railways will open up more of Cornwall for working people wanting to travel to the seaside for day outings?'

'Yes, yes, that's all fascinating,' her grandmother said, not looking at a bemused Mr Hayward. 'Now, if you'll excuse me, I believe Lady Beatrice is trying to attract my attention.'

Grace and Mr Hayward watched her grandmother bustle across the room and join several older women. This was all very peculiar and Grace could only wonder if the pressure was affecting her grandmother as much as Grace and making her somewhat demented.

'Who would have thought Lady Ashbridge would harbour such an interest in railways?' Mr Hayward said, a knowing look on his face as if this was not a surprise at all.

'Yes, that is unexpected,' Grace said, still watching her grandmother. While she nodded along with whatever the older women were discussing, her eyes were firmly on the Duke. Grace followed her gaze, gave a little gasp at what she saw and immediately turned to Mr Hayward as if seeking sanctuary. The Duke was staring straight at her and his glowering expression was not that of a welcoming host.

'I believe you have once again caught the Duke's eye,' Mr Hayward said, his tone suggesting this was not necessarily a good thing.

Grace gave a tremulous smile, her nerves fizzing not just inside her stomach, but throughout her body.

'I assume your grandmother is hoping you'll do more than just catch his eye this weekend.'

Did she detect a note of bitterness in his voice? If she did, she could not think of that now. She had to prepare herself for the possibility that the Duke might approach her.

Smile, laugh, but not too much. Compliment him...talk only of him.

'And I believe your grandmother has discovered the perfect bait so you can do just that,' he added somewhat cryptically, then he smiled at Grace. She so loved that smile, which helped to soothe her jittery nerves. 'But it is of no matter as it is delightful to see you again, Miss Lowerby,' he added.

'And it's delightful to see you again,' she responded with all honesty and a heartfelt smile.

'Are you looking forward to the weekend?' he asked.

It was time to put all honesty aside and give the expected responses. 'Oh, yes, I've heard there's to be horse riding, croquet and so many other activities.' *And during all these activities I will be expected to shine and impress and show the Duke I am born to be a duchess.*

'So I believe.'

'Do you intend to take part in any of these activities?' she asked hopefully.

'No, I will be leaving once the Duke has signed over his land.'

'Oh,' she gasped. 'That is a shame.'

'Not to worry, Miss Lowerby, I suspect you will be fully occupied this weekend and will hardly notice my absence. Your grandmother obviously expects you to dedicate all your time to landing your prey, hook, line and sinker.'

'Oh, will there be fishing as well? I don't believe we packed for that and, to be honest, I hate fishing. I always feel so sorry for the poor fish.'

His smile turned to laughter, a lovely melodious laughter. 'Miss Lowerby, you are a delight.'

Warmth coursed through her, although she had no idea what she had said that was so delightful, but it was lovely to make him laugh.

'I don't know if there will be fishing, but I do know that everyone in this room is trying to reel in something or somebody.'

'Oh,' she said with some embarrassment, catching the meaning of his words. 'But some of us are better anglers than others,' she added. Grace did not need to look towards the Duke to know he was still surrounded by several pretty young women who were more skilled in the arts of capturing a man than she would ever be.

'You have no need to worry on that account. With your formidable grandmother in your corner I can hardly see how you can fail.'

She looked over at her grandmother, who was nodding at something Lady Beatrice was saying, but watching Grace carefully. Then she looked towards the Duke and, to her horror, she could see he was now crossing the room, straight towards her.

'He's coming,' she gasped out, then blushed, having revealed far too much to Mr Hayward.

'Breathe, slowly and deeply,' he advised. She did what he said, but had only managed one long inhalation before the Duke was at her side.

'Miss Lowerby,' he said with a brief nod of his head.

Her held breath came out with a loud embarrassing gush, causing the Duke to frown. This was not going well, but at least she was still on her feet.

'Your Grace,' she said with a small curtsy.

'I hope Hayward hasn't been boring you with talk of business, acquisitions and accounts.'

'Oh, no, not at all,' she said. 'We were talking about…' She bit her lip. 'About fishing.'

This caused Mr Hayward to smile, and she smiled back at him, until she caught the Duke's look of disapproval and drew her features into a more composed countenance.

'Fishing, eh? Didn't know you fished, Miss Lowerby. My estate has several of the finest fishing rivers in this part of the country, you know. Love it myself. If you wish, I can take you fishing tomorrow.'

Grace's stomach did an unpleasant flip. She had been taken fishing once as a child and had hated it. She had even burst into tears when the little fishy had been pulled out of the water, gasping and flapping around, and had begged for it to be returned to the river where it could swim happily away. And now she would have to prove to the Duke it was something she loved as much as he did.

'That's the beauty of owning ten thousand acres,' the Duke continued. 'You have plenty of land so you can fish, shoot, hunt and ride to hounds.'

Shoot? Ride to hounds?

Every inch of Grace's body tensed as she tried to come up with an excuse, any excuse, to get her out of those repugnant activities. Fishing was bad enough, but as for killing innocent little birdies and chasing terrified foxes across the countryside—those activities were abhorrent to her.

'I'm afraid you can't take Miss Lowerby fishing tomorrow,' Mr Hayward said before she had time to formulate an answer that would save her from such a terrible fate. 'She has agreed to take a walk with me so I can show her where the new rail line is to be installed.'

The Duke's lips curled in disdain while relief swept over her. Mr Hayward had saved her once again, this time from the horror of having to kill defenceless little fish and the embarrassment of exposing her abhorrence for blood sports.

'Has she?' the Duke said, his nostrils still flared. 'Has she, indeed? Well, I hope Hayward doesn't just show you where the railway line will go, but also shows you the extent of my estate, which takes in not just the best fishing streams in the county, but also comprises enormous parts of the coastline, several villages, and heavens knows what else. It is one of the largest estates in the country.'

'Then we will have to take a very long walk indeed so we can take in all its wonders,' Mr Hayward said, causing the Duke to smile at the compliment, then scowl.

'Wonders that have been in my family since Tudor times,' the Duke said, a note of venom in his voice.

Mr Hayward gave a small laugh that did not sound amused. 'And some of those wonders won't be in the family for much longer.'

The Duke fixed his glare on Mr Hayward, his fists clenched at his side. She looked from him to Mr Hayward, who was smiling at the Duke in a manner that was almost taunting, then back at the Duke, waiting for his riposte. He said nothing. She looked to Mr Hayward to see what he would do or say next.

'Speaking of losing land, you have some papers to sign,' Mr Hayward added.

The Duke waved his hand across his face. 'Money and business, is that all you ever think about, Hayward? You need to learn to appreciate the finer things in life, the things that money can't buy.' He looked at Grace and smiled. She smiled back, as was required.

Mr Hayward made a dismissive laugh. 'It's lucky for you it doesn't take money for you to attract these finer things, or you'd be struggling, wouldn't you?'

Grace gasped at this insult as the Duke stared at Mr Hayward, his eyes blazing, his fists curled ever tighter. If this look of aggression was meant to cower Mr Hayward, it had no effect. He continued to stare at the Duke, his face impassive.

'Someone needs to put you in your place, Hayward,' the Duke said through gritted teeth.

'I believe you've said that to me before, many, many times, going right back to my first day at school. When do you think that will finally happen?'

The Duke once again looked at Grace. 'Very, very soon.'

Grace waited for Mr Hayward's response. He said nothing. She looked back at the Duke, who was once again staring at Mr Hayward with undisguised dislike.

With her head moving from one to the other, this was starting to feel like watching a rather unsettling tennis match. Or was it more like watching stags during the rutting season, sizing each other up before an attack? Heat rushed to Grace's cheeks at the thought of such a thing and she was pleased the two men were still staring at each other and neither saw her cheeks turn bright red.

'Your Grace… Mr Hayward,' her grandmother said, joining the group.

Both men turned to face her and bowed their heads, still wearing those implacable expressions.

With her grandmother present, Grace knew it wisest to adopt the required sweet smile and a look of interest in everything the men said, particularly the Duke. If her grandmother knew of the level of animosity between these two men she would be outraged and there was the danger she would once again forbid her from being in Mr Hayward's company.

Grace's heart jumped within her chest at that possibility. Being in Mr Hayward's company was the only thing making this occasion bearable. It was so wonderful to talk with him, to laugh with him, and when he looked at her with those deep brown eyes, it was as if there was a connection between them, something intangible, something rather marvellous.

She would almost rather her grandmother forbid her from being in the Duke's company than Mr Hayward's.

Her hand shot to cover her mouth, as if she had expressed that outrageous statement out loud and was desperate to take it back. She looked at the assembled group, fearful that they might have read her mind.

The two men and her grandmother continued to chat in what appeared an almost amicable manner. No one had noticed Grace's inner torment, so she resumed smiling, pleased that in her confused state no more was expected of her.

She looked from one man to the other. Despite the supposedly polite conversation now taking place, there was still that undercurrent of deep-seated discord in everything they said. And what was that reference to money couldn't buy the finer things in life? Were they talking about her? She hoped not. Surely that was not how those two men saw her, as something that could be bought.

She watched her grandmother, smiling at the Duke as if he was the most intelligent, wittiest, interesting man she had ever met, and a horrible thought occurred to her.

Could her grandmother be wrong? Was it the title that she admired, not the man? No, that could not be right. As her grandmother had said, again and again, if a man is at the very pinnacle of society, it is because he is a superior man in every way.

That was why her grandmother was so supportive of her desire to marry the Duke, so she would have the best of husbands and the respect of being married to a man every other debutante had set her heart on.

'I'll bid you two ladies goodnight,' Mr Hayward said, drawing her out of her reverie. 'And I look forward to our walk tomorrow, Miss Lowerby.'

Grace curtsied and kept smiling while looking anxiously in her grandmother's direction to gauge her reaction. Her grandmother was certain to lecture her on the folly of wasting time with Mr Hayward when she was supposed to be pursuing the Duke.

'You are to walk with Mr Hayward tomorrow?' her

grandmother said the moment Mr Hayward was out of ear shot. 'How pleasant.'

What on earth was happening? Everyone this evening was acting in such a peculiar manner and Grace could hardly keep up with what was being said and not being said.

'I would recommend making it a very short walk indeed,' the Duke said with a sneer in the direction in which Mr Hayward had departed, then smiled at Grace. 'Remember, you have promised me a dance tomorrow night.'

Grace could remember doing no such thing, but it was of no matter. If the Duke asked, then of course she would accept.

'Dancing,' her grandmother exclaimed. 'How delightful.'

'Remember, keep the time you spend with Hayward as brief as possible.' And with that final instruction, the Duke excused himself.

Grace braced herself for the inevitable lecture that would follow now that they were out of the Duke's hearing and tried to compose a justification for agreeing to take a walk with Mr Hayward.

'Well done, my dear,' her grandmother said, using that surprising term of affection. 'You are playing this perfectly.'

Grace was unsure how she was supposed to react to that statement. She wasn't playing anything, perfectly or otherwise, but compliments from her grandmother were rare indeed so she would merely accept it as the precious gift it was.

'It will do no harm to encourage Mr Hayward. Nothing piques a man's interest in a girl more than knowing that she is sought after by another. It's a shame that Mr Hayward is not another titled man, but needs must.'

'Yes, Grandmama,' Grace answered in her usual quiet manner, while inwardly dancing a little jig. She was not only being allowed to go on tomorrow's walk, but had just been given permission to encourage Mr Hayward, even if she was unsure what encouraging entailed.

'But just remember, only encourage him so far. It is the Duke's heart you have to win this weekend,' her grandmother added in that more familiar admonishing tone.

Grace was tempted to ask her grandmother how far was too far when it came to encouraging a man, but felt it wise to keep that question to herself. It would not do for her grandmother to think she was pleased to be spending time with Mr Hayward. So she would remain ignorant of the finer details of what was expected when it came to encouragement and just try her best.

Chapter Five

'I believe we have a contract to sign,' the Duke said to Thomas after breakfast the following morning.

Finally.

Once Thomas had what he wanted he could escape this infernal weekend party and get away from these people and all their machinations. It would be a shame to miss his walk with Miss Lowerby, but as she was here to win the Duke it would be no real loss.

Would it?

He paused momentarily as he followed the Duke down the hallway towards his study.

No, of course it would not. He resumed walking. She was not his type in more ways than he could list.

She was a sweet, innocent debutante in search of a titled husband. Every one of those qualities made her exactly the type of woman he avoided. Sweet and innocent were not what he was after when it came to feminine company. The women he enjoyed spending time with were those who flouted the rules of society rather than obeying them to the letter the way Miss Lowerby did. And as for a young lady in search of a titled husband, that put him out of the running on two counts. He had no title and he most certainly was not in search of a wife.

No, his departure was all for the best. He would get the

Duke's land and Miss Lowerby would hopefully get the Duke. And even if she failed in that quest, such an attractive young woman was bound to capture another titled man. Her dance with the Duke at his ball would have been noted by everyone in society, along with this coveted invitation to his house party. That would have drawn the interest of every eligible marquess, viscount, earl and baron after a suitably compliant wife. When it came to finding a husband, she most certainly did not need his help to achieve her goal.

They entered the study, and the Duke collapsed on to the leather chair behind the large mahogany desk. A desk, which Thomas noted did not contain the legal papers they were to sign. It looked like the Duke intended to play yet another of his games before he succumbed to the inevitable.

With a sigh of irritation, he took the facing chair and gave a quick look around the room. Glassed-in bookshelves lined every wall and each shelf was packed with books, none of which Thomas suspected the Duke had ever read. The room carried the lingering smell of cigars and a hint of brandy. That was more likely what this room was used for, as a place where the Duke could pretend he was a man of substance running a well-oiled estate, when, in fact, it was merely another place for him to drink, smoke and while away his endless free time.

But it was of no matter to Thomas what the Duke did with his time. While men like Hardgraves continued to squander the fortunes they had inherited, men like Thomas would continue to profit.

'Right, let's get these papers signed so I can be on my way,' Thomas said, knowing it would not be that easy.

'Not so fast, Hayward, not so fast.'

Thomas swallowed his exasperation, determined not to let the Duke see the effect he was having on him.

'Weekend parties always involve some gambling, so I have a wager for you,' the Duke said, picking up a letter opener and flicking it with his finger.

'You know I'm not a gambling man,' Thomas replied. If he cared one fig about the Duke, he would advise him that he, too, should cease to gamble if he wanted to keep hold of what was left of his fortune. But he did not care even that one proverbial fig for the Duke, so he kept his opinions to himself.

'Oh, I think you're going to want to take this wager.' The Duke stared hard at Thomas, those beady eyes reminding him of a venomous snake he had seen at the London Zoological Gardens, and he suspected, just like the snake, the Duke was planning to strike.

'Miss Lowerby is a rather comely chit, don't you think?'

Thomas's teeth clenched together. So that was what this was about. That should have come as no surprise.

'Indeed,' he replied, not rising to the bait.

'Quite fancy her, do you?'

'I'm not here to discuss Miss Lowerby. I am here to take your land and I am offering more than a fair price for it. You won't get better anywhere else and, as we both know, you need the money.'

The Duke's eyes narrowed further and Thomas regretted the harshness of his tone and the reference to the Duke's precarious financial position. Like a stubborn child, the Duke was liable to cut off his nose to spite his face if he thought he was being insulted and deny Thomas the land.

'Business, that's all you ever think about, isn't it, Hayward?' He looked Thomas up and down as if this was the worst insult he could make on a man's character. 'If you were a gentleman, you would know that weekend parties are about having fun, gambling and entertaining the ladies.'

Thomas could point out *he* was not here at this weekend party for fun, gambling or for the ladies, but he would be pointing out the obvious to the Duke and to antagonise him further would do nothing to shorten these proceedings.

'So I propose we do all three,' the Duke added.

Or we could do none of them and just sign the bloody papers.

'I have a proposition for you. One that involves Miss Lowerby.'

'What about Miss Lowerby?' Thomas snapped back, annoyed at the terseness in his voice.

A satisfied smile curled at the edge of the Duke's lips, as if he had caused Thomas to reveal more than he intended. But his reaction had nothing to do with Miss Lowerby. He was merely irritated by all this unnecessary game playing.

Wasn't he? Yes, of course he was.

'I propose a wager involving her and my land,' he said, a viciously joyful note in his voice. Thomas had heard that tone before many times at school. It usually meant someone weaker than the Duke was about to be hurt.

Thomas clenched his fists tighter. If the Duke proposed anything that would harm that innocent young lady, he would feel the full force of Thomas's wrath, even if it meant losing the land.

'I believe, despite your best efforts, that the young lady knows quality when she sees it and it is with me that her real affections lie. So if by the end of this weekend I have proven that to be true, then I will sell you my land at a lower price. However, if by the end of the weekend she is smitten with you…' the Duke smirked as if this was an impossibility '…then you will have to pay a higher price for my land.'

Thomas forced his face to remain expressionless. Was

the man completely insane? No wonder the Duke was such an appalling gambler if he made bets like this, ones in which even if he won, he lost.

'It will be like a duel that men fought in the good old days when they were allowed to do such things, but instead of swords or pistols at dawn, this will be a wooing duel,' the Duke added, obviously pleased with this imagery. 'One that proves once and for all who is the better man.'

'You're on,' Thomas said, reaching across the desk and shaking the Duke's hand, hardly able to believe the man's stupidity. During their schooldays, Thomas had bested the Duke at both lessons and sports, and had knocked him to the ground on numerous occasions while they were having boxing instructions. Despite that, the Duke could never understand that a title did not automatically make you the better man and it was obvious he still had not learnt that lesson. Now he was so desperate to beat Thomas at something, he would sacrifice his land, even if all he got was the appearance of a win.

So be it. All that would be required of Thomas was to pretend to woo Miss Lowerby, a young lady who had already set her heart on marrying the Duke. Once he had gone through that pretence and inevitably lost her affections to Hardgraves, he would walk away with the Duke's land at a cheaper price than he had originally offered.

The Duke stood up and puffed himself up as if they were about to commence battle. 'Let the best man win the fair maiden's heart,' he said.

Thomas resisted the temptation to laugh in the idiot's face. Not only would losing this bet be to Thomas's benefit, but giving the Duke the impression he was wooing Miss Lowerby would prove no arduous task. In every way, Thomas would come out the winner this weekend.

* * *

As arranged, Thomas met Miss Lowerby at the entrance of the Duke's home so he could accompany her on a walk. And as expected, she behaved in the correct manner of a well-trained debutante and kept him waiting a few minutes. But it was rather worth the wait. If he had to pretend to woo a young lady, he could think of none better than Miss Lowerby. She really was rather lovely and seemed to get more lovely each time he saw her.

Dressed in a pale pink day dress and carrying a lacy parasol in her gloved hands she was as pretty as a picture. She smiled at him. It really was a delightful smile, one that lit up her face and made those big blue eyes sparkle.

He smiled back at her, genuinely pleased to see her and looking forward to their walk around the estate, even if all he would be doing was showing her all that might one day be hers if she did achieve her aim of marrying the Duke.

'Shall we?' he said, offering her his arm.

She placed her arm through his and he led her out through the entranceway and into the formal garden, the dutiful lady's maid following at a discreet distance.

'I dare say the Duke has already told you he possesses one of the most opulent estates in all of England and one of the largest,' he said, unable to keep the sarcasm out of his voice. Thomas had lost count of the numbers of times he'd heard that boast, as if it was proof of the Duke's prowess as a man.

'Yes, I believe he has mentioned that on one or two occasions. Although he said that while his is big, yours is even bigger.'

Thomas laughed out loud. He looked at Miss Lowerby to see if that was a deliberate double entendre, but her innocent smile made it obvious she was unaware of how her words could be interpreted. 'We've never actually got out a ruler and compared, but I'm fairly confident that I have the advantage.'

She smiled politely at a joke she did not understand.

'I take it your grandmother did not object to us taking this walk together?'

Her cheeks coloured slightly. 'I'm afraid I have a confession to make.

He raised his eyebrows. 'You, Miss Lowerby? A confession? What could a young lady such as yourself possibly have to confess?'

'Grandmama has instructed me to encourage your attentions.'

Thomas gave a low chuckle. He was not in the least surprised. That canny old woman had no doubt noticed what would be obvious to everyone except Miss Lowerby—that the Duke wanted what he thought might be denied him.

'And how do you feel about that?'

'Oh, I'm very pleased,' she said with a sincere smile, then her blush grew deeper and she lowered her eyes as if she had done something wrong or revealed too much.

'As am I,' he said, surprised at how true that statement was.

She bit her top lip lightly, drawing his gaze to that rather attractive feature. Soft, full and decidedly kissable, with an intriguing line in the centre of her plump lower lip that gave her an unexpected sensual appearance.

'So how are you going to do that?' he asked, forcing himself to look away from her lips.

'Do what?' She looked up at him in confusion.

'Encourage my attentions?' That teasing question was rewarded with another blush tinging her creamy cheeks.

'Grandmama didn't go into details.' She gave a small, embarrassed laugh. 'What do you suggest?'

'It's not really my field of expertise. Weren't you taught about such things at finishing school? My sister told me that learning how to encourage a man's interest is the only thing a young lady is taught at such institutions.'

'Yes, she's right.'

She thought for a moment, then sent him a pretty smile, one that held a hint of mischief. 'Well, I could flutter my eyelashes at you, I suppose.'

'All right. Let's see your best flutter.'

She stopped walking, attempted to pull her smiling lips into a more serious expression, tilted her head in a coquettish manner, then fluttered rapidly, causing him to once again laugh out loud.

She lightly tapped him on the arm. 'You're not supposed to laugh. You're supposed to be enraptured.'

'So what else do you have in your arsenal so you can reduce a man to a quivering idiot?'

'Well, if I had my fan, I could flutter it lightly in front of my face, hiding all but my eyes.'

'Which presumably would also be fluttering.'

'No, I believe that would be overdoing it somewhat.'

'But there must be something other than all this fluttering you can do. You can't spend all your time looking as if you've got something caught in your eye.'

'I believe you are making fun of me, Mr Hayward.'

'I believe you might be right, Miss Lowerby.'

They exchanged smiles, then she blinked rapidly, not to flutter and enrapture, but to break the gaze which they had held for perhaps a moment too long.

'But you're right,' she continued as they commenced walking. 'Fluttering is not all I've been instructed to do. I could laugh at your jokes.'

'I'd have to say something funny first.'

'Oh, no. What you say doesn't actually have to be funny, as long as it's an attempt at humour.'

'All right, let's pretend I've just tried to make a joke. Let's hear your best laugh.'

Smiling, she placed her gloved hand lightly over her mouth and gave a small titter, a titter which soon turned into a small laugh. Then she was laughing whole heartedly, still trying to cover her mouth with her gloved hand.

'Not like that,' she gasped out as she attempted to stop her laughter. 'No teeth,' she said, failing in her attempt and laughing even more loudly.

'Teeth?'

She laughed herself out, then smiled up at him, a cheeky glint of amusement in her blue eyes. 'A young lady must never show her teeth when she laughs or she is in danger of looking like a horse.'

It was his turn to laugh. 'Whoever said that was a fool. I don't believe I've ever seen a horse laugh.'

'No, neither have I.'

'So, your fluttering has failed to enrapture me. You've committed the unforgivable sin of laughing so hard at my unfunny joke that you exposed your teeth. What else are you supposed to do to encourage my affections?'

'Well, I also have to compliment you.'

'I like the sound of that. Off you go, then.'

Her hand covered her mouth again, but not soon enough for a laugh to escape. 'Why, Mr Hayward, everything you say is so clever,' she said, her laughter making a mockery of her words. 'You are such a learned man it quite shames me to know I am so ignorant by comparison.' This was followed by another round of eyelash fluttering, which caused Thomas to join in her laughter.

'Excellent work. I feel thoroughly complimented and I

particularly liked the flutter at the end which added a certain panache.'

'Why, Mr Hayward, I believe you are flirting with me,' she said, still fluttering those dark eyelashes. 'That's something else we're supposed to say, but it has to be said in a manner that the gentleman knows that you want to be flirted with.'

'And you did it admirably.'

They smiled at each other, and Thomas had to admit laughing with her, teasing her and flirting with her definitely held their attraction.

His gaze lowered to her smiling lips. But she was wrong. If she really wanted to encourage a man all she had to do was pout those lovely full lips, then he would be entirely lost.

Her smile faded and her lips pursed slightly as if she was reading his mind. A jolt of hot desire shot through him as he imagined his lips on hers, his tongue running along that full bottom lip, of her lips parting as he entered her, tasted her, savoured her.

He looked straight ahead.

Where the hell did that come from?

His fevered mind had turned something that was merely harmless fun into something far from harmless. He was supposed to be pretending to woo Miss Hayward. There should certainly be no actual wooing involved, and most certainly no kissing. He did not want Miss Lowerby. He wanted the Duke's land, nothing else.

'But I have another confession to make,' she continued.

'Another one?' he asked, forcing his voice to remain light. He, too, could make a confession about what he had just been thinking, but that was something he would be keeping to himself.

'Well, it's the same confession, but I didn't tell you all my grandmother said. She told me to encourage you as she believes it will further garner the Duke's interest in me. I am so sorry.'

'You have absolutely nothing to be sorry for.' If anyone should be apologising it should be him. Despite enjoying this walk, he was only here for one reason, to get the Duke's signature on that document and, thanks to her, he now had the opportunity to get the land at a lower price than he had been prepared to pay.

But that was something she did not need to know. And surely no harm would come of this. She would get what she wanted. Her grandmother would get what she wanted and Thomas also would get what he wanted. No, nothing was to be gained by making such a confession.

'Your grandmother is right,' he said instead. 'Nothing gets a man's blood pumping faster than a bit of competition.'

That and very kissable lips.

'But it all seems a bit, well, as if we are using you.'

'I'm happy to be used,' he said, meaning every word. Miss Lowerby was not for him, but she was delightful company. She also had an attractive face, decidedly alluring lips and a temptingly curvaceous body. If she wasn't an innocent debutante, he'd be more than happy for them to use each other in every pleasurable way imaginable.

He coughed lightly. 'So your heart is set on marrying the Duke?' he asked, bringing his wayward thoughts back to reality, one in which Miss Lowerby was an innocent young debutante who had to save her innocence for the titled man she married.

'Oh, yes,' she gushed. 'I know I shouldn't say this, but to marry the Duke would make all my dreams come true.'

Thomas's teeth gritted tightly together and his stomach

clenched as if it had taken a punch. Why he should react in such a manner he had no idea. It was what the aristocracy did. They vied to make a marriage that would advance their position in society and no one would advance Miss Lowerby further than the Duke. It was just a shame he was such an oaf who did not deserve a young lady such as she.

'And why would that be?' he asked, annoyed that his tone might be revealing his irritation, but unable to disguise the rancour in his words. 'Is it his wit and intelligence that attracts you? Is it because he is a man of the highest calibre? Is it because he manages his estate with such skill and proficiency? Is it because he demonstrates a high level of integrity in all matters?'

He knew the Duke possessed none of these characteristics. There was only one thing that made him an attractive catch. His title.

He looked down at her, waiting for her answer. Her otherwise smooth brow crinkled in confusion and guilt rippled through him. He should not make sport of her desire to capture a man of the Duke's status. It was what she had been trained for all her life and she would know of no other way to behave.

'What is the dream that you are sure will come true if you marry the Duke?' he asked in a gentler tone.

'It's what I've wanted for as long as I can remember. And it would make my grandmother happy. Very, very happy,' she said quietly. 'And that is what I want, more than anything in the world.'

'And you becoming a duchess is also your grandmother's dream, is it?' That was a question that did not need to be asked.

'Yes.' She nibbled on her lip again and he wished she

wouldn't. He did not need a reminder of how tempting her lips were.

'I don't know if you know much about my unfortunate background,' she continued in that quiet, apologetic manner.

He raised his eyebrows in surprise. He doubted there could be anything in this sweet young woman's background that was unfortunate. In fact, he doubted she even had a background. Young ladies such as she were sheltered from everything until they reached the age of eighteen. Then they were thrust into society where they were measured and compared by all the men in pursuit of a wife.

'Unfortunate?' he probed.

'My father was a piano teacher,' she blurted out as if confessing the most heinous of sins.

He waited for her to continue and reveal her terrible past.

'My mother ran away with him against her parents' wishes.' Her expression was imploring, as if waiting for him to grasp the magnitude of this scandal.

'I see.' It was hardly a crime, but obviously in this young lady's eyes marriage to a piano teacher was an unforgivable act of treachery.

'She could have married anyone, Grandmama says, but she threw it all away.' Her eyes continued to appeal for his understanding.

'And where are these terrible parents now?'

'They died in an accident.'

'I am so sorry,' he said, regretting his jesting description of them as terrible.

'My grandmother kindly took me in. So I owe it to her to pay her back for all she has done for me and to make amends for the shame my mother brought on the Ashbridge lineage by making a good marriage.'

It sounded like a well-rehearsed speech, one her grandmother had presumably made many, many times while she had been growing up.

'Do you remember anything about your mother and father?'

'No, not really. I was only a small baby when they died in a carriage accident.' She looked down and blushed slightly. 'When I was a little girl and exploring my grandparents' estate I found a portrait of my mother that had been put away in the attic. She was rather beautiful and had such kind eyes.'

'Just like you,' he added quietly.

She smiled at him. 'Grandmama has said she was stubborn and disobedient, but she didn't look like that in the portrait. She looked gentle and loving. When I was a child I spent a lot of time up in the attic sitting close to that portrait, especially when I'd done something to displease Grandmama. I'd imagine my mother holding me and telling me how much she loved me.' She looked down at her feet. 'It's silly really.'

'I don't think it's silly in the slightest. And I'm sure your mother would have loved you dearly,' he said, fighting off anger at her harsh grandmother who had failed to see that her granddaughter was sad and lonely.

'But I'm not a child any more,' she said with a sudden determined edge to her voice. 'And I am very grateful to my grandmother and owe her so much. When I was growing up she arranged for a series of nannies to look after me.'

Her teeth clamped on to her quivering bottom lip and Thomas wondered whether she was trying to bite back tears. It was so unfair. Every child deserved to be loved and cared for by their family, not handed over to paid staff who came and went at the whim of their employer.

'And since my debut and my presentation to Queen Victoria, Grandmama has devoted all her time to me.' She smiled at Thomas as if the old lady was bestowing a great gift on her granddaughter, rather than using her to pursue her own aims. 'And before that she did provide me with all the tutors I required so no one would ever know that I had a father who was, well, a…'

'Nobody?'

She bit her lip again. 'I'm sorry,' she murmured.

'No need to apologise. If that's as unfortunate as your background gets, then believe me, you have nothing to be ashamed of. Your father made an honest living and your mother presumably married for love. I can see no shame there.'

Her blue eyes grew wide in surprise. He suspected these were two possibilities she had never considered or, if she had, they were ideas too shocking to be spoken of aloud.

'I'm certainly not ashamed of my background, nor do I see it as unfortunate,' he continued. 'My great-grandfather was a baker. His son expanded the business and moved into other areas of commerce. My father expanded those enterprises substantially, as I intend to do. I'm proud of what they have achieved. Although…' he shrugged '…my father and your grandmother do have one thing in common.'

'They do?' Her eyes grew wider as if she could not possibly imagine that to be true.

'My father wanted a title in the family and he got it. My sister Georgina married the Duke of Ravenswood.'

Miss Lowerby nodded. 'She did her duty by the family. Your parents must be very proud of her.'

This caused Thomas to laugh loudly. 'If you had ever met Georgina, you would know she would never do her duty and, if anyone tried to make her do so, she would take a great deal of pleasure in doing the very opposite. My father was, however, lucky. She fell in love with the Duke he had tried to force her to marry, otherwise it would never have happened.'

'Oh, I see,' she said quietly, her brow furrowed as if she did not really see at all. Then she smiled as if it all suddenly made sense. 'Your sister really did get a fairy-tale ending. It does actually happen.'

Thomas groaned inwardly. She really was a romantic, a sweet, innocent romantic, and he was tempted to let her know what marriage to the Duke would really entail and it would be no fairy tale. But what good would it do? Her heart was already set on the Duke and it was hardly his place to change it.

Chapter Six

Grace was unsure whether talking so freely with Mr Hayward was what her grandmother had meant by encouraging his attentions, but it was rather liberating to not have to watch everything she did and said, and surely it would do no harm. It wasn't as if he could ever be a contender for her hand in marriage.

She had never told anyone about those furtive trips to the attic as a child. Her grandmother would be outraged to know she had ever seen her mother as anything other than the source of the family's shame, but Mr Hayward seemed to understand why she had done it. Perhaps that was why she had told him her secret and why she now had no regrets about doing so.

She sent him another smile as they walked along in silence. Even this comfortable silence was rather pleasant. She closed her eyes briefly, enjoying the gentle caress of the soft breeze on her face, the tweeting of the birds flitting between the trees and the occasional bleating of sheep in the distance.

She felt so light in Mr Hayward's company. Unlike being in her grandmother's company, she was not constantly on her guard to make sure she said or did nothing wrong. Nor was it as taxing as being in the Duke's company where she had to pretend to be exactly the sort of young lady he wanted her to be. She could just be herself with Mr Hayward, although, after years of having to be the person she was expected to be, she had to admit, she wasn't entirely sure who that person was.

It was hard to believe she had actually made fun of her finishing school lessons, but it was so good to laugh, really laugh, without having to worry about how she looked and what impression she was making. She was so thankful to her grandmother for allowing her this precious time with Mr Hayward, even if it was for the rather questionable reason of using him to capture the Duke.

And her confessions had removed a weight that she had been carrying. He would now understand why it was so important for her to marry the Duke. It wasn't just for her own sake. Nor was she being bought by his title. It was because of her debt to her grandmother, a debt that could only be paid by making a good marriage.

It would be nice if she already felt comfortable in the Duke's company, but one day, hopefully, they would be able to spend enjoyable time together, just like this. She looked up at Mr Hayward—perhaps one day he would be walking like this, arm in arm with the young lady he wished to marry and would find the happiness he deserved.

Grace's breath caught in her throat at the thought of this young lady, who, as far as she knew, did not yet exist. Who would she be? Would she be prettier than Grace, more amusing, more accomplished? What sort of young lady would he take as a wife? Grace both wanted and did not want to know the answer to that question.

'Do your parents expect you to make a good marriage, the way they expected your sister to do so?' she ventured, her stifled breath making the words sound awkward.

'Fortunately for me, I cannot bring a title into the family, so I am free to marry whomever I choose.'

'And what sort of woman do you plan to marry?' She forced her voice to remain light, as if this was a question of no real account.

He sent her a quizzical look, and she instantly regretted the question.

'I am sorry, that was forward of me.'

'Not at all. I hope you will always feel that you can ask me anything.'

She smiled, grateful that he had once again made her feel comfortable. 'Well, what sort of woman do you plan to marry?' she repeated, it being the one question she was desperate to have answered.

'If I do marry, and I say if, not when, it will be to a woman who is intelligent and can be a helpmate, rather than one who spends all her days taking tea, gossiping and shopping. She will be a woman I respect and admire.'

'And love?' she asked, her voice little more than a whisper.

He shrugged. 'It's all hypothetical as I have no intention of marrying.'

Grace's breath came easier as that imaginary woman disappeared from her mind, leaving just the two of them walking together and enjoying each other's company.

'You are lucky to have the freedom to choose who you marry and whether you wish to marry or not,' she said, her statement causing her some surprise.

He gave her a considered look. 'Yes, I am, but you also have a degree of freedom.'

'I suppose,' she responded with a small, dismissive laugh. 'After all, I'm not a slave.'

She continued to smile at him, but he did not return her smile.

'No, you are not a slave, nor do you have to marry if you do not wish to do so. Women do have some choices now. My sister has a friend who is an artist, another who runs a successful magazine, another who has established a school for women in the East End of London.'

Her smile died and she stared at him as if he was talking a foreign language. Choices? There was only one real choice for a young lady such as her and that was to marry well.

'You don't have to do anything you don't want to, Miss Lowerby. Remember that. You can make decisions about what sort of future you want.'

'Of course,' she said, unsure what other answer she could give.

Once again they slipped into silence, but this time it was not quite so companionable. What did he mean? She didn't have to do anything she did not want to? She *was* doing exactly what she wanted to. Wasn't she? She wanted to be married and to the best of all possible husbands and that was surely the Duke. And more than that, a good marriage was what her grandmother had always wanted and she deserved such a reward for all that she had done for Grace.

Yes, she hoped to marry a man she loved and while she might not be in love with the Duke, not yet, she was sure, like Mr Hayward's sister, she, too, would grow to love him. She nodded her head to underline this conviction. Yes, that was what she wanted, what she had dreamed of all her life.

They reached a river, over which spanned an ancient arched bridge, moss growing up the pale brown bricks. They paused and looked down at the gently flowing water and the grass banks speckled with flowers.

'Should we return to the house? Your grandmother might be wondering where we have got to,' Mr Hayward asked. 'As might the Duke.'

She looked over her shoulder. He was right. They should return. But it was so pleasant being in Mr Hayward's company. And, she had to admit, it was rather pleasant to be on the arm of a man so sublimely handsome, so charming and, well, such fun.

Her grandmother had instructed her to encourage Mr Hayward in order to capture the Duke, so to spend a little bit longer in his company would surely be what was expected of her.

'But you told the Duke you were going to show me the land you wish to purchase from him,' she said. 'We are yet to see it.'

He raised his eyebrows slightly. 'It's on the far side of these fields and there's not much to see.'

'Still, I'd like to see where the railway will run.'

'As you wish.'

Arm in arm, they crossed the bridge and walked over a grassy field. As they passed a flock of sheep, they lifted their woolly heads from their grazing, assessed the passing couple as being no threat and returned to their contented munching.

It would be so lovely if they could continue on this walk indefinitely and she did not have to go back to the house where so much was expected of her. But after a few minutes Mr Hayward came to a stop and stood looking at the land that appeared no different from any other part of the field.

'This is it. As I said, there is nothing much to see.'

He was right, but she was still pleased they had spent this extra time together.

'Shall we return now?' he asked.

'What is it about this bit of land that makes you wish to buy it?' She was not especially interested, but was determined to delay the inevitable, even if for a few moments longer.

He pointed towards the horizon. 'It's a direct route to the coal mines owned by my family. At present we're having to put the coal on barges to transport it to the nearest rail depot. When we lay tracks over this land, we'll be able to run trains directly from the mines to the port.'

'So it will be much more efficient?'

'Indeed.'

She looked around at the contentedly browsing sheep. 'But where will the sheep go?'

'As you can see, the Duke does not run a particularly large flock, so this loss of land will hardly make any difference. And sheep are not as profitable as they once were. Cheaper wool is imported from the colonies and inefficient farms such as this can't compete.'

'I see.' She bit her lip, about to ask a question she should not. 'Is that why the Duke has to sell the land, because it's no longer profitable?'

'Hmm,' he said as if considering how much to reveal.

She tilted her head in encouragement.

'Unfortunately, the Duke has not learnt that the way in which his family has farmed for centuries, or rather, the way in which his tenants have farmed, is outmoded.'

'But wouldn't it be better to change the way you farm, rather than sell off land that you'll never get back? If he keeps selling off bits here and there, eventually he'll have no land and no way of making money.' She looked over towards a group of cottages, presumably where the tenant farmers lived. 'And what will the people who work on the land do if that happens? Where will they go?'

She looked to him for answers. He was gazing down at her with an expression she had not seen before, not from the Duke, not from her grandmother, not from anyone. It was as if he was taking what she had to say said seriously.

'You are completely right, Miss Lowerby. Unfortunately, men like the Duke seldom realise that, or, at least, not until it's too late.'

'Unfortunate for them, but fortunate for men of business like yourself. I hope he is at least getting a good price for what he is selling off.'

'I have offered the Duke a fair price, although thanks to you I'm hoping that by the end of this weekend I will have made an even better deal for myself.'

'Thanks to me?'

'Yes, I believe you might be my lucky star.'

She smiled, flattered that he should see her in this light.

'But would it not be better if I was your unlucky star?' she said with a laugh, so he'd know she was teasing. 'After all, I should be trying to help the Duke get a better price for his land.'

'I can see you have a good head for business. If you do marry the Duke, I'll have to watch out for that if I make any future deals with him.'

If she married the Duke.

Why was that prospect no longer filling her with such excitement? It couldn't possibly be because of Mr Hayward, could it? Surely not. Yes, she enjoyed his company and, yes, he was the most handsome man she had ever met, and she was flattered that he chose to spend time with her, but it was the Duke she had set her heart on.

Mr Hayward was, of course, kind and undeniably companionable and these were qualities she had yet to see in the Duke, but surely a man as eminent as the Duke would possess such virtues as well. Then, of course, there was her surprising reactions when Mr Hayward looked at her, that strange fluttering that erupted in her stomach, that quickening of her heart, the shortness of breath. But surely she would eventually feel that way about the Duke as well.

And none of that mattered anyway. He was wholly unsuitable. She knew that and her grandmother certainly knew it. They would not be standing together looking at an empty field if her grandmother did not see this walk as part of the plan for her to wed the Duke.

And her own plan, of course, she reminded herself. Marriage to a titled man was what she had longed for since she was a little girl. It was what she lived for and now that opportunity was within her grasp. Any other ridiculous thoughts needed to be pushed firmly out of her head.

'Perhaps we should go back to the house,' she said, knowing it was the right thing to say, even if it was not entirely what she wanted to do.

'What? Have you had enough of staring at an empty field that will one day be a railway track?'

He smiled down at her and, despite her confusing thoughts, warmth enveloped her as she looked up at those smiling eyes, then down to those beautiful lips. And they *were* beautiful. What would it be like to run her finger over their sculptured edge, to feel their softness under the pad of her finger?

The lips stopped smiling and her gaze moved back up to his eyes. As if transfixed, she stared back into his deep brown eyes. Her heart pounding loudly in her chest, blood surging through her body, she knew she wanted to do more than just touch his lips with her finger. She wanted to feel them against her own lips, for him to take her in his arms and kiss her. She wanted to feel his body against hers, his arms around her holding her tightly.

'You're right,' he said, his voice husky and unfamiliar. 'We should return to the house.'

'Yes, yes, of course.' She forced herself to look away. What on earth was wrong with her? She should not be having such thoughts about any man other than the man she wished to marry and, even then, not until her wedding night. And she most certainly should not be having them about Mr Hayward. It was beyond shameful and she could only hope he had no idea where her mind had unaccountably strayed.

He took her arm again and they retraced their steps, her lady's maid still trailing several yards behind them.

Grace attempted to steady her breathing, tried to bring her still rapidly beating heart to order and to stop thinking of how her lips had tingled, nor how her body had throbbed as she had stared into his eyes.

Forgetting such unfamiliar, unforgivable reactions would be so much easier if she was not so close to him. So close she could feel the warmth of his body. So close she could even smell the crisp citric scent of his soap and something else, a musky, underlying scent that was, oh, so masculine. She breathed in gently, loving the way that scent filled her up. Despite her commands not to do so, she inched closer to him.

No further words were exchanged as they once again crossed over the arched bridge and finally walked up the gravel path towards the Duke's looming house. As they drew closer Grace could see two shapes waiting for them at the entranceway: her grandmother and the Duke.

Seeing the two of them brought reality crashing down. She instantly moved further away from Mr Hayward and, if it wasn't such a rude thing to do, she would have dropped his arm so no one would suspect the guilty thoughts that had possessed her. If her grandmother had any inkling of what she had been wanting to do only moments earlier, she would be horrified, not just because they were inappropriate for a young lady to have such desires, but because she'd had them for a man who had no value as a potential husband.

As if about to be punished, Grace braced herself, even though she knew her grandmother could not possibly know what she had been thinking or feeling. They drew closer to the house and Grace could see that her grandmother was smiling. Her tight shoulders relaxed. She breathed easier, but that did not mean she should not be on her guard to ensure she never, ever had such a reaction to any man again—any man, that was, except the Duke.

'Did you have an enjoyable walk?' her grandmother said as soon as they reached the top of the steps.

'Yes, Grandmama,' she answered in the expected manner.

'Good. Then you'll have to tell me all about it over a nice cup of tea.'

After saying their goodbyes to the Duke and Mr Hayward, she followed her grandmother into the ladies' parlour. The moment the door closed behind them, her grandmother took hold of her, still wearing that delighted smile.

'It's working, my dear, it's working,' she said, her words coming out in a rush. 'The Duke was beside himself, wondering why the walk was taking so long, where you had gone and what you were doing.'

'And that's good?' Grace asked.

'Of course it's good. He definitely wants you now and I suspect it won't be long before he's asking for your hand.'

Grace forced herself to smile. She should be delighted. Of course she was delighted.

'So should I keep encouraging Mr Hayward?'

'What? No, I think he's served his purpose now.'

'Oh.' Grace tried to ignore the clenching in her chest.

Her grandmother tapped her chin in thought. 'Well, yes, maybe. If the Duke's interest does start to wane, then encourage him by all means.'

'Yes, Grandmama,' Grace said with a smile.

'Otherwise, have nothing to do with Mr Hayward.'

'No, Grandmama,' she added, clinging on to the hope that the Duke's heart had not been captured, at least not yet.

'Pleasant walk?' the Duke asked as he followed Thomas up the stairs. Was the man going to trail behind him all the way to his bedchamber?

'Perfectly nice, thank you. It's good of you to enquire,' he responded, his voice dripping with sarcasm.

'I'm not an imbecile, Hayward,' the Duke said, causing Thomas to smile to himself. That was news to him.

'I could see the blush on her cheeks and the sparkle in her eyes. It's that look chits get when they're ripe for the picking.'

Thomas stopped walking and turned to face the Duke. The Duke took a step backwards down a stair and raised his hands in a parody of surrender.

'Don't get so upset. I was merely going to say you had the advantage of making the first move. While you may have won this hand, the game isn't over yet. Believe me, I still have a few cards up my sleeve.'

Thomas released an irritated sigh at the laboured metaphor.

'Tonight there will be dancing and by the end of the evening little Miss Lowerby will be mine,' the Duke added with a supercilious smile.

Thomas could inform him that Miss Lowerby was already his. She had been his since before they had even met, but instead he asked, 'Will the dancing take place in the ballroom?'

The Duke's supercilious smile died, as Thomas knew it would. While the ballroom at his Kensington home was pristine, the one at this estate was reputed to be in a desperate state of repair and would need a great deal of money to bring it back to its former glory, money the Duke would not have until he sold his land to Thomas.

'Not tonight, no,' the Duke said through clenched teeth. 'We are a small group of only twenty or so. The blue drawing room provides a more intimate space.'

And doesn't require all those expensive candles to light it. Candles you can ill afford.

'And I take it after you have made your play, we can declare a winner and you will sign those papers.'

'Don't be so hasty, Hayward. If you knew the ladies the way I do, you would know that wooing can't be rushed.'

Thomas stifled a laugh. Did this buffoon really delude himself into thinking the young ladies pursuing him required wooing? Did he not realise they were chasing his title and cared nothing for the man who possessed it?

'As you wish,' he said instead. 'But by tomorrow a winner must be declared or the bet is off and I will look elsewhere for land to buy.'

He took satisfaction in seeing panic ripple through the Duke at the thought of losing that much-needed money.

'Of course. I'm sure by then Miss Lowerby will see who is the better man.'

'I'm sure she will,' Thomas added and continued walking.

Although that does not mean that it will be the better man she will wed.

* * *

Thomas passed the remainder of the day in his room, seeing to correspondence and other business matters and trying to put Miss Lowerby out of his mind, a task that was proving surprisingly difficult. The thought of that sweet, trusting young woman married to that cretin was a torment. But any intervention from him would not be welcome and was sure to prove fruitless.

He paused in his work and looked out the window. There was one action he could take to make her a less desirable catch for the Duke. He could ignore her. Without the incentive of trying to take something Thomas wanted, there was a good chance the Duke's interest would move elsewhere. The man was such a simpleton he was unlikely to appreciate anything or anyone unless someone else wanted it.

But what good would such actions really do? If she didn't marry the Duke, it would be some other titled man and perhaps one even worse than the Duke, if that was possible. And at least she would get to be a duchess. There were certainly advantages to being at the pinnacle of society and, as she said, it was her dream. He just hoped her dream did not turn into a nightmare.

No, he would continue to play along with the Duke's ridiculous plan, endure one more interminable evening, mixing with people he had made a point of avoiding whenever possible and watching the disagreeable sight of the Duke of Hardgraves in the act of wooing the delightful Miss Lowerby.

Chapter Seven

Was it wrong to hope that the Duke's interest did wane, even just a little bit, so that Mr Hayward would once again have a purpose?

That was the question Grace had pondered for the remainder of the day and was still trying to find an answer to when she entered the drawing room for pre-dinner drinks.

The Duke smiled at her from across the room and her heart sank. His interest was not waning, not in the slightest. If anything, it was showing an increased level of vigour. Would that mean Mr Hayward *had* served his purpose? Would she never speak to him again, walk with him, laugh with him?

It should not matter, but the aching in her heart suggested it did matter, a great deal.

The Duke broke from the group surrounding him and headed straight for Grace and her grandmother. 'Miss Lowerby, you are a picture of youthful beauty tonight,' he said, taking her hand and kissing the back. She made the smile she had perfected with many hours of practice in front of the looking glass. One that aimed to be both coquettish and alluring. One she hoped would hide her inner turmoil.

'Thank you, Your Grace,' she said with a curtsy.

The Duke nodded to her grandmother, but his gaze remained fixed on Grace, as if unable to look away.

'And did you enjoy your walk?' he asked, a challenging note in his tone.

'Yes, Your Grace,' she answered, unsure if that was what the Duke wanted to hear.

'My granddaughter was telling me how splendid your estate is.'

Grace had told her grandmother no such thing, but it mattered not. The Duke had been flattered, that was all that was required, even though it was Grace who should have been the one paying him the compliments.

'Yes, quite magnificent,' she added, causing her grandmother to smile in approval.

'Yes, I have ten thousand acres and some of the finest fishing rivers and game reserves in the county,' he said yet again and Grace nodded, smiled and tried to look interested as if she was hearing it for the first time. He continued talking about his estate and Grace was pleased no more was required of her, because, while he was speaking, she was far too conscious of Mr Hayward standing across the other side of the room. She forced herself to keep her focus fixed solely on the Duke and not to look in his direction, but that did not mean she was unaware of him, where he was in the room and to whom he was talking.

Out the corner of her eye, she saw a young lady join his group. Her attempt to maintain a delighted smile wavered and it took every ounce of willpower she possessed not to turn around to see who this young woman was.

He had said he was not interested in marrying, but if he did it would be to a woman who could be his helpmate, one he respected and admired. Did this young lady have those qualities? If only she could find a reason to look in Mr Hayward's direction and satisfy her curiosity.

But it would have to be a very convincing reason to

look away from the Duke. Anything less than an enormous commotion on that side of the room would inflame her grandmother's wrath. After all, *Mr Hayward had served his purpose*. There was no justifiable reason why she should be at all interested in anything he was or wasn't doing, or who he was or wasn't talking to.

The dinner gong rang and the couples lined up to parade down the hallway to the dining room.

'Would you do me the honour?' the Duke said, offering his arm.

She exchanged a quick glance with her grandmother and they both knew what that meant. The honour was all Grace's. That position should have been reserved for the woman present who had the highest title and that most certainly was not Grace.

By taking her arm, he was all but declaring they were a courting couple.

Grace should be ecstatic. This was what she wanted. It was what her grandmother wanted. Her grandmother would now be so pleased with her, she might even hug Grace this time, rather than merely saying she could do so. That was something Grace had longed for all her life. So many times she had tried and failed to make her grandmother proud of her and now she was. She had always dreamed of being courted by a handsome man such as the Duke and now her dream was within her grasp. How could she not be ecstatic?

She sensed, rather than saw, Mr Hayward join the parade on the arm of the young lady he had been speaking to. Who was that woman? What was she to Mr Hayward?

Grace was tempted to turn around to find an answer to her questions or to ask the Duke, but she knew she would do neither.

Mr Hayward had served his purpose. She should for-get all about him. .

So instead she smiled at the Duke and placed her hand on the top of his, all the while fighting to ignore those whirl-ing questions.

The Duke led her to the seat on his right, while her grandmother had been assigned the seat on his left. Once again, he was letting Grace, her grandmother and the as-sembled guests know she was more than just another deb-utante. She was the one he had chosen.

The other guests lined up in front of their place names, with Mr Hayward at the far end of the table.

The footmen held out the seats of the ladies and with much rustling of silk and satin they took their places.

Throughout the twelve-course meal, the Duke continued to talk. Thankfully all he required from Grace was the oc-casional 'Oh, how fascinating!' or 'That is so interesting, Your Grace.' And even for her to once or twice say, 'That was so clever of you.'

At one time she had to bite her lip to stop herself from giggling, remembering her conversation with Mr Hayward when they had joked about such behaviour. With him, con-versation flowed so freely, smiles and laughter came so easily. She so envied the young woman sitting next to him, even though she knew right now she would be the envy of every unmarried young woman in the room.

Despite that, she still wished to know who that young woman was at Mr Hayward's side.

'The table arrangements are simply divine,' she said to the Duke when there was a brief pause in his monologue. Under the guise of admiring the table setting, she tried to look down the table, to where Mr Hayward and that mystery woman were seated at the far end.

More than twenty guests separated them, along with a large floral arrangement in the centre of the table and several tall candelabras made even taller by their flickering candles, all contributing to thwarting her from seeing Mr Hayward's dinner companion.

And as for trying to hear what they were talking about, that was beyond impossible. Any words that might travel down the long table were drowned out by the noise of the guests talking and laughing and the clink of silverware on fine porcelain.

It was a fruitless task, so she turned her full attention once more back to the Duke, where it belonged.

The meal finally over, the ladies rose from the table and retired back to the drawing room, leaving the men to their cigars and brandies. Now she would get her opportunity. The women were all lined up in the order in which they had been seated. Dare she do something as crass as gawping over her shoulder to see which young lady was at the end of the line?

But before she could succumb to temptation, her grandmother took her arm. 'You've done it, my dear, darling child,' she whispered in her ear, barely containing her excitement.

Grace had to think for a moment what exactly she had done to make her grandmother so happy.

'You will soon be a duchess.'

Oh, yes, that. She smiled at her grandmother, wanting to share in her excitement.

They returned to the drawing room and her grandmother rushed over to join her friends, as if bursting to impart the good news and be bathed in their congratulations and envy. Grace watched the group of older women move into a chattering huddle and had no doubts that her success was the topic of their animated conversation.

The footman handed her a cup of coffee. She took a seat beside the fireplace and with gratitude used the time to relax before the men joined them and she would once again have to present herself as the ideal bride for the Duke.

She scanned the other young women in the room. Mr Hayward's companion had been wearing a cream gown, but then, so were at least five of the debutantes. Her chestnut hair had been braided and plaited and piled high on her head, but again, so was every debutante's in the room. She sighed, knowing she was unlikely to know the identity of the woman without doing something unforgivable and asking.

'I hear there is to be dancing tonight,' a young lady seated on a nearby sofa said. Grace quickly scrutinised her. She was thankfully dressed in a pale blue gown and was not Mr Hayward's companion.

'I wonder if Graceless will take another fall and the Duke will realise that if you're born low you stay low-born.'

Grace froze, her cup halfway to her mouth, as the other girls giggled behind their fans, all looking in Grace's direction.

'It's a shame no one has yet told him what a fool she made of herself at his ball,' another added. 'Then he'd know it would be the joke throughout society that someone so lacking in grace and charm was called Grace and it would be, too, too funny for her to become a duchess and for everyone to have to refer to her as Your Grace.'

This caused the girls to giggle even louder while Grace wished she could curl up into a little ball, one so small she would all but disappear. Would she never be allowed to forget her shameful behaviour at the Duke's ball? It would seem not.

The men entered the room. The giggling ceased immediately. The young ladies all sat up straight, adopted the required polite smile, the requisite tilt of the head, and looked towards the men as if they were the sun rising over the eastern horizon.

Grace knew she should follow their example, but those cruel words were still ringing in her ears. The Duke hadn't seen her fall. If one of those girls told him, would he withdraw his attentions from her? And if he did so, would all the affection her grandmother had bestowed on her also be withdrawn? Would Graceless Lower-Born prove herself to be just as much a disappointment as her mother had been?

Thomas returned to the drawing room with reluctance, certain he would have to endure more of the Duke's crowing. That puffed-up rooster had looked so pleased with himself throughout dinner and Thomas had not missed the looks of triumph he had repeatedly sent him while the brandy was being served.

The only way Thomas had managed to squash down his agitation was by reminding himself that everyone was close to getting what they wanted. He would get his land cheaper than he had originally asked, Miss Lowerby would become a duchess and the Duke would get a wife who was far too good for him.

He quickly scanned the room and saw Miss Lowerby, seated alone, her face dejected, her shoulders hunched. Something was wrong. He pushed past the other men crowded around the door, crossed the room and took the seat beside her without being invited.

'Grace, what is it? What's wrong?'

'It's nothing,' she mumbled.

'Is it the Duke? Has he said or done something to upset you?'

'No, no, it's not the Duke.' She looked towards the young women who had hurt her so. 'It's nothing, really.'

The chamber group seated in the corner struck up a tune. Music filled the air and couples lined up for the first dance.

'Dance with me,' he said, offering her his hand. 'And tell me all about it.'

She quickly looked in her grandmother's direction. The old lady was watching them and with a quick nod of her head gave her permission.

'So what has happened that has made you look so sad when so far this evening has been such a success for you?'

'I suppose it's silly really, but those debutantes were laughing about my falling over at the Duke's ball and I suspect they're going to tell him that, you know, I completely embarrassed myself at his ball.'

He released an annoyed sigh. 'You know why they're doing that, don't you?'

'Because they're right. Graceless Lower-Born should never have thought she could possibly marry a duke.' She looked up at him. 'That's what they call me: Graceless Lower-Born.'

'Bullies always aim for what they think is your greatest vulnerability. Remember what I said to you at the Duke's ball? The secret is to not let them see that they have hurt you. If you do, then they will be relentless.'

'That's easy for you to say,' she murmured. 'No one would ever try to bully a man as strong as you.'

'That is where you're wrong. At school I was certainly the target of bullies.'

His mind shot back to those first days at school, to the relentless name calling and the constant threats of violence.

'What did you do?'

'Luckily for me, the bullies picked on something I cared nothing about. They thought my family's lack of a title was my vulnerability, but it was my strength. And you should be the same—make your vulnerabilities into your strength and be proud of yourself and all you've achieved.'

She stared at him with wide disbelieving eyes. 'You think I should be proud because I fell over in the middle of a ballroom?'

'Be proud that despite doing something that would be the ruin of a lesser young lady's Season, you managed to pull yourself up and go on to capture the interest of the most eligible man available this Season.'

'But I didn't pull myself up. You did. But their teasing is all so unfair. Why do they have to be so mean?'

'Because you have what they want. They might call you Lower-Born, but they weren't the ones sitting at his side at the dinner table. They weren't the one to whom he was giving his complete attention.'

'I think that is also because of you and the Duke's jealousy.'

'That's not true.'

She raised her eyebrows.

'Well, not entirely,' he added. 'But he is only jealous because he wants the prettiest, most delightful, most elegant young lady in the room as his own.'

'You certainly know how to flatter, don't you, Mr Hayward? Anyone would think you were the one who attended finishing school.'

She gave a small laugh and relief washed through him. It pained him so much to see her unhappy and he knew that was all he wanted for her. It was just unfortunate that she thought her happiness lay in capturing a man who was so unworthy of her.

'Or should I call you Thomas, now that you've called me Grace?'

He raised his eyebrows at this surprising question.

'When you asked me to dance, you called me Grace.'

'My apologies, that was forward of me.'

'You're forgiven, but only on the condition that you allow me to call you Thomas.'

'I would be honoured, Grace.'

They smiled at each other as they continued to dance, then her smile turned to a slight frown. 'Your schooldays must have been miserable if you were constantly having to deal with bullies.'

He shrugged as if to dismiss all those disagreeable times. 'They would have been, but on my first day I also made two very good friends, Isaac Radcliff and Sebastian Kingsley. They were also outsiders at the school and the three of us took great delight in being the best at everything. I suppose we were trying to prove something, to ourselves and everyone who looked down on us.'

'You're lucky to have friends,' she said, that look of sadness returning. 'But I have a friend now as well, don't I?' she added, smiling up at him. 'A very good friend who always seems to be at hand when I need to be rescued.'

'And if you ever need a friend, at any time, remember, I will always be at your service,' he said, surprising himself with this admission.

But she did deserve a friend and looking out for her was the least he could do to make up for her unwittingly being caught up in a game between himself and the Duke, even if that game did end with her becoming the Duchess of Hardgraves.

She bit the edge of her lip in that now familiar manner. 'So, who were you sitting next to at the dinner table?'

He cast his mind back, trying to remember. 'Lady Catherine and Lady Stephanie, I believe.'

Thomas hoped that was what they were called. All the debutantes tended to look alike, and their conversation was unvaryingly the same and unvaryingly dull. 'Why do you ask?'

'No reason.' She smiled up at him, her eyes glinting in the candlelight. 'No reason at all, except I think you mean Lady Catarina and Lady Seraphina.'

'Yes, perhaps.'

The dance over, Thomas escorted a much happier Grace back to her grandmother, who was standing beside a scowling duke. Good, he should be made to work for the hand of such a worthy young lady and not expect her to be handed to him on a silver platter, the way everything else in his life had.

'I believe you promised the first dance to me,' the Duke said, that childish petulance in his voice.

'My fault entirely,' Thomas answered before she could make an apology, one the Duke did not deserve. She was not his property. Not yet. And she should not have to defer to him.

'Well, let's rectify that situation, what?' the Duke said, taking Grace's arm as if he already owned her.

He led her back out on to the dance floor and Thomas watched as he wrapped his arms around her waist and held her somewhat closer than was demanded for the gallop.

'Don't they make a perfect couple?' Lady Ashbridge said.

'Hmm,' was the only response Thomas believed that comment required.

'My granddaughter is quite smitten with the Duke.'

'Is she?' he responded, still watching the Duke and fighting the temptation to stride across the dance floor and pull him off her. His hand had moved lower down her back and was now resting on the top of her buttocks. Lady Ashbridge must have seen that and must know it was unacceptable behaviour. But she quite obviously did not care.

'Yes, quite perfect,' Lady Ashbridge continued. 'It is her dream to become a duchess, you know.'

'So I hear.'

'Good, because she will never be yours.'

He turned to look at Lady Ashbridge, who, despite her snappish tone, was smiling as if they were having a polite conversation.

'It appears, on that, Lady Ashbridge, you and I are in complete agreement.'

'Are we?' she asked, her voice still curt while her smile never faltered. 'I saw how you were looking at her while the two of you were dancing. But if you have any thoughts of trying to lead my granddaughter astray, then you can put those ideas right out of your head.'

'As lovely as your granddaughter is, I have no intentions of taking a wife any time soon. All I have ever offered her is my friendship. And as for leading her—'

'Good, then you can stop trying to bedazzle her. She is a naive, chaste young lady and a man such as yourself could easily turn her head.'

It appeared his use as bait had come to an end. The Duke's performance this evening had presumably convinced Lady Ashbridge that an offer was imminent and Thomas had become redundant to this woman's plans.

'You have no reason to fear me turning her head, Lady Ashbridge. You have convinced your granddaughter that what she wants more than anything else is to be married to a duke. After many years of being told what to think, what to want and how to feel, I do not believe anything I or anyone else could do would convince her that it is not her own dream, but one that has been imposed on her.'

The polite smile faltered and briefly turned into a grimace, before returning, just as bright and just as false as before.

'You have no right to question anything I do. All I care about is what is best for my granddaughter and I will not have you ruining my plans for her. I saw the way the two of you looked at each other when you danced together. It would be best for all concerned if you have nothing more to do with her.'

Thomas wanted to argue, but perhaps she was right. Despite himself, he had become far too involved in these people's intrigues and stratagems. This was not his world. He did not belong here. He should just get what he came for and withdraw.

'As you wish.'

He and Lady Ashbridge turned back to watching the couple dancing in the centre of the drawing room. Still holding her far too close, the Duke leant down to whisper in Grace's ear while he stared straight at Thomas. Her eyes grew wide, her mouth opened in surprise. She looked over at Thomas, then her gaze moved to her grandmother.

Lady Ashbridge nodded her head rapidly, no longer worrying about the need for discretion or the veneer of politeness.

Grace copied the motion and gave a small nod of her head and he could see her lips form the word *yes*.

It was done. The Duke had made his offer of courtship, maybe even marriage. Thomas was tempted to rush across the room and tell her she was making a big mistake, but it was none of his business. And even if it was, what good would it really do? This was what she thought she wanted and why would she listen to him? She would now be a duchess. Lady Ashbridge would also get what she wanted and would perhaps stop treating her granddaughter simply as a means to achieve her own ambitions, but as someone who should be loved and cherished.

And Thomas would get his land at a lower price. Although right now, that felt like a very hollow victory.

Chapter Eight

Grace fought to maintain her smile while turbulent emotions swirled within her. She should be jubilant. The Season had barely begun and she already had what she wanted. The Duke had asked to court her. Well, he hadn't actually said it was he who wanted to court her. He had asked her if she would like to be courted by him, but surely it was the same thing.

She was not sure why she had hesitated and not given him an immediate yes—yes, yes, of course she wanted it, wanted it more than anything in the world. She wanted him to court her, to marry her, to make her a duchess and give her the fairy-tale marriage she had always dreamed of.

Yet, between him asking and her answering, it had not been jubilation that had coursed through her veins. And why had she looked to Thomas?

She forced herself to smile brighter. She would not think of those things, nor would she focus on the pain in the centre of her chest, or the tightness of her stomach. She was to be courted by a duke, the most eligible man available this Season. She was a success. Her grandmother would be proud of her. She was proud of herself.

'Now that that is settled,' the Duke said, finally removing his stroking hand from her arm, 'will you excuse me? I believe there is a card game in progress.'

Not waiting for her response, he gave a quick bow of his head and departed, leaving Grace to cross the room alone and impart the wonderous news to her grandmother.

Thomas was still standing beside her grandmother, watching her, and his face did not suggest he was happy with what had just occurred. But surely that mattered not. She was not here to make him happy. He had said she should do whatever it was she wanted with her life and this was what she wanted, what she had always wanted, and now it was almost a reality.

'Miss Lowerby, Lady Ashbridge, if you will excuse me,' Thomas said as soon as she joined them.

Her grandmother didn't reply, nor did she curtsy, her focus being intent only on Grace.

'Don't tell me yet,' she whispered. 'Wait until we are alone in your bedchamber, then you can tell me everything the Duke said.'

With that, she took Grace's arm, rushed her out of the room, up the stairs and into her bedchamber with as much haste as possible without actually running.

'What did he say?' her grandmother asked the moment the door shut behind them. 'Did he propose? Am I going to receive a formal offer for your hand?' She tapped her chin with her index finger in thought. 'I suppose it should be your uncle who he makes the offer to, as he is now the Earl of Ashbridge, but I am your nearest living relative, even if I am a woman.' She flicked her hand in dismissal. 'But it matters not. Your uncle will do whatever I tell him to and how could anyone turn down a duke?' She laughed at the impossibility of that idea.

'So tell me, my dear child, what exactly did he say?' She took Grace's hands, stood back and smiled at her, a genuine, warm smile that filled Grace's heart with joy. Then she did what Grace had been longing for her to do her entire life. Pulled her into an embrace. Like a child, Grace sank into her arms. As a child she had yearned to be held by her grandmother, to be cherished and loved, and now she was. All other, confused feelings evaporated. She had made her grandmother proud. She had made her grandmother love her.

'Was it a formal proposal?' her grandmother asked, in the voice of an excited debutante.

'No, not exactly.'

Her grandmother dropped her arms and took a step backwards. 'What? Well, what did he say to you then?'

The churning emotions returned as the need to have her grandmother's approval gnawed at her like a physical ache. 'He asked if I would be agreeable to being courted by him,' she said in a choked voice.

Her grandmother nodded and once again tapped her chin. 'Yes, that will do. It's not as good as a proposal, but it's the next best thing and will inevitably lead to an engagement, then marriage. There is no reason why it should not.'

The finger dropped from her chin and she smiled. 'Oh, my dear, dear child, this is wonderful, more wonderful than I could ever imagine.' She resumed tapping her chin. 'I wonder if the Prince of Wales will attend the wedding, maybe even Queen Victoria herself. After all, it's not every day that a duke marries.'

Grace kept smiling, caught up in her grandmother's excitement.

'I could tell by the way he was touching you when you were dancing that he would have to make an offer of some sort. To not do so would be a disgrace and a man like the Duke of Hardgraves would never do anything disgraceful.'

Grace's confusion once again forced its way up through

her happiness as she remembered the way the Duke had held her far too close while they danced, and how he had kept rubbing his fingers up and down her arm.

'Grandmama,' she said and bit her bottom lip, as she tried to compose questions she was unsure she should ask. 'I don't really like it when the Duke touches me. Is that normal?'

'What?' Her grandmother frowned at the question. 'Yes. I suppose so. It doesn't really matter, does it? It's not your place to like or dislike him touching you. Your place is to do what he wants. Your pleasure comes from pleasing him.'

'It does?'

'Oh, my dear, you are such an innocent. I blame myself. I should have explained all this before the Season began. Sit down, my dear, and let me explain a few things to you.'

She took a seat on the sofa by the window. Her grandmother sat beside her and took Grace's hands, her expression serious.

'The Duke will have his needs and it is your duty to satisfy those needs, whatever they might be. That is all that will be expected of you. Once you are married, he will want you to provide him with an heir and you must submit to him in the bedchamber and do all that you are instructed to do in order for that to be accomplished.'

'I see,' Grace said, not entirely seeing at all and not particularly liking the sound of the words 'submit' and 'doing as she was instructed'.

'But that won't happen until we are married?' she asked, hoping that would be the case.

'Ideally, but now that the Duke has said he wishes to court you he can be granted some liberties.'

'Liberties? What sort of liberties?'

'That will depend on the Duke and what he wants. Just do as he asks. He may have a mistress and not require anything of you, merely that you perform your duties once you are wed. Then when you have provided him with an heir, he might require no more of you. It is entirely up to him.'

'A mistress?'

Her grandmother smiled as if she had said something quaint. 'Yes, men of the Duke's standing often keep a mistress, sometimes several. That is something you will just turn a blind eye to.'

'But—'

Her grandmother held up her hand to stop her objections. 'You will never question anything the Duke does.'

'So if he touches me again, the way he did tonight, that is all right?'

'Yes, and, well, whatever else he wishes to do. And if he does take a few liberties, do not screw your face up the way you did tonight. You don't have to look as if you're enjoying it, you're to be the wife after all, not the mistress, but don't at any time let him think that you find his touch objectionable.'

'I see,' Grace said, suppressing that forbidden look of horror. 'So, what sort of liberties might he take?'

'Oh, for goodness' sake, girl, stop with all these questions.'

Grace's heart lurched and her body tensed, as it always did when she upset her grandmother.

'Just do as the Duke wishes. He is the man and he is a duke. It is your duty to do as he bids.'

'Of course, Grandmama,' Grace replied, causing her grandmother to smile once again and pat her hand.

'Good girl.'

Grace smiled back at her, while questions swirled unanswered in her mind. She really did not like the Duke touching her, nor did she like the idea of him taking liberties, whatever that meant. Kissing, probably, more touching, perhaps. Thankfully, her grandmother had said she was not expected to enjoy it, because she doubted she ever could.

Her thoughts strayed once again to Thomas. If he had been the one to caress her arm, if his hand had slipped lower down her back so it was resting on the top of her buttocks, she was sure she would not object.

Heat pulsed through her body at the thought of Thomas kissing her, of his hand stroking her, of his hand moving to places it shouldn't.

'I can see by that flush on your face that you are thinking of all the ways you can please the Duke,' her grandmother said, once again patting her hand. 'Well, I will leave you alone with those thoughts and tomorrow I'm sure the Duke will be asking me for a quiet word.'

Grace had hoped for another hug, a stroke of her cheek, even a kiss on the forehead, but her grandmother departed without bestowing any of those longed-for gestures of affection.

She rang for her lady's maid to help her undress, then climbed into bed. She knew she should be thinking about this evening's joyous outcome, but all she could think about was how, if it was Thomas she was supposed to submit to, if Thomas was the one she should allow to take liberties, she would be more than willing to do so.

Chapter Nine

'I think we can unequivocally declare me the winner of this wooing duel, can't we, Hayward?' the Duke said when Thomas entered the study the next morning.

'Yes, you won. Now it's time for you to sign those papers.'

The Duke picked up his pen and dipped it in the ink pot, then smiled at Thomas.

'You were never really in contention, though, were you? You should stick to things you know something about, like business and making money, and leave courtship and gallantry to the men who were born to such things.'

'Indeed. Now if you'll just sign the papers, I'll be able to inform my bank to forward you the reduced sum for your land.' Thomas had thought that might temper the man's bluster, but it did not. He still thought he had put Thomas firmly in his place and had finally got that victory he'd desperately been seeking since their schooldays.

'Yes, when it comes to selecting a mate, women always know to go for the most superior man. It's only natural. It's what they're destined to do.'

'Indeed,' Thomas said, pointing to the line waiting for the Duke's signature.

'But you tried your best, I suppose,' he said, shaking his

head as if the insult was a compliment. 'But you have to realise, you can't go chasing after a young lady like you're a tom pursuing a cat on heat. These things have to be done with finesse and that is something that can't be learnt. It is inborn.'

The man really was an insufferable dolt. The sooner Thomas could leave this house and focus entirely on building a railway through his property the better.

'I'm sure you're right,' he added, once again tapping the document.

'I'm pleased you finally can see that I am the superior man.' With that, he signed away his land and ran his blotter over the wet ink. 'Now, you can sign this.'

The Duke removed a piece of paper from his inside pocket and handed it to Thomas. He read the words and sighed. It spelt out the terms of the bet and that the winner was the one that Grace chose.

'Go on, sign it, next to the line that says loser,' the Duke said gleefully, as if the document had some value.

Thomas signed it and threw it across the desk to the Duke, then picked up the document that was actually legal and folded it in two.

'Thank you for selling your land to me for less than I was prepared to pay.' He took great pleasure in watching the Duke's smug smile falter as doubt started to undermine his sense of superiority.

'You do realise you made a bet in which even if I lost I won, and even if you won you lost, but all in all I'm pleased to do business with you. I've now paid much less than I intended for your land and you have missed out on money that you most sorely need.'

Confusion distorted the Duke's features and Thomas could almost see the effort it was taking for him to come to the realisation that he had just squandered part of his inheritance on a ridiculous bet.

'So when will you be announcing the engagement in the newspapers?' Thomas asked and, despite himself, he could not entirely mask his displeasure.

'Oh, all in good time, all in good time,' the Duke said, eyeing him suspiciously.

'You are intending to marry Miss Lowerby, aren't you?'

'Why, Hayward, despite me winning her outright, I believe you're still hankering after the pretty little thing, aren't you?'

Thomas placed the document in the inside pocket of his jacket. 'I'm merely pointing out that for a man who puts such an emphasis on gallantry and courtliness, it would be bad form to lead the young lady on.'

The Duke's smile returned, more gleeful than before. 'You do care for her, don't you? Everything you said about not being able to lose our bet was just balderdash to cover up the fact that you lost what you really wanted. Well, you did lose and I won. You can't have her. She wants me, not you.'

Thomas was sorely tempted to plant his fist in his smug face, but that would do nobody any good. And he was right. Grace was his and Thomas could not have her.

Instead, he leant over the desk, his face mere inches from the Duke. 'You will treat her well, you cretin, or I will ruin you, do you understand?'

He shouldn't have taken so much pleasure in the look of fear that crossed the Duke's face, but then, as the man pointed out, Thomas was from a class that knew nothing of gallantry.

Having made his point, he departed, certain the Duke would take heed of his words. He had promised Grace he would always be her friend and he intended to look out for her, whether she was aware of it or not.

While it was tempting to make a quiet departure, it would be remiss of him not to say goodbye to her, so once he had given instructions to his valet to pack his bags he went in search of her.

Finding her seated in the morning room, staring out the window, he paused briefly at the door and watched her. She did not look like a young woman in love, but one who had been abandoned on a distant shore and was looking out for a ship to come sailing over the horizon to save her. She turned to look in his direction.

'Thomas,' she murmured, then smiled forlornly. 'Won't you join me?'

He took the seat beside her. 'I have heard the news about your courtship and have...' he paused '...I have offered my congratulations to the Duke.'

She nodded and gave him a small smile. 'Thank you.'

'You now have all your heart desires,' he added, fighting to keep any cynicism out of his voice.

'Yes,' she said. 'And what of you? Did you achieve all you wished for and can now extend your railway over the Duke's land?'

'Yes,' he responded, trying to ignore the guilt over how he had achieved that wish. 'And now I intend to depart, but I did not want to leave without saying goodbye.'

'Oh, but I will be seeing you again during the Season, won't I?'

'I don't usually attend such social events. I only attended this one because the Duke left me little option.'

Her brow furrowed. 'Oh, I see. I was hoping... Well, I will miss our talks.'

'Our talks might not be acceptable now that you are to marry the Duke.'

'He didn't say he would marry me. He just asked if I would be agreeable to a courtship.'

'And you said yes—that means spending time with other men will no longer be acceptable.'

'Oh, I see.' The furrows in her brow deepened.

'Goodbye, Grace.'

'Yes, goodbye, Thomas.'

He remained seated. 'Always remember, you are a beautiful, intelligent young lady and the Duke is lucky to have you.'

She smiled at him, the first real smile he'd seen since he entered the morning room.

'You will make a perfect duchess, one who I suspect will eventually be running this estate much better than the Duke ever could. Never, ever think you are not worthy of the position of duchess.'

'Thank you,' she murmured.

'Goodbye, Grace.' And with that, he stood and departed before he said anything more that he should not.

Grace watched him go, suddenly feeling more alone than she had felt in years. If he did not attend society events, then she was unlikely to ever see him again. She blinked to flick away some ridiculous tears that were threatening to fall. She was being silly. She was about to be courted by a duke, no less. Her Season was already more glorious than she could possibly have hoped for.

She turned to look out of the window. This was where she would stay for the rest of the morning, so she could get a final glimpse of him as he drove up the gravel pathway and departed from her life.

'Is this where you are hiding yourself away?' her grandmother said from the doorway.

Grace turned towards her and tried to smile.

'Now, now, now,' she said, taking the seat beside Grace. 'There is no need to look so despondent, my dear. The Duke is a busy man. He can't spend all his time in your company and he does have other guests to entertain.'

'Yes, Grandmama.'

'Now, come and join me and the other ladies in the drawing room. We've got a lively game of whist going and I'm sure everyone is anxious to ingratiate themselves to the next Duchess of Hardgraves.'

'Have you told them?' Grace asked, shocked at her grandmother's lack of propriety. The Duke had not yet made their courtship formal.

'Of course I have done no such thing, but everyone could see the way he was looking at you and no one missed that quiet conversation the two of you had last night. You've made a lot of debutantes very jealous and a lot of mothers extremely annoyed,' her grandmother said, as if these were admirable accomplishments. 'So come along, dear, don't dally.'

Grace gave one last look out the window, before following her grandmother down the hallway and into the drawing room. She was greeted with a row of polite smiles as false as her own. But her grandmother was correct. While they chatted over the card table, everyone deferred to her as if she was a woman of high status and not the daughter of a piano teacher. Even the debutantes who had mocked her were now solicitous, asking her opinions and listening as if everything she had to say was of the greatest interest.

Was this what the rest of her life would be like? Would

she never again know who really liked her for who she was and who only acted as if they did because of her title?

She looked towards the window, wondering if Thomas had left yet.

A footman informed the ladies that luncheon had been served and they joined the men in the dining room, where she was once again the focus of much smiling and looks of admiration from people who had previously shown her no interest.

When the meal finally came to an end, everyone retired to their rooms to change for their trip home. Grace's lady's maid's mood seemed as despondent as her own as she helped her into her dark blue dress, scarf and travelling coat.

Her grandmother entered her bedchamber and dismissed Molly with a flick of her hand. 'He hasn't had a quiet word with me yet,' she said, scowling at Grace as if she were to blame.

Grace shrugged one shoulder, not knowing how she was expected to respond.

'Don't do that,' her grandmother snapped. 'It's most unbecoming in a lady.'

Grace could point out it was a gesture her grandmother often made, but knew better than to do so.

'Perhaps he'll have a word with us as we depart. Yes, that's probably what he'll do. He'll take me aside and have a quiet word with me then.' She nodded her head, but continued to frown. 'Well, come on, make haste, the train won't wait and we don't want to have to hurry our departure.'

They joined the assembled guests at the entrance way, where goodbyes were being exchanged, cheeks were being kissed and promises of 'we must meet again, soon' made.

The Duke was present and was fully occupied, laughing with his male guests. A line of carriages arrived, some to take those who lived nearby home, others to transport guests to the railway station. The Duke helped each young lady and her escort into their waiting carriages.

When there was only one carriage left, Grace and her grandmother walked down the steps to where the Duke was standing by the open door of the carriage.

He helped Grace in and, as he had done with all the other debutantes, lightly kissed the back of her hand. 'Goodbye, Miss Lowerby,' he said. 'It has been a delight having you as a guest in my home.'

Grace waited, expecting him to say more, but he merely smiled at her, so she climbed into the carriage.

'I believe we need to have a conversation,' her grandmother said, standing at the foot of the carriage and rather rudely taking hold of the Duke's arm.

'All in good time, Lady Ashbridge. All in good time.' Still smiling, the Duke pulled his arm away. 'I wish you a pleasant journey home.'

Her grandmother was left with no other option than to climb into the carriage and take her seat. And with that, the Duke walked away and out the window Grace could see him join a group of male friends and the sound of their loud laughter reached them as they drove off down the gravel pathway.

Grace bit her bottom lip and looked tentatively at her grandmother. She was sitting ramrod straight on the leather bench, outrage written large on her face.

'He will probably send a letter as soon as he returns to London,' she finally said as the carriage approached the small country station. 'Yes, that would be more appropriate.'

Grace chose to say nothing. She had no notion of how a courtship was to be conducted, she just wished the Duke had been more attentive to her, as she hated to see her grand-mother looking so distressed.

The train journey home seemed even longer than the trip to Cornwall had been and was made even more trying by her grandmother's continued ill temper.

As she looked out at the passing scenery, Grace wondered where Thomas might now be, what he would be doing and who he would be seeing. Although he said he did not attend society events, maybe there would be a chance that they would see each other again. Maybe he would want to buy more land off the Duke, or would be in attendance when the rail tracks were laid through what had once been the Duke's land.

And if they did meet again, surely there would be nothing wrong with greeting an acquaintance. After all, they *had* been formally introduced and he *was* a friend of the Duke's, or at least had been a guest in his house.

After an interminably long journey, the train pulled into Paddington Station, the noise and bustle a shock compared to the quiet of the countryside. Trains arriving and leaving from the platforms sent out large gusts of hissing steam, a platoon of porters urgently raced up and down, countless passengers moved in every direction and a cacophony of voices and whistles filled the air.

She followed her grandmother down the platform to their waiting carriage, then travelled through the busy London streets to their quiet townhouse. Now all she had to do was wait until the Duke contacted her and their courtship could begin in earnest.

At breakfast the next morning her grandmother urgently flicked through the first post of the day.

'I didn't really expect a note from him. Not yet. He might not even be back in London,' her grandmother said, the disappointment in her voice contradicting her words. Leaving the unopened letters lying on the table, she went back to eating her breakfast.

The second mail delivery of the day also contained no letter from the Duke, nor did the third.

Days passed with no note from him. Her grandmother's temper grew worse. An unpleasant atmosphere permeated every area of the house and, like Grace, the servants walked around as if on tiptoes, their bodies tense, just waiting to be on the receiving end of some criticism from her grandmother.

A week had passed and still there was no note, no visit. Nor were there any cards, flowers, or invitations, all the things her grandmother had said one would expect from a man who was courting a young lady. It was as if the offer had never been made.

With each passing day her grandmother's rage increased until Grace could hardly bear to be in the same room. But bear it she must.

The arrival of the mail was particularly tense. It became a familiar pattern. The footman would enter with the letters on a silver tray and his sympathetic smile at Grace would tell her all she needed to know before her grandmother took the letters. There was still no note from the Duke.

When they entered the second week with no message, her grandmother finally exploded over the breakfast table, her fist hitting the table, making the cups, saucers and egg cups jump.

'He has made a fool of me,' she all but screamed, glaring

at Grace as if this was all her fault. 'He has made a fool of
you. He made a promise and now he has all but rescinded
it.' She threw down the letters she was holding, and they
scatted across the table. 'We are going to have to accept
that the Duke is not courting you.'

Grace stared back at her grandmother, hardly able to
believe what she was hearing. Her grandmother never conceded defeat, but she was now. She would not have to marry
the Duke. That was terrible. Grace knew it to be, yet her
shoulders relaxed slightly and that churning in her stomach
that had been her constant companion since the Duke had
whispered to her in the drawing room calmed somewhat.

There would be no more waiting anxiously for his letter,
hoping it would come so her grandmother's temper would
be pacified, but dreading its arrival because so much would
then be expected of her.

'Thankfully society has no knowledge of your shame,'
her grandmother continued, as if talking to herself. 'As far
as anyone knows, the Duke still showed you special favour,
but no actual offer was made.'

'Yes, Grandmama,' Grace said dutifully, all the while
thinking, *It's over.*

'And there is no reason why you can't be in favour again
and be favoured to such an extent that he has no choice but
to make a formal proposal of marriage.'

The churning in her stomach rumbled back into life.

'And we know exactly how to get him to do that, don't
we?' Her grandmother smiled at her, a smile that suggested
victory was imminent.

'We do?'

'We need Mr Hayward.'

At the sound of his name, Grace's heart skipped inside
her chest. 'Mr Hayward?' she asked, loving being able to

say out loud the name of the man who was constantly in her thoughts.

'Yes, Mr Hayward's presence seems just the catalyst needed to remind the Duke that you are the one he wants.'

Grace placed her hands on her stomach, preparing herself to ask the difficult question. 'Does that mean I'm to encourage Mr Hayward again?'

Please, please, say yes.

'I can see you're starting to understand how this works,' her grandmother said.

Grace smiled at the compliment, not caring that her grandmother thought she wanted to see Thomas again so he could once again be used to incite the attentions of the Duke. She was going to see him again. That was all that mattered.

Chapter Ten

'A Lady Ashbridge has requested to see you, sir.'

Thomas looked up from his desk at his secretary standing by the door.

Lady Ashbridge? What could that dragon possibly want with him? But there was only one way to find out.

'Show her in, thank you, Worthington.'

The man bowed and departed and soon Lady Ashbridge bustled in, all strained smiles and false politeness, putting Thomas on his guard. He stood behind his desk and indicated for her to take a seat, which she did with much rustling and flouncing of her skirt.

'How lovely to see you again, Mr Hayward,' she said, causing Thomas to raise his eyebrows in disbelief.

'And what a delightful office you have.' She looked around, taking in the bookshelves full of bound ledgers lining the walls, the leather furniture, then back to his oak desk, with its piles of papers awaiting his attention as soon as she left.

'This looks like quite the hive of activity.'

Thomas stifled a sigh of impatience. 'And to what do I owe the pleasure of this visit?' he said as he took his seat, aware that it was unlikely to contain any pleasure for either of them.

'I believe I owe you an apology, Mr Hayward,' she said, her smile fading and an equally false look of regret crossing her usually stern features.

'Apology?' he prompted.

'Yes, at the Duke of Hardgraves's weekend party I was perhaps a tad rude to you.'

A tad. The lady was certainly one for understatement.

'Yes. I believe I told you to stay away from my granddaughter. That was very rude of me.' She sighed lightly as if unable to believe that she could do something so out of character. 'Especially as you had shown my granddaughter nothing but your friendship.'

Thomas looked at the elderly woman over his desk and made no comment, waiting to discover exactly what game she was now playing.

'My granddaughter is fond of you and I believe if you wished to continue with this friendship, then that would be acceptable.'

Thomas continued to say nothing. Lady Ashbridge moved uncomfortably in the plush leather seat.

'Very acceptable,' she added, her smile becoming increasingly strained.

He remained silent, enjoying her discomfort.

'If that is what you wish, Lady Ashbridge, then, yes, I am prepared to continue with our friendship, but I ask one thing of you.'

'Oh, and what might that be?' she asked, tilting her head as if she really did care about anything he might ask.

'Honesty.'

She all but jumped back in her chair and stared at him, her brow furrowed as if this was a concept unfamiliar to her.

'I'm assuming things have not gone quite so smoothly

with the Duke of Hardgraves as you had hoped or you would not be here in my office.'

'Oh, no, my granddaughter has—'

He held up his hand to still her words. 'Honesty, Lady Ashbridge.'

'Oh, all right then,' she said, lifting her nose and pursing her lips. 'The Duke has made no contact with Grace since our return from his estate.'

A sense of relief swept over him, to be quickly replaced with concern for Grace. She must be devastated, humiliated even, that the Duke should reject her after his offer of courtship. And it was all because of that bet. This was all his fault.

'And what do you wish me to do to rectify that situation?'

'I believe if we are being honest then you know the answer to that question,' the canny older woman said.

'You wish me to what, pay court to Miss Lowerby, to reignite the Duke's interest?'

'Yes,' came her brief and undeniably honest answer.

'And I assume you then wish me to graciously bow out when she does recapture his interest.'

'Yes.'

He remained silent while he digested this outrageous request.

'And is Miss Lowerby in agreement with this?' he finally asked.

'Of course she is. Despite everything, she is a sensible girl. She could see as clearly as I could the effect spending time with you had on the Duke. And she has, well, some affection for you, so to spend time in your company will not be arduous for her.'

And he, too, had some affection for Grace, perhaps too much affection, and found her company far from arduous. Since he'd left Hardgraves's estate, he had been doing something he had never done before—scouring the society pages to see any mention of her being seen in the company of the Duke. And he had to admit he was somewhat relieved when their names were not mentioned.

But did he really want to be used in this way?

'I wouldn't ask, but this has all been so humiliating for my granddaughter.' Lady Ashbridge pulled a lace handkerchief out of her reticule and dabbed the corner of her eyes. It seemed honesty was now being replaced with play-acting.

'She had to endure that awful incident at the Duke's ball, which I believe everyone saw, and now it appears the Duke has abandoned her.' She gave a small sniff.

Despite the theatrics, Thomas knew what she was saying was correct. Both events would be humiliating for Grace and at future social events those bullying debutantes would be certain to not let an opportunity pass to further ridicule her.

'It was her dream to become a titled lady, but now that the Duke has spurned her, she is receiving no invitations, no expressions of interest from any other young gentlemen,' Lady Ashbridge pleaded. 'It has been a disastrous Season for her and she is so intensely sad.' The dabbing continued along with a few more sniffs. 'All her dreams have been destroyed.'

'You make a fine actress, at least for a melodrama, Lady Ashbridge,' he said curtly, causing the older woman to drop her handkerchief from her eyes and glare at him. 'Although I believe the sniffling was rather overdoing it.'

'Well, are you going to help or not?' she snapped at him. 'You did say you were her friend. Isn't this what friends do? Help each other out in their times of need?'

'Yes. I will do as you request.'

'Excellent,' Lady Ashbridge said, standing up. 'I'll tell my granddaughter to expect you at three o'clock this afternoon so the two of you can take a walk in Hyde Park.' Having got what she wanted, she briskly walked out of the office.

Thomas looked back down at the pile of papers on his desk. He had work to do and, unlike the aristocracy, he did not fritter away his afternoons promenading and socialising, but it would not hurt to take off one afternoon, especially if it meant seeing Grace again.

'He has agreed to escort you on a walk around Hyde Park this afternoon,' her grandmother announced the moment she arrived home.

It took every ounce of willpower Grace possessed to not react to this news and remain seated demurely on the sofa while continuing to embroider the delicate flowers on her sampler.

She was to see him again. After these long days and nights when she had thought of nothing but his laughter, his voice, the touch of his arm as they walked together, she was to see him again.

'That is indeed excellent news,' she said, hoping her voice had not revealed her excitement.

'Now remember, make the walk as public as possible,' her grandmother added as she took her seat. 'The more people who see the two of you together, the more the likelihood that it will get back to the Duke.'

'Yes, Grandmama.' She placed her sampler on the side table. 'I suppose I should change into a suitable dress and get Molly to style my hair.'

'Yes. You need to look as attractive as possible.'

Grace fought to restrain her smile when what she really

wanted to do was laugh with joy and maybe even dance and sing. She would be seeing him again. It was almost impossible to believe and she had the Duke and his absence to thank for bringing him back into her life.

With as much decorum as possible, she left the drawing room, then rushed up to her bedchamber and pushed the bell to summon Molly. She then flew to her wardrobe to inspect the gowns that he had not yet seen, determined to select the most flattering.

Molly knocked on the door, entered and curtsied.

'Oh, Molly, I have to look my very best for a walk in Hyde Park. What do you suggest I wear?' she asked, pushing the gowns along the rail as she searched for perfection.

'It is good to hear the Duke has finally contacted you, miss,' Molly said as she joined her at the wardrobe.

'What? No, he hasn't. I'm to walk in Hyde Park with Mr Hayward.' She bit her lip as if she had revealed too much. 'Grandmama says it is what I need to do to once again gain the Duke's affections, so I must look my best.'

'I believe the blue-and-white-striped gown brings out the colour of your eyes.' Molly went over to the dressing table and picked up the curling tongs. 'If we have the time, I could style your hair with soft ringlets around your face and I could sweep the remainder up into a high, full bun on the top of your head and weave it with blue and white ribbons. That would look ever so feminine and sophisticated.'

Molly smiled as she waited for her answer, seemingly bubbling with as much excitement as Grace. 'Yes, let's do that,' she said, pulling the blue-and-white dress out of the wardrobe while Molly summoned a servant to heat up the tongs. 'After all, the Duke must see me at my very best,' she added in case Molly thought there was any other reason for all this fuss.

'Of course, miss.'

The two women set to work and Grace watched herself transform in front of the looking glass. Molly was as usual correct in all her choices.

'This style is perfect,' she said as Molly held up a hand mirror to show her the back of her head in the looking glass.

'Thank you, miss. I'm sure no man will be able to resist you.'

Grace smiled at her lady's maid, then suddenly remembered that Thomas was due at three o'clock. She collected her lace gloves and returned to the drawing room to await his arrival.

Her grandmother gave her an assessing look as she entered and with a nod of approval declared her suitable.

Her heart racing, her stomach fluttering, she took her seat, picked up her embroidery and attempted to give the appearance this was simply another afternoon, one where nothing of any particular importance was happening.

The footman entered and announced Mr Hayward's arrival. It was mere luck that Grace did not plunge the embroidery needle into her thumb, so shaky were her hands.

'Show him in,' her grandmother said, as Grace placed the embroidery on the side table, then picked it up again, sat up straighter, then once again returned the embroidery sample to the table.

He entered the room and Grace had to suppress a little gasp of surprise. Had he always been this sublimely handsome? Was his hair always that black? Were his eyes always that dark and intense?

Her heart did the seemingly impossible and beat even faster as her gaze moved to the angular lines of his jaw. She imagined running her finger over the dark stubble.

What would it feel like? Soft? Spiky? Her fingers were itching to find out.

He strode across the room, drawing her eyes to his strong body, his long slim legs and powerful shoulders. It was a body she remembered leaning into during their walks, a body she had been unable to stop thinking about all the time they were apart.

Her gaze remained fixed on him and she hardly heard the greeting he made to her grandmother. Then he turned to her and bowed.

'Miss Lowerby,' he said in that lovely, warm voice she remembered so well. 'It is a pleasure to see you again.'

'Yes, a pleasure,' Grace parroted, like an inarticulate nincompoop, looking up into those alluring brown eyes and that charming smile.

'Shall we?' He offered her his arm.

'You young people go off and enjoy the delightful weather,' her grandmother said as Grace stood up and placed her arm through his. 'And remember all that I said to you.'

Grace was unsure whom she was addressing, but it mattered not. She was to spend the afternoon with Thomas and she had her grandmother's blessing to once again do whatever it took to encourage him.

Chapter Eleven

'You look lovely today,' Thomas said as he helped Grace and her lady's maid into his carriage. And so she did. Had he forgotten just how beautiful she really was and the effect that beauty had on him?

She had done something different with her hair, and the loose blonde locks appeared almost golden in the afternoon sunlight, her skin almost translucent, just as he imagined an angel to look. Her delicate features and innocence made him want to protect her from all the harms of the world. Yet, when he looked at her full lips, his thoughts were not innocent, nor were they angelic.

But he was not here to think of her lips or indulge in any fantasies of kissing her or caressing her lovely, curvaceous body. He was here as a friend, to save her from the humiliation of being briefly courted, then immediately abandoned by the Duke, a humiliation that was all his fault, and to help her find the husband she and her grandmother desperately wanted. If not the Duke, then some other titled man. And she would not find that man seated at home waiting and pining. She needed to be out in society. She needed to be seen. Society needed to know that she was not ashamed of anything that had happened, but was an attractive, vibrant young lady, that any sensible man would be pleased to call his wife.

He signalled to the driver, and they moved off through the streets of Knightsbridge, towards Hyde Park.

'It is so delightful to see you again, Mr Hayward,' she said, turning towards him and smiling. 'I could hardly believe it when Grandmama said we were to take a walk in the park together.'

'You do realise what your grandmother's game is, don't you?'

'Of course I do, but I don't care,' she said with a delighted laugh that made him smile. 'She is hoping the Duke will finally start to court me, but it matters not what her reasons are, I'm just so pleased to see you again.'

Unlike the grandmother, the granddaughter did not have to be instructed to be honest. It was yet another of her endearing qualities that he adored.

'I take it the Duke has made no attempt to follow through with the promises he made at his estate.'

'No, we haven't heard a thing from him,' she said with a shrug of her shoulder.

Thomas should be angry with the cad for leading this sweet young lady on and then so unceremoniously discarding her, but he was far from angry. How could he be angry when it had led to him spending more time in her enjoyable company?

'You don't seem particularly upset by this outcome,' he probed.

'Well, I don't really know what to feel, but I know Grandmama has been furious and that always makes me very upset.'

Thomas did not doubt that.

'Well, you're out of the house, away from your grandmother, and we're going to have an enjoyable afternoon.'

She moved in closer and he inhaled lavender and rose water, a scent both innocent and enticing, just like the young lady herself.

'Yes, we are, aren't we,' she said with a small, contented giggle.

The sudden desire to place his arm around her shoulder and draw her into an intimate embrace crashed down on him. He longed to hold her close, to feel her body against his, to taste those lips.

He moved across the bench, putting a wider space between himself and temptation. With thoughts like that invading his mind, Thomas had to wonder whether this was such a good idea after all. Would a man who was merely offering friendship really have such thoughts? That was a question Thomas knew the answer to.

He looked over at the lady's maid, staring out at the passing scenery, and gave a silent thanks for her presence. He needed to focus on the one and only reason he was here, to help Grace achieve her dream. No, make that two reasons. To help her and to soothe the guilt that had been gnawing at him since the Duke won her in that inappropriate bet.

They drove through Hyde Park's ornate wrought-iron gates and Thomas could see that almost all of society was doing what society did best, frittering away their endless time in pointless pursuits. Although, in reality, their pursuits were not entirely pointless. Like Grace, they were here to see and be seen. The young ladies were all dressed in their finery, strolling under their lacy parasols and showing off their charms to the eligible young men.

And soon he would lead Grace into that milieu, placing her on display, so the dukes, marquesses, earls, viscounts and barons could weigh her up, compare her to the other young ladies on the market and decide whether she was worthy.

Bile burned up his throat at the thought of these men who dared to judge her, who dared to want her. He swallowed it down.

That is what she wants. Remember.

And as her friend that was what he would help her achieve.

The carriage came to a halt. He jumped out and held out his hand to her. As she lowered herself down from the carriage her chest came dangerously close to his own, so close he could feel the warmth of her body, so close he could imagine her breasts against him. He swallowed a groan as he imagined what those breasts would feel like: soft, full, irresistible.

Friend. Remember.

He helped the lady's maid descend from the carriage, then took Grace's arm and they joined the parade. Thomas had to admit, it was pleasant to be out of the office, away from his work and taking in the crisp air. Although he'd prefer it if the park was not full of other people, laughing and chattering away, and all but drowning out the birds singing above them, oblivious to the artifices of the high and mighty walking on the paths below them.

'It's rather crowded, isn't it?' she said, echoing his thoughts. Their progress was halted by a couple in front of them who had stopped to chat to a group walking in the opposite direction. 'Isn't there somewhere a bit more private we could walk?'

Thomas looked down at her. What was she suggesting? That she wanted to be alone with him? If that was what she wanted, then Hyde Park on a sunny afternoon was not the place to be.

'I believe being among the crowds is the whole point. One is here to be seen as much as to enjoy the surroundings.'

'Yes, I suppose so.' Did he imagine the disappointment in her voice?

'I believe that is what your grandmother wishes.'

She sighed gently. 'Yes, I know. She's gone from being over the moon with happiness when the Duke offered a courtship, to being even more angry and disappointed in me than usual.'

'You have done nothing wrong. The fault is all with the Duke of Hardgraves.'

And with me for using you to win his land at a reduced price.

'I don't believe my grandmother sees it that way.'

'No, perhaps not, but you should not blame yourself.' He struggled to keep his voice nonchalant as he composed the questions he was burning to ask. 'And what of you? Do you still have your heart set on marrying the Duke?'

She shrugged one slim shoulder. 'It's not really up to me, is it?'

'I believe whomever you choose to marry is entirely up to you, or indeed if you choose to marry at all.'

She laughed as if he had made a joke, which had not been his intent.

'But let's not talk of my marriage.' She lowered her parasol and tilted her head towards the sun, closed her eyes and sighed. 'Let's just enjoy this glorious afternoon and the pleasure of each other's company.'

Thomas stared at her as if transfixed. She looked so content, like a woman relishing in sensual pleasure. A vision of her lying in his bed invaded his mind: her blonde hair cascading over the pillow, her head tilted back in just this manner, her eyes closed and that same smile of fulfilment playing on her lips.

He coughed to drive out that image. He was in the company of an innocent young lady, albeit an attractive and rather tempting young lady. But she was still an innocent and had to preserve that innocence until she married.

She opened her eyes and smiled at him, then caught the way he was still looking at her. He tried to look away, but failed to follow that simple command. She was so beautiful, with the sun shining on her golden hair and turning her creamy skin a soft, honey colour. Her lips parted and her teeth ran gently along her bottom lip.

Was she trying to torment him? If she was, it was working. Hungry desire raced through him. It was wrong, so wrong, but he wanted her so much, wanted to kiss her, to trace his hands over her body, to explore her with his lips and tongue, to take her entirely. He knew he wouldn't do it, but he had to admit he wanted to.

With more strength than he had thought himself capable of, he drew his eyes away, in a fervent attempt to break the spell of those bewitching lips.

'We should walk,' he said, not looking at her, determined to continue their stroll, like any other couple out enjoying the summer's day.

She walked beside him and he hoped and prayed she was so innocent she could not tell the effect she was having on him. The mere fact she was still at his side suggested she was ignorant of his thoughts and feelings. If she'd had any idea of what he wanted to do to her, what he wanted her to do to him, she would have demanded that he take her back to the safety of her grandmother immediately.

He was both thankful she was so innocent, while also frustratingly annoyed that she was.

* * *

Grace moved as close to Thomas as propriety would allow—closer, if she was being honest. She wanted to be near him, wanted to touch him, wanted him to touch her, or at the very least wanted him to look at her again the way he just had.

He had tried to disguise it, but when she had opened her eyes she had caught him staring at her with such intensity, such passion. That was not the look of a friend. That was the look of a man who desired a woman, who wanted her. It was a look that sent heat throbbing through her, had made her body yearn for him to do more than just look, but to act on his desires.

Her grandmother had said once they were courting the Duke would be free to take liberties with her. The thought of it had filled her with trepidation and not a little abhorrence, but that was not what she thought with Thomas. If he wanted to take liberties, she knew she'd be powerless to say no. If he wanted to kiss her and relieve the tingling of her lips, she would say yes. If he wanted to wrap her in his arms, she would say yes. If he wanted to caress her body, she would say yes.

Yes, yes, *yes.*

It was such an unfamiliar sensation, thrilling but tinged with a hint of delicious danger. Her body was seemingly crying out for him. Her skin was aching to feel the touch of his hands. She had never been so aware of her lips or her breasts and had never before felt that demanding throbbing tension between her legs.

She could not marry him, could not even be courted by him, her grandmother would never countenance that, but she had been told she must encourage him once again. Did that mean she should allow him to take liberties, the way her grandmother had said she should allow the Duke to do so? She wasn't going to marry Thomas, but would that really matter?

Surely, one could see it as a type of training, so she would know what would be expected of her when she did finally marry. After all, her grandmother had given her no instructions on what that would entail. She had merely said she should let the Duke, or whomever it was she married, do what he wanted with her and not screw her face up the way she had when the Duke had caressed her naked arm and placed his hand inappropriately on her buttocks.

Well, if she was to give the appropriate response and avoid making the terrible mistake of looking disgusted or surprised, she needed to be prepared for what was to come. It made complete sense. And Thomas, a man who had said he was her friend and would always be there when she needed him, was just the man to teach her what to expect.

She moved a little closer, hoping that would encourage him, but drat it all, he moved further away. He was not averse to her, she knew that. She had seen the way he had looked at her. Was it because he knew they were never to wed, that they would never be more than just friends?

Somehow, she was going to have to make him forget all about that and do what she was certain he was longing to do as much as she was.

But that was not going to happen while they were here, in this public place, surrounded by all these people. For now, she would have to be content with his company and wait for the opportunity when she could encourage him to move beyond merely looking at her with desire.

'Shall we walk to the Serpentine?' she said, keeping her tone light.

'As you wish,' he said and she smiled at the hoarse tone of his voice. He was still in the grip of that desire. Good.

In silence, they walked towards the lake, its water glistening in the sunlight. They were both still lost in their own thoughts, while the hubbub whirled around them. Grace could only hope his thoughts were travelling down the same path as her own. That he, too, was wondering how they could be alone so he could act on his passions and take those liberties she was desperate to surrender to him.

He led her to a bench and they sat under the draping leaves of an oak tree and watched the swans gliding past, the people rowing on the water and the small children playing with their toy sail boats.

'I believe Grandmama is hoping this is the first of many times we are to be in each other's company,' she said, relishing the prospect.

'She wishes you to be seen in public with a gentleman to incite the interest of titled men, particularly the Duke of Hardgraves.'

Was he trying to remind her of the real purpose of this walk, of what she was supposed to be focusing on, or reminding himself? It mattered not. Grace cared nothing for why they were to spend time together, only that they would continue to do so and hopefully not always in public.

'And it appears to be working,' he said, looking around at the people promenading past.

'What is working?'

'You have attracted many glances from men throughout the day.'

'Have I?' Grace had not noticed, but she had seen the sideways looks of many a young lady directed at her handsome companion. She should be outraged at their behaviour, but she was not. She knew exactly how they felt. How could one not look at a man like Thomas? He was so much more handsome than any other man she had ever seen. Despite now knowing he was a complete gentleman, perhaps too much of a gentleman, when she looked at him she still saw that dashing pirate she had imagined when they first met. It was that ink-black hair, those dark, intense eyes and the sculptured cheekbones and jawline that gave him such a wild, rugged look.

A delicious shiver rippled down her body. Didn't pirates have a reputation for ravishing young maidens?

'Yes, many men have tried to catch your eye,' he continued. 'I believe it won't be long before you are receiving many offers and perhaps even the Duke's interest will spark back into life.'

'Do you think so?' Grace tried to keep all displeasure out of her voice. It was what she wanted, of course it was, but not just yet. She had been promised more time with Thomas and she wanted more time, much more time.

'Of that I am certain.'

'But Grandmama said we could go to the theatre together, perhaps be seen riding in your carriage, and for us to take many more walks like this. We could perhaps attend the same balls. I know you said you don't attend balls, but as my friend, surely you will attend any that I am invited to so I have at least one person to dance with.'

Grace was babbling, her words tumbling out in a desperate attempt to make him agree to see her again, but she could not help herself. It would be terrible if this was the last time they were to be together.

'I would be honoured to escort you to the theatre and if you wish me to attend any balls to which we are both invited, then, of course, I shall do so. That is what friends are for.'

'Yes, friends,' she said, feeling rather pleased with herself.

'Now that we have been seen in public by enough people, I believe it time I return you home so you can tell your grandmother what a success today has been.'

Grace bit down a laugh. She would not be telling her grandmother about everything that happened today, nor the decisions she had come to, suspecting her grandmother would not quite understand her reasoning when it came to Thomas and the taking of liberties.

But if her grandmother really thought it through as logically as Grace had, she was sure she would come to the same conclusions. It was essential when the Duke, or some other titled man she was engaged to, wanted to take liberties that she react appropriately and not put him off the thought of marrying her. So there could be nothing wrong with encouraging Thomas to prepare her for that eventuality. Then she would know what to expect. After all, that would surely help her catch a titled man for a husband. If she did have to explain this to her grandmother, that was what she would say, but it was probably best to keep that to herself for now.

Chapter Twelve

Thomas knew he should take her home. Now. And he should not have committed to further outings, not when frustrated desire continued to rampage through his body.

It was so wrong to think of her in any terms other than as a friend. She was not his and never would be. The Duke didn't know it, but he had got his revenge. He had won that ridiculous bet after all. Thomas wanted her and he could not have her because she was the Duke's for the taking.

Anger at that undeserving buffoon surged up within him and he was grateful for its ferocity. That was what he would focus on, not her lush mouth, not her golden hair, not the tempting curves of her body.

He looked out at the Serpentine, hardly registering the quacking ducks, the colourful rowboats or the throngs promenading around its edges. All he was conscious of was the woman sitting beside him, so close they were almost touching.

'Shall we walk?' he said, standing up and not giving her an option. He had to get moving. Activity would surely quell the appalling thoughts that kept invading his mind.

'Yes, let's.' She stood up, took his arm and smiled up at him. Was her smile different? It almost had a complicit look to it, as if she was aware of what he was thinking, what he was feeling, and had no objections. No. It had to be his imagination. If she could read his mind, he knew she would not have placed her arm through his in such a trusting manner and would not be standing so close to him.

'Shall we walk over there? It looks rather idyllic.' She pointed to an area where trees and shrubberies concealed the path.

A wicked jolt of desire ripped through him at the thought of what he could do if they were alone, away from all prying eyes.

'I believe the point of this walk is for you to be seen by as many people as possible,' he said, surprised at how prim and proper his voice sounded. 'That would not be achieved by taking such a path.'

'No, but it would be fun.'

He looked down at her, wondering at the meaning of her words. Surely her thoughts were not running along the same lines as his own. No, of course they were not. She was an inexperienced young lady. He was misinterpreting her words to suit his own carnal longings.

'I suspect your grandmother would not think that.'

'My grandmother is not here.'

'But your lady's maid is and she is sure to report back.' He looked around. Where had that lady's maid got to?

'Oh, it seems Molly has wandered off,' she said with a cheeky smile.

'Be that as it may, we will remain where others can see us.' By God, he sounded like the most anxious of chaperons. And like a good chaperon he was ensuring she remained in public to preserve her virtue, because with the powerful need to feel her soft skin and to taste her lips coursing through him, he was unsure if he would be able to control himself if they found themselves alone.

She shrugged one slim shoulder. 'Some other time, then.'

He commenced walking, feeling as if he had just avoided stepping into a very deep quagmire from which there would be no escape.

'I believe it is time we returned home,' he said.

'Oh, so soon?'

'Yes.' He was still sounding like that strict chaperon. 'Your grandmother must be wondering why we have been away so long.'

Since when did you care about Lady Ashbridge? You coward.

'I suppose so,' she agreed and allowed him to lead her back to the carriage, where thankfully the lady's maid was waiting, chatting amicably with some friends and failing to do her duty in protecting her mistress's virtue.

Not before time, they arrived at her grandmother's home. He escorted her up the path, then bowed goodbye as the footman opened the door.

'Won't you come in?' she asked. 'I'm sure Grandmama would love to see you again.'

Thomas doubted that very much. He hesitated, but knew it would be rude not to at least exchange a few words with the older woman. Thomas could only hope that she did not notice the effect her granddaughter was having on him. He had accused Lady Ashbridge of dishonesty and theatrics, now he was going to have to put on a consummate performance of a man who could be trusted implicitly with her granddaughter.

He entered the parlour, but remained standing to indicate he had no intention of staying any longer than necessary.

'Did you have a nice walk?' Lady Ashbridge said, the real questions unasked. Was the Duke present? Was my granddaughter seen by a sufficient number of the aristocracy on the arm of a gentleman?

'Yes, the park was extremely busy,' he said, causing Lady Ashbridge to smile.

'Did Grace mention that she has been just dying to see the latest play at the Savoy Theatre? I am unfortunately unable to attend, but perhaps you could escort her.'

'It would be my pleasure to escort her.' It *would* be his pleasure, perhaps too much of a pleasure, but at least they would once again be in a public place and there were no private tree-lined paths to tempt him into doing what he knew he should not. 'Now I must say goodbye.'

'Yes, of course, you'll have your business to get back to,' Lady Ashbridge said with arched eyebrows, as if to remind Thomas of something he already knew only too well: that he was not a titled man and would never be in contention for her granddaughter's hand. He was here to serve a purpose and should not see his association with Grace in any other light. And on both those points Thomas could do nothing but agree.

He bowed to Grace and her grandmother then departed.

Now that was over, he could return to his work and not think about Grace's lips, her skin, her hair and certainly not her shapely body. Nor would he remember all the images that had been unleashed when she closed her eyes and smiled so contentedly.

He groaned. That was not going to be easy, especially when all that unsatisfied lust was still pounding through his body. He could relieve his unsated hunger by visiting one of the women he often kept company with, but he would not insult them by using them in such a manner. And it was not them he wanted. He wanted Grace. He wanted her naked beneath him, writhing under his touch, opening herself up to him and giving him the release he desperately needed. He wanted to feel her loving touch on his skin, to see the ardour in her eyes when they made love, to hold her afterwards in an intimate embrace as they relished in the pleasure of having satisfied their passion for each other.

But that was not going to happen. He would have to deal with his lust in the time-honoured fashion of frustrated men, then think of ways in which he could stop acting like a lecher and remember what his role was. To be her friend, nothing more.

'Did you see him?' Grace's grandmother asked as soon as the door closed behind Thomas.

It took a moment or two for Grace to think whom she was referring to. The Duke. Of course she was asking about the Duke. 'No, unfortunately we did not see him, but the park was very busy so I'm sure he will hear I was out walking with Mr Hayward.'

'Good, good,' her grandmother said, tapping her chin. 'And the Duke is sure to be at the opening of that new play at the Savoy.' She smiled at Grace. 'He is so discerning and such a great patron of the arts.'

Grace resisted the temptation to frown and certainly resisted the temptation to contradict her grandmother. They would be attending the latest Gilbert and Sullivan comic opera. Hadn't her grandmother previously said such performances were a travesty? That they were low art that should never be allowed on the respectable stage. Grace was sure she had dismissed them as the preserve of the hoi polloi and not suitable for genteel ladies and gentlemen.

But it now seemed if the Duke approved, then they, too, would approve. If he enjoyed something, then they, too, would enjoy it.

But instead of doing something she had never hitherto done and suggesting her grandmother was being a hypocrite, she did what she always did and smiled. 'Yes, he must be a man of refined tastes if he enjoys comic operas and Gilbert and Sullivan's musicals are said to be such rollicking fun.'

Her grandmother's smile became strained and Grace could not resist teasing a bit further. 'I believe I read somewhere they are quite the satirical take on society and its manners. I wonder if that is what the Duke likes about them?'

Her grandmother's nostrils flared, even as she kept smiling. 'You will hopefully soon have a chance to ask him for yourself, but when you do, remember, do not give your own opinion. Ask the Duke what he thinks, then tell him you agree completely.'

'Of course, Grandmama,' she answered dutifully, unable to quell a satisfied smile of amusement at her grandmother's predictable answer. With Thomas she would never have to tell him what he wanted to hear. She could have her own opinions and that was so invigorating.

Her grandmother's eyes narrowed. 'I hope spending time in Mr Hayward's company is not making you wilful.'

Panic twisted in Grace's stomach. It had been a mistake to behave in such a manner. She must not give her grandmother any cause to stop her from seeing Thomas again.

'No, Grandmama,' she answered quickly.

'You are not wanting to go to this play because it will mean spending time with him, are you?'

Grace had never lied to her grandmother before, but if her grandmother felt it acceptable to not entirely tell the truth when it suited her, surely it was not wrong for Grace to follow her example. 'No, Grandmama. I am merely excited about the prospect of attending a performance where the Duke will be present and hopefully of renewing our acquaintance.'

Her grandmother said nothing, just continued to stare at her in that disconcerting manner. The silence between them stretched on and on, becoming increasingly uncomfortable.

Grace attempted to swallow down her anxiety without her grandmother seeing and fought to maintain her false smile.

'You're not developing feelings for Mr Hayward, are you?' her grandmother asked, her eyes narrowed.

'Of course not,' Grace shot back and attempted a dismissive laugh.

'That's not why you're so eager to go to this play, is it?'

'No, Grandmama, of course not, Grandmama.'

Lies were piling on top of lies. She did want to see Thomas again, yearned to see him again.

'Need I remind you that he has no title?'

'No, Grandmama.'

'His only purpose is to help you find a suitable husband.'

'Yes, Grandmama.'

'And once you are courted by another, then you will never see him again.'

Grace's hands flew to her stomach as she gasped in a breath. She knew that. She had always known that. She had to marry a titled man. Thomas would never be anything more than a friend. A good friend.

'Yes, Grandmama,' she said quietly with lowered eyes.

'Good, and never forget it. That is the one and only reason I am permitting him to accompany you to this play.'

The turmoil in her stomach started to ease. She had her wish. She would be able to see Thomas again and the longer it took for the Duke or any other man to express his interest in her, the more she would see of him. She could only hope and pray that took a very, very long time. Not every young lady married in her first Season—some spent as many as five Seasons or longer in search of a suitable husband. There was no reason why that couldn't happen to Grace.

But she had nearly taken a misstep and ruined everything. She must never do that again if she was to continue seeing Thomas. From now onwards she must watch every word she said.

'On the night of the play you must look your very finest, as you might not get another chance to capture the Duke's heart,' her grandmother continued.

'Perhaps I can wear the sapphire-blue gown.' Grace held her breath, waiting for her grandmother's answer.

She nodded slowly. 'Yes, that would be perfect.'

Grace exhaled quietly, and the two women smiled at each other as if joined in a conspiracy. The blue gown was the most daring of her collection and one that Grace had thought she would never be so bold as to wear. It was cut lower, exposing a hint of décolletage, and the straps of delicate silk made her shoulders appear almost naked.

She knew her grandmother would see that gown as one to tempt the Duke, but there was another man Grace hoped would find the sight of her dressed in such a revealing manner a temptation impossible to resist.

Chapter Thirteen

It was obvious from the moment Thomas stepped into the drawing room of Lady Ashbridge's home to escort Grace to the theatre that her reappearance in public had had its desired effect.

'Look at all these gifts from admirers,' Lady Ashbridge said, indicating the bouquets adorning the various tables dotted around the drawing room. She picked up a card, nestled inside a display of brightly coloured flowers. 'This one is from Howard Seymour, the Earl of Whitecliff, an eminent and very suitable man.' She moved across to the sideboard and another bouquet. 'And this one is from the eldest son of Baron Morsley, such a refined young man.'

'Nothing yet from the Duke of Hardgraves?' Thomas already knew the answer to that question. If that man had sent flowers, the Earl of Whitecliff and Baron Morsley's son would not get a mention, and tonight's outing to the theatre would have been regretfully cancelled.

'No, not yet. Although I have heard from a reliable source he, too, will be attending tonight's performance.'

Thomas had heard the same rumour and knew what it meant. Grace was about to be placed on display and expected to reel the Duke back in, and Lady Ashbridge expected him to help her do so.

He was tempted to turn around and walk out the door rather than be caught up in this appalling game, but despite his contempt for the scheming and artifice of the aristocratic marriage market, he had made a promise to Lady Ashbridge and it was no more than he owed Grace after using her for his own ends in that bet. If this was the only way he could pay her back, then so be it.

She entered the drawing room and any thoughts of walking away from this evening's commitments evaporated. She was nothing short of a vision of loveliness. It was the way the blue gown matched the colour of her eyes, making them sparkle, that caught his immediate attention. Quickly followed by the plunging neckline, revealing the swell of her creamy breasts. If she was trying to gain a man's admiration, there were few ways better to achieve it than this. His own reaction was testament to that.

He had spent far too many tortuous hours speculating as to what she looked like under her layers of clothing. Now he had a tantalising hint of what reality would be like and could now see it would be irresistible.

But resist he must. She had not dressed to impress him, to tempt him or incite his desires, even if that had been the unintended effect. She was on display for the Duke's appreciation. Not his.

'Doesn't my granddaughter look like a duchess tonight?' Lady Ashbridge said.

'Yes, you look very nice, Miss Lowerby,' he replied, those words wholly inadequate in describing her enchanting appearance.

'Thank you,' she said, giving him a sweet, innocent smile and reminding him that, despite her appearance, she was a young debutante, an untouchable woman, someone with whom he would never, ever be anything more than just a friend.

'I think she's bound to catch a certain man's eye tonight,' her grandmother added in an almost coquettish manner.

Grace smiled up at him, a pretty flush tinging her cheeks. There was no denying she would catch the Duke's eye. How could she not? It was going to take every ounce of self-control Thomas possessed to stop his eyes from straying to that enticing décolletage. Somehow he was going to have to stop not just his eyes, but his mind from straying, to not think about what her breasts looked like released from the gossamer-thin silk, what they felt like cupped in his hands, what they tasted like when he caressed them with his tongue.

He gritted his teeth tightly together and dug his fingernails into his clenched hands to drive those images out of his mind.

'The Duke is expected to be in attendance tonight and I'm sure he will be enchanted,' Lady Ashbridge continued, staring hard at her granddaughter. 'That is what we are hoping, isn't it, Grace?'

'Yes, Grandmama,' she said with lowered eyes.

Lady Ashbridge turned her attention back to Thomas and narrowed her eyes. 'Grace is so excited about the prospect of reacquainting herself with the Duke.'

There was no possibility of missing the intent of her words. He was being reminded, even though it was not required, that she was not for him and there was only one reason why he was present tonight.

Lady Ashbridge continued to show what a cunning old fox she was. She had packaged her granddaughter up in this revealing manner so the Duke would be able to see what was on offer. Now she was to be sent out with Thomas, making her even more desirable to a man who couldn't bear the thought of others having what he believed was his by right.

'Shall we?' he said, offering her his arm and leading her out to his carriage, followed, of course, by her discreet lady's maid.

The moment they left the drawing room, she looked up and smiled at him. 'This is so exciting. I've never been to the theatre before. I am so looking forward to it.'

'And you'll be pleased to know that my private box is directly across from the Duke of Hardgraves's.'

'Yes, so my grandmother has informed me, repeatedly,' she said as he helped her into the carriage.

Thomas looked at her in the dim light of the carriage lamp. Her tone did not suggest this was as an exciting prospect as her grandmother had implied. Was she starting to question the wisdom of her grandmother's wish to marry her off to this Season's most eligible man?

Hope swelled up inside Thomas. Not for himself. Of course not for himself. Despite his undeniable attraction for her she was an untouchable young lady. Only one man would taste the sensual delights of those luscious lips and alluring body. The man she married and that would never be him. But she deserved a better man than the Duke of Hardgraves.

'Do I sense some reluctance regarding the Duke?' he asked, keeping all hints of expectation out of his voice.

She shrugged one shoulder, drawing his gaze to the naked skin, covered only by straps in the thinnest of sheer fabric.

'Grandmama is still certain that all the Duke needs is a gentle reminder of what he said to me at his estate and he will make good on his promise to court me.'

'And what of you, Grace? Is that what you want?'

She turned towards him in the intimate space of the carriage. 'Well, I do want to make my grandmother happy, but I also want to experience some happiness of my own.'

'And how are you going to achieve this happiness?' he asked, staring into those blue eyes so his eyes would not stray to where they wanted to go.

'I'm not sure. Perhaps you can show me,' she stated, still looking at him with an unfamiliar boldness.

Desire ripped through his body. He wanted to show her all the ways a man could make a woman happy. He wanted to teach her how to lose herself in the taking and giving of pleasure, but he would never do so. Her words might have caused erotic images to rampage through his mind, but that was where they would remain—he would never act on them.

He flicked a look at the lady's maid, who was staring out the carriage window as if fascinated by all that was happening outside. She might not be as focused on her charge as she should be, but Thomas said a silent thank you for her presence.

'Happiness is so elusive.' He coughed to clear the restriction in his throat. 'I believe we all have to find it in our own way.'

'Oh, yes, that is what I intend to do,' she said with a mysterious smile.

The carriage came to a halt in front of the theatre. That enigmatic smile lingered on her lips as the attendant opened the carriage door. Her behaviour tonight was decidedly out of character. While he applauded her new-found determination to find happiness, he could only hope this inexperienced young lady knew what she was doing and she did not make such a request of any other man, particularly the Duke.

* * *

He had said happiness was elusive, but Grace knew he was wrong. She knew exactly what made her happy. Being with Thomas made her happy. She was all but bubbling over with that wonderful emotion and just wished she could feel like this for ever.

The bubbles deflated slightly. This would not last for ever, only tonight, or for as long as she failed to attract the attention of the Duke.

Perhaps he *was* right. Perhaps happiness *was* elusive. Once he was no longer in her life, did that mean she would never be happy again? She gave a little shake of her head. That was too upsetting to contemplate, especially on a magical night such as this, and she simply would not ruin things by focusing on the future.

She would just enjoy their time together and maybe, just maybe, she would find some way to make it last for ever, while still doing her duty to her grandmother and making her proud.

Achieving that, she suspected, would be more elusive than happiness, but she would think of that another time. Tonight she would forget all about such things and just enjoy herself.

As she stepped down from the carriage, she leant forward under the guise of lifting the bottom of her gown, knowing exactly what would happen. Thomas's eyes lowered briefly as if they were no longer under his control.

A delicious sense of power rippled through her. This, too, was happiness. Knowing he wanted her. He desired her.

She smiled at him, a smile she hoped he would interpret in the way it was intended. *If you want me, you can have me.*

It was decidedly naughty of her and she knew it, but she

had nothing to feel guilty about. Not really. Her behaviour was exactly as her grandmother had prescribed.

She had instructed her that, when meeting the Duke, she was to make a very low curtsy and, rather than keeping her back straight as would normally be expected, she should lean forward ever so slightly.

'If the gown gapes open that is hardly your fault,' her grandmother had said with a wink. 'And if the Duke happens to look down at your décolletage, then by all means let him. After all, you're just enticing him with what will one day be his.'

At the time she had thought her grandmother's advice shocking, but when she had seen the way Thomas had looked at her when she entered the room, where his eyes had gone, she could see the value of her grandmother's stratagem.

It had been marvellous to have him look at her like that and she wanted him to do so again and again. And if he wanted to do more than just look, well, that, too, was something she would not object to.

She took his arm, moved in close to him and gave a little sigh at the thought of his hands moving to where his eyes had strayed.

It was such a scandalous thought, but one that sent a delicious throbbing sensation coursing through her body, as her nipples tightened against the soft caress of her silk gown.

Arm in arm, they joined the procession entering the theatre's foyer. Excitement bubbled up within Grace and she gripped his arm tighter. Being out on a night like this was enchanting, like being a princess in a fairy tale accompanied by her handsome prince. She looked up at the high ceiling and elegant chandelier bathing her and the other guests in warm, sparkling light, then gazed around at the other elegant patrons, and the smartly dressed ushers in their military-style uniforms.

'I wonder which play we will see tonight,' Grace said, looking at the posters lining the walls, showing beautiful actresses and handsome actors in an array of exotic costumes. Despite her question, she cared not the slightest what play she saw, just loving the experience of being here.

'Tonight's performance is *The Mikado*,' he said, stopping to buy a programme and handing it to her.

She clutched the memento of what she knew was going to be a glorious evening to her heart as Thomas led her up the plush carpeted stairs and along the hallway to his private box. Her lady's maid took a seat at the back against the wall and he escorted Grace to the front, where they settled into their velvet seats, overlooking the theatre below.

It was as if they were alone together, while still in a noisy, crowded room. She looked down on the other members of the audience taking their seats in the auditorium, then to the stage, hidden by a thick velvet curtain, then at Thomas. He was smiling at her, enjoying her excitement.

'This is marvellous,' she said. 'Thank you so much.'

'It's my pleasure,' he said and lightly touched her hand.

Even through their gloves, it was as if his skin was caressing hers and a small thrill moved up her arms and lodged itself in her heart.

She smiled at him again and looked back around the room, at the crowd below and at the orchestra pit, where the musicians were tuning up, the cacophony of so many instruments playing at once failing to drown out the laughter and chatter from the excited audience.

Movement in the box directly across from them drew her gaze and she saw the Duke of Hardgraves entering his box, along with another man who had attended his weekend party, and two young ladies, one of whom was Lady Octavia, the bully who had called her Graceless Lower-Born.

She looked away immediately, her happiness dissolving, then flicked another glance over at the Duke's box. He had not yet noticed her presence, but Lady Octavia had. She was staring straight at Grace, a smirk distorting her otherwise pretty face.

As if sensing her discomfort, Thomas reached over and gently squeezed her hand. Grace sat up straighter, lifted her chin and stared across the auditorium at Lady Octavia. The lady stared back at her, her lips curling into a deeper sneer. But Grace would not be cowed. Not this time.

So what if I fell over at a stupid ball? So what if the Duke said he would court me, then turned his back on me?

She would not let Lady Octavia or anyone else think of her as Graceless or Lower-Born.

Lady Octavia shuffled in her seat, then turned to the man sitting next to her, who was paying her no attention, but laughing with the Duke. She sent a quick look at Grace, who was not going to look away until that bully knew her days of intimidation and teasing were over.

Once again, Lady Octavia squirmed in her seat, picked up her programme and lowered her head as if absorbed by its contents.

'That is all it takes,' Thomas said, giving her hand another squeeze. 'Once they know they can't hurt you, the coward underneath the bullying exterior is quickly revealed.'

She squeezed his hand back in response, letting him know she was thankful for his words of advice and encouragement, then looked back at the Duke's box with a sense of triumph.

The other man in the box was looking in her direction while talking into the Duke's ear. The Duke stopped laughing and looked towards her. But it was not Grace he stared at. It was Thomas, and the Duke did not look pleased to see him.

Grace couldn't help thinking that his sullen expression bore a striking resemblance to a child who had been denied his favourite toy. Had she seen that sulky expression before and, if so, why had she not noticed it?

'It looks like your grandmother's plan is working,' Thomas said. 'You once again have the undivided attention of the Duke of Hardgraves.'

Grace was not so naive as to think it was she who had drawn the Duke's attention. After all, she had done that before and had lost it. The Duke's only interest in her was because she was with Thomas.

'Yes, so it would seem,' she murmured.

'Don't let it unnerve you,' he said, his voice soothing in reassurance. 'If the Duke can't see that you are a young lady more than worthy of him, then he is a complete fool.'

'Thank you. I won't.' The only thing unnerving her was the thought that the Duke might renew his interest so soon and this would all come to an end. It would make her grandmother happy, but would it make Grace happy? She knew the answer to that. No. Only Thomas could make her happy. But what choice did she have? She had to make a good marriage and there were no marriages better than one to a duke.

'For now, let's forget all about him and just enjoy the performance.'

'Yes, let's,' she said, turning back to the stage as the curtain raised and the orchestra struck up a lively tune.

She moved closer to him, determined to do as he suggested and not think about the Duke, her grandmother, or anything else, and just enjoy tonight's performance.

Chapter Fourteen

Thomas knew he should heed his own advice and focus entirely on the performers acting, dancing and singing their hearts out on the stage below.

But that advice would be easier to follow if Grace was not sitting so close to him. So close her breast was almost skimming his arm. So close he was enveloped in her scent of lavender and rose water. So close he could almost feel the warmth of her body burning into him.

Drawing his eyes from the man singing about being a wandering minstrel while incongruously dressed as a samurai, he looked over at the Duke of Hardgraves. He, too, was not watching the performance, but staring straight at Thomas.

Thomas nodded his head, in a parody of greeting, causing the Duke to almost snarl his dislike.

If he needed any reminder of why he was here tonight and why Grace was almost pressed up against him, it was there, in the box across from him. This was all about luring the Duke back in and getting him to make good on his offer of courtship and Thomas would do well to never forget that.

She had said she wanted to do what would make her happy, and he knew what that would be. To do as her grandmother wished and become a duchess.

She turned to face him and smiled, her eyes glinting in the soft light, her look almost inviting.

It's all for the Duke's sake, he reminded himself as he smiled back.

He refused to let himself look over at the Duke to see his reaction to that exchange, but had no need to do so. He knew exactly how the Duke would be reacting. If he thought he couldn't have her, then he would want her. If he thought Thomas wanted her, then his desire to have her would be all the greater. If he thought he could put Thomas in what the Duke considered 'his place', then he would not miss an opportunity to do so.

But what the Duke wanted and what Thomas wanted were of no matter. All that mattered was what Grace wanted. She claimed it was her happiness and the happiness of her grandmother she wished for. The second would be achieved by marriage to the Duke, as for the first, whatever Grace thought would achieve her wish of happiness he would accept, even if it did irk that a man such as Hardgraves should be the one to win her hand.

He focused on the stage below him and tried to follow the plot which seemed to involve arranged marriages, people falling in love when they shouldn't, men being punished for lusting after forbidden women and characters getting caught up in various nefarious plots. It all sounded horribly familiar.

After a series of songs and lots of dancing, some witty banter and much running around the stage, the curtain descended for intermission and the auditorium was filled with the sound of gloved hands clapping enthusiastically.

Thomas saw the Duke stand and leave the box and he knew what he had to do, even if it was not really what he wanted to. He had to provide Grace with the opportunity to shine in front of the Duke, so the promised courtship could begin in earnest.

'Shall we take some refreshments?' he asked her.

'Oh, can't we stay here? Perhaps Molly could go and get us something to drink.'

She turned to look over at her shoulder at her lady's maid, who was rising from her seat.

'The Duke has left his box and I believe your grandmother would want us to take the opportunity to exchange some words with him.'

'Oh, yes, I suppose so,' she said, picking up her shawl and fan and taking his hand as he helped her up from her seat.

They strolled down the corridor, Grace on his arm, and still just a tad closer to him than etiquette demanded. She really was determined to arouse the Duke's jealousy. He just wished she wouldn't come so dangerously close to arousing *him* in the process.

'There you are, Hayward,' he heard the Duke's booming voice from the end of the corridor. 'Thought I saw you. Thought private boxes were reserved for the aristocracy. Didn't know anyone could buy one, what.'

The guests parted to let him through, not daring to stand in the way of a duke's progress.

'Miss Lowerby,' he said when he reached them. 'How delightful to see you again.'

She performed a small curtsy, her back so ramrod straight she was almost leaning backwards, and murmured, 'Your Grace...'

'I've been quite remiss in not visiting you since your return from my weekend party. Tell your grandmother I will be paying the two of you a visit soon.'

'Yes, Your Grace,' she said quietly, like the obedient young woman she had been trained to be.

Once again, it looked like Thomas's role as bait was about to come to an end.

Grace continued to keep her eyes lowered while the Duke smirked at Thomas, knowing that his status meant there was nothing to stop him from taking her off him if that was his wish.

Thomas glared back at him, his body tense as if readying for a bout of boxing. Hardgraves pushed out his chest and lifted his chin, his curling upper lip exposing his teeth. Teeth Thomas would so love to push down the back of the puffed-up fool's throat.

For several long seconds they remained like that while the noisy audience swirled around them.

'Well, won't keep you,' the Duke finally said, turning to the prize he intended to take from Thomas. 'And remember, Miss Lowerby, expect a visit from me very, very soon.' With another contemptuous sneer in Thomas's direction, he turned and strode off, the patrons once again parting so they would not impede the progress of the titled clod.

'I believe your grandmother will declare tonight a success,' he said once the Duke was well out of hearing distance.

'Yes, I'm sure she will,' she murmured, then turned to her lady's maid. 'Molly, will you arrange for some refreshments to be sent to Mr Hayward's box.' She looked up at him and shrugged. 'We've achieved the purpose of joining the throng. I for one would be much happier if we returned to the privacy of your box.'

'And your happiness is all I care about,' he said, taking her arm as the lady's maid rushed off in the opposite direction.

'Good,' she said, that enigmatic smile returning. 'I intend to hold you to that promise.'

They returned to their box. She took her seat and looked over towards the Duke's box, her smile disappearing.

'Is everything all right?' he asked as he took the seat beside her.

'Oh, yes, perfectly. It's just, well, sometimes this game can become a little tiresome.'

'That's one way of describing it.'

'I thought the Season was going to be such fun. I didn't realise I'd have to take part in all this pretence and intrigue. It's more complicated than all the tangled threads of this play,' she said, pointing towards the stage.

'Then I don't believe your grandmother did her job properly and explained to you what it would be like.'

'No, all she said was I had to marry a man with a title, preferably at least an earl if not higher.'

'What? A baron isn't good enough?'

She gave a small laugh. 'Well, a baron would do at a pinch, but after the Duke's offer of courtship I suspect my grandmother would be very disappointed with such a lowly title. It's almost as if it is now the Duke of Hardgraves or nothing.'

'And nothing is not an option, I suppose.'

'No, of course not.' She laughed as if this was something that would only ever be said in jest. 'Although sometimes I wish it was.'

'Always remember that, whatever you decide to do, it is your choice. You can choose whom to marry, or you can choose not to marry if you wish.'

'Yes, that's what you said to me when we were at the Duke's estate. But what do you suggest I do? Become a piano teacher like my father?'

'Would that be so bad?'

She stared back at him with a look of incomprehension.

'Grandmama said that when my mother married my father, the shock was so bad that it sent my grandfather to an early grave. I could never do such a thing to my grandmother.'

'I suspect your grandmother is much stronger than you think and is more than capable of bearing a shock or two,' he said, certain he was speaking the truth and that tale was simply that manipulative old dragon's way of using emotional coercion to ensure her sweet granddaughter did exactly as she was told. 'You have every right to what you want even if at times it runs counter to what your grandmother wants for you.'

That enigmatic smile once again played around the edges of her lips. 'Yes, perhaps you are right.'

Molly entered the box, followed by two waiters carrying a bottle of champagne in an ice bucket, two glasses and a tray of canapes.

'Oh, lovely, but can you bring another glass for Molly,' she informed the waiter, who bowed and departed.

She really was rather special. Apart from his sister, he knew of few young women of her class who would ever consider the enjoyment of their servants.

He waited for the third glass to arrive, then poured the champagne and handed one to each of the women.

'To us,' Grace said, raising her glass.

'To us,' Thomas echoed, although he doubted that after tonight, once the Duke had visited Lady Ashbridge's home, there would be an 'us' to celebrate. But in the meantime he might as well enjoy this last evening in her company.

The curtain rose, the orchestra started playing, the cast began singing and Grace wished this evening could go on for ever. Then she could stay as she was, seated beside Thomas, champagne and happiness making her giddy.

She moved a fraction closer towards him, close enough so the naked skin of her arm was skimming his jacket, so close her thigh was all but touching his.

This was perfection. Well, almost perfection. What would make this evening perfect would be if it wasn't his jacket that was caressing her arm, but his fingers. Her arms tingled as she imagined them tracing a line up her arm, then slowly moving over her body.

She closed her eyes and sighed, pleased that laughter from the audience covered the sound.

He looked at her and smiled at something amusing that had happened on stage. She smiled back at him. His gaze moved to her lips and she willed him to do it, to kiss her. No one would see. Everyone, including Molly, was watching the play.

He turned back to watching the performance and she silently cursed his respectable behaviour.

He should kiss her. Now. Tonight.

If the Duke did start to pay her court, she knew what would happen. Her grandmother would insist she see no more of Thomas. Tonight might be the last time she was in his company. This might be the last time she would have an opportunity to discover what it was like for him to hold her, to kiss her, to feel his caresses. It was an opportunity she would not waste.

If he would not take advantage of the dark and his private box, she would have to find some other way to get him to do what she wanted and what she was sure he must want as well.

The performance came to an end. Grace joined in the rapturous applause as if the entire thing had been an absolute delight, even though her thoughts had been on other matters and she had failed to follow the story line. The cast took bow after bow. Even Mr Gilbert and Mr Sullivan made appearances and received standing ovations. Eventually, the electric house lights were turned on and it was time to go.

They left the box and joined the exuberant crowd departing from the theatre, all loudly discussing the performance and laughing at the antics of the cast. Like herself, Thomas remained silent, as if he, too, was lost in his thoughts.

It had been a magical evening, but all Grace could think was they might never again walk arm in arm.

The carriage was waiting for them at the entrance and they drove home through the busy streets, still full of traffic at this late hour, the pavements packed with people walking under the glow of the gas lamps.

The journey was annoyingly short and they arrived home far sooner than she had hoped. This was it. She would now say goodbye to him and if the Duke made good on his promise to call, they might never see each other again.

He helped Molly down from the carriage, then held out his hand for Grace. She placed her hand in his. The strong fingers curled around hers. Was he thinking the same as she? Was he regretting the likelihood they would never again be in each other's company? Was he thinking they had to make the most of these last precious moments together?

She looked into his eyes to try to answer those questions. He gazed back at her and there was such warmth in his look, such intimacy, she was sure he was feeling the same.

She lowered herself to the ground, her body coming temptingly close to his. How she longed to know what his body felt like up against hers. She'd had hints of the strength and power of his arms and chest when they'd walked and danced together, but she wanted to know what his muscles felt like under the touch of her fingers.

'You can go ahead, Molly,' she said, not looking in the direction of her lady's maid. 'I shall be in shortly.'

The door opened, light briefly filled the path, then with a soft click the door closed. They were alone in near darkness. No one would see them now. Grace continued to stare up into his eyes. She knew he wanted to kiss her. She could see it in the intimacy of his gaze.

Do it, she silently urged.

She parted her tingling lips in invitation, her breath turning into gentle sighs.

His hand moved tantalisingly slowly up her arm, over her elbow-length gloves to her naked skin, further kindling her burning need for him. She had to feel his lips on hers, his body up against hers. She yearned for him to relieve this pounding desire for his kisses, for his caresses.

She moved in closer, closed her eyes and tilted back her head.

'We can't,' he whispered, his lips so close she could feel his warm breath feather-light on her cheek.

'Yes, we can,' she whispered back. 'It's what I want. No one will see. No one will know.'

Then his lips were on hers, hot, hard and hungry.

She kissed him back, unleashing the pent-up longing that had been building up since she had first danced with him, loving the taste of him, the feel of his rough cheeks on hers and relishing the sensation of his strong muscular chest against her soft breasts.

Oh, yes, this was what she wanted.

She wrapped her hands around his head, her fingers weaving into his thick hair, holding him tight as her kisses gave full vent to her passions.

His tongue ran along her bottom lip, causing her lips to part so she could fully experience the pleasure of that arousing touch. Kissing her deeper, holding her tighter, he let his tongue gently enter her mouth and she was sure that if he hadn't been holding her so tightly, she would have swooned with the sheer sensual thrill of such intimacy.

His masculine taste was so intoxicating, the feel of his body pressed against her was maddingly enticing, but it was still not enough. She wanted more than his kisses. She wanted his caresses. Her breasts yearned to feel the touch of his hands, the throbbing between her legs demanded release, a release only he could give her.

His kisses moved to the sensitive skin of her neck and she pressed herself against him, silently urging him to continue in his exploration of her body.

'Miss… Lady Ashbridge insists you come inside, now,' Molly said, her voice urgent.

He all but jumped backwards.

Grace had not heard the door open, nor the arrival of her lady's maid, and as fond as she was of Molly, she cursed her for her unwanted interruption.

'I'll be in shortly,' she said.

'Yes, miss.' The door opened and closed and they were once again alone, but he remained standing frustratingly apart from her.

'You must go inside before Lady Ashbridge comes looking for you,' he said, his voice a hoarse rasp.

Grace released a sigh of exasperation. 'Yes, I suppose you're right,' she said, but did not move.

'I'm sorry, Grace. That should never have happened.'

'You have nothing to be sorry for,' she whispered back.

'You have my assurance that no one will ever know.'

She shrugged. 'I don't care if everyone knows.' Why

should she care if everyone knew about something that had given her so much pleasure? Surely the world should be allowed to share in her joy.

'Yes, you do,' he said, his voice surprisingly stern. 'You do not want your grandmother to know. You don't want anyone in society to know. You will be ruined. Your chances of marriage will be destroyed.'

Again, what did she care?

'Go inside, Grace,' he said quietly. 'We'll talk of this another day.'

'Yes, yes, you're right, I suppose,' she said, her voice full of disappointment. 'Thank you,' she added, unsure what she was thanking him for: for bringing her back to reality or for kissing her and showing her what true pleasure was like. But she knew he was right, she had to go.

'Goodnight, Grace,' he whispered.

'Yes, goodnight, Thomas,' she replied and continued to stare up at him, until he opened the door for her and she knew she had to depart.

The door closed behind her and she released a long, euphoric sigh. That had been more captivating than she had imagined kissing a man could possibly be. She had thought she would not know what to do, but it had all come so naturally, as if they were made for each other.

And she would be seeing him again. He said they would talk of this another day, but she did not want conversation, she wanted more of his delicious kisses.

Smiling to herself, she walked down the hallway towards the drawing room where her grandmother would be waiting, expecting to hear of everything that happened tonight.

She would tell her grandmother the Duke planned to call. That was what she wanted to hear, but she certainly would not be telling her grandmother anything else that had occurred. That was to be her secret. Her delicious, glorious secret.

Thomas climbed back into his carriage as if in a daze and signalled for the driver to take him home. He could hardly believe he had done something so forbidden. He had kissed a debutante. No man in his right mind did such a thing. But he hadn't been in his right mind when he'd looked down at those tempting lips. He hadn't been in any mind at all, right or wrong, as he'd been incapable of thinking. He had just wanted. Wanted her so fiercely it drove out all rational thought. He had wanted to feel her lips on his, wanted her soft body pressed up against his and wanted more, much more than he was entitled to. He had longed to explore every contour of her shapely body with his hands, his lips, his tongue.

Thank God they had not been in a private place, as he had doubts that he would have been able to stop himself from doing what he really wanted to do, lifting her up, parting her legs and finding release deep within her soft feminine folds.

He put his hands on his head and groaned. He could not believe the depths of his moral decay. She was an innocent debutante, a young lady who knew nothing of the world and nothing of men, and she was expected to remain that way until she was married.

Yet she had made it clear she wanted his kisses and the way she had reacted did not suggest she was quite as unworldly and naive as he had assumed. A vision of her beautiful face before he kissed her appeared in his mind. With her lips parted in invitation, her body arched towards him, her head tilted and her eyes closed, she gave every impression she was offering herself to him. And he had been in-capable of resisting the irresistible.

But it was still wrong, so wrong as to be unforgivable, and nothing could justify what he had done. Under normal circumstances such behaviour would have to be followed by an immediate proposal of marriage, but Grace did not want marriage to him and Lady Ashbridge most certainly did not want him to marry her granddaughter. She had set her sights much higher than Thomas and after tonight was likely to get her wish.

And once the Duke did come courting again, Thomas's role as Grace's escort would come to an end.

He groaned again at the memory of her lips, at the fem-inine taste of her, of the spicy, womanly scent under her floral fragrance. Now that he'd experienced her kisses once he wanted them again, wanted more than just her lips on his, but that could never be.

His carriage pulled up in front of his townhouse, but he signalled to his driver to take him to his club. He did not need the quiet of his home, where he would spend what re-mained of the night being tormented by what he had done. What he needed was a stiff drink, several stiff drinks, and some raucous masculine company to divert his mind from his appalling behaviour.

Arriving at his club, he walked up the stone stairs to-wards the highly polished black doors as if approaching a sanctuary. Only men could be members of the Eldridge Club and, while his sister and her friends constantly railed against such institutions, tonight he gave thanks for it.

He nodded to the doorman as he entered and headed across the foyer, his footsteps muffled by the deep crim-son carpet. He entered the dimly lit bar and was pleased to see his two oldest friends seated in an alcove, sharing a bottle of claret.

'Thomas, where have you been hiding out?' Sebastian called out while Isaac signalled to the waiter to bring another glass.

Thomas sank gratefully into a leather chair. This was just the diversion he needed.

'No, I haven't been hiding. It's just been business as usual.' He poured himself a glass of wine, downed most of the contents and poured himself another.

His friends exchanged looks at his uncharacteristic behaviour, but thankfully made no comment.

'I heard you had bought a sizeable chunk of Hardgraves's land,' Isaac said with a satisfied smile.

'Yes, and I got it for much less than I was prepared to pay.' Thomas took another large sip of the claret and forced himself not to think of how he managed to make such a good deal.

'I saw him tonight, at the theatre, looking as pompous as ever,' he continued, then cursed himself. He did not want to think about tonight. Not the theatre and not that kiss. Definitely not that kiss.

'You weren't at The Elysian,' Isaac said with mock disapproval, referring to the music hall of which he was the manager.

'No, I was accompanying a debutante, so I don't believe The Elysian would have been appropriate.'

Sebastian and Isaac looked at him with raised eyebrows, their lack of comment speaking volumes.

'I was merely doing her grandmother a favour,' he said, hoping that was enough of an explanation.

The eyebrows were not lowered.

'Hardgraves was there as well,' he added, desperate to change the subject.

'I hope you were at a pantomime,' Isaac said. 'I doubt if that buffoon would be able to follow anything more complicated.'

Thomas smiled at the jest, while inwardly cringing that Isaac was talking about the man Grace might end up married to. She deserved so much better than Hardgraves. She deserved a man who would cherish and appreciate her. That would never be Hardgraves.

He took another long swallow of his claret while the others laughed about all the times Hardgraves and the other aristocrats had tried to get the better of the three of them when they had been schoolboys. They had arrived at school at the same time, three lost young boys. They instantly found they were all outsiders and soon became firm friends. A friendship that continued to endure to this day.

Isaac and Sebastian were both sons of aristocrats but were still seen as 'not up to snuff' by the other boys, Isaac because his mother was an actress and Sebastian because his family had been tainted by scandal for several generation, scandals he chose not to discuss. That had always mattered more to the other pupils and the schoolmasters than the boys' academic achievements or their sporting prowess.

Talk of school soon moved on to other topics and it wasn't long before they were laughing loudly as Isaac regaled them with ribald tales from his music hall. Thomas said a silent thanks for having such friends, who could so easily divert his brooding mind from what he should and should not have done, and what he should and should not do in future.

They were saving him ruminating, at least for the moment. He knew as soon as he left the club he was going to have to do some serious thinking about what had occurred tonight and come to some important decisions. But for the rest of the evening he would just drink and laugh with his friends and try to forget about everything else.

Chapter Fifteen

Grace had hardly been able to stop smiling from the moment she left Thomas on the doorstep. She had gone to bed with a silly grin on her face, had spent the night revelling in the most glorious of dreams and had woken still smiling with delicious contentment. Then continued to smile as she joined her grandmother in the breakfast room.

'You're in a very good mood today, my dear,' her grandmother said, looking her over her teacup. 'I take it that seeing the Duke again has put that smile on your face.'

'Yes, Grandmama,' Grace replied dutifully with the only response her grandmother ever wanted from her.

The footman entered the room with an enormous bouquet of flowers.

From Thomas?

Grace could only hope their kiss had affected him as deeply as it had her and these were a token of his affection.

She jumped up from the table, rushed over to the footman and removed the note. She forced herself to keep smiling as she saw the crest. 'They're from the Duke of Hardgraves.'

'Oh, my dear, darling girl,' her grandmother said, rushing to join Grace, taking the embossed card from her fingers and placing her hand over her heart. 'This is wonderful, wonderful news.' She looked back down at the card. 'And he wishes to call on us this afternoon. This is it, my dear, this is it. You're about to become a duchess.'

Grace should be dancing with joy. She should feel as if she was floating on air. She should be tingling all over as if unable to contain her happiness. She should be feeling how she felt last night as the memory of Thomas's kiss played out repeatedly in her mind. What she should not be doing was having to force herself to keep smiling, nor should she be thinking of ways to get out of this afternoon's visit.

'Should we invite Mr Hayward as well?' she said quietly. 'So, well, so the Duke doesn't think he's got things all his own way?'

Her grandmother looked up from the card, still smiling, then placed her finger briefly on her chin, before shaking her head. 'No, I believe that man has served his purpose. You won't need to see him ever again.'

A heavy weight descended on Grace, making her shoulders slump. Her legs suddenly seeming incapable of carrying her. She wanted to cross the room and collapse on to the nearest dining chair. This could not happen. To never see Thomas again would be torture. She simply *had* to see him again. It was as if her very life depended on it—certainly her happiness did. It was imperative that her grandmother change her mind.

'But wouldn't it be better to continue to make the Duke jealous? I mean to say, he has shown me such favour before and withdrawn it. Perhaps he will do the same again this time.'

'We will just have to make sure he doesn't,' her grandmother said, lightly stroking Grace's cheek. 'You will have to do everything in your power to make sure he doesn't. And I mean, everything.' It was a gesture of affection Grace always longed to feel, and under normal circumstances it would be enough to make her do and say exactly what her grandmother wanted, but not this time. This was too important. She could not lose Thomas, not now.

'Grandmama, I have something I have to tell you.'

'Hmm, what is that, my dear?' Her grandmother placed the card back in the flowers and took her seat at the dining table.

Grace joined her, pleased that she was finally able to sit.

'Last night…' She gasped in a breath to give herself strength.

'Yes, last night?' Her grandmother signalled to the footman to pour another cup of tea.

'Last night I kissed Mr Hayward,' she said, forcing her words to come out in a rush before her constricted throat prevented her from speaking.

'Leave us,' her grandmother barked at the footman.

Grace clasped her hands together in her lap to stop them shaking. She was tempted to lower her head in shame, knowing how disappointed her grandmother would be in her, but how could she be ashamed of kissing Thomas? She had wanted to do it. She had encouraged him to do it and wanted him to do it again.

She breathed in deeply to try to slow her racing heart and looked across the table at her grandmother, who was glaring at her with dagger-sharp eyes, seemingly speechless with rage.

'It wasn't Mr Hayward's fault,' she rushed on. 'I encouraged him. I wanted him to kiss me.'

'Did anyone see you?' her grandmother said, her voice ominously quiet.

'No, we were outside the house, the entrance was in darkness and there was no one in the street.'

'Good.' Her grandmother looked towards the door, then

picked up the silver bell beside her plate and gave it a vigorous ring.

The footman appeared immediately. 'Samuel, I have decided to increase your wages. I have always appreciated your discretion and loyalty and believe it needs to be rewarded. Do you understand what I am saying to you?'

'Yes, my lady,' the footman said with a bow. 'Thank you, my lady.'

'But I also believe in punishing disloyalty and indiscretion. Should I, say, hear that the servants are gossiping about something they should not, then I would have no hesitation in sacking the culprit responsible for spreading unfounded rumours and throwing him out on to the street without a reference. Do you still understand what I am saying to you?'

'Yes, my lady,' the footman said with another bow.

'Good, you can leave us now.' With that, her grandmother turned the full focus of her displeasure back on Grace.

'No one saw what happened. No one knows what happened. No one needs to know what happened. I will make sure Mr Hayward says nothing. You've been a stupid, stupid girl, but it should not harm your prospects.'

'But—'

'No buts. We will never mention this again and, of course, you will never, ever see that man again.'

'But—'

Her grandmother held up both hands to stop her words.

'But I love Mr Hayward,' Grace blurted out before she even had the chance to think about what she was going to say. But it was true. She did love him. She loved being with him, loved the way he made her feel, loved the way he made her laugh, loved the way she could rely on him, loved everything about him.

A smile spread across Grace's lips, a glorious, blissful smile. She was in love with Thomas. Of course she was. That was why the world seemed like a better place the moment she saw him. That was why she thought of him constantly. That was why she felt complete when she was with him.

She was in love with Thomas Hayward. And she wanted to spend the rest of her life with him. Not the Duke, not any other man. To marry another would be a travesty, for herself and for the man she did not and never could not love. It had to be Thomas, only Thomas.

Surely even her grandmother would be able to see that.

'Don't be ridiculous,' her grandmother all but snarled back at her. 'You don't know the meaning of the word love. The man was just using you.'

'He was not. He's not like that,' she said, defiance welling up inside her at this unfair criticism.

'Oh, isn't he? He kissed you last night, didn't he? He took an enormous liberty that no man should take with a debutante, but did he send you a bouquet of flowers this morning?'

Grace looked over that the enormous bouquet from the Duke.

'No,' her grandmother answered for her. 'When he kissed you, did he ask for your hand in marriage, as any real gentleman would?'

'No,' Grace whispered.

'Or did he take what he wanted, then run off into the night feeling pleased with himself that he had taken liberties with a silly debutante?'

Grace chose not to answer.

'He did, didn't he? Then he probably went and boasted

to his friends as to how you had all but thrown yourself at him and he had merely taken what was offered.'

Heat rushed to Grace's cheeks at the memory of how she had indeed offered herself to him, desperate for his kisses.

'And is he here today, offering for your hand in marriage, making right on the wrong he committed?'

Again, Grace did not answer, the pounding of her heart and the burning of her cheeks making thinking all but impossible.

'No. The man does not love you, Grace,' her grandmother said in a softer tone. 'He could just see that you are a stupid, naive little girl who could be taken advantage of. You're just lucky that a kiss was the only thing he took.' She narrowed her eyes and stared at Grace. 'That is all he took, wasn't it?'

Grace nodded, trying to take in all her grandmother had said. There *was* no bouquet from Thomas and certainly there had been no mention of marriage, except when he had first told her he had no plans to do so. Could her grandmother be right? It seemed there was only one thing for it, she would have to ask him herself.

'And you can put any thoughts of trying to contact that man again right out of your mind,' her grandmother said as if reading her thoughts. 'If you do see him again or write to him—and believe me, if you try such a foolhardy action I will hear about it—then I will cut you off. You will have nowhere to live and no money to live on. Then you really will find out whether your precious Mr Hayward is actually enamoured with you or was just taking advantage of your stupidity. You will discover whether he is prepared to take in a waif with nowhere else to go. You'll know for certain whether that one kiss was enough to make him want to take you as his wife.'

Grace gripped her hands tightly in her lap, her heart racing, her stomach tying itself into ever tighter knots.

'Or you can continue to live in my home, where nothing more is expected of you than to marry well.'

Grace made no reply.

'And this afternoon you can show me just how grateful you are for all that I have given you by being charming to the Duke so he knows that it is he, and he alone, that you wish to wed.' She narrowed her eyes again. 'And you will never, ever mention that kiss again or speak Hayward's name in this house. Do I make myself clear?'

Again Grace made no reply.

'Or do I need to show you what life is like for a young woman such as yourself who is thrown out of her home after shaming her family? Do you think you will actually be able to survive out there?' She pointed towards the window. 'Can you imagine what would have happened to you if I had not taken you in and given you a home and the best of everything?'

Grace looked down at her trembling hands.

'Good. Then we will pretend that this conversation never happened.' With that, her grandmother rang for the footman. 'Samuel, my tea has gone cold,' she barked at the young man. 'Make another pot.'

The footman took the teapot and hurried out of the room.

'I believe you can spend the rest of this morning in your bedchamber, thinking about all I have said, while Molly helps you prepare for your important visitor. Tell her the lavender gown will be appropriate. You should be dressed in a manner suitable for receiving an offer.'

Grace remained quiet, staring down at her hands.

'Right, you are excused.'

She stood up and moved away from the table.

'And remember,' her grandmother added, stopping Grace just as she took hold of the door handle, 'you will smile throughout this visit. You will let the Duke know you are flattered by his renewed interest and you see him as the most charming, most intelligent, wittiest man you have ever met, or you will face the consequences. Do I make myself clear?'

'Yes, Grandmama,' Grace said as she walked slowly out of the room on legs seemingly made of lead. Her entire body ached as if she was coming down with influenza and even in her childhood, she had never felt more confused and alone that she did right now.

While Molly took to her hair, backcombing, curling, sweeping it up, pushing in pins and flowers, Grace stared at her reflection in the looking glass and chewed on her bottom lip in thought.

Her grandmother was wrong. Thomas had not used her. She had to be. He had not seen her as a silly, naive debutante and taken advantage of her. Well, she *was* a silly, naive debutante, but that was hardly her fault. She knew nothing of the world. She'd been cloistered away in her grandmother's homes for the last eighteen years. Her only experience of life was at the social events she had attended during the Season and there had been woefully few of them, and what she had seen out the window of their carriage.

But her grandmother was right about one thing—many of the sights she had seen as they had travelled through London had been grim indeed. Even in the wealthier areas she had seen some shocking sights, children begging on the streets, people dressed in rags, desperate women trying to sell flowers, blind men selling trays of matches.

She would never survive if she was tossed out into that

world. But nor did she want to stay in this world, one where she had to marry a man she did not love and hardly knew and see nothing of the man she did love.

If only she knew how Thomas really felt about her. If only he had sent her a note declaring his love. If only he had asked for her hand in marriage. If he did love her as much as she loved him, they could wed and she could still have her fairy-tale ending. It might not be what her grandmother wanted, but it would still be glorious, and maybe, just maybe, when her grandmother came to see what a remarkable man Thomas was, she, too, would come to see how perfect such a marriage could be.

She released a loud, slow sigh. That would never happen and there was no point pretending it would. Thomas did not have a title. It did not matter how perfect he was, the possession of a title was all that mattered to her grandmother.

Her hair styled to perfection, Molly helped her into the lavender gown her grandmother had insisted she wear. It was a gown Grace had simply adored when the dressmaker had presented it to her, but now it felt like she was being clapped in irons rather than adorned in satin, and being taken to her execution rather than receiving a visitor for afternoon tea.

'You look lovely, miss,' Molly said. Despite the compliment, her lady's maid's voice reflected Grace's sadness.

'Thank you, Molly,' she said, releasing a low sigh.

Molly hesitated, as if there was something she wished to say, then curtsied and departed. Grace waited until she was summoned. Then, with a heavy heart, walked down the stairs and entered the drawing room, where she found her grandmother and the Duke of Hardgraves seated on the sofa, their heads close together as if deep in conversation.

The Duke stood as she entered and smiled at her. She

flicked a quick look at her grandmother, who glared at her, then sent her a false, beaming smile. Grace knew she should imitate her grandmother's expression, but her lips refused to move.

'Your Grace,' she said with a curtsy, then kept her eyes lowered as she took her seat. Hopefully, that was all that would be required of her for the rest of the afternoon.

The Duke asked whether she had enjoyed last night's play and how she was enjoying the Season, which she responded to in as few words as possible.

He then went on to discuss the changeable weather and how much he was looking forward to the hunting season once the social Season was over. To which Grace made the required non-committal responses.

'I am aware that you have been keeping company with Mr Hayward and believe you have developed a certain fondness for the man.'

At the mention of his name, Grace's gaze fixed on the Duke, both interested and wary as to where the conversation would now go.

'I believe I would be remiss in my duty if I did not inform you as to that man's true character,' the Duke said, shaking his head slowly and frowning.

'Really, Your Grace?' her grandmother said in mock surprise. 'We were under the impression that Mr Hayward was an honourable gentleman and he has been so attentive to my granddaughter.'

'Yes, he no doubt was able to deceive such a trusting soul as yourself,' the Duke said, the furrows in his brow deepening. 'But I should inform you that, unfortunately, that man is neither honourable nor a gentleman.'

Grace stiffened and forced herself not to blurt out that he was both. He had been the one to restore her dignity when she had fallen so ignominiously at the Duke's ball. He had given her the strength to stand up to that bully Lady Octavia. And his behaviour towards her had always been honourable. Some might say he should not have kissed her, but that had been what she wanted so he could not be criticised for such behaviour. And, yes, perhaps he should have made an offer of marriage, but, well, maybe he just hadn't had the opportunity to do so yet.

'Is he not honourable?' her grandmother said, placing her hand over her heart and tilting her head, as if hanging on the Duke's every word.

'Yes, I'm afraid the man is quite disreputable and I can tell you things that perhaps a young lady should not hear.'

'It is good of you to spare my granddaughter's delicate feelings, Your Grace, but it if is something she needs to hear for her own protection, then I believe you should tell her all that you know.'

Grace was beginning to wonder if this was a discussion they had already had and were now merely putting on a performance for her benefit.

'Mr Hayward is a covetous man who always wants what other men have.'

To Grace this sounded like one of those occasions her old nanny would have described as the pot calling the kettle black.

'He knew that I had, shall we say, an attraction for you,' he continued and gave a small smile. Her grandmother tittered behind her hand while sending Grace a steely gaze of disapproval, a look that Grace returned.

'That is why he appeared to be so interested in you at my weekend party.'

'Appalling, simply appalling,' her grandmother said, shaking her head in disapproval as if this was something about which she was unaware and not something she had orchestrated as part of her plan to capture the Duke.

'But it is worse than that, I'm afraid.'

'Oh, surely not,' her grandmother said with a gasp of feigned shock.

'Yes, the man had the audacity to suggest to me we use Miss Lowerby in a shameless wager.'

Grace's gaze shot to the Duke, her body suddenly numb, even as her heart thumped loudly in her chest.

'Yes, it's true,' the Duke added, looking in her direction. 'And I'm ashamed to say, I accepted his bet, but only because I knew that I would win.'

Her grandmother tilted her head once again, as if to say, please go on, and despite herself, Grace also wanted to hear what the Duke had to say, even though she suspected, or hoped, it was all lies.

'He challenged me in a contest to see who could woo Miss Lowerby and gain her affections, and, in his words, to make things more interesting, that we should bet on the outcome.'

Grace covered her mouth with her hand to stop herself from crying out, *No, he would not do that.*

'I took the bet because I knew just how greedy the man was and because, well…' he shrugged and smiled at her '…I was intending to woo you anyway.' He pulled his face into a more serious expression. 'But I told him that if he won he would have to pay me more for the land I no longer required, the land he so desperately wanted for that railway thing of his, but if I won, I would sell it for a lower price.'

Grace stared at him, her heart pounding hard, as the ramification of that bet crashed down on her. Hadn't Mr Hayward informed her when they were out walking that he expected to get the Duke's land at a lower cost? She had enjoyed that walk so much, but was he merely playing a role? It could not be true. It simply could not be. Surely she would have known if he had been merely toying with her. The fun they'd had together, the way they had laughed and teased each other, that could not have all been artifice. Could it?

'I can see you are now starting to understand what sort of man he is,' the Duke said, shaking his head in disapproval. 'I knew he would merely go through the motions of wooing you, but let me win so he could get my land off me for less than he had originally offered. That's the sort of man he is. One who only cares about business and will do anything to get what he wants. Whereas I was prepared to sacrifice my land for a lady's honour.'

'Oh, Your Grace,' her grandmother said, both hands over her heart. 'That was so noble of you. And dare I say rather romantic?'

'Well, I did have my own selfish reasons.' He smiled at Grace. 'I actually wished to win the fair maiden. That was much more important to me than land or money ever could be.'

Her grandmother sighed loudly, while Grace tried to take in all that he had said.

'I don't believe you,' she seethed, finally finding her voice.

'I can understand that,' the Duke said, once again shaking his head dolefully. 'It would be hard for a young lady as kind and gentle as you to believe someone's behaviour could be so disreputable, but I have the altered contract and a written document that attests to the bet if you wish to see it.'

'I'm sure that won't be necessary,' her grandmother said as Grace continued to stare at the Duke in disbelief. Could it be true? Had Mr Hayward used her so he could buy the

Duke's land at a reduced cost? Was that all she had ever been to him? A means to advance his own business interests?

He had mentioned his expectation of making an even more advantageous deal than he had expected, that she must be his lucky star and would be the one to make it happen. She had felt so flattered at the time. Had he been making fun of her? Had it all been just one big joke at her expense?

'I'm so sorry you have had to hear this and I can see it has been a shock for you,' the Duke said. 'But people are not always what they seem.'

Grace gave a small, mirthless laugh. That was becoming increasingly obvious.

'But even though I lost the bet I feel like a winner,' he continued. 'And that is why I am here today. I hope I will continue to be a winner.' He turned towards her grandmother. 'At my weekend party I asked if your lovely granddaughter would be amenable to a courtship. To my delight she said yes. Now I wish to ask whether she would be equally amenable to my offer of marriage.'

'Oh, Your Grace,' her grandmother said. 'Of course my granddaughter would be amenable, more than amenable.' She laughed as if this was all so amusing. 'Wouldn't you, Grace?'

They both looked at her and Grace knew she had no option. She had thought she loved Mr Hayward, but he was not the man she thought he was. She didn't love the Duke and suspected she never would, but as her grandmother said, what did she know of love? Nothing.

There was no point pursuing the foolish dream of being with Mr Hayward. In fact, there seemed no point in anything. It was time to accept her fate.

'Yes, I accept your proposal,' she said, her dreams of happiness as shattered as her heart.

Chapter Sixteen

Thomas had received no response to the note he had sent Grace containing a clumsy attempt at an apology for his outlandish behaviour. He had not gone as far as to offer his hand in marriage, but he had made it clear he would do whatever was required to make amends.

When another day had passed and he had still received no reply, his concern continued to mount. Had Lady Ashbridge intercepted the letter and destroyed it? Or had Grace received it, but not replied? Had he offended her by not immediately proposing marriage? Would his presence at her home be welcomed or rebuffed?

It was a bizarre situation in which he found himself. He did not obsess over women. Apart from the occasional pleasant reminiscence, he gave his romantic encounters scarcely a second thought. Yet he couldn't get Grace out of his mind, nor could he stop wondering why he had heard nothing from her and speculating over what she might be feeling.

By the third day he resolved to visit her and find out for himself what she was thinking and feeling. When a letter arrived in the morning post bearing an unfamiliar feminine handwriting, he opened it with relief. Finally, his questions would be answered.

But that relief soon turned to dismay when he read the contents.

It was not from Grace, but Lady Ashbridge, informing him that Grace had accepted the Duke's proposal of marriage and their engagement was soon to be announced. She went on:

> *My granddaughter confessed all regarding your de-*
> *plorable indiscretion and has my full forgiveness.*
> *Under the circumstances, it is advisable for you to*
> *have no further contact with my granddaughter and,*
> *if you care anything for her well-being, you will act*
> *as an honourable gentleman and do or say nothing to*
> *jeopardise her future with the Duke of Hardgraves.*

He reread the letter, hardly able to believe the words, then crumpled it into a tight ball and threw it on to the table.

It was done. The Duke had finally made good on his offer. Grace and her grandmother had achieved their goal. Thomas had served his purpose and was no longer needed.

He stood up and paced the room, angry energy making it impossible to remain seated. Had this all been just a ruse? Had that kiss meant nothing at all? Was it merely a bit of fun before she committed herself to marriage? A goodbye gesture, perhaps?

Whatever it was, it mattered not. It was over.

He shot an angry glare at the note and went back to pacing. Instead of being angry, he should be thanking Lady Ashbridge. He had kissed a debutante, but there would be no demand for a proposal, quite the opposite. She had given him his freedom.

His life could return to the way it was before Grace had tumbled into it. And that was what he would do. He would put her behind him, forget all about her and let her get on with her life with the Duke.

He stopped pacing, picked up the note, smoothed it flat and read it yet again. The words remained the same, but he wondered as to their real intent. It was from Lady Ashbridge, not Grace. Was this what she really wanted or was it being forced on her?

Was she at home now, waiting for him to save her from this terrible fate?

The way she had kissed him had not been that of a young woman set on marrying another. Nor had it felt like just a bit of fun, or a goodbye kiss. It had contained real passion. It had been obvious in her response she was yielding to a powerful desire, a desire that had mirrored his own surging need.

And yet she was now to wed the Duke of Hardgraves.

This was surely happening against her will.

Clenching his fist, he crushed the letter in his hand.

If she was being forced to marry the Duke against her will, he would not stand for it. He would not take Lady Ashbridge's letter at face value. He had to hear from the young lady herself that she was willingly entering into this marriage. And if she wasn't he would…he would… He resumed pacing the room, a tumult of thoughts churning in his mind.

He stopped walking. What would he do? Would he offer to marry her himself?

He looked down at the tightly crunched paper in his hand.

Would that be such a bad thing?

He had never considered marriage before, but then, he had never met anyone like Grace Lowerby before. He'd never met a young lady who could cause him to forget himself in the way she did. The idea that he might one day kiss a debutante would not so long ago be ludicrous. And yet he had done so, knowing where that must lead.

Marriage.

Every man knew the consequences of kissing a debutante. He had known it when he kissed her and that had not stopped him. Was it because that was what he really wanted?

Of course he had wanted her. His body ached for her, his dreams were full of her. When they were apart she was all he could think of. And that kiss—by God, that kiss had been like nothing he had experienced before. It wasn't just the sensuality of such an intimate act, it was more, so much more, something that transcended the mere physical.

But marriage?

It would mean spending every day with Grace, waking up to her each morning, going to bed with her every night. He smiled at the prospect. She would be in his life permanently. He would see her smile every day, hear her lovely voice, her laughter.

They would be husband and wife, lovers, friends, companions for the rest of their lives.

He smoothed out the letter, folded it up and placed it in the inside pocket of his jacket. His mind was made up.

The first thing he would do was find out what was really happening, and if, as he suspected, she was being coerced into this marriage and it was not what she wanted, he would offer for her hand.

He patted his jacket pocket where the letter sat over his heart and smiled to himself.

The smile faded. But what if she was doing this willingly? He released a long sigh through flared nostrils, then dismissed that idea.

It was extremely unlikely. A woman who wishes to

marry another does not kiss with such ardent passion and surrender so fully and fervently.

Did she?

If he wanted that question answered, and he most certainly did, he was going to have to ask the lady herself. And if she did tell him she was entering into a marriage with the Duke willingly he would wish her every happiness in her future life as the wife of the Duke of Hardgraves. Then he would follow Lady Ashbridge's demands and do or say nothing to endanger her future with the Duke.

But he knew that outcome would be unlikely.

Grabbing his gloves and hat, Thomas took his carriage over to Lady Ashbridge's townhouse to have a conversation he would once have thought he would never have. One where he would soon be an engaged man, a man about to make an innocent debutante his wife. A man who was surprisingly not just resigned to the idea, but rather pleased by the prospect. More than pleased. And if she consented to be his wife he was sure that pleasure would turn to euphoria.

His carriage pulled up in front of their home. He rushed up the path, rang the bell and composed himself, trying to think what one says in these circumstances.

When the door opened, he handed his card to the footman who returned a few moments later to inform him that Lady Ashbridge was not at home to him. Ignoring the man, he pushed past him, entered the drawing room, and was faced with a furious Lady Ashbridge.

'I believe I told you—'

'Grace,' Thomas interrupted Lady Ashbridge and strode across the room where she was seated beside the window, embroidery clasped in her hands. 'Your grandmother has told me that you have accepted a proposal from the Duke. Is this true?'

She lifted her chin and met his gaze with steady eyes. 'Yes, it's true,' she stated clearly.

Thomas paused, his unformed words dying before they could be uttered. This did not sound or look like a woman who was being coerced.

'But is it what you want?'

'Yes, it is.' She continued to stare at him without coyness or artifice. 'The Duke has won my hand, fair and square.'

Thomas remained staring at her, trying to make sense of her words.

'Are you sure? Have you been forced into this?' He looked over his shoulder at a now preening Lady Ashbridge.

'No. I have not been forced. I am to marry the Duke of Hardgraves,' she continued. 'He has won my heart.'

'I see,' he said, not really seeing at all. He wanted to ask, so why did you kiss me with such passion? She was such a chaste young lady he could not imagine she would do so for any flighty reasons. It had to mean something. Didn't it? Surely her words did not mean what they were saying. There must be a hidden message in them. Somehow they had to be a cry for help, to be rescued, but he couldn't for the life of him see how her words could be interpreted in any other way than an admission that she actually wanted to marry the Duke.

'Is it really what you want?' he asked again.

'I believe I have made myself clear, Mr Hayward,' she said, her tone becoming terse. 'The Duke is my champion. He is the one who values my affections above everything else. He took a chance on winning my love and he secured his prize.'

'But, Grace—'

'My granddaughter has answered your questions repeatedly, Mr Hayward, and made her feelings very clear. Now, would you please leave my drawing room. You were not invited and I would rather not have to call my footmen to eject you.'

'If that is what you want, Miss Lowerby, then I wish you every happiness with the Duke,' he said softly and bowed to both ladies. 'I promise you will see no more of me.'

He had expected a reaction from her, something, anything, but she kept her head high, and stared straight ahead, not even looking at him.

There was nothing for it. He had his answer. It was time to go.

Lady Ashbridge followed him out the room and grabbed hold of his arm as he reached the front entrance.

'I'm assuming that despite that reprehensible display to which you have just subjected my granddaughter, you are still capable of being a gentleman and will give me your promise that you will forget about anything that may or may not have happened between the two of you, and never, ever mention it to anyone.'

'You have my word I will discuss nothing of what occurred between myself and your granddaughter,' Thomas said, giving the only promise he was capable of keeping. While he would say nothing, he could not honestly say he would never think of the kiss they exchanged.

'Good, then I will say goodbye to you, Mr Hayward.'

With that, he left, the footman closing the door behind him with a decisive thud.

Now it really was over. She had stated clearly that none of this was against her will. It was what she wanted and it seemed she even had a strange affection for the Duke, seeing him as her champion who had won her heart. It was difficult to believe, but believe it he must.

He should be relieved that she was not being coerced and

was doing what she wanted. And he supposed he should be pleased. He was once again free. He had never wanted to marry. He had never wanted to kiss a debutante and put himself in such a perilous position. But as he drove back to his home it was not a sense of freedom he was experiencing.

Nor was it relief. She wanted that buffoon, the Duke of Hardgraves. She had kissed him, but she wanted the Duke. She even saw the Duke as her champion. As if that imbecile could be a champion at anything. He had despised the Duke since he was a boy of seven, but never so much as he did now.

How could she believe herself to be in love with a man who was so beneath her?

Anger surged up within him. The Duke was beneath her in every way except one. He was a man with a title.

She was about to do what countless generations of aristocratic women had done before her, marry one of her own kind.

And there was nothing he could do about it. He could not capture her, run off with her and marry her against her grandmother's and, so it would seem, her own wishes. He would simply have to accept her decision.

He called out to his driver to take him to his office. It was time to get back to his old life and put this entire episode behind him and he knew the best way to do that. He would bury himself in his work and forget all about Miss Lowerby, Lady Ashbridge and the Duke of Hardgraves. Compared to the scheming and double-dealing of the aristocracy in search of marriage partners, the affairs of business seemed so much more straightforward.

'Well, of all the nerve,' Grace's grandmother said, taking her seat. 'Barging into our home like that. It shows an appalling lack of manners and breeding.'

Grace chose not to answer and continued staring out the window, not seeing anything of the garden.

'Thank goodness you'll never have to see him again. Believe me, I let him know what's what before he left. We won't have to put up with displays like that ever again.'

'Yes,' she murmured, sure that her grandmother was correct. What was the point of seeing a man who lied to her and used her in such an outrageous manner? She should be angry, offended, hurt at all he had done.

Instead, she felt nothing, as if all feeling had died. The man she was certain she loved was not who she thought he was. He was a man who could use her as part of a callous bet. And she had just given him enough opportunity to tell her she meant more to him than just a means to get a better deal on the Duke's land. But he had not taken that opportunity.

Why hadn't he said *he* was her champion, that he wanted to win her heart, that he prized her above everything else, including that damn piece of land? But he had said nothing of the sort. Merely accepted that she was now to be the Duke's.

'But you conducted yourself admirably, my dear,' her grandmother continued. 'You put him in his place and let him know how things stand. He now knows the Duke has won you fair and square and is the champion of your heart. It's all perfect.'

'Yes,' she responded automatically, still staring out the window.

'You'll have to tell the Duke what you said. I'm sure he'll get a lot of pleasure in knowing you gave that upstart a good telling off and let him know he will never measure up to the Duke of Hardgraves.'

'I thought you said we were to never speak of Mr Hayward again?' she said, turning to look at her grandmother.

'Well, yes,' her grandmother spluttered. 'Yes, I suppose you're right. There's no point bringing him up and we most certainly wouldn't want the Duke to get the impression Hayward means anything to you.'

Her grandmother narrowed her eyes. 'He doesn't mean anything to you, does he?' Her stern expression made it clear there was only one correct answer to that question. 'All that ridiculous talk of love is forgotten now, isn't it? You've come to your senses, haven't you?'

'Yes. He means nothing to me.'

'Good. And you're right. We should never talk of him again. You can just put all thought of him and the very short time you unfortunately spent in his company completely out of your mind. It's time to focus on the future. Your future as a duchess.'

Grace turned back to the window. Never talking about Mr Hayward was going to be easy. She was hardly going to want to discuss him with her grandmother or the Duke, but as for never thinking about him, that was going to prove more difficult.

She lightly stroked her lips.

'We've got so much to do in preparation for your forthcoming marriage I believe there will be no time to think of anything else.'

'Yes, Grandmama,' she answered, hardly knowing what her grandmother had said, her mind completely taken by the memory of that kiss and how it had made her feel. Would the imprint of his lips on hers ever leave her? Would she ever forget how it felt to have his arms encasing her, holding her tightly in an impassioned embrace? Heat erupted deep within her at the memory of the burning passion they had shared. She ran her tongue along her bottom lip, remembering the masculine taste of him and how it had set off a desperate throbbing need throughout her body.

Would she ever feel like that again?

Kissing him had transported her to such an ecstatic state it was hard to believe it all meant nothing to him. She had merely been someone he had played with. Her grandmother had been right. She was a stupid, naive little girl who had no idea what love was and knew nothing of men and the world.

And it had taken the Duke, of all people, to open her eyes to what he was really like. Mr Hayward was a businessman who thought only of profit, success and winning.

'Grace, Grace,' her grandmother interrupted her thoughts. 'Have you heard a word I have said?'

'Sorry, Grandmama, what were you saying?'

Her grandmother smiled benevolently at her. 'You were thinking of the Duke and your wedding day, no doubt. It's perfectly understandable that you should get a bit distracted.'

Grace made no response.

'I was saying that the days leading up to your marriage are going to be the most exciting of your life. Well, the most exciting days until you are actually married and become a duchess.' Her grandmother placed her hand over her heart and smiled. 'You really are the luckiest of young ladies and you are going to have the most wonderful life imaginable.'

Again, Grace made no response, merely turned back to stare out the window.

She had agreed to do her duty, after all, what choice did she have, but it would be asking the impossible for her to actually enjoy doing so or to see it as the most wonderful life imaginable. She could easily imagine a more wonderful life, but that was one denied to her, one that had never really existed.

Chapter Seventeen

As he did every morning, Thomas strode up the stairs towards his office like a tiger seeking sanctuary in his lair. That was where he was comfortable. Not in the ballrooms mixing with society, not in drawing rooms taking tea with the ladies, but in his place of business where he knew the rules and how to always come out the victor.

Thank goodness for his work, he muttered to himself. He had plenty to keep him occupied now that he was no longer involved in helping Miss Lowerby achieve her dreams. Now he could focus on what was important to him. And there was one project demanding his immediate attention—the surveying and construction of a railway line on the land that was once the Duke of Hardgraves's.

He entered the reception area and came to an immediate halt. Seated on one of the leather chairs in the waiting room was his sister, Georgina. It seemed he was not going to be able to take immediate refuge in his work after all.

'Georgie, how lovely to see you again,' he said, kissing his sister's cheek. 'I hope you haven't been waiting long.'

'That is all right. Mr Worthington and I have been having an interesting conversation while I waited.'

He looked at his secretary, whose face remained professional and impassive, although Thomas suspected the poor man had just been disturbed from his work and subjected to a long monologue from his sister on whatever topic was presently fascinating her.

'Shall we go into my office?' He placed his hand gently on his sister's back and escorted her through the open door, smiling as he spotted a sign of relief cross Worthington's face.

'Tommy,' she squealed with delight as soon as they were alone in his office. 'What are all these rumours I've been hearing about you?'

Thomas cast a look at the solid oak door and hoped the squealing had not carried through to the outer office.

'How are things with the Duke of Ravenswood, and with the children?' he asked, hoping to divert the subject away from himself.

'Fine, fine.' She waved her hand in circles to indicate she would not be distracted from what she really came to talk about. 'So, what is this I hear about you being seen round town with a certain young lady?'

It was Thomas's turn to wave his hand as if it was nothing. 'I was merely escorting a young lady to a few social events as a favour to her grandmother.'

'That's not what I heard.' There were few things his sister enjoyed more than a good gossip. Usually Thomas remained unaffected by this, seeing it as one of her silly indulgences, but then he was not usually the subject.

Georgina settled herself on the leather couch and sent him an enormous smile, her hands clapping lightly together as if unable to contain her excitement.

'What I heard was you danced with Grace Lowerby at the Duke of Hardgraves's ball, that you were seen walking together at his estate. Alone.' At this, Georgina raised her eyebrows as if to underline the importance of her statement.

'That you were spotted walking in Hyde Park together, and…' she paused, presumably for dramatic effect '…you escorted her to the Savoy Theatre and were seen drinking champagne in the family's private box. All and all, this indicates you are courting. So why do I have to hear about this from my spies? Why have you not introduced her to the family?'

'Because I am not courting her and the young lady in question will be soon announcing her engagement to the Duke of Hardgraves.'

'No,' Georgina squealed even louder, as if he'd just announced they were about to face a life-altering catastrophe. 'Oh, Tommy, you must be heartbroken.' She rose from her chair and started to approach him. He waved his hand back at the sofa. The last thing he wanted was his sister's condolences.

'I know how that feels,' she said, thankfully taking her seat once more. 'It's devastating. And, yes, I can see that you are suffering.' She paused and tilted her head, her lips turned down in sympathy.

'So, how can I help you win her back?' she added, once again becoming animated. 'I'm very good at doing that. I've helped all my friends and they're all happily married now.'

Thomas couldn't help but raise his eyebrows. He doubted that Georgina's friends had benefited from any of her help, which tended to run to outrageous plans that caused more problems than they solved.

She continued to look at him, with that eager expression he had seen many times when they were children, the one that usually came before she was about to indulge in an act of mayhem.

'I am not heartbroken and I do not need your help,' he stated as emphatically as possible, hoping against hope she would listen to him.

'Of course you're heartbroken. What you need to do is declare your love to her in a heartfelt manner, preferably accompanied by a magnificent and sincere gesture that she cannot ignore. That always wins over a young lady.'

She stood up and began pacing the room, her brow furrowed in thought. 'Adam made a grand, if rather dangerous, gesture when he declared his love for me. I was so touched I just couldn't resist him.'

Thomas found it hard to believe the sensible Duke of Ravenswood would do anything dangerous, but under Georgina's influence anything was possible.

'You could challenge the Duke to a duel. No, that might be a bit much,' she added before Thomas had a chance to tell her what a ridiculous, not to mention illegal act that would be.

'Maybe you could serenade her under her window.'

Thomas released a low groan.

'Yes, you're right. You've got a terrible singing voice. You could write her poetry.' She stopped walking and turned towards him. 'Do you know how to write poetry? You've never really seemed like the poetic type, too busy with ledgers and all of that.' She indicated the books open on his desk, books he was desperate to get back to.

'Stop, Georgie,' he said, louder than he intended. 'I do not need to make a sincere and magnificent gesture of love. I do not need to win the young lady's heart for the simple reason I am not in love with her. I was merely helping her capture the man she really wanted, the Duke of Hardgraves. He was one of those bullies from school who always resented the fact that someone from my background achieved so much more than him. I was merely making him jealous so he would see Miss Lowerby as a desirable marriage prospect.'

Georgina stared at him, her mouth open, but for once not speaking, her eyes boring into his. 'How could you possibly be so heartless?' she finally said.

'What? Heartless? I was being gallant. I was helping a debutante achieve her dreams.' Thomas knew that was only half the story, but there was no point giving Georgina the full details. She would only react in her usual dramatic fashion and make more of this situation than it deserved.

'You have fobbed her off on a man you describe as dim-witted and a bully. How could you?'

'She had her heart set on marrying a titled man and that is exactly what she is going to do.' He strove to keep the bitterness out of his voice. 'It's what they all do.'

They might toy with the lower orders, they might kiss them, but they marry to advance their position in society.

'The Duke may be a dim-witted bully,' he continued while Georgie stared at him wide-eyed, 'but he is a duke—that makes him a highly desirable catch as far as any debutante is concerned.'

'Nonsense. Love transcends such things.'

He sighed at his sister's romantic fantasies. 'Whatever you might like to think, the Duke is the man she wants to marry.'

'Well, you need to show her she is making a mistake.'

He stared at his sister as if she was the dim-witted one.

'Don't look at me like that, Tommy. I've known you long enough to be able to read everything you are thinking.'

Georgina might think that was the case, but she was deluded.

'You have feelings for Miss Lowerby, strong feelings. I can see it in your face. And if my spies are correct, she most certainly has feelings for you. I was told she was sitting so close to you at the theatre she was almost in your lap.'

'I believe that is an exaggeration.' He was certainly

pleased her so-called spies had not seen them on the door-step outside Miss Lowerby's house.

'No, no exaggeration. I never exaggerate.'

Thomas merely shook his head at this delusion.

'So what are we going to do about this situation?'

'*We* are going to do nothing about a situation that only exists in your head. *You* are going to go and do whatever it was that brought you to London. *I* am going to get back to work.'

'No, you have to tell her how you feel. You can't let her marry the wrong man.'

'Don't you have some shopping to do, or something?'

'Yes, and I'm meeting my friends for afternoon tea, but first we have to sort out your problems. So, what do *your* friends think of what has happened? What have Sebastian and Isaac advised? Whenever I have a problem I always talk it over with my friends and get their advice.'

Once again, Thomas shook his head in disbelief. 'Unlike you, I do not get together with my friends to discuss my love life.'

'Ah ha.' She pointed her index finger at him. 'You admit it. It is your love life we are discussing.' She resumed pacing before Thomas could counter this claim. 'But Seb and Isaac would be of no help anyway. They're as useless with women as you are.'

This time, Thomas shook his head and rolled his eyes at his sister's ignorance. The only problems Isaac and Seb had when it came to women was dealing with the large numbers they had in and out of their beds, but that was not something he wished to discuss with his sister.

'I can see it is going to be all up to me to solve this problem.'

'There is no problem. Nothing needs to be solved and, as I have already said, I do not need your help.'

He stood up, crossed the room and opened the door. 'But thank you for coming. Now, I won't keep you from joining your friends and give my regards to your husband and my love to the children.'

Georgina was about to say something more, but he sent her a warning look and tilted his head towards Worthington seated in the outer office, as if to say he did not wish this to be discussed in front of his secretary. To his immense surprise, she did as she was bid.

'Goodbye, Georgina, it was a pleasure as always.' He kissed her cheeks and guided her towards the stairs.

'I'm not finished with you yet, Thomas Hayward,' she said in a voice she no doubt used when calling her step-children into line, but one entirely wasted on her brother.

'Goodbye, Georgina,' he repeated, and with relief watched her walk down the stairs.

Thomas returned to the sanctuary of his office, where under normal circumstances no one discussed love, court-ship, magnificent gestures, or any other frivolous matters. He picked up his pen, then lowered it and stared out the window.

His sister was wrong, as usual.

He had not been courting Miss Lowerby, far from it. If it hadn't been for her falling over at the Duke's ball, he would never have even considered talking to a debutante, never mind dancing with one. If the Duke hadn't made that ridiculous bet and if he hadn't been tempted by the chance of getting the land at a more advantageous price, he would not have spent so much time in her company. If her grand-mother had not come to him with that request to be seen in public with her, and if he hadn't been feeling uncharac-teristically guilty over that bet, he would not have escorted her out in public.

That was the truth of the matter. Not all this romantic rubbish his sister was spouting.

Well, not entirely the truth. Yes, Georgina was right that he did have feelings for Miss Lowerby. And, yes, he had kissed her, which he would never do with a debutante if he hadn't been irresistibly attracted to her and, yes, it had crossed his mind to offer his hand in marriage as a result of that kiss, but it mattered not one iota. She was to marry the Duke of Hardgraves and that was the end of it.

He picked up his pen one more time and stared at the contracts in front of him. This would be his focus from now onwards, the uncomplicated world of business, not love, romance, grand gestures or any of that other baffling nonsense.

Chapter Eighteen

Her dream had come true, but like all dreams it was all an illusion. Grace was now engaged to a duke. Her grandmother couldn't be happier and showered her with praise and affection as if she were a princess. She had craved such attention when she was a child with a desperation that had made her ache. Now she had it. It should be making her content.

You should be happy, she had told herself yet again.

She had everything she had ever wanted. And surely, if she had never met Mr Hayward, she *would* be happy. But she *had* met him and he had ruined everything.

'Not long now,' her grandmother said over breakfast, having once again counted down the days until Grace would be married.

'Yes,' Grace responded with the only answer possible. It would not be long. The engagement had been announced, the banns had been read. Soon she would be walking up the aisle in her beautiful white gown, for which no expense had been spared.

'I don't suppose I will be seeing the Duke again today,' Grace added, stating something else that did not need to be said.

'It's of no matter.' Her grandmother took a sip of her

tea, then resumed smiling. 'You are engaged. It's been announced in all the papers. He cannot back out now. You will soon be a duchess.'

'And married to a man I never see.'

'Some women would see that as a blessing.' Her grandmother gave a little laugh. 'I've already explained all that to you, my darling child. All that is to be expected of you is to do your duty and provide an heir and maybe a spare. Once you have done that, then the two of you can live separate lives. That is the way it has been done for countless generations and will continue to be done for countless more.'

'Good.' That at least was some consolation, although the thought of actually providing the required heir and spare was something Grace would prefer not to think about.

Her grandmother studied her over the top of her teacup. 'I can see the thought of being a duchess is already starting to change you. You are becoming so much more confident and self-assured. It won't be long before you are someone completely suited to being at the very pinnacle of society, someone to whom all others have to defer.'

She gave another little laugh, like an exuberant child. 'When you do become a grand lady I hope you don't forget your dear old grandmama and all she sacrificed for you so you could achieve everything you ever wanted.'

Grace took a sip of her tea, wondering who was actually doing the sacrificing.

'Anyway, if you are missing the Duke, you will see plenty of him when we visit his estate.' Her grandmother sighed. 'Soon to be your estate. Then you will have the chance to show him how much you have missed him.'

A shudder ripped through Grace. She just hoped the Duke continued to treat her with the same indifference he had of late. She would hate for him to take those liberties her grandmother said she should now grant him.

Once again that kiss she shared with Mr Hayward invaded her mind. She drew in a long, deep breath in an attempt to slow her suddenly racing heart. She could almost feel his lips on hers, his arms around her, his body pressed against hers. Her fervid imagination could all but taste him, and that taste was intoxicating.

She shook her head lightly, to drive out that image. She would not think of him. She would focus on the future, not the past. Yes, he kissed her. Yes, he made her feel things she did not know it was possible to feel. Yes, she had thought herself to be in love with him. But it was all a mirage. He was not the man she thought him to be.

Whether she was having reservations or not about marrying the Duke, it mattered not a bit. She was now engaged. It was official. There was no getting out of it now. It might not be the fairy tale she had imagined as a child, but she was not a child any longer. She was an adult. A woman about to become a bride and one day a mother. It was time to put aside all childish fancies and do her duty.

Forgetting about Miss Lowerby was proving far harder than Thomas had imagined, harder than anything he had done before. Especially as his working day now started with a ritual that doomed him to failure, scanning the society pages of the newspapers for any mention of the Duke and Miss Lowerby.

Thomas never read such tittle-tattle in the past, but as the weeks passed he found himself reading the goings-on of society with increasing focus. The Duke and Miss Lowerby did not feature as often as he would have expected and, when they did, it was a disappointment. The journalist always failed to mention how she appeared. Was she happy, sad, excited, regretful? Nor was there any mention as to whether the Duke was treating her well and acting in the correct manner of a man courting a lady. Instead, there were gushing descriptions of what she was wearing, as if that was all that mattered.

He had read the announcement of their engagement and, with trepidation, each day he braced himself for the announcement of their forthcoming marriage.

Despite these preparations, when it came, the impact winded him like an unexpected punch to the stomach.

He gripped the paper tighter as he reread the words. Their wedding was to be held at the local church near the Earl of Ashbridge's property, in one month's time, with the wedding breakfast to follow at the Earl's estate. Thomas threw the paper across his desk, not needing to read any further about the distinguished guests from the highest echelons of society who were expected to attend. Nor did he need to read how it would be the wedding of the Season between a beautiful young lady and a man of illustrious standing.

It was all but done. She was almost a duchess. She was to get the prize that every other young debutante had been seeking this Season. At least she would have well and truly put those bullying debutantes in their place. That provided some satisfaction, he supposed. But not much.

And the Duke was wasting no time in getting his fiancée up the aisle. If he was worried that Thomas might sweep in and steal her away, he was misguided. Or was it the thought of the dowry that was prompting such haste? Thomas placed his head in his hands and refused to believe they were actually in love and desperate to be man and wife.

He stood up and paced around the office, unspent energy coursing through him and refusing to let him settle. He should be pleased it was now a done deal. He could now do what he had been trying to do these past weeks, put her firmly in the past where she belonged and get on with his life.

He paced back to his desk, picked up the newspaper, screwed it up and threw it into the rubbish basket.

It was time to get back to work and stop wasting time on things that no longer concerned him.

He sat down. Stood up, paced over to the window and looked down at the busy London street below him, then paced back to his desk.

This would not do. He could not stay cooped up like this, pacing back and forth like a caged animal. He had to be outside. He had to be active. He had to be working, doing something physical to burn off all this unspent energy.

'Worthington,' he called out to his secretary. 'Send a telegram to the works manager. I'm heading down to Cornwall to inspect the progress on the construction of the new rail line.'

'Very good, sir,' came the reply.

While his secretary was off organising that, Thomas stuffed the papers he was supposed to be working on in a leather folio and stormed out of the office. He took a cab back home to pack some essentials, then headed for the train station.

As he travelled through the countryside, he tried to focus on the documents he had taken with him, but found himself staring at the changing scenery outside the window, unable to get his wandering mind to focus.

The telegram had obviously arrived as a carriage was waiting for him at the station. As he travelled up the recently laid track on what was now his land, he ignored the overbearing presence of the Duke's house and focused instead on the work site ahead of him.

When he saw the gangs of men hard at work, he released a satisfied sigh. This was where he needed to be, among men dedicated to achieving physical goals and as far away from society events and white weddings as it was possible to get.

In the previous weeks, the land had been changed beyond recognition from the way it had looked when he had escorted Miss Lowerby around the Duke's estate.

Large carts carrying metal railway tracks and wooden sleepers were parked beside makeshift workers' camps. Teams of labourers armed with pickaxes were levelling the land, others were laying the sleepers, while a group of burly men were hammering the tracks into place.

Thomas could see his input was not necessary, but it was good to be out in the open, among the noise of industrious men. But it was not enough to just watch. He had energy to burn off. Energy that *had* to be burnt off.

'We're making great progress,' the manager shouted over the noise of men's voices and the clanging of hammers on metal.

'I can see that. I hope you don't mind, but I feel the need to do some physical labour.'

Surprise crossed the manager's face, and Thomas felt the need to explain. At least, to explain as much as the manager needed to know.

'When I first joined the family business my father made me spend some time doing labouring work, so I would know the business from the ground up. Sometimes, when I'm stuck in my office, I miss it and feel the need to get my hands dirty again.'

He expected the manager to continue to look at him as

if he was insane, but instead he smiled. 'Yes, sometimes you just have to get back on the tools, don't you? Well, we could do with someone to help with driving in the spikes.'

'Perfect.' Thomas took of his jacket and shirt and tossed them to one side, picked up a sledgehammer and joined the line-up of men, rhythmically driving in the metal spikes.

Yes, this was exactly what he needed. He could not think of Miss Lowerby when he was working up a sweat and using every muscle in his body in hard physical toil.

The day passed quickly, Thomas's muscles becoming satisfyingly tired with each passing hour, his mind mercifully fixed on work that demanded his full concentration.

In the afternoon he heard the familiar sound of coach wheels crunching over gravel. He paused in his work, wiped the sweat off his brow and looked across the fields to see a parade of carriages rolling up towards the Duke's home.

He turned his back and continued pounding in the spikes with increased vigour. It mattered nothing who the Duke planned to entertain at his home. If it was Miss Lowerby, he would think nothing of it.

He was on his own land, engaged in his own work. He had no need to see or speak to the Duke while he was here. And thank goodness for that. The last thing he wanted to see was that churl's gloating face.

'And to think, all this will soon be yours,' Grace's grandmother said, not for the first time, as the carriage made its way up the drive towards the Duke's country home.

'Just one more month and you will be the Duchess of Hardgraves,' she added, as if this, too, was something she had not repeated more times than Grace could count.

'Last time we were here you were just one of many debutantes attending a weekend party,' she continued, smiling fit to burst. 'And you outshone them all to win the man every other young lady had set her heart on.'

Grace shuddered, wishing her grandmother would not use words like 'win'. Not when it reminded her of what had really taken place the last time she had been at the Duke's Cornwall estate.

She looked out the carriage window as memories of that weekend party flooded her mind. She had driven up this same path full of nervous excitement and trepidation, as if about to embark on an adventure. It was a far cry from the resignation she was now feeling.

She glanced up at the grand, imposing house, remembering all that had happened, the euphoria of walking and dancing with Mr Hayward, the despair of being yet again the victim of bullies, the sense of security that came when Mr Hayward saved her from their taunts, and then the confusion of the Duke's offer of courtship.

But so much more had gone on that weekend of which she had been unaware. There had been that bet. That terrible bet. The one where she was pitted against a piece of land.

At the time ignorance had been bliss and she had thought Mr Hayward was spending time with her because he was her friend and, dare she admit it, was interested in her romantically. She had naively been flattered and delighted. But the only thing he had been interested in was building a rail line so he could increase the profitability of his coal mines.

She quashed down her anger, determined not to let it consume her.

'And you will have the Duke completely to yourself this weekend,' her grandmother prattled on.

'Yes, that will certainly make a change.' Whether it would be a good change or not Grace was yet to discover. They had barely spent time in each other's company since his proposal. It had become increasingly obvious the Duke much preferred gambling and consorting with his rowdy friends. That should be making Grace miserable, but strangely it did not.

She knew the real cause of her despondency. Mr Hayward. Despite her determination to forget all about him, that man was constantly in her thoughts and had even taken to haunting her dreams. Everything that happened in her life, she imagined talking over with Mr Hayward. Every time she dressed in her finery for another social event, she could picture him looking at her the way he had when they had attended the theatre, with such admiration and desire. And as for that damn kiss, when was it going to stop tormenting her?

It was beyond ridiculous to be so obsessed with a man she despised. He had used her in such a cavalier manner. He cared nothing for her and had made a complete fool of her. The anger she had been fighting to control welled up inside her, along with an overwhelming, infuriating wish to see him again.

'There's no need to be nervous.' Her grandmother patted her knee, completely misinterpreting Grace's feelings. 'I'm sure the Duke will behave like a perfect gentleman this weekend.' She sent Grace a coquettish smile. 'And if he doesn't, it matters not. You'll soon be his wife and he's entitled now to show you a little of what will be expected of you.'

Grace couldn't help but grimace.

'Now, don't be like that,' she said, wagging her finger in a playful manner. 'There is nothing wrong with the Duke taking a few liberties now that you are so close to being married. In less than a month you'll be his. It won't be a liberty then. It will be your duty.'

Grace fought to pull her face into a more impassive expression.

'I know, my dear,' her grandmother said, once again patting her knee. 'You are such an innocent and this is all going to be a bit of a trial for you. But just accept it as your lot in life and think of what you are getting in exchange.' She returned to looking out the window as they pulled up in front of the house. 'It's more than worth the sacrifice.'

Grace was not convinced. Her grandmother had told her what would be required of her so she could do her duty and produce the necessary heir. She had described what went where in a clipped tone, her nostrils flared, as if it was all too distasteful to discuss, let alone do.

The main instructions Grace had been given was to lie back, give her body to the Duke and submit to whatever he wanted to do. As she spoke, all Grace had been able to think about was doing so with Mr Hayward, of giving her body to him, of letting him do whatever he wanted. But that was something she knew she must never think of again, not if she was to end this self-inflicted suffering.

The footman helped them down from the carriage and once again the Duke was not waiting to greet them, and once again her grandmother chose not to mention this lapse in etiquette.

'Make haste, dear,' her grandmother said as the footman helped them out of their travelling cloaks. 'We do not want to keep your future husband waiting.'

'No, that would be terribly rude, wouldn't it?'

Her grandmother raised one eyebrow as she registered Grace's sarcasm, but said nothing.

They retired to their bedchambers to change out of their travelling clothes. Molly removed an ornate day dress from the trunk, one of the excessive number that had been packed for the two days they were to be at the Duke's house.

With a sigh, Grace surrendered to being trussed up in an even tighter corset, weighed down with layers of fabric and having her hair pulled, combed and braided into the ornate style her grandmother deemed suitable for a future duchess.

When Molly was finished, she held up a hand mirror so Grace could see the back of her hair, but she waved her lady's maid away, rose and joined her grandmother. They descended the stairs together, her grandmother's elevated head and stately posture suggesting she felt this grand house and estate already belonged to her.

They entered the drawing room to find the Duke staring out the window, looking out over his estate. He did not turn around when they entered. Even when the footman announced their presence he did not greet them.

'That damn man is here,' he said, still staring out the window, his fists clenched behind his back.

Grace sent a quick look in her grandmother's direction. She abhorred cursing, seeing it as something only the lowest tradesman would do, but she made no reaction to the Duke's words, merely tilted her head as if in concern.

'Who is present, Your Grace?' her grandmother asked.

'That man Hayward.'

The mention of his name sent heat rushing to Grace's cheeks and caused her heart to jump.

'He's actually out there working on my land, like a common labourer,' the Duke continued.

Grace could mention it was not the Duke's land any more. He had lost it in a bet and had won her instead, but his angry posture suggested that right now he did not see that as much of a victory.

Instead, along with her grandmother, she crossed the room and joined him at the large sash windows. In the distance she could see a group of men laying the rail tracks and one of them was undeniably the tall, strongly built figure of Mr Hayward.

Grace stifled a gasp before it escaped. He was not wearing his shirt. Desire and panic warred within her as she watched him rhythmically pounding the ground with a large hammer. She should look away and end this anguish, but she remained frozen at the window, staring at him, as if under a spell.

'I know exactly why that man is here.' The Duke finally turned from the window to address Grace and her grandmother. 'He must have known my intended would be here this weekend and he thinks he can still win her. The man has no decency and was never able to accept when he had lost.'

Win her? Why would he still think he could win her? He had his land and that was all he ever wanted.

'Well, he *has* lost,' her grandmother said. 'But you are right, Your Grace. The man is beneath contempt and this display merely demonstrates that despite his wealth he is little more than a peasant.'

As their disparaging words whirled around her, Grace continued to watch Mr Hayward as he worked beside the other men. Even from this distance she could see the whip-like strength of his body as he lifted the hammer high over his head and brought it down with considerable force.

'Well, he needs to be taught a lesson, yet again. Miss Lowerby, will you accompany me on a walk?'

Grace tore her gaze away and looked at the Duke, who was offering her his arm.

'What? Now? Where?'

'I merely want to inspect my land and make sure those ruffians are causing no damage to my estate.' He sent Grace a knowing smile.

The last thing she wanted was to be anywhere near Mr Hayward. She looked towards the window, her teeth nibbling lightly on her bottom lip.

But as he now owned the land adjacent to the Duke's it was inevitable that at some stage their paths would cross. Perhaps it was better to get it over with and done with. And if she was on the arm of the Duke, if she could show him that she had what she wanted, he would see that his winning that appalling bet had not been his victory, but hers.

Yet it would still mean seeing him again and ensuring she made no reaction. She could not let him see she harboured even the slightest regret that he was no longer in her life. That would be beyond mortifying.

'What a good idea.' Her grandmother's words cut across her confusion and somehow she managed to both smile at the Duke while glaring at Grace. 'Go for a nice walk and stretch your legs after that long journey.'

'Of course,' she finally acquiesced, taking the Duke's arm.

At a rapid pace, he led her straight out the house and across the fields towards where the men were working, all the while muttering curses about Mr Hayward. That was what Grace assumed they were from his tone. Whatever it was he was saying, they were expressions she had never heard before and ones she suspected even those tradesmen her grandmother looked down on would be loathe to use, especially in front of a lady.

As they drew closer, Grace fought to keep her heartbeat and breathing steady. She did not want Mr Hayward to see that he affected her in any manner, but she was still curious as to how he would react to seeing her again and on the arm of the man she was to marry.

Would he have any reaction? Would he even care?

They reached the work site and came to a halt. Mr Hayward looked up from his work. Grace froze, her breath caught in her throat, as his gaze moved from her to the Duke and back again. Then he resumed his work, pounding in the metal spike with increasing vigour.

She had her answer. He didn't care. She meant nothing to him.

'Hayward, I see you've reverted to type,' the Duke called out, causing Mr Hayward to stop once more and wipe the sweat off his brow. Grace knew she shouldn't, but she couldn't stop her gaze from moving over his naked chest, taking in those lean, hard, sweat-slickened muscles.

He cares nothing for you. Look away. You were just a means to gain this land he is now working on.

It would be so much easier to follow those commands if he wasn't so potently masculine or if her fingers would cease aching to run themselves over those powerful, naked muscles. Her gaze followed a trickle of sweat as it ran down his chest and over his firm stomach. A shocking image entered her mind of her tongue tracing its path.

She forced her eyes to do as her mind demanded, returned her gaze to his face and adopted what she hoped was an imperious look, while she fought to ignore the burning heat consuming her body.

It would be so much easier to maintain that haughty pose if loneliness wasn't gnawing at her resolve. The time she had spent with him was the happiest of her life, even if it had all been pretence. She had felt cherished and admired. They had talked so freely, had laughed together so easily and she had enjoyed every minute she was in his company. She had even foolishly thought she loved him. She *had* loved him, at least, loved the man she thought he was. Even if it had all been an illusion it had felt so genuine and it was hard to turn off those feelings just because they aren't real.

'I believe congratulations are in order,' he said, lowering the sledgehammer and taking a step forward. It took Grace's muddled brain a few moments to realise he was congratulating the Duke on their engagement.

'That is almost gracious of you, Hayward,' the Duke said, placing his arm around her waist and pulling her close. She pulled against him, mortified that he should act in such a familiar manner in front of this group of men.

'I hope you are very happy together,' Mr Hayward said with a look of derision.

'Yes, we will be. I can promise you that.'

Before Grace knew what was happening, the Duke pulled her into a clinch and his lips smashed hard against hers. Grace gasped in horror, her mouth opening, giving the Duke the opportunity to plunge his tongue inside.

He was kissing her. In public. In front of these workmen. In front of Mr Hayward.

She struggled against him, but he held her tighter. His hands cupped her buttocks, pushing her hard against his hips and he rubbed himself against her. It was as if he was going to take her, here, in public.

This was unconscionable. A gross indecency.

Wedging her hands between them, she gave his chest a hard push.

He flew backwards with more force than she thought herself capable. Gasping in mortified breaths, she watched as

Mr Hayward's fist landed in the middle of the Duke's face and he fell to the ground, blood streaming from his nose.

The Duke was instantly on his feet. He took a step towards Mr Hayward, his clenched fists raised. Then, registering the anger burning in his eyes, the coiled fury in his taut muscles, he took several steps backwards. The men had all stopped their work and were watching the scene unfolding before them as if it were entertainment provided for their benefit.

'You will treat Miss Lowerby with the respect she deserves,' Mr Hayward seethed, his words as tense as his body.

'She's mine and I'll do whatever the hell I want with her,' the Duke said, his voice muffled as he tilted his head backwards and tried to staunch the flow of blood.

He took another step towards the Duke, his fists raised, his breath coming in loud, rapid gasps. 'You will treat her with respect, you blackguard, or you'll pay the consequence.'

'I'll treat her anyway I want,' the Duke said, taking another step backwards. 'She's to be my wife. I won her fair and square and you lost. Just accept it, Hayward.'

That bet.

They were still arguing about that offensive bet.

Grace looked from one man to the other. That was all she ever was to both of them, a prized possession to be fought over, a possession made all the more valuable because they thought the other wanted it. But neither really wanted her. They just wanted to get the better of each other and she had been caught up in the middle of their rivalry.

She was the one who had been insulted and subjected to a gross act, yet they both appeared to have forgotten all about her. All they cared about was their hatred of each other and this senseless feud.

Well, she would leave them to it. With that, she turned and strode across the field back to the house.

Chapter Nineteen

Thomas was tempted to chase after Grace, to make sure she was all right, but the Duke was correct. She was his and would soon be his wife. It had been her choice and it was not Thomas's place to comfort her. It was this sorry excuse of a man who was nursing a much-deserved bloody nose who should be rushing to her side and trying to make amends for that unforgivable affront.

But he looked as though he had no intention of doing so, so it was up to Thomas to teach him where his duty and responsibilities lay.

'I don't care if she is your fiancée and will soon be your wife,' he seethed. 'You will treat her with the respect she deserves and will continue to do so once you are married.'

'Or what? You don't frighten me.'

Thomas took a step towards him and the Duke quickly took several back. 'You should be frightened of me. You have debts up and down the country. All I have to do is buy those debts and I could take more from you than just the land to build this railway. I could ruin you.'

The Duke smiled in triumph. 'And in the process ruin Miss Lowerby and cause her to live in poverty. Is that what you want?'

Thomas drew in a slow, deep breath and fought not to

let this witless churl see how right he was. He would do nothing to harm Miss Lowerby.

The Duke's smile turned into a sneer. 'I knew it. You're in love with her. You're in love with the woman I will marry. My God, I really have beaten you, haven't I.' The sneer became a leer. 'That's going to make my wedding night even more enjoyable. Every time I bed her I'll have the additional pleasure of knowing that I'm having her and you're not.'

Thomas's fist flew out again and with a satisfying crunch connected with the Duke's face. He raised his fists again, but several firm hands on his shoulders prevented him from doing what he longed to do and giving him a beating he would never forget.

As he attempted to shrug off the workmen, the Duke turned tail and literally ran back to his house.

He knew he should respect Miss Lowerby's choice, but how could he do so when it was so obviously the wrong choice? Surely that display had shown her what sort of man he was, a man she could not tie herself to, a man who would treat her appallingly at every chance he could, if for no other reason than to torment Thomas.

She could not marry him and Thomas had to stop this outrage before it was too late.

'You're back sooner than I expected,' her grandmother said as Grace strode into the house. 'And where's the Duke?'

Ignoring her grandmother, she continued walking towards the stairs.

Her progress was stopped when her grandmother grabbed her arm. 'What has happened? Did you see that Mr Hayward again?'

Grace shrugged off her grandmother's arm, but nodded, her rage making words impossible.

'Oh, my poor, dear girl. I can see you're upset. Tell me all about it.'

Grace doubted her grandmother could offer her any comfort, but she allowed her to lead her into the drawing room.

Her grandmother indicated the chairs beside the unlit fireplace and Grace collapsed into one, suddenly more exhausted than she had ever felt before.

'So, what did that terrible man do?'

'He kissed me and rubbed himself up against me.' Shame washed through Grace at the memory of that appalling encounter.

'What?' Her grandmother screeched, standing up, her hand flying to cover her mouth. 'This is an outrage. I hope the Duke dealt with him in the manner he deserved.'

'What? No. I mean the Duke kissed me and rubbed himself up against me, in front of all the men working on the railway, including Mr Hayward.'

'Oh, I see.' She lowered her hand and once again took her seat. 'That is rather unfortunate behaviour. I can see why you are upset, as any well-brought-up young lady would be.'

She nodded and placed a comforting hand on her roiling stomach. 'It was disgusting.'

'Hmm, but we have already had this conversation. The Duke is to soon be your husband. You have to take your lead from him, even if sometimes it makes you feel, well, perhaps a little uncomfortable.'

'A little uncomfortable?' Grace repeated, her voice growing loud. Had her grandmother really just dismissed something so offensive, something that was impossible to tolerate, as a little uncomfortable?

'Did you not hear what I said? He was rub—'

'Yes, I heard what you said.' She held up her hands as if pushing the words away. 'It does not need to be repeated.'

'He was trying to prove to Mr Hayward that I was his possession and he could do whatever he wanted with me. Even kiss and fondle me in front of him and all those other workmen.' Surely even her grandmother could see this was behaviour unacceptable from any man.

'I see. Well, that explains it. The Duke is right. You are his now and it is time that Mr Hayward realised it.'

She stared at her grandmother in disbelief. It was one thing to allow the Duke to take liberties before they were married, but for him to do something so obnoxious, to treat her in that manner in front of other men, was beneath contempt. How could her grandmother possibly condone such behaviour?

Her grandmother smiled at her, as if that was to be the end of it, causing Grace to shake her head slowly from side to side, words being inadequate to express her contempt at what the Duke had done and at her grandmother for not seeing it as unforgivable.

It was obvious her grandmother was never going to side with her. No matter what the Duke did, her grandmother would accept it and expect Grace to do the same. Like the Duke, like Mr Hayward, her grandmother only saw her as a means to an end.

'But you should not allow yourself to get so upset,' her grandmother said in a soothing voice. 'Perhaps you should retire to your bedchamber for a while and have a lie-down to compose yourself.'

Grace gave a mirthless laugh.

A lie-down? Did she really think this could be cured with a lie-down?

'I'll send Molly up to you with a sedative to calm your fit of the vapours.'

Without responding, Grace flew out of the room and stormed up the stairs to her bedchamber, then commenced pacing, fury coursing through her. Her grandmother had shown her true colours. She cared nothing for Grace and probably never had. She expected her to submit to anything in order to marry a duke. Well, she would not do it. She would not marry him. She would not let that odious man near her ever again.

Molly soon arrived with a glass of warm milk and a cloth soaked in lavender oil.

'I don't need any of that,' she said, louder than intended, startling her lady's maid. 'I'm sorry, Molly,' she said in a calmer voice. 'But I don't think warm milk and cool cloths are going to solve anything.'

'No, but it might help,' Molly said, placing them on the table. 'And shall I loosen your corset? You are quite flushed.'

Grace doubted that loosening her clothes would help to alleviate her agitation, but she did as her lady's maid suggested, and with the corset removed her rapid breathing was eased somewhat.

'I am so sorry to see you upset, miss. Shall I brush out your hair?'

Grace suspected that would not help either, but allowed Molly to lead her to the dressing table.

With soothing fingers, Molly undid the clips from her hair and brushed out her long tresses. Under the lady's maid's gentle strokes her agitated state began to dissipate slightly.

'You do deserve to be happy,' she said, her voice gentle.

'Thank you, Molly, that's very kind of you,' Grace said, closing her eyes.

Molly drew in a breath and paused in the rhythmic brushing. 'I never knew your mother, but some of the older servants did and they say she, too, was a lovely young woman. They were all so pleased she married for love, rather than marrying the man your grandmother had chosen for her.'

Grace's eyes flew open at this revelation.

'As was your grandfather,' Molly added.

'What?' Grace spun round on the stool and faced her lady's maid. 'No, Grandmama said the shock of her bringing such shame on the family sent him to an early grave.'

Molly shook her head sadly. 'That's not what the older servants say. They say he was pleased his daughter had found such happiness and it was her sudden death in the carriage accident that broke his heart and caused his rapid decline.'

Grace turned back to face her reflection. Had her grandmother really lied to her all her life? And if she lied about that, what else had she lied about? 'Have the servants said anything else about my mother and father?'

'Well, everyone remembers what a talented pianist your father was.' Molly smiled. 'They also say he was so kind to your mother and everyone adored him. Well, everyone except your grandmother. She was so angry when your grandfather gave them his blessing along with your mother's dowry. And when you were born he made provisions so you, too, would never have to worry about money.'

Grace stared at a reflection she hardly recognised, her face drained of blood, her jaw tight. She gripped the edges of the stool. 'I have money of my own?'

Molly shrugged. 'That's what the servants say.'

Her grandmother had lied to her, repeatedly. She had lied about her parents, lied about her grandfather's death. And lied when she said that without her grandmother giving her a home, Grace would be living on the street and trying to fend for herself. This was almost more than Grace could take in. She'd spent her entire life trying to make up for the so-called sins of her mother, had tried desperately to repay her grandmother's generosity, and all because she was being deceived by a woman who she had desperately wanted to please, a woman whose love she had ached for and had constantly been denied.

'Will there be anything else, miss?' Molly said quietly when she had finished brushing out her hair.

'No, thank you, that will be all,' she said in little more than a whisper. She turned on her stool to face her lady's maid. 'And thank you, Molly, for everything.'

Molly nodded and departed. Grace stared at her reflection, fury once again boiling to the surface.

She would love nothing more than to confront her grandmother and throw her lies in her face, but it would do no good, and might do a great deal of harm. Her grandmother would know this revelation came from the servants, and Grace knew how her grandmother treated staff she considered to be disloyal.

But it did mean everything Grace had thought about her parents, all she had done to make amends for the shame her mother had brought on the family, had been for nothing.

She thought of that painting in the attic, of that woman with the gentle eyes and kind smile, and couldn't help but wonder what her life might have been like if she had been raised by two loving parents instead of a woman who cared nothing for her.

She continued to stare at her reflection. She really had been naive. Everyone she thought cared about her had been lying to her and like a gullible fool she had accepted those lies and did exactly what the liars wanted her to do, allowing them to sacrifice her so they could achieve their goals.

So what did she do now? One thing her grandmother was correct about. She did need to calm down before she made any decisions about her future. To that end, she climbed on to her bed and placed the lavender-scented cloth on her head, trying to digest all she had been told.

The Duke's behaviour, the fight, her grandmother's reaction and Molly's revelation spun round and round in her head, making rest impossible.

She climbed off the bed and paced backwards and forwards, trying to walk off her rising anger, but that was as fruitless as resting. What she had to do was face the people who had caused her wrath, to let them know she would no longer be a pawn in their manipulative games.

She left the room and all but collided with her grandmother, who was standing outside her bedchamber about to enter her room.

'You did not tell me Mr Hayward had assaulted the Duke,' her grandmother hissed, as if it had been Grace who had thrown the punch. 'This is outrageous and, instead of sulking in your room, you should be offering comfort to your future husband.'

'Don't be so absurd. Of course I won't comfort that despicable pig of a man.'

Her words caused her grandmother's mouth to fall open in a manner that would almost be comical if Grace felt like laughing.

She pushed past her grandmother, strode down the stairs and walked past the open door of the drawing room, where a young maid was tending to the Duke, wiping away his blood.

She humphed her disapproval and headed out the front

door, determined to walk and walk until she had walked off her anger and had composed the words she needed to say to these people. Words that would make it clear that things had changed irrevocably and they were just going to have to get used to it.

What she would do then she had no idea, but first she needed to get this surging anger out of her body so she could think more clearly and decide what she was to do with her future.

Her walk took her past the fields where the railway tracks were being built. Mr Hayward dropped his hammer on the ground, grabbed his shirt and, pulling it on, raced after her.

'Miss Lowerby, wait,' he called out.

Curiosity caused Grace to halt her progress. She turned to face him, anger still coursing through her, but wanting to hear what he had to say.

'I'm sorry,' he said when he caught up with her.

That was a good start, but hardly enough to quell her anger at him, at the Duke, at her grandmother, at the entire world.

'What exactly are you sorry for?'

'For punching your beloved in the nose.' The small smile that quirked at the edges of his lips made a lie of that apology.

'He deserved it. It's just a shame I wasn't the one to deliver the blow.'

Just like her grandmother, his look of surprise was almost comical, then he laughed. She had forgotten how lovely his laugh was, warm and comforting, and despite herself she smiled back at him.

'That I would have paid anything to see. Do I take it that he can no longer be described as your beloved?'

'I believe we both know that term could never be used

when describing our relationship,' she countered, her anger once again bubbling up inside her.

'I am truly sorry,' he repeated. 'You deserve so much better than him.'

That was something Grace was starting to see. She had done nothing to deserve the way she had been treated. All she had tried to do was make others happy and to do her duty like an obedient young lady.

'Yes, I do,' she stated emphatically.

'So the marriage is off?'

'Of course it is off.'

He released a long breath and nodded. 'Good.' He looked over her shoulder and frowned. 'And it looks like you're about to get the opportunity to tell him so yourself.'

She turned towards where he was looking and saw the Duke striding across the field, followed by her irate grandmother.

'What is the meaning of this?' her grandmother called out. 'Get away from that man and come back to the house immediately.'

'It looks like the Duke is not the only one who needs telling of your change of heart,' Mr Hayward said.

'Miss Lowerby, as my betrothed I forbid you from consorting with this man,' the Duke said the moment they reached her. He puffed up his chest and attempted to look formidable, but his quick, nervous glances at Mr Hayward undermined that stance.

'I'll consort with whomever I choose,' Grace shot back.

'You will not. Not if you are to be my wife.'

'Well, that is easily solved if I'm no longer your betrothed,' Grace said, surprised by how calm her words sounded.

'Stop this at once,' her grandmother screeched. 'I don't know what's got into you, but you know better than this,' she added in a slightly quieter tone. 'Return to the house, now, and we will forget all about this peculiar behaviour. Won't we, Your Grace?' she said, smiling obsequiously at the Duke.

Grace released a long sigh of exasperation. 'No, Grandmother. I have no intention of doing anything you order me to do ever again.'

Once again, her grandmother's mouth fell open in that comical manner before she slammed it shut, to the sound of teeth hitting teeth, and glared at Mr Hayward. 'This is all your fault. You've put these ideas into my granddaughter's head. Shame on you.'

'Perhaps you should, for once, listen to what your granddaughter has to say,' Mr Hayward said, turning to Grace with a smile of approval.

'Well, what have you got to say for yourself, and I want none of your nonsense,' her grandmother said, her glare of disapproval moving between Mr Hayward and Grace.

Grace took in a long breath as she tried to order her thoughts. 'Grandmother, I appreciate everything you have done for me in terms of giving me a home when my parents died, giving me shelter, clothing and an education.'

'Well, for goodness' sake, show that appreciation. Come back to the house and stop behaving like a spoilt brat.'

'As I said, I have no intention of following your orders ever again. While I appreciate what you have done for me, I will no longer be manipulated or taken advantage of by you or anyone else. I will not be used so you can elevate your position in society. I will not be used so you can right the supposed wrong you think my mother committed by marrying for love. I will not be sold into a loveless marriage to a man who cares nothing for me and just sees me as a way to get the better of a man who he knows is in every way his superior.'

'Now, see here,' the Duke spluttered. 'I will not allow you to—'

'Shut up and listen,' Grace said, surprising herself as much as the Duke and her grandmother. They both stared at her with matching bulging eyes, horrified that anyone, especially a powerless debutante, would dare to speak to them in such a manner.

'I was used by you, just as much as I was used by my grandmother and I will not stand for it, not for a moment longer. You're a despicable man who lacks even a modicum of honour and that obscene display in front of the workmen proved it.'

'What? What?' he gasped, his lips flapping like a fish who had just been pulled out of the comfort of the water.

Mr Hayward smiled at her in approval and clapped his hands in admiration of her performance. 'Well said, Grace, well said.'

She turned and glared at him. 'And I don't know what you're smiling at. You're no better than either of them.'

As expected, the smile died, the clapping stopped, and he, too, looked taken aback by her words.

'I know all about that bet you had with the Duke, the one where I was in competition with that piece of land. It was despicable.'

She pointed across the field to where the workmen had stopped in their labours and were looking in the direction of the commotion. 'That was so unforgivable I barely have words to express how repugnant it is. You used me to get a better deal on this land. You didn't care that I'd be married off to a man who only wanted me because he thought *you* wanted me. You led him on so that he would want to marry me even though you knew exactly what my marriage to him would be like. You had no reservations when it came to selling me off to this buffoon so you could increase the profitability of your business.'

His look of shock now matched that of the Duke and her grandmother. It was obvious he, too, did not expect to be spoken to in this manner, nor did he expect to be called to account for his behaviour, and especially by someone as powerless as herself.

All three started talking at once, the Duke to declare he was not a buffoon and as a duke would not tolerate such lack of respect, her grandmother to desperately attempt to reprimand Grace and call her to order and Mr Hayward to repeat his empty apologies.

'Well, I've had it with the lot of you,' she said, cutting across their babble. 'I want nothing to do with any of you, ever again.' With that, she strode off across the field, determined that it was all over and she could now start a new chapter in her life. One where she made her own decisions, ones that suited her and no one else.

Chapter Twenty

Thomas watched her retreating figure, awe, amazement and a sense of shame waging a war within him.

'This is all your fault,' Lady Ashbridge spluttered. 'You've put these outrageous ideas into her head.'

'All I can say is thank goodness I found out what the chit is really like before I married her,' the Duke added. 'Wouldn't want a wife with a temper like that. Lucky escape, I say.'

Thomas was tempted to once again plant his fist in that oaf's face, but this was not time to think of what he wanted to do. It was more important that he talk to Miss Lowerby, to ensure she was all right. He needed to reassure himself she knew what she was doing and to apologise with all his heart for what she had rightly called his despicable behaviour.

To that end, he left Lady Ashbridge, trying to soothe the Duke and convince him that Miss Lowerby's outburst was just some sort of pre-wedding nerves and her granddaughter would very soon come to her senses, while the Duke put on a familiar display of petulance.

Entering the house, he stopped a passing footman. 'Which room is Miss Lowerby staying in?'

The man looked him up and down, obviously reluctant to answer.

'It is vital I see her. She is in a state of distress.'

His plea had no effect on the man, who continued to scrutinise Thomas, taking in the mud on his trousers and the inevitable dishevelled appearance that followed hard physical toil.

'I am Thomas Hayward and am a guest of the Duke of Hardgraves.' Thomas was stretching the truth somewhat, but needs must.

'Of course, Mr Hayward,' the man said. 'I'm so sorry I didn't recognise you. You were at His Grace's recent weekend party, I believe.'

'Yes, I was and please excuse my present appearance. So where would I find Miss Lowerby?'

'She's in the second room after the first corner at the end of the hallway. If you wait here, I'll get her lady's maid to—'

Thomas did not hear the rest of the sentence, but rushed up the stairs two at a time and all but ran down the hallway, determined to find her room within this maze.

He passed an open door and saw her standing beside her bed, pushing gowns into an open trunk.

Without knocking, he entered, stood in the middle of the room and tried to compose what he was to say.

'I suppose you've come to give me a lecture as well,' she said, not stopping in her task.

'No, I have come to make sure you are all right and to once again apologise.'

She pushed another pile of silk, satin and taffeta into her trunk. 'You can save your apologies. I have no need of them.'

'So where do you plan to go? What do you intend to do?'

'I have no idea. All I know is I want to get as far away from this house and everyone who has ever used me.' She punched a silk gown that was refusing to sit neatly in the trunk.

'And do what?'

She picked up a lace shawl, bundled it into a tight knot and glared at him. 'I have no idea, not yet, but weren't you the one who told me women have choices nowadays? Didn't you say they don't have to marry if they don't want to?'

'Yes, but they usually have a plan.'

'I might not have a plan, but I'm not completely useless. My training to make me an ideal wife for a man such as the Duke means I can speak four languages fluently. I could teach. I could give piano lessons like my father.' She shrugged one shoulder. 'All I know is I will survive and no one will ever use or manipulate me ever again.'

'Good.'

She stopped her packing and stared at him. 'Good?'

'Yes, you deserve to live your own life the way you want to and you are an intelligent woman who has just proven herself to be strong and determined. I am sure you will be successful in whatever you choose to do.'

'I will,' she said, resuming stuffing gowns into her trunk. 'Anyway, I've recently discovered my grandfather left me some money, which my grandmother neglected to inform me about. Perhaps I'll start my own business. I don't know, but I'll think of something.'

'But before you leave, I have to say I am sorry. Truly sorry for what I did.'

'Yes, so you said, but what are you sorry for really? For taking that bet or for being caught out?'

'Yes, you're right, for both if I'm being completely honest. And I deserve your condemnation. I wanted the land, but I should never have agreed to the Duke's proposition.'

She stopped in her packing, a silk gown crunched in her hands. 'The Duke's proposition?'

'Yes, when he suggested that offensive bet, I should have said no. I knew it was wrong at the time and yet I still agreed. That was unforgivable.'

'The Duke made the proposition?' She tilted her head in question. 'What exactly was the proposition?'

Thomas's jaw clenched tightly. He did not want to spell it out to her. His behaviour was too shameful.

'Tell me the truth. You owe me that much, surely.'

He exhaled a long breath. 'The Duke challenged me to what he called a wooing duel. If I won your affections, I would have to pay more for the land than we had agreed. If the Duke won your affections, then I would get the land at a cheaper rate.'

Her hands clasped more tightly around the gown. 'It was the Duke's idea?' she asked quietly.

'Yes, and I should have said no. I should have told him it was an outrageous thing to do. To have not done so was unforgivable and you have every right to be angry with me.'

'You're damn right I have. You had a choice, me or cheap land. You chose cheap land.'

Thomas flinched as her words hit him. 'I'm so sorry. At the time I let our childish rivalry blind me to what I was doing and I tried to justify myself by saying no one would be harmed. I told myself you would get what you wanted. Marriage to a duke.'

'You thought no one would be harmed?' she said, her eyes enormous as she shook her head in disbelief. 'You thought I would not be harmed if I married a man like him? You thought I would not be harmed if I married a man who never really wanted me, just didn't want you to have me? You thought I wouldn't be harmed if I married a man capable of behaving the way he did out in the field? You knew what he was like and you happily let me be courted by him all so you could get that land at a better price.'

His muscles clenched tighter with every word. She was right. What he had done to her was appalling and he deserved no less than her wrath and disdain.

'I am so, so sorry. I tried to justify it to myself by saying that it was what you wanted, but I was fooling myself. I was wrong, so very wrong.'

'Why didn't you tell me what he was like?' she said quietly. 'Why didn't you try to stop me from marrying him?'

'Yes, I should have. That, too, was unforgivable.'

'Yes, it was.' She stuffed another dress unceremoniously into her trunk. 'But the Duke had told me the bet was all your idea. That was why I agreed to marry him, because I thought you had betrayed me.'

'He lied.' Thomas took a step towards her. 'It was never my idea. You have to believe that.'

She shrugged as if it made no real difference and she was right. It didn't.

'But I should never have agreed to it. After the Duke announced you were courting I thought that would be the end of it. Then your grandmother encouraged me to see you again.'

'She only did that to pique the Duke's waning interest.'

'Yes. She told me you wanted the Duke desperately, that it was your dream to be a duchess, and his jealousy was the only way to capture him.'

She snorted. '*My* dream? That's what she said, was it?'

'After that bet I felt so guilty I thought I owed you, that it was my duty to help you achieve your dream.'

She snorted again and shoved the crumpled silk dress into the trunk.

'No, that's a lie,' he added. 'That was what I told my-self at the time. I did feel guilty over the bet, but I agreed to what your grandmother asked because I wanted to see you again.'

She stopped pounding the dress so it would fit in the trunk and looked up at him.

'You did?'

'Yes, and the brief time we spent together has been the happiest time of my life.'

'It was?'

'Yes.'

She ran her teeth lightly along her bottom lip. 'I suppose I have an apology to make as well.'

He shook his head. 'You have nothing to apologise for.'

She waved away his objections. 'I knew my grandmother was using you to renew the Duke's interest. I knew it was wrong, but I did nothing to stop it because I, too, wanted to see you again.'

She looked down at the trunk, then back up at him. 'And you are right. As stupid as it now seems, I thought I did want to become a duchess. I thought that was what would make me happy. I thought it was what would make my grandmother love me.'

'Oh, Grace, you never deserved to be treated this way, by anyone. Your grandmother should have loved you for who you are, a lovely, kind, clever young lady, and not seen you as merely someone to further her own ambitions.'

He paused, wondering whether he could say what was really in his heart. 'She should have let you marry for love, to a man who appreciates you for who you really are.'

She gave a mirthless laugh. 'That was never going to happen. My mother married for love and she never forgave her, even though my father was apparently a good man who loved my mother and made her happy.'

'It sounds like your mother was a strong woman, just like her daughter, and followed her own path.'

She looked up at him, unshed tears making her eyes sparkle. He so wanted to take her in his arms and comfort her, but he had proven himself unworthy of her and had no right to do so.

'I so wish I had known her,' she said. 'I so wish I hadn't made such a mess of everything.'

Despite his command to not comfort her, he moved closer and took her hands in his. 'You have done nothing wrong. You were trying to do what your grandmother wanted, what you thought was your duty. All I was doing was trying to get the better of the Duke and increase my family's business assets.'

This might be the last time he would ever see her, so he knew he had to be completely honest or he might never get another opportunity. 'When I made that bet I thought getting the better of the Duke was all that was important and I could not see beyond making a fool of him and getting a good deal on the land I wanted. Now I know that neither of those things mattered. There is only one thing that is important. You.'

She looked up at him, blinking rapidly as if trying to make sense of what he was saying. He stepped closer to her, desperate to make her see that these were not idle words.

'Now I know there are more important things in life. You showed me that. And I no longer want the Duke's land, not when it reminds me of how I hurt you. I'll give it back to him and be done with it.'

'Don't do that. Why should that man profit from any of this?'

'Then I'll give it away to a rival railway company. I don't care. I don't want it. Not when it reminds me of how callous I have been.'

He lightly stroked the back of her hand. 'I mean what I say. You have made me see that there are more important things in life than petty revenges and acquiring more and more money. You've shown me that love is so much more important.'

'Love?'

'Yes, love. I love you. And all I want is for you to be happy and to live an independent life that will allow you to be who you really are and not the person you think other people want you to be.'

It was Thomas's turn to be surprised when she lifted herself up on tiptoes and kissed his lips. The sweet taste and gentle touch of her lips drove out all other thoughts. If this was to be their farewell kiss and the last time he had her in his arms, he wanted it to be a kiss to remember. He gently wrapped his arms around her shoulders and held her close to him, loving the feel of her soft feminine curves against his body and kissed her back.

If she wanted him to stop, he would do so and be grateful for this one, sweet parting kiss. But he hoped she did not. Not yet.

Her lips parted, making it clear she wanted him to continue. He gladly accepted the invitation and ran his tongue along her full bottom lip. She released a soft sigh and he entered her mouth, holding her close, loving the way she moulded herself into him, as if this was where she belonged.

Then to his immense disappointment, she pulled back from him. But that, too, was something he was going to have to accept. It was all over. He had hurt her. He did not deserve her forgiveness and he certainly did not deserve her kisses.

'You said you want me to be happy,' she said, looking up at him, still in his arms. 'This is what makes me happy. Being with you. Being in your arms. I had thought that being with the Duke would make me happy. I had thought that giving my grandmother what she wanted would make me happy, but it didn't. And you are the only person in my life that even cares whether I am truly happy or not.'

'And that is all I care about,' he whispered as he pushed a stray lock of her long blonde hair off her face.

'I love you,' she whispered back. 'I love you so much I never want to be away from you.'

He stared down at her, hardly believing what he was hearing. 'Then marry me,' he said, the solution so obvious. 'You can still live the life you want to live. You can still be the independent woman you want to be. Gracie, you can be anything you want to be, but I would love to be part of your life.'

She nodded, giving him hope.

'I'd love to be part of your life because I love you, everything about you,' he said, encouraged by her smile. 'I think I've loved you from the moment I saw you sprawled out on the ballroom floor.'

This caused her to laugh lightly.

'I could see how much we were alike even if I hadn't realised it at the time. We are both outsiders, both people who have to fight for our place in the world.'

'But it was you who taught me how to fight back and stand up for myself.'

'No, I think you learned that all by yourself,' he said with a laugh.

'I did, didn't I,' she said with a cheeky smile. 'And I intend to keep standing up for myself for the rest of my life. You had better take that into account if I'm going to be your wife.'

'I would hope for nothing less, but does that mean you accept? That you will marry me?' he asked, hardly able to believe it could be true.

She nodded.

'Oh, Gracie, I love you.' Those three words hardly enough to describe the strength of the feelings rushing through him.

'And I love you.'

She stepped back from him and sent him another wicked smile. 'My grandmother has said, many, many times, that once a man has agreed to marry you, he's allowed to take liberties.' She gave a small laugh, walked over to the door, closed it and turned the key in the lock. 'And, as you know, I always follow everything my grandmother says.'

He took her in his arms and kissed her waiting lips, knowing this was what he wanted. What he had always wanted.

Chapter Twenty-One

Grace could hardly believe it was actually happening. It was what she had dreamed of since she had first met him and those dreams had only become more intense since he had first kissed her.

Now she was back in his arms, his lips were on hers. This was where she had to be and where she intended to spend the rest of her life, in love and married to this glorious man.

Her entire body aching for his touch, she moulded herself against him, loving the feel of her breasts hard against his chest as she kissed him back, unleashing a burning desire that had been smouldering within her since they had last kissed.

'Oh, God, I want you so much,' he murmured, as his lips left hers and he kissed a line down her neck. 'But if you want to wait until we are married, I understand.'

She shook her head, shocked that he could say such a thing. 'No, I want you now,' she said, her voice raspy with desire. 'I need to have you now.'

His kisses left her neck and he smiled at her, a smile that sent tingles of anticipation rippling up and down her spine.

'And you have me, my love, heart, mind and soul.'

'And body,' she added.

'Yes, and body, definitely and body.'

And that was what she wanted as well. She wanted to feel his body against her, his warm skin against hers. She needed to be out of the restricting clothes that were creating a barrier between them.

Her trembling fingers moved to the buttons of her gown and she tried to release herself from the restricting fabric.

'Allow me,' he said, removing her hands. 'I want to unwrap you like the precious gift you are.'

He undid the buttons down the front of her dress and slipped it off her shoulders. Kissing each shoulder, he pushed it lower over her hips where it dropped to the ground. His lips returned to hers, and through the fabric of her chemise, her body moved against his, the friction turning her nipples hard and sensitive. Throbbing anticipation mounted inside her, rising to an almost unbearable pitch as he continued to kiss her with ravenous longing.

'Lift your arms,' he murmured. 'I want to see you naked.'

She did as he commanded. He lifted her chemise over her head, tossed it to one side and pushed her drawers down over her hips. She stepped out of them and looked up at him. She was standing in front of him dressed only in her silk stockings and garter belts, as he slowly looked her up and down. She could see the raw desire sparking in his eyes, intensifying her own pounding need for him.

He desired her. He wanted her. He was going to take her. And she wanted it with an all-consuming wildness that was intoxicating and thrilling.

'You are perfect,' he said, his voice a husky rasp. 'You are even more beautiful than I had imagined.' He smiled at her. 'And believe me, I have a vivid imagination.'

His hand lightly stroked across her breasts, a feather touch on her nipples. She released a soft sigh and closed her eyes, focusing on that touch.

'Yes,' she murmured, that one word saying so much.

He scooped her up into his arms and carried her across the room, placing her in the middle of the bed. She lay back on the feather mattress, loving the way she was offering herself to him, loving the intensity in his gaze as he feasted himself on her body while he ripped off his clothes.

With the shedding of each item she watched as more of his body was exposed to her hungry gaze. He was perfection, like a marble statue of a Greek athlete, all sculptured muscles and sinews, and the promise of sensual pleasure.

She reached out her hands towards him, wanting to touch that hard, muscular body, to run her hands, her lips, her tongue over his skin.

'I love you so much,' he said, looking down into her eyes.

'So prove it,' she said, her breath coming in short gasps as her heart pounded hard within her chest.

He smiled down at her. 'My pleasure,' he said as he joined her on the bed and took her in his arms. Then he kissed her again. Warm naked skin against warm naked skin, his lips were on hers, hot and ravenous.

She kissed him back, giving expression to her fervent, untamed desires. Her hands ran down his strong back, loving the feeling of those rippling muscles under her fingers.

His lips left her lips, gliding to the sensitive hollow under her ear and tracing a slow line down her neck. She writhed under him, every inch of her body alive, every inch craving his touch.

His lips moved lower, tracing a line of kisses across the mounds of her breasts. Grace released a sigh of exquisite pleasure as he cupped each breast, kissed each tight bud in turn, then took one in his mouth, his tongue and lips tormenting the aching peak.

She took hold of his head, her hands running through

his thick black hair, her breath coming in louder and louder gasps, his caressing tongue sending surges of ecstasy cascading through her.

As she released a loud sigh, pleasure shot through her, leaving her gasping in its wake. His lips were once more on hers and she kissed him back, unable to believe that his lips and tongue could give her so much pleasure, but desperate to know how much more this magnificent man could show her.

His hands exploring her body, she arched towards him in longing and expectation. His hands swept over her breasts, down her stomach, over her mound to the cleft between her legs. Not thinking, just reacting, she parted her legs, showing him where she wanted his caressing hands to move, letting him know how much she needed him to relieve the tight, throbbing tension that was once again mounting within her.

His hand moved between her legs. She released a *yes* on a soft sigh as his fingers parted her and slowly, gently entered her.

He lifted himself up off her, and she opened her eyes. Surely he would not be so cruel as to stop now?

'Are you sure, my love?' he asked, his voice gentle.

'Oh, I'm more than sure,' she said, placing her hand over his and urging him to continue.

'If you want me to stop at any time, just tell me.'

'Don't you dare stop,' she said, causing him to smile slightly before he kissed her again.

His lips moving to the soft skin of her neck, he cupped her feminine folds and rubbed against her sensitive spot, his fingers entering her deeper with each rhythmic stroke. Her gasps of pleasure matched the rhythm of his hand, growing louder and louder as raw need surged up within her. His hand moved faster, the pressure harder, taking her higher and higher, until exquisite pleasure crashed over her. Calling out his name, she collapsed back on to the bed.

He kissed her again, his body blanketing hers, and her desire for more of this glorious man was instantly sparked back into life.

'That was divine, but isn't there more that we can do?'

He laughed slightly and held her closer. 'Are you sure? Don't you want to wait until your wedding night? Then we will be husband and wife and in our own bed.'

'No. I want to be your wife right now. We can get those bits of paper later.'

'You really do know your own mind now, don't you?' he said, smiling down at her.

She rubbed her inner thigh against his leg and watched the effect on his face. 'I certainly do,' she said, smiling back at him.

He gently placed his hand on her inner thigh and she did what she knew he wanted, parted them wider and wrapped her legs around his waist.

'If this hurts, tell me and I'll stop,' he said. She nodded and felt his tip against her opening.

'Promise me you will let me know if I hurt you.'

She looked up into his eyes. 'I promise you.'

Gently, he pushed himself inside her. She gasped at the unexpected feeling of him stretching her, filling her up. He instantly withdrew.

'No, don't stop,' she said, sliding her hands down his back and cupping his firm buttocks so he would not escape her.

'Are you sure this is what you want, my love?' he whispered.

'Yes, I'm very sure.'

He pushed further into her and Grace released a long,

slow sigh. This was perfect. They were joining together as one. He was hers. She was his.

Slowly, he withdrew and pushed inside her again, again and again, each time her body relaxing further into the heavenly feeling of having him inside her. The thrusts became faster. They penetrated deeper until Grace lost herself in the throbbing of her body as her gasping breaths matched his thrusts.

Gripping his buttocks tightly, she wrapped her legs further up around his waist so he could enter her deeper, harder and faster, taking her higher and higher with each thrust. Pleasure mounted up within her, like an ever-rising wave. Just as she thought she could bear no more, it crashed over her, sending intense euphoria flooding through her body as she cried out his name in passionate ecstasy.

'Oh, Grace, my darling Grace,' he said as he reached his own release and collapsed on to her.

She lay back panting, residual shivers of pleasure rippling through her as he held her tightly.

'You are now mine, for ever,' he said before once again kissing her still-gasping lips.

'And you are mine. For ever,' she murmured as he nuzzled her neck.

When his heartbeat finally slowed down and the fog of passion lifted, the reality of where he was and what he had done dawned on Thomas. He was in the Duke's house, in bed with the woman the Duke was expecting to marry, the woman Thomas loved and would soon make his own wife.

While it mattered nothing to Thomas what the Duke or anyone else thought, that did not mean Grace would be as equally relaxed about such a scandalous breach of etiquette.

He rolled on to his side and gazed at her. Had he ever

seen a more beautiful sight? No, he knew he had never seen anything so wondrous as the woman he had just made love to. She was perfect in every way and she was his. He didn't know what he had done to deserve such good fortune, but he would be eternally thankful that fortune had smiled on him and granted him this precious gift.

He picked up a coil of her long golden hair, spread out over the pillow, just as he had imagined it so many times, and wrapped it around his finger.

'I doubt if we're going to be welcome in the Duke's house,' he said, causing her to give a small laugh. 'I can go and tell the Duke and your grandmother we are to marry and while I'm facing their wrath you can continue packing. Then we can make a hasty retreat.'

She rolled on to her side. 'No, let's tell them together.'

He lightly kissed her shoulder. 'Are you sure? I doubt if your grandmother is going to be pleased.'

'I've spent my entire life trying to please my grandmother and all that's resulted in is me being completely miserable.'

He lightly stroked her cheek. 'Are you certain? I don't think she will take the news of our marriage at all well.'

She laughed. 'I *know* she won't take it well, but the sooner we get it over and done with, the sooner we can leave this house and the sooner we can marry.'

He smiled at her, his brave, independent Grace.

They climbed out of bed and he helped her to dress, then tried as best he could to help her knot her hair up into a bun. As he did so, he had to resist the temptation to kiss the back of her neck again. He knew where that would lead—straight back to bed—and she was right, the sooner they were out of this house, the sooner they would be married.

Hand in hand, they walked down the stairs and into the

drawing room, where they found the Duke standing in the middle of the room, his nose raised high in the air, his lips pursed and his arms tightly crossed over his chest, still muttering about what an outrage this all was, while Lady Ashbridge tried to reason with him.

They both looked towards the door as Thomas and Grace entered. Both sets of eyes grew enormous and two mouths fell open as conversation ceased mid-sentence. If those two hadn't both behaved in such despicable ways, Thomas would almost feel sorry for them, they looked so stunned.

'Grandmother, Thomas and I wish to inform you that we are to marry,' Grace stated in a clear voice. 'I will be sending you an invitation to the wedding and you will be most welcome to attend.'

Lady Ashbridge's eyes grew even larger and she stared at her granddaughter as if she could hardly understand the language she was speaking.

'No,' she gasped out, placing her hand over her heart and staggering towards the nearest chair. 'You can't do this to me.'

'Yes, I can. I intend to marry for love, just as my mother did.'

'You'll get nothing,' Lady Ashbridge said, pointing a finger at Thomas. 'I'm sure you're aware of how generous my granddaughter's marriage settlement is, but you will not get your hands on one penny of it.'

'I care nothing for that,' Thomas said, giving Grace's hand a gentle squeeze. 'I'm marrying Grace because I love her, love her with my heart, mind and my soul.'

'And your body,' she whispered beside him, causing him to smile.

'Never wanted the chit anyway,' the Duke added, his nose once again lifting high into the air. Thomas took a step towards him, but was stopped when Grace placed a hand on his arm.

'He's not worth it,' she whispered. And she was right. The man was bitter and angry. And as he was responsible for bringing his lovely Grace into his life, in a strange way Thomas owed him a debt of gratitude.

'That's all we came to say,' Grace added. 'We will take our leave now.'

'No, Grace, you can't,' her grandmother cried out. 'You've ruined your chances with the Duke, but there are other suitable men. There's the Earl of Whitecliff and Baron Morsley's eldest son.'

They left the room while her grandmother continued listing men she deemed more suitable than him to wed her granddaughter.

Thomas arranged with the footman to have her trunk loaded on to one of the carts used on the railway site and for the retrieval of his own possessions, then they climbed aboard and headed off to the local train station.

'When we get to the station, I'll buy you a first-class ticket,' he said and looked down at his rough attire. 'But dressed as I am I'll have to join the other workmen in the third-class carriage.'

'No, you won't. We'll both travel third class. Don't the marriage vows say for richer or poorer, for first class or third class?'

He laughed loudly and wrapped his arm around her shoulder. 'You are precious. But this is hardly the most auspicious start to our life together,' he said as the roughly built cart rattled and creaked through the countryside.

'Yes, it is. It's perfect,' Grace responded with a smile. 'This is everything I have dreamed of since I was a child,' she added, leaning her head on his shoulder. 'I always pictured myself running away with my handsome prince, knowing that he loved me as much as I loved him.'

Thomas kissed the top of her head. She was right. This was perfect and like a dream come true.

Epilogue

No wedding could be more like a fairy tale, of that Grace was certain. Just as she had always dreamed of doing, she had won the love of a handsome prince. He didn't have a title, but in her eyes, Thomas was every inch her prince charming.

And soon he would be her husband.

On the arm of her uncle, the Earl of Ashbridge, she walked up the aisle of the small stone church near Thomas's family estate in Somerset as an organ played the wedding march. Unlike her grandmother, her uncle did not see this marriage as a travesty and, when asked to give her away, had been delighted. 'Your mother would be so happy for you, as would your grandfather,' he had said. 'And it would be my honour to stand in for your father and grandfather, two men I admired greatly.'

Each member of the congregation smiled at her as she passed, reflecting her happiness. Even the old stone church seemed to radiate joy, with the pews bedecked with ivy and white roses, and colourful floral bouquets adorning every corner.

She reached the altar and her uncle handed her over to her husband-to-be and took his seat in the front row next to Thomas's parents.

His parents had made her feel so welcome and Grace

now felt as if she finally had the loving family she had always wanted and a place where she belonged. From the moment she stepped down from the carriage when she first arrived at their estate they had taken her into their fold.

'Me dear, I am so pleased to have another daughter, one I am sure is going to make my son so happy,' she said, encasing her in a warm hug, as Thomas's father shook his hand and offered his congratulations.

'I knew one day a lovely lady would capture your heart,' he said before turning to Grace and kissing her on the cheek. 'Welcome to the family, Grace.'

Then Thomas's sister also hugged her.

'This is simply splendid,' Georgina had gushed. 'I just know that you and I are going to be the best of friends, but you're going to have to tell me, how did Tommy finally win your heart? Did he do as I told him and challenge the Duke to a duel? Did he serenade you and shower you with love sonnets?'

She had looked towards Thomas, who was smiling and slowly shaking his head in amused disbelief.

'No, but he proposed in a manner that did make me very, very happy,' she had said, sending Thomas a quick wink. 'Happier than I had realised it was possible to be.'

'Good, and he better continue to do so or he'll have me to answer to.'

'Believe me, I intend to make my new wife just as happy again and again, at every opportunity,' Thomas had said with a devilish smile, causing Grace to blush slightly.

And soon he would make good on that promise. Soon she would be his wife.

'You look like a princess,' he whispered as she smiled up at him through her lace veil.

* * *

Throughout the ceremony, Thomas held her hand and Grace tried to adopt a suitably solemn expression as the vicar took them through the service, but it was hard to keep that ecstatic smile off her face. And every time she looked up at Thomas, he, too, was smiling with unrestrained joy.

Finally, the vicar told Thomas he could kiss the bride. Gently, he lifted the veil, leant down and kissed her lightly on the lips. Grace closed her eyes and released a gentle sigh, and heard the congregation sigh along with her, basking in the sight of two people in love.

Still holding her hand, he led her back down the aisle to the sound of joyous church bells, and the moment they were on the threshold of the church they were showered with rose petals.

It was all so magical and Grace found herself both laughing and crying, until Thomas once more took her in his arms and kissed her, much to the pleasure of the assembled guests and villagers who had come out to witness the happy occasion.

A flower-bedecked carriage awaited them and, as they drove off to their wedding breakfast, Thomas once again kissed her. Now they were alone, the kisses were longer and deeper, heightening her excitement of the wedding night to come.

Flowers decorated the house and, when they pulled up in front, the servants were all waiting outside, baskets of rose petals in their hands, and they were once again showered with those delightfully scented flowers.

Hand in hand, they rushed up the stairs. Thomas pulled her behind one of the pillars and kissed her deeply, taking the opportunity before the other guests arrived.

'I love you with all my heart,' he whispered before kissing the soft skin of her neck.

'And I love you,' she gasped back. As much as she was looking forward to sharing the joy of her marriage with their guests, she couldn't wait for the wedding breakfast to be over so they could be alone together and start their life as husband and wife.

Georgina and Thomas's two closest friends, Sebastian and Isaac, were the first to arrive. Georgina had been right when she had said they would soon become the best of friends and had bubbled with excitement when Grace had asked her to be her bridesmaid.

'It will be the fourth time I've been a bridesmaid,' she had declared. 'I'm obviously very good at it.'

Sebastian and Isaac had performed their roles as best man and groomsman admirably, even if they had been unable to completely hide their surprise when Thomas had told them he was to marry.

The rest of the family, including her grandmother, were next to arrive. Grace had been surprised she had accepted the invitation to the wedding. She wanted to see it as her grandmother finally accepting her choice of husband, but suspected it had more to do with her grandmother discovering that Thomas was the brother-in-law of the Duke of Ravenswood. But whatever the reason, Grace no longer cared. Her grandmother had hurt and bullied her throughout her life and she knew that no one would ever do that again. She was now married to a man who loved and cherished her, a man who had shown her how to be strong and independent, and nothing would ever change that now.

As the wedding party were walking up the stairs, Thomas smiled down at her. 'I love you, Mrs Hayward,' he said.

'And I love you,' she responded with all her heart.

Georgina paused at the top step, sighed and placed her hand over her heart, while Isaac and Sebastian gave small, embarrassed coughs.

'Don't be so cynical,' he called out to his friends, laughter in his voice. 'Love is the best thing possible. It makes the world a better place. It makes you a better man.'

Instead of replying, both men rolled their eyes, linked arms with Georgina and led her inside.

'I think those two need to be alone together,' they heard Seb say as he walked into the entranceway.

'Agreed. There's only so much of this lovey-dovey business I can take,' Isaac added, causing Thomas and Grace to laugh.

'They will learn,' he said, looking over at his retreating friends. 'And when they do, they'll discover how love can sneak up on you in the most unexpected of places and steal your heart.' He looked down at Grace and smiled. 'And then you become it's happiest, most willing captive.'

With that, he kissed her again and Grace was certain her parents were smiling at the happy occasion, pleased that, just like them, she had married for love.

* * * * *

The Lady's Proposal For The Laird

Jeanine Englert

MILLS & BOON

Jeanine Englert's love affair with mysteries and romance began with Nancy Drew and her grandmother's bookshelves of romance novels. When she isn't wrangling with her characters, she can be found trying to convince her husband to watch her latest Masterpiece/BBC show obsession. She loves to talk about writing, her beloved rescue pups, and mysteries and romance with readers. Visit her website at jeaninewrites.com.

Author Note

Some books write themselves and this book was one of those. Ironically, Rowan was a hero I have had in my heart for over ten years, and I think his book was never published before because I had him paired with the wrong heroine.

Perhaps he knew this well before I did.

It wasn't until Susanna appeared in *The Highlander's Secret Son* that I had even an inkling of a new love match for him. Then, once I wrote Iona and Royce's story, *A Laird without a Past*, I realized Rowan and Susanna were the perfect pair. Each of them was fierce, relentless, and full of emotion and passion that teetered on the edge of chaos. All in all, they needed a partner with equal fire, not complementary parts.

It is like that in life sometimes as well. You wait and wait, rather certain you are on the right path, and then suddenly you blink and a different route appears. It is only then you realise it was the one you should have been on all along.

Wishing you the right path at just the right time, my dear readers.

DEDICATION

To my critique partner and dear friend,
Tanya Agler:

You have been an integral part of my writing
journey, and I know I would not be where I am today
without you. I am so grateful for meeting you at
Georgia Romance Writers back in 2013 and for
being able to share in the joys and heartbreaks
of publication that only another fellow author
knows and understands.

I thought it was fitting to dedicate this book to you,
as Rowan has been a character you have known as
long as I have, for better or worse, throughout
a variety of story drafts.

His book and this heartfelt thanks
to you are long overdue.

Prologue

October 1745.
Loch's End, Glencoe, Scotland

'She must marry, brother. It is the best way to protect her. In truth, it may be the *only* way to protect her.'

Susanna Cameron scoffed and halted her descent on the stairs at the sound of her eldest brother's voice from the cracked door of the study below. Her blood cooled as her hand clutched the wooden finial of the railing, her slippered foot hanging in mid-air, frozen by his words. Moonlight streamed in through the stained-glass windows, casting blotches of colour on the stone and on her dark gown, as she stood on the landing and listened. Surely her brothers were not discussing *her*. She needed no husband, nor any man's protection. She was a Cameron after all. She frowned. But who else would they be desperate to marry off for protection? Her youngest sister was already married with her first bairn due next year.

'She will not have it, as you well know. *Especially* if you attempt to force it upon her.' Rolf answered with a chuckle rounding out the end of his words.

Susanna smiled as her younger brother Rolf came to her defence, and then frowned with the realisation and confirmation that it *was* she who was being discussed. She squared her shoulders, turned on her heel, and took a step onto the bottom set of stairs prepared to tell them exactly what she thought about their scheme to marry her off. In simplest terms, she wouldn't agree to it.

Ever.

'I do not want to force it upon her, you know that, especially after Jeremiah,' Royce added in low tones. 'But surely her safety trumps all. She must have another family to back her in case the worst happens—and we are no longer here to protect her.'

Susanna stilled. Her throat dried and her stomach dropped. She blanched. *No longer here to protect her?* She had never heard her brothers talk in such a way. The politics and unrest in the Highlands were precarious now to be sure, but Royce, her eldest brother and laird of the clan, feared nothing and no one. The Camerons were one of the most powerful clans in the Highlands, if not *the* most powerful. Who would dare attack or threaten them, especially now? And what reason could they possibly have to do so? They had alliances with almost every surrounding clan.

'You cannot even entertain such thoughts. You have a bairn on the way.'

'That is exactly *why* I must think such,' Royce countered. His boots echoed along the stone floor. 'And you must prepare yourself. Our sisters may become targets once all is revealed. So might Iona and our babe. If something happens to me, you must be ready to carry on. No matter what.'

'You know I will protect all of them with my life, but such talk is extreme. It may never come out, brother. All this worry and planning may be for naught.'

'While I hope you are right, Rolf, my gut tells me otherwise,' Royce replied. 'And once all is revealed, the Highlands may become the battleground we feared, and instead of the British being at odds with us, we will all be fighting one another.'

Chapter One

Two weeks later.
Argyll Castle, Glencoe, Scotland

Laird Rowan Campbell slammed the forging hammer down with force, the clash of metal against iron reverberated through his body. He relished the ache the repeated pounding created in his forearm. His nightly visits to the forge had become his place of peace, not unlike a religious man's house of worship. He set aside his hammer and turned the rough metal blade that would become a sword in his grip and frowned. The piece was becoming too cool to shape and would fracture if he wasn't careful. Setting it aside, he grabbed the shovel, scooped up a heaping pile of hot bright orange coals, and then added them to the forge before sliding the metal blade beneath them.

'This is the last place I thought to search for you, yet here you are.'

Rowan stilled at the sound of the familiar female voice behind him. It was a voice he had not heard for over two years. One he had not ever wished to hear again but wishes were fickle things prone to shatter much like hot metal when it cools too quickly and isn't properly tempered. And that was Susanna Cameron: fire and ice within the same breath and a woman quite prone to breaking things and relishing in her destruction.

'Susanna,' he replied, shifting the coals evenly over the flame in the forge, not eager to face her. He needed a moment to gain his bearings and counted to five as he ran his soiled hands down the leather apron protecting him as he worked. Then, he turned, and his body thrummed and heated at the sight of her like the first time he'd set eyes on her when he was fifteen years old with the beginnings of scruff on his cheeks. She stood framed by the doorway of the forge, covered in her signature dark hooded cloak, her glistening ice blue eyes gathering all the light in the room while her pearly skin and lush pink lips reflected the firelight and sent a surge of need straight through him.

Deuces.

His body didn't remember what his mind always did: her cruelty. He fisted his hands by his sides.

'You look far better than the last time I saw you,' she said, her gaze slowly assessed him head to toe as she pulled at the tips of her gloves one at a time to remove them from her hands.

She'd skilfully landed her first blow. He knew more was to come.

'What do you want, my lady? And how did you manage to get past my guards? And where are yours?' He wiped his forearm across his brow to keep the sweat from stinging his eyes as they swept the room. She was alone.

'Always to the point,' she replied, smiling at him as if she were about to steal from his pocket. Knowing Susanna Cameron, she already had, and he just didn't know it yet.

'Merely eager to get back to my work.' It had been over two years since his last bout with insanity, and he planned to keep it that way, despite her prodding. The forge brought him calm, salvation, and sanity, and his nightly visits were a necessary part of his recovery. Her presence was interrupting all of that.

She scoffed, her gaze flicking about the forge as if it were a dirty, forlorn place. 'You are laird. You have men to tend to these needs.'

'Perhaps it is *I* who need *it*.'

Her brow lifted for a moment, her interest evident, before she cast it aside. 'I need your assistance.'

'I doubt that. You have men to tend to your every need, and you have a way of bending them *to* your needs. Otherwise, you would not have been able to enter this forge.' He would deal with his men that allowed her entry later. Much later, after his temper had cooled.

She frowned. 'Perhaps, but not for this task. It requires discretion.'

'Then why come to me, a man who would relish in the idea of exploiting your clan's secrets for my own benefit.'

'Because I have no other options.'

She looked away and fidgeted with her hands, an odd display of weakness from a woman never prone to it. Her cool, calm, and icy demeanour slipped away to reveal a brief momentary glimmer of the young vulnerable lass he had known and thought he once loved many years ago before her mask fell back into place.

Curious. Now he *was* interested.

'A Cameron without options is an odd situation indeed,' he replied. 'Why would I be willing to help you? Perhaps you have forgotten our last exchange?'

Susanna's gaze met his, but she didn't answer. They both

knew well what that last exchange was, but she was loath to speak of it. So was he.

He set aside his tools and turned away to shovel a new scoop of coal into the forge and the blast of heat sent goose-flesh running along his wet skin. His tunic stuck to his flesh, soaked in sweat from his hour of labour. The sun had long gone down, and the nearby families in the village were tucked in preparing for bed, but not him. He had another hour in the forge, perhaps two, before his body and mind would be exhausted enough for sleep. This unexpected visit might well set him back another hour.

The barn door slid closed, and he lifted his brow in surprise as he stoked the coals and used the tongs to hoist a new strip of metal he needed to shape into the bright orange heap. There was a slight sizzle as sweat from his forehead dripped onto the hot embers.

'Do you not worry about your reputation? Being an unmarried woman alone with a laird in a forge, especially a man like me.' He faced her and was stilled by the desperation and agony in her gaze. He had only seen that expression once before.

'Instead of plaguing me with your barbs, I need you to listen,' she replied, her tone softening.

She had his attention now. He came closer, so close he could see the dark circles under her eyes and the tight agitated hold of her hands in front of her waist. She hadn't been sleeping and probably not eating either. He knew well the signs of prolonged desperation and worry.

'I am listening,' he said, crossing his arms against his chest.

'My brothers are keeping something important from me and my sister, and I need you to unearth what it is.'

He chuckled. 'You came all this way in the dead of night because you need me to find out a secret for you?'

Surely there was more to it. Susanna Cameron was not prone to care about such trivial matters, and nothing was ever as it seemed at first glance with a Cameron. Ever.

'Aye. It is undermining our family, and I don't know why. It consumes my brothers, especially Royce. I fear it will shatter us if I do not figure out what it is that plagues them so.'

'They are probably scheming as you lot are prone to do,' Rowan added.

'Nay. It is far more than that. I know it. They are even conspiring to marry me off to ensure I have the proper protection, whatever that may entail. Imagine me, a Cameron, in need of protection.' She shifted on her feet, another symptom of her growing agitation. He set aside his annoyance.

'And when did this change in their behaviour begin?' he asked.

'After they returned from Lismore a month ago, but it has grown worse in the last two weeks. They have been secretive and meet for hours at a time locked in Father's old study. They will not utter a word about it to me, and with Catriona no longer at Loch's End, I find I am shut out of my own family. I want to know why.'

'That merely sounds like Royce to me,' he replied with a frown.

Susanna's eldest brother was serious and rather unyielding like Rowan was. He had heard the rumours about Laird Cameron's disappearance over the summer. It was an odd recounting of Royce having suffered a head wound and memory loss before returning to his home at Loch's End with his brother Rolf after being missing on the mysterious isle of Lismore for over a month. No one knew why he'd travelled there in the first place.

'The old Royce perhaps, but when he returned from Lismore he was a changed man, and he still is. He is kinder, happy even except for this. He is married now with a bairn on the way. It is this one secret that I do not trust. I still do not even know why he was there. He will speak of it to only Rolf.'

'Why are you asking me to help you? Why not enlist a trusted warrior or guard within your ranks to assist you in this intrigue? Surely, they are better equipped to gain access to and information from your brothers.'

'Nay,' she shook her head. 'It is too great a risk. My gut tells me it is of a far more serious matter than what can be trusted to a soldier, even one within our clan.'

'And to ask my question again: why me, and why on earth would I help you?'

She lifted her chin and pulled back her shoulders like a bird splaying its feathers to make itself appear larger. It didn't really work for Susanna as she was far too petite, but her intention was clear: she would not be refused. 'Because I was promised a favour by your brother when he was laird years ago, any favour of my choosing when I need it, and I plan to collect on it. Tonight.'

'As you well know, my brother Brandon is not laird any more. I am.'

'But as *you* well know you are beholden to fulfil the promise he made to me two years ago as the new laird of Clan Campbell.'

He clenched his jaw. *Devil's blood.* He knew exactly what promise she was referring to. She had offered up her men to help rescue Brandon's son and the babe's mother

Fiona in exchange for an open favour that could be claimed for whatever purpose Susanna needed later. Without her men, Brandon's now wife and son would have been killed. Her assistance had saved their lives.

But that didn't mean it had not been a foolish and risky promise to make as a laird. The Camerons could not be trusted. Rowan had found that out when he had begun courting Susanna when they were teens. His opinion upon them had not wavered. If anything, it had grown more resolute.

He sighed, fisting his hand by his side. Brandon would want and expect Rowan to uphold their end of the agreement with her, no matter how much he wanted to deny Susanna. Honour was not something to be trifled with. She knew he could not balk at fulfilling such a request as it would put his lairdship and clan at risk.

One's word was almost all that mattered in the Highlands, especially now. And he still had much to prove as the reinstalled laird. Even though two years had passed since he had regained his title, the clan elders and villagers still scrutinised him and his decisions.

The woman had him finely wedged between duty and honour and she knew it. Exasperation didn't begin to describe his feelings. He felt trapped and his skin began to itch. He had to find some means of escaping her demands.

'And if I were to fulfil this promise, how do you plan for me to get your brothers, who generally despise me on a good day, to share their most pressing secret with me? I feel you have not thought all of this through, Susanna. Your brothers will see me upon their doorstep and slam the door in my face before I dare utter a syllable. I should know. I would do the same.'

Her gaze lifted to him, and her slow, seductive smile warned him of the danger that would fall next from her lips, but nothing could have prepared him for her words.

'You will offer for my hand, and we will be betrothed until I discover the truth.'

Chapter Two

Rowan's laughter surprised Susanna most. It was a deep, heavenly sound, and it echoed through the large, heated barn that served as the clan's main forge. Despite the ugliness that had passed between them before, her attraction to him had never waned, ever since the first time she'd seen him when she was a young lass on the cusp of womanhood. He was a large, powerful, handsome man used to getting his own desires met, and that ferocity had always made her pulse quicken and throat dry. She was glad to see him back to his old self. Remembering him as the fragile broken man of two years ago in Argyll Castle made her shiver. Rowan was never meant to be anything other than the substantial, formidable wolf amongst men that he was now.

While she knew he would balk at her request, she hadn't expected this odd response. He had always been overly serious and prone to brooding just like her eldest brother. She wasn't quite sure how to manoeuvre. Ranting, refusal, and dismissal she could counter, but laughter?

Curses.

Finally, his laughter subsided, and he wiped the wetness from his eyes. 'I must thank you. I have not laughed aloud like that in years. Now, please tell me your *real* plan.'

'That *is* my real plan.'

He scrubbed a hand through his dark, damp, wavy hair that had grown a bit past his shoulders, far longer than she could ever remember. His muscles rippled along his torso and forearms exposed by the rolled sleeves of his shirt; her gaze unable to resist following the movement. His body strained against the transparent material of his tunic that was soaked through by his labours. It had been far too long since she had been comforted by a man's touch, and sadly her body had always had an overly strong reaction to him. She pressed her thumbnail into the flesh of her index finger so she could focus on the pain of it rather than her emotion. A trick she had learned and mastered over the years. It quelled the flush of heat rushing through her skin and helped her focus on the task at hand: gaining his agreement.

'Susanna, there is no way this will work. Surely, you realised that before travelling all this way to me.'

'Nay, it will work, but it will require your commitment to the role. They are eager to find me a husband, and your clan is powerful enough to fulfil that need.'

'I am no performer. You have the wrong laird for such a part.'

'Nay. You are the perfect candidate for the role. People fear you and wouldn't dare question you. And because of your recent past, people will not doubt your—changefulness towards me.' She bit her lip on her word choice. It could have been better. Perhaps he would not pick up on her allusion.

He looked down at his hands and shook his head before finally lifting his bright blue gaze to glare at her. 'Ah. You believe this will work because of my previous bout with insanity. No man will question the irrational acts of a man who has struggled with his faculties once before.'

He winced. 'Quite the cut, even from you.' He rubbed the back of his neck.

Her skin heated. Aye, it was a cruelty to use his weakness against him in such a way, but she was desperate. Far more desperate than she wanted him to know.

The future of her clan might rest in his hands. The thought of it turned her stomach.

'And what shall you tell your family?' he asked. 'How will they believe you have fallen for a laird whose reason and sanity are questionable at best, especially after our fractious history together. You rejected my proposal to marry you more than ten years ago. We ended on horrid terms. We are not even friends. How and why would they believe *you* have changed *your* mind and chosen to attach yourself to *me*?' He pointed a finger to his chest.

She had practiced this part, knowing full well he would challenge her scheme and attempt to poke holes in her plan. 'For power. I will tell them you are weak and that I can control you once we are married and use it to further our claim in the Highlands.'

He cursed and walked away from her. He stoked the coals and turned the metal he was heating with the tongs. She knew this would be the most perilous part of their conversation. No man and no laird would want to be perceived as so weak and without control, especially a man like Rowan. But she had no choice. 'You cannot expect me to agree to this, promise or not.'

'Aye. I do. Your brother and I had an agreement, and I will hold you to it.' She lifted her chin.

He glared back at her.

'If I had other options, I would seize upon them,' she offered, her confidence gaining even as his agreement waned.

'But I have thought through them all. It is either you or my family, and as you well know, I will always choose them.'

He turned and his steely gaze seared through her. 'Aye. You made that clear to me when we were teens and you rejected me. I have not forgotten. But this—this is low even for your standards.' He threw down the tongs and stalked towards her. He stood so close she feared, and half hoped he might touch her or kiss her, but he did neither.

'If you *knew*…if you truly understood what I have been through to crawl back from the pit of grief I was in after losing Anna and our son four years ago. If you understood what I have been through to get to where I am now as laird after all I lost, you would not ask this of me. You would not ask me to put myself in such a position of weakness amongst my clan.' He swallowed hard. 'Not even you would be so cruel.'

'As I said,' she whispered, commanding herself to stand her ground under the swell of heat and emotion in his eyes. She could not acknowledge his past grief for fear of being dissuaded by her mission. 'You are my only option, and your brother promised me I could call in the favour I am due at any time for any reason. And this is how I wish to do it. You do not have to like it, but you must uphold your end of his agreement to me as the Laird of the clan.'

'And you are as cold of a wench as they come, Susanna Cameron.' His eyes glistened in the light, the hatred for her burning brightly in his gaze.

She held fast, gripped her cloak, and absorbed his words. Too much had passed between them to be unwound now and she dared not try. She almost had his agreement despite how repulsed he was by her tactic of calling in her brother's favour. It was time to lay her final card out on the table to seize his agreement. She stepped closer.

'What if I said in return for your agreement in this and as a gesture of good faith, I would aid you in your revenge upon Laird Audric MacDonald? He does not venture out of his lands much these days, as you well know, but he will be meeting with my brothers in the coming weeks and months to recommit to our alliance and to set a firm boundary to a disputed portion of our shared border wall. If we are betrothed, your access and presence at Loch's End will not be of consequence, and he will be within your grasp finally. I am sure you could concoct a plan for his demise that would not be suspected, especially at his advanced age. You could finally avenge the death of your wife and son and so many others from that horrid day.'

Rowan stilled and an eerie unnatural quiet fell throughout the forge. His gaze met hers, his cobalt blue eyes brilliant and fierce in the light, as he spoke to her. 'Then, I would say, you have your betrothed. When do we begin?'

Now that she had his agreement, Susanna scarcely remembered what to say and do next. She blinked back at him mesmerised by the rhythmic rise and fall of his chest, the heat emanating from him, and the ferocity in his gaze. Those eyes of his had always had a way of seeing through her and she had to fight against the unnatural pull she always felt in his presence and resort to what had always helped her gain her objectivity: cold and brutal detachment. She took a step back and turned away from him as she nestled further into her cloak. The distance helped, and soon she felt her blood cool and pulse settle.

'When can you come to Loch's End?' she asked. 'How soon would a visit be possible?'

'You think me simply arriving at your doorstep and asking for your hand will make this believable?' he scoffed.

She turned to him. 'Aye. Why would it not?'

'I have not been an unattached man for some time, but even *I* remember a man must court a woman properly to be taken seriously before one offers for her hand. Especially, if that hand is to be yours. Your family never approved of me or our previous relationship, and you have refused a proposal from me already. They will suspect this sudden change of heart and reject it if it is forced upon them too soon without merit. They are not fools.' He untied his leather apron and sat on a nearby bench. He leaned forward and pulled his soaked tunic away from his chest, revealing a glimpse of the hardened muscles that hid beneath.

Susanna averted her eyes, unwilling to address her past treatment of him. She also didn't wish to tell him the truth about it. Not yet. 'What would you suggest then?'

'When is the next sizeable Highland clan gathering?' he asked, staring down at his hands before wiping them with an old rag. 'One where it might seem that we could run into one another naturally?'

She frowned. 'I do not keep up with social events.' Such manoeuvrings were quite taxing and boring to her.

'Perhaps now is a fine time to start. For both of our sakes. Look at your recent invitations and I will as well. Then, we can craft when we will encounter one another at one such gathering. Choreograph a scene, if you will, of where and when we meet again for all to see.'

She shook her head and lifted her brow in surprise. She had not expected such forethought from him, but perhaps she should have. He was smart and a soldier. Strategy came naturally for him. Perhaps too easily. She would need to be careful. 'And here you said you could not play such a part?'

He lifted his head and met her gaze. 'To finally have revenge against Audric after four long years—' he paused '—and to have the opportunity to punish him for killing my wife and son during his attack on Argyll Castle and our clan, I can and will do anything. I will hold you to your promise, Susanna. Nothing will stand in my way of finally ending him. Not even you. Do you understand me?'

The hatred in his stare cooled the room, and she froze before she nodded in agreement. She would not begrudge him his revenge. Not after what he had lost that day. Even she was not so heartless, even if the rage emanating from him frightened a small part of her. She had to use it as the weapon it was to gain what she needed: information from her brothers about what secret they held from her and her sister before it fractured them entirely.

'Say it,' he ordered, rising to his feet, and walking towards her.

She held her ground as he approached, her pulse beginning its uneven cadence once more. Lifting her chin, she did not yield to him. Not yet. She needed to maintain the power she had over him as long as she could. Otherwise, he would overwhelm her with his sheer will, and she would not allow anything other than an equal share of power in their pact.

'Say it,' he ordered again, a pitch lower this time as he stood before her. Desperation and rage duelled in his eyes, and his lips parted. His fingertips skimmed the back of her hand, and her pulse picked up speed. He gripped her wrist, the pressure firm but not hard, eliciting a slow pooling heat to travel through her. He leaned in close to her ear. 'Say it,' he whispered.

Her eyes closed and she savoured his touch, the feel of his warm, strong fingers along her skin, the calluses from his labours in the forge gliding along her smooth unblemished flesh. It had been far too long since any man had touched her and somehow even after all these years her body remembered him and longed for his touch as much as she was loath to admit it.

As much as she hated to acknowledge the power he held over her.

'Aye,' she whispered, leaning even closer before she could halt the reaction, the heat from his body warming her own. Her lips almost touched the skin along his collarbone. 'I understand,' she answered. 'Nothing will stand in your way.' Her breath hitched. 'Not even me.'

Rowan closed his eyes at the feel of her warm breath along his shoulder. He dropped her wrist, commanding himself to withdraw from his proximity to her. Susanna always did this to him, and he didn't know if he hated himself or her more for it. Perhaps he hated the heavens that had made her the most. She was a force that could pull him in and drive him to say and do things he didn't like: such as commanding her to say she understood, as if he had any right to touch her or demand for her to say anything at all.

Devil's blood.

He held his breath and stepped back. Scrubbing a hand through his hair, he turned away from her and faced the forge, resting his hands along his waist. The heat and flickering flames beckoned him, and he needed to hammer out his budding desire and rage before he would be able to sleep at all this eve.

'I'll be in touch,' she said before leaving. 'Do not tarry

in your reply to my letter. You know I do not like to be kept waiting…for anything.'

The barn door slid closed behind her, and Rowan exhaled in relief. He leaned against the work table, clutching at the solid, steady presence it provided him with, and counted to ten.

Focus on the present. Focus on the present. Focus on the present.

He chanted the phrase in his mind over and over until his pulse slowed and he felt calm again. Then, he donned his leather apron and set about the task of finishing the blade he had hoped to complete this eve. He would craft strategy as he worked.

If he was to survive this plan with Susanna to be her betrothed *and* exact his revenge on Audric, Rowan would need to utilise his mind and body and focus them both on strategy *while* maintaining his sanity. He had come too far to lose the foothold he had regained in his life. And he sure as hell would not relinquish it now. Not even for the likes of Susanna Cameron.

His mind spooled back to the memory of her as a bonnie lass when they'd met. The first time he'd seen her, all of him had stilled. His body, his heart, and his gaze had been absolutely transfixed and arrested by her beauty and the power that had emanated off her as if she were fire itself. It had been a cold, autumn day, the trees burnished gold, and mist had swallowed up the rolling green hills of the meadow coloured with the last lingering purple hues of heather. He had stormed out of the castle, angered by his father's demands of him, and walked down to the meadow to explore the grove of rowan trees that had been planted when he was born, a tribute to his future but also a noose of expectation of what he was expected to achieve for the clan. Such expectation hung tightly around his neck, despite the beauty and peace the sight of the grove always brought him.

Susanna had been a dark ethereal cloaked creature amongst the black, silvery tree trunks and their reaching limbs, and the setting sun had glowed out of her as she had turned and faced him. Her blue eyes, pale skin, dark hair, and full rosy lips made her the most beautiful and enchanting woman he had ever seen. When he discovered she too had fled the castle walls of Loch's End due to a dispute with her controlling father, Rowan had thought they were kindred spirits. He had seen himself in her and recognised her struggle and she had seen his own. He had kissed her that day, his first kiss as well as her own. The feel of her warm lips on his and the slight pressure of her hand against his chest had made his body feel weightless as if they had transformed—into the mist themselves. He released a breath at the memory. Even now, he didn't know if it had been a trick of the light or her sheer power and beauty that had reflected just so in that moment.

Did it even matter?

He blinked back to the present. Despite that heady kiss and the many that followed after that, she had refused him when he had asked for her hand in marriage. Soon after, she had fallen in love with a Cameron soldier named Jeremiah and made her affection for him well known. Unfortunately, their affair had a brutal end as he had died in battle.

After Susanna's rejection, Rowan's heart had healed—ever so slowly. A year later, he had met Anna, and married her soon after. *Anna*. A woman he had loved more deeply than he ever thought possible. They had shared a life and built a life together with their two children. Her brutal death and the death of their son had brought Rowan to his knees and thrown him into the depths of grief and madness.

Aye, Susanna had been his first kiss and first love, but she had made her decision to be without him long ago. So had he. Much time and heartache rested between them now, and none of it could be undone.

Fool.

He slammed the hammer along the metal blade and smothered the memory of the moment of their first meeting, knowing full well it was the romanticised version of his youth, not reality. The real Susanna Cameron was the one he saw today. Cold. Heartless. Selfish.

She was the woman who had rebuked him when he was at one of his lowest points of grief and loss two years ago. The memory of their brief encounter at her and his brother's sham of an engagement celebration still stung. Not only had the engagement been orchestrated by Susanna's father to punish her for not marrying the man of his choosing, but it had also been a reminder to Rowan of how low and useless he had become after losing his title as laird. The only blessing of the eve was that his brother Brandon had come to his senses and such a marriage to Susanna had never happened—and that her harsh words that eve had set Rowan about a different course. One that may have saved his life.

'You do not deserve to be a laird or a father,' Susanna had seethed, her ice blue gaze taking in the sight of him, roving from the tips of his boots to his face with disapproval. *'Despite your fine clothes this eve, I know what you have become, Rowan. Perhaps no one else dares to tell you such truths, but I will, despite how estranged we*

have become. You are weak and selfish and no father for that wee girl. It is as if the lass has lost both of her parents, but do you even care or notice? What Anna would think of you now,' she'd said bitterly. *'I for one am glad she is dead, so she doesn't have to look upon you like this. You are not the man you used to be.'*

She'd held his gaze for one more beat of time before turning away from him, the tail of her long dark cloak whipping around and making her look like the serpent she was.

In that moment, her words had cut through him and set him alight with anger. Who was she to challenge him, especially after not seeing one another for so many years? But, as he watched her go, her cloak gliding along the stone castle floor, her words had echoed in his mind and shaken him to his core—for deep down he knew they were true. He was no longer the man Anna had married and was no father to his daughter Rosa. He'd been stripped of his title as laird due to his own ineptitude. Consumed by anger and self-pity after his wife and son's deaths, he had cast all responsibilities aside, even that of being a father. All he had thought of was his need for revenge against Laird Audric MacDonald, the man responsible for killing them. No other life or purpose had mattered to him at the time: not even the love of his daughter.

The realisation had stopped him cold.

Later that eve when he'd had the choice to rescue his nephew or chase after Audric for revenge, he had chosen to save his nephew, wee William. It was a decision he had never regretted. It had led him back to the journey of remembering his duty as a father and laird. Soon after, Brandon had stepped down as laird and convinced the elders that Rowan was a changed and capable leader once more.

All because he had been able to set aside his grief and rage for the purpose of saving William.

Something he should have instinctively wanted to do.

But if Susanna hadn't spoken to him that eve, would he have made a different choice? Would he have cast aside his nephew's welfare and sacrificed him to kill Audric and have his revenge?

Rowan shuddered to think upon it. He wanted to believe he would have done so without her words, but in truth, he would never know.

The irony of Susanna lobbing the option for him to now fulfil that quest for revenge against Audric was not lost on him. Perhaps that cruel moment years before had been her putting him and what was best for him and his daughter first for once although it hadn't felt that way then. Could she have said it to help him?

Was she capable of such a kindness? Of such friend-ship even after how their relationship had ended over a decade ago?

It was hard to imagine, but perhaps she was. Perhaps some small part of her had still wanted him to be happy and cared for him and his daughter Rosa despite all the unsettled and rocky past between them. He scoffed and shook his head. Now *that* was a fool's musing. One he should keep at arm's length. Just like he should keep *her* at arm's length.

Susanna was the same cold, calculating woman she had always been. And he would do well to remember that, lest he get his heart ripped to shreds.

Chapter Three

Midnight kicked up dirt and mud as Susanna rode her
filly hard across the valley, cresting one hill and then the
next in a flurry of speed. The wind whipped along her
cheeks and tugged strands loose from her dark plait, the
hood of her cloak having fallen back to rest on her neck
miles ago. Her two most trusted soldiers, Lunn and Cynric, rode ahead of her as the pastel streaks of dawn threatened. She slapped the reins to close the gap between her
and them. She had to be back inside Loch's End before her
brothers rose. No one could know of her adventure, except
her two guides, and they had even been sworn to secrecy.
She only hoped they would mind their word to her out of
duty to Jeremiah, the man she had loved more than any
other. A man they had been loyal to until his untimely end
in battle almost five years ago. Their mutual affection and
loss had bound them to each other in an odd way, but she
never took their loyalty and care for granted. They knew
how much she had loved Jeremiah and how deep her grief
had been when her father had stood between her marriage
to him and sent him away to fight to punish him for daring
to offer above his rank for her hand. Her chest tightened.
And such actions had ultimately led to his death.

Even when her father lay dying a few months after her

botched engagement to Rowan's brother Brandon and asked
for her forgiveness for keeping her from the man she loved,
she had not granted it. Now, she would have released him
from such guilt and grief as her heart had finally loosened
its fierce and angry grip on the past. She understood regrets
and had her own about Jeremiah's loss. But she could not
undo such regrets. No one could.

Not even God.

The glorious looming profile of Loch's End came in
view, and she breathed a sigh of relief. She would make it.
As she crested one rolling meadow and then the next, she
slowed, clucking her tongue at Midnight as they approached
the large new barn erected in honour of another fine fallen
soldier: Athol. The man had given his life to protect her
older brother and laird, Royce, just as she would risk all to
keep her siblings and clan safe. The reminder of Athol's
sacrifice only steeled her resolve and affirmed that she was
doing the right thing for them all.

She stared upon the smooth silver crest with its crossed
dirks above the door honouring him. She could not help
but think he was now alongside Jeremiah still watching
over her, her brothers, and dear sister. That they were war-
riors even in spirit guiding them alongside their journeys.
She didn't wish to imagine them as buried in the earth in
foreign lands. A shiver lit up her spine and she shook off
the unease such a flicker of thought gave her and followed
Lunn and Cynric towards the barn. Lunn dismounted and
approached her, reaching up to assist her in descending
from Midnight. His gaze reflected the resolve and strength
it always had. 'Was your journey a successful one, my
lady?' he asked.

'Aye. I achieved all I hoped for. Now, I must be patient and let things play out.'

As her boots rested on the ground, he released her hand and chuckled.

'I know. Patience is not my strong suit, but I shall try.' She pulled off her gloves and breathed in. The cool air invigorated her as it always did. So did the possibility that she might be one step closer to figuring out what her brothers were up to.

'That will be a sight to behold,' Cynric added with a smirk as he approached them.

Such informalities between them were common although they reverted to utter formality whenever anyone else was near. She smiled. 'Aye. It will.' She stepped closer. 'Thank you both for daring to accompany me this eve. As always, I owe you far more than I can ever repay.'

'And you know we would do anything for you, my lady. 'tis what Jeremiah would want.' Lunn glanced down and shifted on his feet.

'I am grateful for such loyalty,' she answered quietly.

'You shall always have it,' Cynric replied with a nod.

Emotion tightened her chest, and she pressed her lips together. She did not know if they would despise her once they realised what she had done. Even they didn't know all her plan. Only Rowan did. It was risky to not include them, but she didn't want to lose their friendship. They were a tether to her past with Jeremiah, and she wasn't ready to let go of it or her memory of him.

She doubted she ever would be.

For it was one thing to feel attraction and desire for a man like she had this eve with Rowan, but it was quite another to give a man her heart. And the one time she had done that with her beloved Jeremiah and lost him, it had broken her. It was best to never take such a risk again.

Ever.

'I will take care of the horses if you'll escort her in,' Lunn said, taking the reins of Midnight from Cynric.

'Aye,' he answered. His other hand rested atop the hilt of his blade in his waist belt. Even now, he was on his guard scanning their surroundings for any possible threats. Times were perilous in the Highlands. Even such a short distance to the castle was one Susanna no longer took alone at night. Desperation and unrest had made once good men into thieves, and the grief caused by the British pressing in ever closer to them all made it even worse. Even her sister-in-law Iona had ceased her daily swims in the loch, no longer willing to risk such with her bairn on the way.

Susanna's hand slid to her stomach. She wondered what such a blessing would feel like. To have a wee bairn growing within her belly. She had had so many dreams with Jeremiah. One of them was being a young mother and carrying a babe with the best of them both. Perhaps a wee son with his crooked smile or a daughter with his solitary dimple. Her eyes filled at the reminder of what she had lost. Her hand dropped away, and she pressed her thumbnail into the fleshy pad of her index finger once more until she collected herself and blinked away any possible tears.

As she reached the back entrance to the castle, she pulled up her cloak to help her hide within the shadows of the many corridors. No doubt some of the servants would see her, but they would never tell Royce. Over the years, she had either earned their devotion or their fear. Both suited her purpose: their silence. Cynric opened the door for her, allowed her to pass through, and sealed the door tightly behind her. Knowing Cynric, he would stand watch for ten more minutes just to ensure her safety. She smiled at the thought of it. Jeremiah's friends were the best of men, just like he had been.

She rounded the corner, removed her cloak, and added it to the many hooks near the door. She travelled silently through the main foyer, her gaze casting left and right, but she saw no one. As she approached the hallway to Royce's study, light emanated from the room. His lanterns were already lit.

Curses.

She stopped, lifted her skirts, and turned back to take another stairwell to her room.

'Up so early, sister?' Royce called. The mild censure in his voice was mixed with amusement.

She stiffened. While subduing the desire to curse aloud, she let go of her skirts and turned to face him. Her brother sat in shadow behind her in a large, oversized chair before the hearth, which had yet to be lit. She shivered and alarm set her on edge. Would her ruse with Rowan end even before it began? Was her brother here to tell her the name of her future husband? Had he attempted to tell her last night and noted her absence even then?

She swallowed hard. She needed to choose her words carefully. Royce was no fool.

'Aye. Just taking Midnight out for an early ride,' she offered. It was *almost* the truth.

'All night long?' he asked and rose from his seat. He was impeccably dressed as if he had just awoken, but his eyes held a fatigue that warned otherwise.

She said nothing, but clasped her hands in front of her

and waited for whatever further questioning was to come. Or whatever news of her future remained.

'No answer?'

She pressed her lips together.

He lifted his brow and sighed. 'And here I thought we were building bridges back to one another and not keeping secrets.' He rested his hand on the back of the chair.

She scoffed. 'Says the man who hides with Rolf for hours in your blasted study and will tell me none of your clan dealings.'

'That is not the same.' His voice hardened.

'Oh, no? It seems such to me.' She crossed her arms against her chest. 'If you and Rolf have secrets, then so shall I.'

''Tis your choice, sister,' he replied, a weary edge to his tone. 'I have far more pressing issues to tend to this day.' He let the matter drop, which concerned her. It was very unlike Royce to drop anything. Her pulse picked up speed.

'Has something happened?' she asked.

He nodded. 'Iona cannot keep down her meals as of late.'

She approached him and sat across from him on the edge of an identical chair, her heart fluttering with unease. Iona's carrying had been more difficult than expected. Her sickness in the morning these early months of her pregnancy had been as difficult as what Susanna remembered for her mother, who had lost not one, but two babes before they were due. It struck urgency in Susanna, but she tried to suppress it for Royce's sake. He would no doubt remember what the outcome had been for their mother as well.

'The doctor only left an hour ago,' he added. 'I had gone to your chambers to fetch you for help. You have a way of comforting Iona that she prefers.' He chuckled and scrubbed a hand through his hair, sending strands in all directions. 'She says I fuss over her too much and make her worry more. When you were not there, it only compounded my worry.'

She squeezed his hand. 'I am sorry, brother. What did the doctor say? What can I do now?'

She would not explain herself, but she would help. She cared deeply for her sister-in-law and her eldest brother. She also could not wait to have a sweet niece or nephew. She secretly hoped for one of each.

'She needs rest. He also left some tonics to set her stomach at ease. She had one and now sleeps. We will try to get her to eat again later when she wakes. I am utterly helpless to her, and I hate it.'

'Aye. You are, but just be there for her. She and the babe will be fine. I know it.' She met his gaze and smiled. While she did not know anything for certain, she would do her best to will a happy outcome. The two of them deserved nothing less than a beautiful, healthy baby.

'So, you will not tell me what you were about this eve?' he asked.

'Nay. But you do not have to worry about me, brother. I can take care of myself.'

'That is something else I wished to speak to you about. Perhaps it is not the perfect time, but there will not be one, as I know you do not wish to discuss it.' He rubbed the back of his neck as he was prone to do when worried. She braced herself for the words she feared.

'You must take a husband. It is time, Susanna. Past time if I am to be honest. Long enough has passed since Jeremiah. You must marry and be settled—and protected,' he added.

'Why now?' she scoffed.

'Why not now?' he countered.

'You know I do not wish to marry,' she pushed her nail into the pad of her thumb, trying to quell the emotion bubbling within her.

'Aye,' he sighed and met her gaze. 'But you must. I have begun enquiries as to possible matches. Ones that may benefit you and the clan since I know you will not marry for love.'

'And why might that be, brother?' she countered, her anger getting the better of her.

'Susanna,' he replied, his voice softening.

'Why did you not just allow me to marry Jeremiah? Why did you have to side with Father? You could have stood up to him.' Her words were sharp prickly arrows she hurtled at him.

'I was not strong enough then, Susanna. I did not understand,' he replied simply. 'I am sorry. I know you loved him. And when I think of how I would have felt if Iona had been taken from me in such a way...' he could not finish but looked upon her with sympathy.

To his credit, he absorbed her censure without rebuke. He was indeed changed. It made her eyes well and she bit her lip, trying to keep the emotion at bay. She was moved by his kindness but embraced her anger instead. 'Then, you shall marry me off to a stranger to make it up to me?' she rose from the chair and paced the room, her energy vibrating through her.

'Nay,' he replied. 'I will give you some time to offer up some additional candidates for us to consider for you. It is the best I can do right now. Times are perilous for us.

You must trust me.' Royce's tone held a pleading note that softened her. The rebuttal she had planned faded away.

When she did not answer, he rose from his chair and approached her.

He pulled her into a side hug and kissed the side of her head before releasing her. 'I know you do not understand, and I know I cannot bring Jeremiah back. Just take this opportunity to choose and try to open your heart to the possibility of it.'

She cherished this new Royce and his kindness, but the idea of a husband was unfathomable.

'I must get some sleep before Iona awakes. I will expect your list in a week or so. Promise me?' he asked her before pulling away.

'I promise,' she replied crossing her fingers behind her back. She watched him turn the corner, and then hustled up the opposite staircase to her own chambers, lifting her skirts so she could climb the stairs two at a time. She had much to attend to. Sleep could wait.

So could that blasted list of his with the names of future husbands.

Susanna opened the door to her chamber and her lady's maid, Tilly, cast her a curious glare. One she was quite familiar with. Susanna looked away and pressed her lips together. The woman had been more of a mother to her than her own, and she knew all facets of Susanna, even the ones she wished she could have kept hidden. To her credit, Tilly completed folding the extra bedding before lobbing her first question.

'And just where have ye been, lassie?' That single solitary eyebrow that Susanna had grown to fear as a girl raised its ugly head at her. The censure and judgement obvious. 'Ye are not a young woman any more. What ye do at night outside of this castle could cause ye ruin, but ye know that already, don't ye?' Tilly gave the folded sheets one final blow to pat them into submission, a bit harder than necessary, before she tucked them into a drawer.

How many times had they had a similar conversation? Enough that if these words were coin, she would be swimming in money.

Susanna rolled her eyes and flopped dramatically on the bed. Nothing could send her back to her teenage self faster than a rebuke from Tilly. Suddenly, she was thirteen all over again having sneaked out for the first time and been caught upon her return. She refused to answer Tilly's questions for she knew it would aggravate her maid further.

Old habits were hard to break.

'Nothing to say for yerself?' she walked over to Susanna and popped her hands to her plump hips, a few wisps of grey hair escaping her cap.

Susanna blinked up at Tilly's looming figure and shrugged.

'Exasperating as always,' Tilly muttered and shook her head before turning to open the large heavy blue curtains that framed the double windows that looked out at the loch far off in the distance. 'Suit yerself. Ye know where to find me if ye have need of me.'

'Thank you, Tilly,' Susanna called as the woman left the room.

Sun swathed the room. Susanna stretched and stared at the ceiling, the large wooden beams solid and sound like every inch of Loch's End. The castle was an impenetrable fortress in the Highlands just like her clan itself. Or at least she had always thought it was. But the way her brothers had spoken that night she'd overheard them in the study unnerved her. What if they were not as strong and protected as she always believed? What would she do then?

She sat up.

She would refuse to concede to such a thought. Period.

Facing the loch with its rising sun, she squinted. It would be a very long day, but she could not begrudge its beauty or what she had accomplished with her evening meeting with Rowan. Soon, she would know what secrets lurked in this castle and her family would be safe.

And that was all that mattered.

She settled into her writing desk, delighting in the cool smooth wood of her favourite chair and the orderly arrangement of parchment, ink pot, and quill. Sleep would have to wait its turn for she had far more important matters to attend to, namely crafting her betrothal plan. If she was to create a believable match, she would have to be careful and thoughtful in her approach and tread carefully with Rowan. A fragility still rested in his eyes. One akin to weakness. And weakness might lead them both to ruin.

And she would not allow it.

She scratched out her list:

Phase One: The Accidental Encounter
Where?
When?
How accidental should it be?
How many observers should be there to make the
encounter worth the effort?

She frowned. She hadn't thought much past getting him to agree to the ruse. Now that she had his agreement, it did sound a bit complicated. But it was necessary. She had to know what her brothers were hiding from her, and she had to prevent some unseemly marriage arrangement by implementing their fake betrothal sooner rather than later despite how abhorrent the idea of being anyone's betrothed was. She shivered.

In the last week, correspondence had been heavy, with a larger than normal volume of letters coming in and going out from the castle. And a bit of investigating had led her to note a trend in the enquiries: eligible lairds and second sons. There was also only one reason a sea of enquiries were sent out to so many lairds and second sons at once: to see who dared take her as a bride. Royce had confirmed her suspicions this very morn.

She hoped the list would be small. Very small.

And most likely it would be. She smiled. She'd done her part in distributing her share of rejections and refusals when she had tried desperately to marry Jeremiah, much to her father's displeasure years ago, and no one would mistake her for a soft, compliant bride.

Bride.

The thought of it made her throat dry.

She gripped the quill, sat forward, and straightened her back, newly inspired to work on her plan. While she was fine with being someone's fake betrothed for a while, the idea of being a real bride turned her stomach. Even though motherhood appealed to her, she had no one in mind that could fill the role of husband. And one seemed to preclude the other, did it not?

She sighed, staring down at the dark blot of ink on the parchment from where she'd stilled the quill. The ink bled out much as her grief had years ago.

Jeremiah.

He had been the one to win her heart, and when she lost him, her heart had been buried with him. And she planned for it to stay that way.

Chapter Four

'Papa?' Rosa called from outside the study door.

'Aye, love,' Rowan answered without looking up from his work. Soon, he heard the worn study door creak open, the familiar pitter-patter of small bare feet on stone, and giggles bubbling in the air as his eight-year-old daughter climbed up his legs and crawled onto his lap.

He set aside his work and smiled.

This was his favourite part of the day: these first moments when his daughter was awake and she looked upon him like he was a good man, hell a great man, and he could set the course of his day by trying to prove her right, trying to be the father she deserved. The one she believed he was.

Nothing else mattered.

She wrapped her soft warm arms about his neck and pressed a sweet wet kiss to his cheek. Her small hand scrubbed along his scruffy face, and she giggled again. 'It tickles,' she said.

'Aye. Your papa needs a shave,' he answered, wrapping his arms around her as she settled into his lap and stared up at him.

'Did you sleep well, my little pitcher?' he asked, running a hand over her long chestnut hair, the curls lopsided and still rumpled from sleep.

She shifted on his lap and nodded. 'I dreamt of Mama,' she said and rubbed her eyes. 'She looked just like the painting,' she said turning around to point to the portrait of Anna that hung in his study on the opposite wall, where he could stare upon her whenever he wished. 'It was lovely,' she continued. 'We played along the meadow and made daisy chains. I could feel the warm sun on my cheeks.'

Rowan's heart lurched in his chest, and he caught his breath, steeling himself for the emotion that always swelled within him at the mention of his late wife. He counted to five and answered. He knew talking of Anna was important to Rosa, and he wanted dearly to keep the memories of her mother alive and well within her no matter the cost to him.

'Do you remember such a day?' he asked gently as she snuggled her back against him, so they could both look upon Anna's portrait.

'Aye,' she answered. 'She made me a beautiful crown and I made her a necklace.'

He chuckled. 'Aye. I remember now. You made one for me as well as Mr. Hugh.'

She cackled. 'And Mr. Hugh broke his. Flowers went everywhere.'

'Aye. They did.'

She leaned back against Rowan's chest and sighed. 'I miss her, Papa.'

His throat clogged with emotion, but he swallowed it down. 'I do too.'

She turned and smiled at him. 'I love you, Papa.'

'And I you, my Rosa,' he murmured, pulling her into a tight hug.

She returned his embrace, and he smiled. 'What do you plan to do today?' he asked.

She pulled back. 'Cook said she would teach me how to make pies.'

'Pies?'

'Aye.' She leaned close and whispered in his ear. 'Auntie Trice's birthday is in two weeks, and I want to learn how to make her a pie. Don't tell her,' she added. 'It will be a surprise.'

'Your secret is safe with me. Off with you to Cook then. And if it helps, apple pie is her favourite.' He winked at her, and his daughter scurried out.

'But put on some shoes first,' he called after her, but she was already gone. He chuckled and shook his head. His daughter hated shoes just as he had when he was a boy. In truth, he couldn't blame her. He was tempted to pull off his own and savour the feel of the cool stone beneath the soles of his feet right this minute. Something about it always made him feel anchored to the world.

'Good morn, Mr. Hugh,' Rosa called down the hallway.

'Good morn to you, my lady,' Hugh replied. The sound of his heavy booted footfalls growing louder as he approached.

Evidently, Rowan's fancy of having bare feet this morn would have to wait.

With his brother away on clan business with his family in the northern Highlands, Rowan had much to discuss with Hugh Loudoun, the clan's second in command. Namely this farce of a plan with Susanna that he'd agreed to last night. *Deuces.* How exactly would he begin to explain? He scrubbed a hand through his hair. He wasn't altogether sure, but he would have to. Hugh was no fool, and if Rowan didn't enlist his help with crafting such a charade, it would fail before it even began. Rowan couldn't do it alone. It would require far too much coordination.

And subterfuge.

He set aside the maps that cluttered his desk, glanced at Anna's portrait, and stilled. What had he been thinking? He hadn't been. The thought of exacting revenge on the man that had stolen Anna's life and the life of their son had consumed all reason and he'd agreed in an instant. That was what the thought of Audric did to him. In a moment, he'd been set back years in his recovery of grief. The flash of hate and vengeance had lanced through him like a thunderbolt in the sky, hungry to hit its mark and singe whatever was in its path. Even now the thought of it made his pulse increase in anticipation. He rolled his shoulders. He was well enough that he could do this. He just didn't dare do it alone. Hugh would keep him in check and ensure he wasn't drifting too far afield from sanity. That he was staying focused on his health, his daughter, and the well-being of the clan. It was a daunting task, but if there was a man who could muster it, it was Hugh.

The man might also try to change Rowan's mind and convince him to fulfil Susanna's favour without exacting his revenge on Laird Audric MacDonald. Rowan shifted in his chair. Even in the wee hours of the morn after a night's sleep, his desire to follow through with Susanna's plan to exact his revenge on Audric had not wavered. The peace and healing it would give him would allow him the sleep of a lifetime. As ridiculous as it was, he still wanted and needed justice despite how hard it would be for him to maintain his well-being.

Managing extended periods of time with Susanna Cameron would break any man.

He almost chuckled aloud at his own joke.

'What has you smiling this morn?' Hugh asked as he crossed the threshold to the study.

'Ah, a new plan. Close the door,' Rowan commanded without making eye contact with Hugh. His friend would be none too pleased when he heard of his arrangement.

'I had to speak to the men on duty at the forge last night,' Rowan began.

'Oh?' Hugh asked, crossing his arms against his chest, his stance prepared for the unexpected.

'I had a surprising visitor.'

Hugh furrowed his brow and his jaw tightened. He said nothing but waited for Rowan to continue. As expected, Hugh would wait until all was revealed before commenting on anything. It was what made him such a great leader and strategist. He listened while others talked, and he had no compelling desire for power.

Unlike most soldiers he knew, Hugh desired peace above all else.

A solely unexpected and unusual trait for any soldier in the Highlands. And one Rowan never took for granted.

'Susanna Cameron.'

He shook his head and craned his neck towards Rowan. 'Sorry, did you say, Susanna Cameron?'

'Aye. She appeared in the forge close to midnight as I was working. Sneaked past our soldiers and entered unbidden. Seems her soldiers created a compelling distraction that allowed her to sneak in. Our men still don't even know she was here. Only you and I do.'

Hugh sat in the chair opposite Rowan with a thud. 'Why?' He shifted in the chair. 'She has not set foot on these lands since her sham of an engagement to your brother two years ago.'

'I remember. I was just as surprised to see her.'

Hugh studied Rowan's face for a few moments and frowned. 'I'm not going to like her reason for being here, am I?'

'Most likely not. She asked me to marry her.'

His friend's eyes widened, and then he laughed.

Rowan smiled and waited for the laughter to dissipate before he continued. 'I had the same reaction, but it is no jest. Even called in her favour from Brandon to compel me to follow through with it. *This* is what she wants in return for helping us to rescue Fiona and William the night of that sham of an engagement.'

Hugh leaned forward in his chair and narrowed his gaze at Rowan. 'But she hates you. Why would she *compel* you to marry her? Does she truly wish for you to be unhappy that much? Seems extreme even for a woman such as her.'

'Although I am not entirely clear as to what has made her so worried, she says it is so I can help her extract information from her brothers. There is a secret troubling her.'

'All of this to unearth a secret?' Hugh scoffed. 'Are you sure there is not a different motive at play here? It seems too far-fetched to be believed, and she is a Cameron after all.'

'I thought the same. The added threat to her is that Royce is threatening to marry her off to keep her safe from whatever this secret danger may be. By pretending to be engaged to me she can keep that from happening as well.'

'A pretend engagement? Now you've lost me.'

'Aye. I am to *pretend* to be engaged to her until we discover this secret of her brothers. Then, our affair can run itself into the ground and be over. She has no real desire to *actually* marry me, which is quite a relief, truth to be told.'

'To me and you both.' He ruffled his hair and sighed. 'Night and day with her might put us both into an early grave.'

Rowan laughed.

'But this still seems an odd plan. No one will believe you are serious about one another, especially after your last encounter here.'

'I said the same to her, but she is quite determined, and she made an additional offer I could not refuse.'

'Oh?' He leaned backwards in his chair. 'Now I am intrigued. I could not imagine there would be anything that could make you agree to such a farce, especially with her.'

'She can give me access to Audric. I can finally have my revenge.'

Hugh stilled and studied him before shaking his head. 'Rowan, you cannot entertain such an idea. Killing him would incite a war we would never recover from. It would turn the Highlands into a battleground, and not with the British, but with ourselves. You cannot be responsible for such despite how much he deserves such a fate. You know this.'

Rowan dug in. He knew Hugh wouldn't like this part. Perhaps he shouldn't have told him, but the man was no fool. He would have deduced it soon. 'This is the chance I have been waiting for. Surely you can see that?'

'I can see your pride talking. *That* is what I see.'

Hugh's words hit their mark.

'Aye,' he answered. 'I would be lying to pretend otherwise. But it is also what Anna and my son deserve.'

Hugh's gaze softened. 'But is that what they would want for you and Rosa? For the clan?'

Rowan stared upon Anna's portrait. He knew the answer. She wouldn't have. But she wasn't here living with the brutal agony he carried each day. Knowing he hadn't been enough. That he had failed at his most important duty: protecting his family.

But he couldn't say that aloud. Not to Hugh. Or anyone. It cut too deep and wide, and even now he could hardly breathe at the mere thought of it. He steeled himself and clenched his jaw.

'Then it is a good thing you don't have to make such a decision,' Rowan replied, his tone hard and unyielding. While there was much he could be persuaded to do, letting this go was not one of them.

Ending Laird Audric MacDonald was a mission as necessary as his love for his daughter, and he'd not let it go. Not while he drew breath.

Hugh nodded and let the matter drop, as Rowan expected he would. There was providing counsel to the Laird and then there was contradicting him, and Hugh knew his place as second in command. He'd not challenge Rowan on it further.

'But as to the matter of Susanna,' Rowan continued. 'I will need your help in devising a strategy to make our farce believable. That is why I have enlisted your help. As you know, I am far removed from the expectations of courting.'

Hugh chuckled. 'And you think I know better?'

'You know something of it, which is more than I can say. You also have a bevy of men you could ask such advice from and not be questioned, whereas such enquiries from me would create quite a stir, especially from Trice.'

Hugh laughed at that, the good humour and rapport between them easily restored. 'Aye. Your sister would love it, and you would never hear the end of it. I will see what I can find out. What thoughts do you have so far?'

Rowan turned the parchment he had been writing and sketching ideas on for hours around so Hugh could see it. He smirked and squinted at it before glancing back up to Rowan.

'This looks like a battle plan.'

Rowan smiled. 'It is.'

Chapter Five

'Yer correspondence, my lady.' Lunn murmured close to Susanna's ear, pressing a small letter into her palm as he helped her down from Midnight after their morning ride. A glimpse of the maroon wax seal stamped with what looked to be the Campbell crest sent her heart fluttering, the response surprising her.

It was about time. A week had already passed.

'Aye. Thank you for asking. I had a lovely ride this morn,' Susanna replied, loud enough for any stable boys to hear as she alighted to the ground and handed off Midnight's reins to Lunn. She slipped the note into her gown pocket quickly before removing her gloves in case other gazes were upon them. While she wished to rip into the note unbidden, she dared not risk being seen. Without secrecy, her plan would fail before it even began.

Her heart skittered with a mix of relief and irritation. While she was thrilled to finally receive some correspondence from Rowan, his lack of urgency had tested the limits of her withering patience. Her brothers continued their daily talks without her, despite her protests, and the uncertainty fed her doubt much like air to a starved fire.

She ran her fingers over the edge of the letter in her pocket. She would have to break her fast and wait before reading the letter in private. Too many eyes and tongues were about Loch's End.

Climbing the hillside, she took in the glorious, lush green grass and soft turning of the leaves on the trees. Soon, the valley would be awash with autumnal shades of reds, golds, and browns. And not long after the once violet fields of heather would be dark green hillsides carrying the winds of winter along with their subtle whispers and howls along the loch. Her favourite time of year was almost here. She sighed and her heart slowed. This was the quiet peace she sought.

If only she had the man she had loved at her side to share it with.

Even now she could feel his touch heating her bare skin and the feathery trace of the back of his hand along the nape of her neck. She shivered as a breeze kissed along her cheek.

Jeremiah.

She smiled.

'When the wind whispers softly along your cheek, it is me, love, sending my kisses until I return.'

Her chest tightened and she blinked back the tears burning the back of her eyes. Those were the last words he'd spoken to her before he'd left for battle. His gaze revealing he had little hope of returning to her. If she were honest with herself, she had known it too. Her father had been angry, and he was a brutal man. Jeremiah had dared love her, the daughter of the Laird, a woman well above his station, and Father would not suffer such insolence.

He had sent Jeremiah to a battle along the Borderlands as punishment, but they had both suffered and lost. Lost one another. For ever. She clenched her fists at her side. While she'd always been prone to hardness and suppress-

ing her feelings, a consequence of her father's own cold-
ness and cruelty, Jeremiah's death made Susanna's edges
rougher and her anger sharper. She'd turned into a woman
who preferred to use her sharpness and edges to keep all
other suitors at a distance, for there was no replacing Jeremiah and no one who would ever be worthy of giving
her heart to again.

She frowned. The joyous mood from her ride and the
walk through the beautiful early morn of the day was evaporating away like the morning dew the closer she came to
the castle. Rolling her shoulders, she set her mask of indifference in place and entered, nodding to those servants
she passed, as she headed to the dining room. If she were
lucky, her brothers would have already broken their fast
and she could eat alone.

Entering the room, she frowned. She was not to be so
lucky this morn.

'Sister,' Rolf said, nodding to her in greeting before
popping what remained of a piece of bread into his mouth.

'Good morn,' she replied, her gaze flitting briefly to
meet his. When his eyes cut to their brother Royce and then
back to her without a word, her heart skipped a beat and
then sped up. It was her younger brother's way of warning her that Royce was not to be trifled with this morn.
They had used such code since they were children. She
walked quietly to the buffet to see the spread set out for
them. The usual meats, cheeses, breads, and jams greeted
her. She picked up a plate and set a slice of bread upon it
before Royce launched into his speech.

'It has been a week since we spoke, sister. I have granted
you time. Have you prepared a list of suitable candidates
for marriage as we agreed?'

She clutched the plate, hoping her fierce hold would not shatter the fine porcelain into bits. Rather than fear, anger filled her gut. She counted to ten and then answered. 'Aye. I have a list.' After plunking a sausage, cheese, and a slathering of marmalade to her plate, she dropped her plate loudly on the table, sat down with a rather unlady-like plop, and set what she hoped was her best withering gaze upon him.

'And?' Royce asked, matching her ire.

She glanced to Rolf who shook his head slowly at her as if in warning to swallow the angry words brewing from her lips, but she lifted a single brow at him instead and he sighed, knowing what was coming for they had spoken about such a list just the evening before.

She removed the small, folded paper from her pocket, careful to leave the correspondence she'd received tucked safely within. After setting the note on the table, the maid poured her some tea, and Susanna thanked her.

Royce opened the note and sighed.

Susanna stifled the smirk on her lips and took a sip, the liquid scalding the tip of her tongue. Perhaps it served her right.

'Close the door upon your leave,' he ordered. The maid nodded and sealed them within the room.

'It is blank,' Royce stated coolly.

Rolf met her gaze, also suppressing a chuckle.

'You knew as well?' Royce set his glare upon her younger brother.

'Did you expect anything else? I didn't.' Rolf toyed with the rumpled linen napkin beside his empty plate.

'Aye. I did,' Royce answered, his tone dark and deep. 'I provide you the option to pick your husband and you lob the offer back in my face in reproach with a blank piece of paper. Perhaps I shall marry you off to Dallan MacGregor. I hear he has not secured a match.'

Rolf intervened, a growl entering his voice. 'That is too far, brother, and not a joke to be made.'

Royce shook his head. 'Apologies. You are right. I never should have said such. Not even in jest. Not after what happened.'

Or *almost* happened to their younger sister, Catriona. Thank God Ewan Stewart had saved her that day at the Grassmarket in Edinburgh. Otherwise… Susanna's skin crawled at the thought of such a horrid man like Dallan MacGregor being anyone's husband.

Royce scrubbed a hand through his hair, and the room stilled.

'Despite the crassness of what I just said,' Royce began, 'and how lack of sleep is impacting my judgement, the result is still the same. You *must* pick someone, sister. While Rolf and I cannot divulge the entirety of why, you must marry within the year, for your own safety. The Highlands is an uncertain place now. We need to know you are protected.' His gaze was soft, his voice pleading, and the alarm that was slowly bubbling within her started a slow boil. Angry, roaring Royce she knew and understood, but this—this she did not, and it terrified her.

Rolf reached over and squeezed her hand. 'We know you do not wish to marry after losing Jeremiah, but it is important, sister. Please choose someone and soon. Please.'

The second please and desperation in their gazes cut her to the quick. Before she knew it, she was nodding. 'Aye. I will. And soon.'

Her hunger was squashed by their conversation; she rose from the table.

'You did not eat,' Rolf said and gestured to the spread of food.

'I find I am no longer hungry,' she answered. 'And there are other matters I must attend to.' She left before they launched into any enquiry. The last thing she needed was more poking and prodding or encouragement to choose a spouse. Her stomach soured, and she climbed the stairs, reaching her chambers in record time. Tilly assisted her with changing into a more proper day gown and out of her riding clothes, the hems now soiled and splattered with the mud and dirt from her extended ride.

After Tilly left, Susanna walked to the window and opened her palm. She had hidden the letter there while she'd changed, and the parchment had warmed and softened, moulding to the curving shape of her hold.

She pressed her lips together before breaking the wax seal on it, a feather of worry clouding her. It had been a week since her visit to his forge. Had Rowan changed his mind already? Or perhaps he had a plan in play? With Rowan, her chances of success equalled her probability of failure. Despite his agreement at their initial meeting, uncertainty had consumed her. It was a large request, and he was a man known for his moods well before losing Anna. Her loss had only exacerbated his changefulness. He was unpredictable, which made him a dangerous choice for such a secretive plan, but he had been her only option for this ruse for three reasons. First, he was the only man who would never really marry her because he despised her because she had refused him before. Second, he was so honest that he was incapable of going back on his word.

Lastly and to Susanna's chagrin, despite all that had happened between them, he was the one man she dared trust outside of her family, Lunn, and Cynric, and she could not involve Jeremiah's friends in such a scheme.

Unfortunately, that had not changed. Over the last week, she had thought upon her options for a real husband, and they were—less than appealing. She said a quick prayer and opened the letter.

Suze,
I have thought further upon your request and made
some plans which may interest you. I dare not risk
including them here. Meet me at the old grove two
nights from now at midnight.
  If I do not see you, I will assume you have had
a change of heart and abandon any further plans.
Ro

Susanna's heart skipped at the sight of his use of their nicknames for one another when they were young. No one had called her that in over a decade. Some small part of her flickered to life at the memory of his voice calling her that all those years ago, as if her young self was reawakened and yawning to life.

She bit her lip and swallowed before reading it once more and closing it. Who knew what sort of plan he had concocted by now. Rowan was a creative strategist and strong warrior. Or at least he used to be. Grief had dulled his sharpness. She had seen that even at their initial meeting. The Rowan of old would not have been startled by her arrival at the forge. He would have heard the first squeak of the barn door sliding open and drawn his blade. But the

Rowan of old also would have dragged her out of the forge and not heard her out at all.

She'd have to take both sides of his newness as they came and hope the damage from grief years ago had weakened him just enough to be malleable but not so much that he could not lead her in such an endeavour when required. Only time would tell.

She sat at her writing desk and began a sketch of her own plans, so she'd have a clear idea of her own thoughts before she heard out his own two nights from now.

Ugh.

Her shoulders slumped.

She'd also need to do the unthinkable: ask for any social correspondence. Perusing the latest invitations was essential, despite how much she loathed the idea of being a part of societal manoeuvrings. Although, such a display and effort would set her brothers more at ease as she would seem to be complying with their latest request: to attempt to find a husband. She tugged on the rope near her writing table to summon one of the servants.

While she was quite capable of going down a flight of stairs and sorting through the correspondence herself, making a show of the request would work in her favour. Word would spread through the servants at Loch's End and filter on to her brothers about her renewed and unexpected interest in the upcoming social events of the season. If she were lucky, it might even spread well beyond and out into the Highlands. She smiled widely and wriggled her toes in her shoes.

This would look exactly as she wanted it to.

She would appear to be soft and compliant, while scheming and setting her own plan in motion.

It would be perfect.

A knock sounded at the door.

'Come in,' Susanna answered.

One of the maids entered and stopped before her. 'Aye, my lady?'

'Can you bring me all the recent social correspondence from the last week or so? I'd like to peruse it.' Susanna smiled and attempted to look as innocent as possible, which felt far more forced than she expected.

The young lass's eyes widened briefly before relaxing again. She paused and then replied. 'Aye, my lady.'

'Thank you. That will be all.'

The young woman took a moment to move, but soon she regained her faculties and left.

Based on the wide-eyed disbelief in the young woman's gaze, the first move in Susanna's plan was now well in motion. She could sit back for a minute and watch it unfold.

She had scarcely begun to sketch out a list of ideas for her plan when a knock sounded at the door again.

'Come in,' she replied, shoving the used parchment into the drawer of her writing desk before closing it softly.

She stood and stilled at the sight of her sister-in-law Iona at the threshold. She smiled deeply and hurried to her.

'You shouldn't be up,' Susanna fussed.

Iona flashed her a wicked smile and glanced behind her before quietly closing the door. 'I have made an escape from my room while Royce was downstairs,' she whispered as she stepped further into the room. 'I cannot spend one more hour in that chamber. I fear I am watching the dust settle with boredom,' she continued in her normal voice. A few rogue waves escaped her long dark plait of hair, and her eyes gleamed with mischief despite the hollow pallor of her skin.

Susanna grasped Iona's hand and pulled her into a gentle side hug. 'But you must rest, sister.'

'I know, but I do not have to wither away. I am restless and my limbs ache to move about. I dream about swimming in the loch once more, but I know Royce will have none of it. Nor would the doctor. Perhaps you could walk with me outside? Take in some fresh air?'

'Aye,' she replied. 'Although we will take one of my men along with us, so Royce does not fret.'

Iona met her gaze, her brow furrowed.

'So he will fret *less*,' Susanna corrected and chuckled.

Iona glanced over Susanna's shoulder at the open writing desk and the materials upon it. 'But I have interrupted you. I can come back later.'

'Nay. You will do no such thing. Your arrival will aid me in postponing the inevitable.'

Iona smiled. 'And what is that?'

Susanna sighed. 'Reading through correspondence once it arrives and deciding which social endeavours I shall attend.'

Iona's mouth gaped open, and she stepped back. 'Why?' she asked, a note of suspicion in her voice.

Despite not knowing Iona long, she evidently knew Susanna well enough to know her disdain for such a task. 'To find a husband,' she replied, her voice dropping so low and in such an indiscernible murmur that it was indecipherable.

Iona cocked her head. 'To find a what?'

She felt like stamping her foot like a three-year-old demanding more sweets, but she didn't. She squared her shoulders and said clearly, 'To find a husband.'

Iona crossed her arms against her chest and frowned. 'Why?'

When Susanna failed to answer, Iona surmised the truth. 'Because of Royce,' she muttered, settling on the settee near the writing desk. It was more of a statement than a question.

Susanna nodded and sat next to her, settling back into the soft cushions.

Iona rolled her eyes. 'You would think he would have learned after Catriona. He pushes and shoves his notions into decisions without thinking sometimes. I will speak with him.'

Susanna smirked at Iona's certainty in being able to sway her husband. Before her, Royce could not be swayed into much of anything. The petite healer was strong, intelligent, and formidable, and Susanna was often in awe of how easily she had slipped into their family after bringing Royce back from certain death after being ambushed on her tiny isle of Lismore.

Despite being far too rational now to have such romantic notions, Susanna couldn't help but wonder at how fate had brought the two of them crashing together, much like the waves upon the shore of where Iona found Royce that night. If she hadn't rescued him and nursed him back to health, her eldest brother and laird of the clan would be dead. The thought of such a loss made Susanna shiver. She had come to love this new and improved brother of hers. Iona had softened his hardened edges, well some of them, which was far more than she could ever ask for.

'I appreciate your willingness, but I do not believe Royce movable on this issue. He claims it is for my own safety and well-being.'

'A man would say such,' she said with a chuckle of her own. 'But I believe we both know not every man can provide such comforts, but the right man can. I do wish that for you.'

'I do not hold out such hope for myself,' Susanna replied.

'I had not either but look at me now. Seems I just had to get out of my own way. My doubt almost cost me everything.'

'Meaning?'

Iona met her gaze and gifted her a soft smile. 'I did not believe I deserved his love or your family's love for that matter. That is why I did not come when he first invited me here to be his wife.'

The confession stilled Susanna.

That wasn't her, was it?

She didn't have a husband because there was no replacing Jeremiah. The two things were not the same.

Were they?

She looked down at her hands and picked at her nail.

'Sometimes I wonder if you have denied yourself for the same reason.' Iona's words were soft. 'But it is not for me to say. Just know that I will support you in whatever you do. You are my sister.'

Tears heated the back of Susanna's eyes. Why did she feel like crying? She never cried.

Perhaps she did need some fresh air, despite returning from a ride only a few hours ago.

'Still longing for a walk?' she offered, avoiding the implication of Iona's statement.

'Aye,' she replied, gripping Susanna's hand. 'Although I cannot promise I will not be sick in the bushes at some point.'

Susanna laughed aloud, the feeling of it a joyful release of emotion in the moment. 'And I promise not to tell Royce if you do.'

'Deal. Let us go before anyone can stop us.'

Correspondence could wait.

Chapter Six

Crunch. Crunch. Crunch.

Rowan frowned at the sound of leaves being crushed beneath boots. Despite her usual stealth, Susanna and her guards were as loud as Rosa trying to catch him in a game of 'Where am I?' where he hid, and she tried to find him. Rowan clenched his jaw and stared at the bright moon above him and the intermittent clouds that eased effortlessly across the navy sky. Tiny stars dotted the darkness, like an array of breadcrumbs leading to the heavens. He smiled. Or at least that was what Anna always used to say.

He blinked back the emotion that accompanied the memory and remained hidden behind one of the many large rowan trees spaced along the hearty grove and watched Susanna advance. He wished to observe *her* this time before they spoke as opposed to what happened during her visit to the forge at Argyll Castle. He needed to see if she could be trusted before he ventured further into their plan together.

A Cameron was a Cameron after all.

Perched high in the opposite direction from the hillside, Rowan spied Hugh scanning the surroundings to ensure Rowan's safety and determine who else accompanied Susanna. As a skilled soldier and bowman like himself, Hugh could fell a man from a great distance with impressive accuracy. And despite his reluctance to take part in this scheme with Susanna, Hugh was loyal and willing to protect Rowan and the clan at all costs, even in this ridiculous ruse.

The crunching grew louder and the upper leaves on a tree quivered to his left as a bird took flight, spooked by her approach. Rowan held his breath as Susanna slowly emerged into his sights. Cloaked in all black, her steps were careful, methodical even, and she scanned the area before her as she advanced. A glimmer of metal flashed from a drawn blade, and Rowan caught sight of one and then the other Cameron soldier accompanying her this eve. They had fanned out behind her in a 'V' formation to ensure privacy but were also close enough to strike quickly in her defence if needed. While the men's facial features were too far in shadow for him to discern their identity, perhaps Hugh would have better luck at distinguishing who they were. He wanted to know who the woman trusted enough to accompany her. It would help him with his backup plan, if indeed he needed to use it.

Susanna stopped and stilled like a doe in the wood as it listens for a predator. Rowan watched, unable to look away at her exquisite yet fragile profile set in the darkness. A small curling of chilled breath escaped her lips, otherwise she might have blended into the surroundings of the wood and disappeared entirely. This duality of her strength and softness had been a fascination for him since their first meeting all those years ago when they were young, and even now he held his breath.

A slow smile formed on her lips. 'I know you are there,' she said just above a whisper. 'I can feel you watching me.' She turned in his direction a quarter step and pushed back her cloak hood to reveal her face and the loose dark locks framing her features.

Gooseflesh rose along his forearms as her gaze met his own.

He stepped from behind the tree and set a glare upon her, frustrated at being discovered before he wished to reveal himself and by the thrumming attraction his body had to her presence.

'You may need to work on your stealth, my laird,' she murmured as he approached.

'As you may wish to work on your couth, my lady,' he countered, glowering at her.

She shrugged. 'I have never claimed to be kind. Why would you expect such now?'

'Because we are to pretend to be betrothed,' he said as loudly as he dared, so as not to be overheard. 'No man would allow themselves to be cut and cuckolded by the woman he plans to wed. Surely even *you* know such.' He lifted his brow at her and settled his hands along his waist belt. 'Otherwise, this ruse of yours shall be over before it begins.'

She said nothing and pressed her lips into a thin line, a tell that his words had hit their mark and served their purpose.

'Your plan?' she finally asked. Her light blue eyes set upon him as cool and piercing as a pike thrust into frozen ice.

He looked away and pulled the rolled parchment from his waist belt and gestured for her to follow him up to a small spot in the grove where they could be partially hidden by the canopy of two trees yet still sit on the large boulder there and read by the full light of the moon. This was not his first midnight rendezvous, and he knew the grove as he knew the battle scars along his body. Every tree within the neatly arranged orchard had grown in unparalleled precision just as he had and this place had become a haven and part of who he was, as if it were a fixture of his identity.

For all intents and purposes, it was, for it was planted on the day of his birth. A tribute to him from his father and a beacon of hope and luck for a clan attempting to recover from its troubled past. Just as he was now.

He gestured for her to take a seat on the large boulder, weathered smooth by wind and rain. Her cloak flared out before she sat, reminding him of a peacock showing its feathers to assert itself. He smothered the beginnings of a smile. While they had both changed, in some ways they were each profoundly the same. When he joined her on the boulder, there was little room between them. He frowned. He didn't remember this boulder being so small and…intimate. Shifting away from her a bit, he unrolled the parchment. She leaned closer to him, and he stilled before turning to glare at her.

She matched his glare and lifted an eyebrow. 'I cannot see it clearly with you so far away. Either I move closer, or you do.'

'We both will,' he conceded, and they both slid in until they were seated hip to hip. Her warmth was an unwelcome distraction. After a few moments, he commanded himself to focus on the plan at hand: settle upon terms for their arrangement, agree to the first step in said arrangement so it can be set in motion, and leave. His gut told him to skip the first two steps and leave, but he could not sacrifice the idea of exacting revenge upon Audric and giving Anna and his son the justice they deserved. He ran an open palm down his trews to centre himself and began.

'This is the plan I wished to share with you,' he whispered. 'Once we agree upon it, we can set the first step in motion.'

Susanna scanned the document and then frowned. Shifting closer to him, she rummaged in her right gown pocket, teetering into his side. He clutched her shoulder to keep her from rocking back and toppling off the boulder before righting herself. 'And here is *my* plan,' she countered. She unfolded her document slowly and then held it out to him. 'I will analyse yours and you mine, and then we shall come to some sort of an agreement.'

He sighed, making no effort to accept the parchment she held out to him. 'I am a laird. Making battle plans is what *I* do. We need not look upon yours. I have a well thought out plan that can be easily executed.'

'And may *I* remind *you* this is *not* a battle plan, but a betrothal,' she replied, letting her parchment drop to her lap. 'It requires more...delicacy.'

'Are you sure?' he asked. 'Neither of us excels with delicacy.'

'While you are not altogether wrong, we must try. Just read it.' She extended her plan to him again. 'Please. The outcome of this is important. It must be successful.' The desperation he saw at their first meeting came into her gaze again, and he shifted, uncomfortable with and unused to her pleading. He preferred her demanding and irrational.

He took the document from her. 'Under the condition that you will agree to the best plan, not your own.'

'As long as you agree to the same.'

'Aye. I will.'

They settled into silence as they read. While her plan was sound, Rowan preferred his own much as he expected he would.

'Meow?' Susanna said murmuring under her breath and chuckled.

Rowan paused his reading and turned to her. 'What?'

She laughed. 'Your plan is M. E. O. W. As in 'meow' like from a cat.' Her laughter intensified until she had an unladylike snort. Then, she met his gaze, her eyes as bright blue as a clear summer sky, and his breathing faltered at the simple joy in her features. Had he ever heard her laugh so? Perhaps when they were young, but since then? Never. He stared at her transfixed and bewildered all at once. What had her in such a state?

'I don't quite...' he began, but she interrupted.

'My apologies. I am reading. Do not mind me.' She breathed out and collected herself, smoothing back her hair from where it had fallen about her face.

He shook his head. He had no idea what she was on about, but it had given her some joy. Perhaps that was something. He twisted his lips. But he couldn't remember crafting anything that was even remotely entertaining or humorous.

'Are you laughing at me or my plan? Or both?' he asked, his words tainted with a bit of anger, in case she was mocking him.

'Neither' she replied, setting the plan aside. 'It is a solid plan. I just happened to have made a word from the first letter of each of your steps, a memory tool that has served me well over my years, and it happened to reduce to 'meow'. And knowing you, since you are nothing close to a cat at all, well, it made me laugh.'

'Meow?'

'Aye. Your steps break down as Meet by chance, Engage with the enemy, Openly woo, and Win her, meaning my, hand publicly. If you take the first letter of each, it creates the new word meow.' She awaited his response as if what she had said made all the sense in the world, which of course it didn't. Not even close. In truth, she sounded like a woman too deep in her cups or addled, but he knew she was neither.

Or was she?

He sniffed her breath. 'Have you been drinking? I know you enjoy—' He coughed as she elbowed him in the side.

'I've not been drinking you fool. Let us get on with our discussion otherwise we might be here until dawn.' Her eyes darkened. Her mood soured as quickly as it had previously sweetened.

He cleared his throat and straightened back up. 'Your thoughts on my plan other than meow?' he asked.

'Reasonable. Although I do think you have left out many details such as *when* we will meet by chance, *when* you will engage with the enemy, *how* you will openly woo me, and *how* you will win my hand. Care to share those finer details with me?'

'I left the details of what we needed to work out and agree on together for our meeting now. How would I know what events might be suitable for a woman such as yourself to go to for our first 'meet' or how you would like me to engage with Audric and your brothers, as enemies to our future relationship?'

'Simple. First, I will go to whatever social event is the soonest, so we can begin this ruse as quickly as possible. It has no bearing to me as to which one it is. I loathe them all equally. Second, you must remain an enemy to them all, at least at first. Audric and my brothers will instantly distrust any kindness you relay to them too soon. But your meanness and arrogance?' she chuckled. 'Such behaviours will put them at ease, and they will not expect the web we are beginning to spin around them.'

'You speak as though we are a spider and they insects caught in our netting.'

She pondered the suggestion and then nodded. 'They are. And my well-being and the clan's well-being depends upon how well we thread and weave our deceit.'

His stomach soured. The more she spoke of their 'deceit,' the more ill he felt. He was a man of honour, not deception. To win at battle through skill and strategy was one thing, but to win through deceit was quite another. 'Are you not at all worried about what will happen when our deceit is uncovered? Are you sure you wish and need to proceed in such a manner? Perhaps there is another more direct and ethical solution.'

'I have thought upon it over and over into the wee hours of the morn. This is my only option.' Her tone was level and serious with an edge of certainty that surprised him.

'You do not fear your brothers' anger after such deception?' Curiosity was getting the best of him. His gut still told him there was more to her story than what she had shared.

'Aye. They will be livid,' she corrected. 'But I would rather deal with their anger than for them to be dead.'

'Dead?' He faced her. She glanced away from him, worrying her hands in her lap. He clutched her forearm gently. 'Look at me.'

She didn't at first, but when he gently squeezed her forearm, she turned back to him, her eyes bright and wild.

'What are you talking about?' he asked. 'You said you feared for *your* well-being, not theirs? You said you did not wish to marry. That you wished to uncover a secret. Why are you now talking as if the lives of your brothers rest in our hands and the success of this plan?'

She held his gaze before answering. 'Because they do.'

'Explain.'

'I have told you all I can for it is all I know. My brothers will not reveal to me all that threatens them and us, but merely their urgency for my union.'

She still held back from him. He could sense it. But why?

'Then, I will be myself and allow them to see the arrogance and anger that hounds me each day. Shall that work?' he asked, anger roiling in his gut. This meeting with Susanna was becoming even more vexing than expected. He needed to know everything if their plan was to be successful.

'Then, plan on bringing your anger and self-righteousness to the Tournament of Champions at Glenhaven at week's end.'

His head fell back in exasperation briefly before casting her a glare. 'Why must *that* be our "meet by chance" moment? I am no young buck in search of haughty praise by lasses as I throw a hammer. And you are no young prize to be won. Surely there is a better event than that.'

Her back stiffened. 'While you might be no prize, my laird, I am the unmarried daughter of the previous laird of Cameron and sister to the current one. I *am* a prize. And if my brothers are to believe I am serious about finding a husband and you serious about claiming a new bride, we must go to an event that has been flaunted as such a meeting place for decades.' She levelled her gaze at him, and he shifted on the rock.

She was right and he hated it. He held his tongue.

'And besides, gossip has it this may be the last year they host the event. Why not enjoy the last endeavour of it?'

He frowned. 'Perhaps because I never enjoyed the previous *endeavours* of it.'

She scrunched her brow and bit her lip. 'But you met Anna there.'

His chest tightened. 'I know, Susanna. And that is exactly why I do not wish to attend again.'

'I well understand your hesitation. I am not insensitive to it. But think of how much romance and believability it would provide our scheme weeks from now. Us meeting there after a decade when you met your first wife there. Me suddenly opening my heart to you after not doing so with anyone else for years after losing Jeremiah.'

He hated her for asking so much of him.

But he couldn't begrudge the logic of her plan. It *was* a fine strategy from a battle standpoint. He scratched his head. But it would wreak havoc on him. 'On one condition.'

She waited for him to continue.

'My sister Beatrice, Hugh, and my daughter will accompany me. Hugh to maintain my sanity and Trice to help care for Rosa. This could be an opportunity for Rosa to see a part of the Highlands tradition she has not yet experienced before it is gone.'

He could also share with her some of his past with her mother. They could experience and remember Anna together. He swallowed hard. If he could bear it.

'As long as you do not become too sentimental or act too much a grieving widower,' she countered. 'Our awareness of each other must be noticed.'

'Susanna…' he warned.

'You are doing this for Anna are you not?' she asked leaning towards him.

'Aye. But I will not dishonour her memory in the process,' he replied, his tone harsh and low, his face a whisper from her own. His pulse increased as he continued. 'I cannot pretend she was not my wife, that I did not love her, that I am not a widower.'

Susanna touched his face, a gentle wisp of fingers along his cheek as one might do to calm a child. 'And I would not ask you to,' she said softly. 'This is a deception, nothing more. All we must do is make people believe in it. So, a small part of us must believe in it too. That is my point. You must act as I must for this plan of ours to work. For me to discover what secrets plague and threaten my family and for you to finally excise the devil that has wreaked havoc upon yours.'

Her touch ignited longing in him, and he fought the urge to cover her hand with his own and hold it to his face. Despite how much he still missed Anna, there was no denying his loneliness and how much he missed the consoling soft caress of a woman. He leaned forward yearning for the touch to continue, but her hand was gone before he blinked again. His cheek was cool, vacant. When she stared back at him quizzically, he started and pulled away abruptly.

'Seems we have a plan, my lady,' he said coolly. 'I will arrive at Glenhaven on Friday in time for the evening meal. If our chance meeting doesn't happen then, find me on the fields for the games on Saturday.'

'Shall I pretend to swoon at your hammer throws?' she replied with a playful eye roll.

'Nay,' he replied. 'You shall not need to pretend.' He turned away and caught himself smiling as he went to find Hugh.

Then, he cursed himself for being such a fool and his smile fell flat.

They *were* only pretending, and he'd be wise to remember it was a small part of him fulfilling his clan's promise for a favour as well as his larger plan for revenge for Anna and their son.

Nothing more.

He had to stay focused on his purpose.

Chapter Seven

'I still cannot fathom that you are here in Argyll with us, sister,' said Catriona Stewart as she enveloped Susanna in a fierce tight hug. Susanna returned her sister's warm embrace on the landing of Glenhaven, the site of the Tournament of Champions to be held this weekend. Despite it being only a year since Catriona's marriage to Laird Ewan Stewart, Susanna still felt that she was making up for all the lost time between them. Catriona had been lost to their family for well over a decade due to the cruel fates of the sea. Having her back in her life had renewed some of Susanna's belief in goodness and hope. Susanna looked up to Catriona's resilience, kindness, and strength.

Susanna pulled back to look upon her sister's face, the glow of expectant motherhood reflected in her fuller physical features just as happiness reflected in her eyes. Contentment flooded Susanna's heart, and there was nowhere else she wished to be in this moment. She swallowed back her reservations about lying, and then answered, 'I felt it was high time to find a husband, and this seemed the best place to begin my search. I also thought it was a fabulous reason and excuse to come see you. I hope you do not mind the last-minute request to come stay with you and Ewan.'

'I could not have been happier to receive your letter and

to see you here now.' She clutched Susanna's hands in her own and squeezed them. 'The bairn continues to grow and the doctor says we should expect a February arrival.' She winked at her and tucked her elbow within her own as they walked further into the castle. 'So why are you really here? I do not believe for a moment it is to find a husband.' She narrowed her amber eyes at Susanna, and her lips quirked into his smile.

Susanna stiffened momentarily and then released a nervous chuckle. While fooling her brothers might not be so challenging, convincing Catriona of her plan might be near impossible. The woman was gifted in reading people and discerning the truth, a skill that had kept her alive in a string of difficult circumstances prior to Ewan finding her a year ago at the Grassmarket in Edinburgh.

'I will explain everything, sister, but first I would love to get settled, change into more appropriate clothes, and refresh myself before we dine. I want to take advantage of what time I have with you and Ewan this evening before everyone else descends upon Glenhaven tomorrow for the Tournament.'

'Aye. I will take you to your chambers. But I will still wriggle the truth out of you,' she replied.

'Alas, I know you will.'

Which was exactly what Susanna feared.

Susanna did her best to hide her displeasure at Rowan not being in attendance for the evening meal the previous night or this morn as she broke her fast before the games began. How had the man not been here in time for two such optimal moments for them to formally meet again in front of her family? Time was slipping away, and they needed to take advantage of every moment of this weekend to make their plan a success. She lifted her skirts and strode down the familiar hillside to the events, assisting Catriona as they went. With every heavy footfall, she reminded herself that she could throttle the man later—after he arrived.

'Thank you for helping me,' Catriona offered. 'I find myself a bit more unsteady now that I struggle to properly see my feet.'

'I wonder how you will be able to walk upright once Hogmanay comes,' Susanna replied with a chuckle. Leave it to her sister to distract her from her worries.

'We've had quite the turnout this year,' Catriona added, gesturing to the fields full of young lairds and their men preparing for events, unattached ladies watching from afar and whispering to one another, and a scampering of children all hustling about as the events were being set up for the day.

'It does look rather crowded. Is this the norm or because rumour has it that Ewan is set to give them up next year?' Susanna added.

Catriona laughed. 'I knew such a rumour would catch fire if he let it.' She shook her head. 'He has no such plans.' She leaned closer to Susanna and whispered into her ear. 'But he also took no pains in dispelling the rumour when he heard it. He was hoping it would attract more people to help bring us together this season with all the strife and unrest throughout the Highlands. It seems to have worked.'

'I would say so by the looks of it.'

'Just this morn, Laird Campbell even arrived with his daughter in tow. Who would have thought that possible? Ewan has told me many a story of the man's past. I was pleased to see him here and looking so well.'

Susanna's hold on Catriona's arm tightened and then relaxed in relief. *He was here.* All was not lost. She released a long breath as they reached the bottom of the hill. 'That is a surprise. He is not a very social man. Why is he here do you think?'

'I have some theories, but I will keep them to myself. I have gossiped far more than I should have already. Ah, Ewan is waving me over. I will catch up with you in a few minutes. I am overjoyed you are here.' She released Susanna's arm and pressed a kiss to her cheek.

'Aye. As I am pleased to see you.' Susanna replied and watched her sister and Ewan heading towards one another. Seeing them so happy was such a blessing. One she never took for granted. He was a good man, and she would always be grateful for what he did to save Catriona and return her to her family and the Cameron clan. But she also knew Catriona was a Stewart now. She was on the cusp of beginning a family of her own, and soon her attentions would be upon that. Being a Cameron would become second.

Susanna bit her lip, watching the couple walk hand in hand down to the playing field. Could she have that? Did she even want it? Her heart ached with an answer she didn't wish to acknowledge.

Aye. She did.

But creating a family of her own would be risky. Susanna sighed. She'd need to find a man she could trust, dare to rely on him, and wade into the murky waters of marriage and hope she could even carry a bairn. Her mother had had her own difficulties with such matters, having lost two babes to miscarriages in the first months of pregnancy after having Susanna and before having her younger sister Catriona. Would Susanna face the same challenges? And would she be able to handle them? Her mother had struggled greatly after the back-to-back losses of her bairns.

'Beautiful day, is it not?'

The familiar husky, deep voice from behind stilled her, shattering her thoughts and musings over a future she dared not long for. She wasn't up to such disappointment, not right now, anyway.

She closed her eyes and set her veil of indifference in place, despite the relief coursing through her. Now that he had finally arrived, their charade could begin.

'About time, I might add,' she replied and turned to him, crossing her arms against her chest.

He narrowed his gaze at her but flattened the irritation she spied through his flared nostrils. 'If we are to appear to be enjoying our little meet here, then you will need to set aside that glare you have upon me now. No one will believe we are anything like a couple, if you only send me daggers, my lady.' He nodded and gave what may have been his version of a smile, as lopsided and awkward as it was.

She fidgeted and let her hands fall to her sides. *Drat.* He was right. She squared her shoulders and lifted her chin to him, pushing back the hood of her cloak. 'Good morn, my laird,' she said, sending him what she hoped was her most dazzling and affecting smile, before offering her hand to him.

His gaze heated and he smiled as he lifted her hand into his own and kissed it, a soft but ardent pressure of his warm lips against her flesh. A tingle of awareness travelled along her fingers and arm. She fought a shiver. As he let her hand go, he lowered his voice. 'That is the bewitching minx I know. Just do be careful not to flash your intentions too brightly. It must be believable after all. We have not been in each other's lives in a long time. Or at least that is what everyone else will believe. Our attraction and intent cannot be too sudden, despite how attracted you may be to me.'

She wanted to stomp her feet and shout in frustration. 'Are you trying to bait me?' she replied in a low voice matching his own, her teeth almost clenched. 'You just asked me to soften to you, and so I did.'

'This is a wooing, Susanna,' he said, taking a step forward. 'It will take time to make it believable, especially *you* softening to the likes of *me* with our history—and if I remember correctly, you are not a patient woman on any count. This shall be great practice for you in building that skill.'

Now she wanted to throttle him. She resisted the urge to grab him by the tunic or pound a fist against his chest. The man was infuriating. 'Aye. It shall take some effort on my part.' She smiled, turned on her heel, and took one step to advance down the rest of the hillside.

'Do you not wish to send me some good luck?' he called. 'Or perhaps provide me a ribbon of your favour before I set upon my first event, the stone put?'

'I do not wish to appear too eager, my laird, do I?' She continued, smirking before she could stop herself.

He was an arse. Plain and simple. There was no manoeuvring around such, but perhaps this ruse of theirs could be a distraction against her real worries about her brothers, an arranged marriage, and the clan's welfare. She paused. She might even have fun. She shook her head and continued. That was yet another ridiculous notion. This was Rowan Campbell she was talking about. He didn't know how to enjoy himself—neither did she.

Together they would be lucky if they could create anything close to the believable farce of being a couple. The man was impossible.

Chapter Eight

The woman was impossible. Rowan stalked down to the field and joined the other competitors, most of whom were almost a decade younger and scarcely had scruff that would make the likeness of a beard. He grumbled, attempted to stretch before the first event, and was grateful to spy Hugh chatting with Garrick MacLean, a man well respected in the Highlands. One of the few lairds Rowan liked. He was honourable and had brought his clan back from the dead after losing everything years ago while he was a soldier away in the Borderlands. While he'd been a second son and never destined to be laird, he had taken on the mantle of duty without complaint or issue when his father and elder brother had died.

Rowan walked over to the pair of men, so similar standing side by side with their sandy brown hair and large build that they could be mistaken for brothers. 'Morn, you two. Good to see you, MacLean. It has been a few years.'

Garrick MacLean gifted an easy smile and shook Rowan's extended hand. 'Far too long. I am pleased to see you here.'

Rowan replied to his unspoken question. 'As am I, but I felt it was time to get out and enjoy this last Tournament of Champions before it ends.'

Garrick chuckled and stepped closer. 'Brenna tells me

it is only a rumour and not truth, but it has brought us all together has it not? Ewan's plan has worked.'

'Oh? What plan is that?' He furrowed his brow.

'It was in an effort to have us all united in the Highlands. There are murmurings that a battle against the British is imminent. Based on the last few years, I am not surprised to hear such. Neither are you, it seems, by your lack of reaction.' Garrick sighed.

'Nay. Not surprised.' Although it was the last thing Rowan wanted. Years of strife within his own personal life had taken their toll on him along with the Campbells' historic feud with the MacDonalds. He was eager for peace, despite how unpopular the idea would be. The Highland lairds were hungry to end the British hold over them, and war seemed the only way it might be obtained, but that didn't mean he wanted it. Great men would be lost, and he'd had his fill of loss.

'Where is your wife, MacLean?' Hugh asked, scanning the area.

Garrick smiled. 'She is ill.'

Hugh balked. 'Is that something to smile about?' he enquired, his confusion evident.

Rowan was equally baffled by the man's jovial statement of his wife's sickness.

Garrick shook his head. 'Aye, but nay,' he sputtered. 'She is carrying another bairn and has the sickness before she breaks her fast, like she did the last time. I am pleased to have another babe on the way, not that she is ill.' He ran a hand through his hair and a slight colour rose in his cheeks.

Hugh clapped him on the shoulder and smiled. 'Congratulations. That is fine news.'

'Aye,' Rowan echoed, also pleased for his friend's good

fortune. While he had never known his wife well, he assumed her to be a good woman to have caught the eye of MacLean.

'Thank you. We are expecting the bairn next summer. June perhaps.'

Rowan's chest tightened. Would he ever have another bairn? Most likely not. Loving a woman and risking the birth of another child along with the thought of possibly losing either again immobilised him with fear. Rosa was enough, he knew that. But it did not take the sting of the loss of his wife and son away. Nothing ever would.

'Rowan?' Hugh asked.

'Aye?' Rowan replied as his friend's voice pulled him back from his memories.

'They are lining up. Do you still plan to throw?'

'Aye,' he replied begrudgingly. He had no desire to be shown up by young bucks, but he had also promised Susanna he would make his presence known and participate in some of the events. The stone put seemed harmless enough.

'Papa!' Rosa called cheerfully.

Rowan turned to the growing crowd a distance from the throwing field. When he spied his daughter waving at him with Trice by her side, he couldn't help but wave back, his heart filling with pride at having her here. He pulled back his shoulders and walked to the line. He would throw well for Rosa's sake.

Catching Susanna's gaze as he walked to the line, the heat from her stare sent a thrill of awareness through him all the way through his core and down to his fingertips. He opened and closed his fist. The woman drove him to madness, but the physical attraction between them was still palpable after all these years. He wondered if others could sense it too. Whatever tether had existed between them as teens had not been entirely severed.

Not yet anyway.

There were still many days to contend with her before the ruse would be complete. But first, he needed to get through this one. A young laird whose name escaped Rowan sauntered back after his throw, knocking his shoulder into Rowan's as he passed and muttering, 'Luck, Seanair.'

The Gaelic word for Grandpa could not be misinterpreted, and a few other men glanced their way, interested to see what might come from the overt insult. Rowan's blood heated, and he fisted his hands by his sides again. It was obvious disrespect, and he saw Hugh's posture tighten from afar. The old Rowan would have seized the impotent dolt by the tunic and thrown him to the ground, pinning him there by the neck until he begged for mercy. Rowan rolled his neck and focused on his breathing. His daughter was here as well as his sister, and he could not be a good candidate for Susanna's betrothed if he killed a man at the first event of the games. Susanna's brothers would be here somewhere, and they would hear of his behaviour, even if they didn't witness it. He counted to ten and continued walking to the line. He would use his anger to throw the stone farther and teach the lad a lesson in humility and what it meant to be a real man.

He stared downfield at the fabric strips fluttering in the wind marked with the previous throwers' tartans. He glanced back at the lad who had passed him: a Macpherson. The orange hue in the tartan a giveaway as to its origin. His flag sat the furthest from Rowan. He stared at it for a few seconds, set his heart on matching or exceeding its distance, and exhaled a breath as he set his feet into position, careful to set them heel and toe length apart for traction. He lifted the heavy oblong stone with his right hand and tucked it under his neck, adjusting the weight until it was comfortable in his hold. The coolness of the stone against his skin settled him. His heart slowed as he twisted his body back and down to the right with his left hand high and outstretched behind him. Exhaling a final breath, he noted the silence of the crowd as they waited for his throw. He imagined the distance once more, envisioned the stone flying with ease, and turned his body with force, releasing the stone in the air along with a guttural yell of effort. He watched its flight as his body followed through on the throw. To his joy, it sailed past Macpherson's mark, sending dirt flying in the air as it landed and flipped to a stop. The crowd cheered, and little Rosa jumped to her feet as did Trice. After he raised his hand in celebration, his gaze caught Susanna's. To his surprise, she had also jumped up to cheer his throw as had many other specta-tors. Such praise for him was an unexpected and welcome response. His chest tightened in joy and remembrance.

The last time he had been here, Anna had been cheering for him after such a display with the hammer throw, and he had been smitten by her unbridled support of him. Such a memory complicated his feelings now, but he tried to set them aside and focus on this moment and no other. Only one other man was preparing to throw. Rowan stepped aside and allowed him the time and space to do so. With hands on his hips, Rowan watched as the stone travelled along the same arc as his own. When it stopped just short of his mark, Rowan released a breath in relief.

'Papa!' Rosa called out and clapped just before the

crowd did the same. He raised his hand in thanks and nodded to Rosa. He covered his heart with his hand and then pointed to her, so she would know he was her champion. She smiled in delight and Trice's eyes glistened with tears. Perhaps she alone knew how much this moment meant to him as she had been here when he had been a lad trying to woo Anna and win her hand all those years ago, just a mere year after Susanna had dashed his hopes and refused his proposal. Anna had been the bright light of hope for him and being here reminded him that he still had hope and a future ahead of him, even without her being here. Trice met his gaze and smiled. He nodded to her that he understood.

'Quite a throw for a *seanair*, eh?' Rowan whispered as he passed the Macpherson laird to leave the event.

The lad had no answer, and Rowan revelled in the fact that he had made his point without brutality or lowering himself to Macpherson's childishness as he might have done but years ago. Rowan had shown his strength and demanded his respect in a far different way. One that only maturity could provide. Perhaps his age could be seen as the gift it was rather than the hindrance he sometimes believed it to be.

Rosa rushed to him, and he bent down to scoop her into his arms. She hugged him fiercely, and every care in the world melted away.

'Papa! You did it! You bested them all! I knew you could do it!' She pulled back and kissed him on the cheek before looking into his eyes.

'It is because you were here,' he said, tucking her dark wavy hair behind her ear.

'Me?' she asked, scrunching her face.

'Aye. You cheered me to victory just as your mama did

the last time I came here. It is here that we met, and I knew that I would offer for her hand.'

She smiled, her eyes wistful as she took in the surroundings. 'Then this is a special place, isn't it?'

'Aye. It is.' he replied.

'Thank you for bringing me. I love it here already! Will you tell me more stories about the games? About Mama?'

Rowan's heart tightened, but he smiled away the discomfort. 'Of course, my little pitcher. Your Auntie Trice and I will fill your ears with such stories while we are here.'

'Aye,' Trice agreed. 'We will. Shall we get you some refreshment, brother?'

'I will meet you at the tables. I just need to gather some things.' He gestured behind him.

He didn't need to gather anything other than his wits. He needed a moment to recover from the rush of emotion winning and thinking of Anna thrust upon him.

'See you there, Papa!' She tugged Trice along and they headed back up the hill in search of sweeties and refreshment.

After receiving congratulations from many of the Lairds, Rowan gathered his fabric marker and tucked it into his tartan.

'Quite the start, my laird. The ladies in my section were swooning over your exchange with your daughter. You even had me a bit misty, and I have no heart as you well know.'

Rowan smiled and faced Susanna. Her gaze searched his. Words rested quietly tucked away in her eyes, and he longed to know what she wished to ask as much as he feared what the question might be. One never knew with Susanna or with any Cameron for that matter.

'Care for some refreshment?' he asked, delaying whatever it was she wished to say.

'Aye. I will walk with you. I am to meet my brothers there. I am sure they will love to hear of your victory and become reacquainted.'

He laughed. 'That I know to be untrue, but I look forward to seeing just how eager they are to become *reacquainted*, as you put it. I have a feeling it would be akin to how eager they might be to sit through a series of dress fittings or a trip to the milliner. Shall we go?' He offered her arm.

She hesitated and then accepted. 'It may be too soon, but perhaps this will help test the waters as to how well my brothers will receive you.'

Chapter Nine

By the time Rowan and Susanna reached the refreshment area, the makeshift tents and benches for seating were already full and overflowing with people as they took their fill before the next event was set to begin. It was a colourful spectacle of tartan, pageantry, music, and a bit of revelry as men and women began to fill their stomachs with ale and food as they chatted and mingled with one another.

'I hardly know where to look,' Susanna said, her gaze skipping from one person to another unable to focus on just one of the many sights and sounds around her.

'It is definitely not the forge,' Rowan muttered, a frown tugging at his lips.

'That is no look for a champion,' she teased.

'What look?'

'The scowl, my laird. While you are not required to smile, I would lose the glare. It may set people off the new charming laird guise you are trying to build.'

'Charming has never been used as a word to describe me,' he said releasing her arm and shifting on his feet.

'That I know, but it does not mean it couldn't be. I saw everyone's response to you with Rosa. You have a heart. Allow people to see it. That alone might make you charming.'

He scoffed. 'Perhaps you should take your own advice,'

he replied as he greeted Hugh and another laird she could not remember the name of. There were far too many to remember. Her sister waved at her from across the way, and she left Rowan to join Catriona and her brothers, who watched her approach with interest. Perhaps her plan was already at work. There was only one way to find out. She steeled her spine and increased her pace.

'Was Laird Campbell bothering you, sister?' Royce asked, his gaze set on Rowan rather than her as he asked the words and then sipped from his tankard.

'Nay, brother. I merely congratulated him on his win at the stone put and he offered to walk me up the hill for refreshment.'

Catriona's scrutiny was so intense Susanna had to look away at a colourful red pennant flapping from one of the tents. Her cheeks heated.

Why am I embarrassed?

She was a grown woman. She didn't have to explain herself to anyone, let alone her brothers.

'And you allowed him to?' Rolf countered in disbelief.

'Aye, I did,' Susanna answered.

All three of them focused on her.

'What?' Susanna finally asked, unable to endure more silent and confusing scrutiny.

'Did he say or do something inappropriate? If he did, I'll—' Rolf began.

She set her hand on his forearm and held his gaze. 'He escorted me up a hill. We exchanged pleasantries. Nothing more.'

'Pleasantries?' Royce scoffed. 'Rowan Campbell? He isn't capable of such. Never has been. It was a blessing when

Father commanded you to refuse him when he offered for your hand years ago.'

'Aye,' Rolf agreed. 'And a further blessing when the marriage planned for you and his brother Brandon also failed, despite his slight in refusing you. Otherwise, we would be bound by marriage to the Campbells.' Rolf feigned a shiver.

Susanna rolled her eyes. Rolf could be a touch dramatic at times. 'People can change,' she replied, the need to defend Rowan and his clan name a sudden and curious development that surprised even her.

Rolf quirked his head, his lips falling open in surprise. 'Are you defending him? Are you unwell?' he asked.

'Is everyone enjoying themselves? I cannot tell you how happy it makes me and Ewan that you are all here.' Catriona grasped the shoulders of Susanna as well as Rolf, interrupting their exchange. Her message to remember where they were and who was watching was unmistakable and well timed. Even Royce turned his scowl into a neutral indifference before he drank more ale. Once again, their sister had saved them from themselves. A skill she was quite adept at.

Susanna released a breath and sent a glance of thanks her sister's way.

Catriona winked back at her. 'Anyone up for the hammer throw? It is the next event. Setting up in the lower fields in the next quarter hour for the event at half past.'

'Perhaps the stone put champion will take part. Unless he has already pulled a muscle in his efforts,' Rolf chided. He bit into a tart and glared behind Susanna.

Her heart dropped. Rowan must be right behind her.

'I may be older than you, Cameron, but I am far from dead or elderly for that matter. Perhaps we should take part in it together. What say you, my lady?' He paused by Susanna's side, so close the fabric from their clothes touched. The proximity didn't go unnoticed. The hackles on her brothers rose as they might on a hound sensing danger.

'Seems a fine idea, does it not, brothers? You could prove to the Laird how wanting he might be.' Susanna smirked at Rowan, who frowned back at her. She bit her lip. She kept forgetting they were to be friendlier towards one another. Baiting him would be a hard habit to break.

'So little faith in me, my lady?' Rowan shook his head.

'Why would she have any faith in you, Campbell? We will not have you sniffing about our sister. She has other plans than the likes of you,' Rolf replied.

'I do, do I?' she countered, irritation ruffling her. They spoke of her as if she was not there and incapable of a thought of her own.

Royce balked and stepped closer. 'Aye. You do,' he replied. 'Campbell needs to set his sights elsewhere. I have heard the rumours, Campbell,' he stood almost toe to toe with him now. 'Eager to secure your footing as head of the clan by finding a bride to sire an heir with before your brother steals your seat as laird again?'

Rowan's jaw tightened, and Susanna pressed her elbow against his own, hoping that pressure might signal a reminder of their plan for the day, and deter him from falling into her brother's trap of baiting him into a true and horrid scene in front of most of the men and women of import in the Highlands. While it was one thing to make their meeting noticeable to people, so that their later betrothal seemed logical, it was quite another to squabble or worse in front of their peers.

The silence between the men lengthened, and neither

man seemed willing to concede to the other. Susanna's throat dried and her muscles tightened. The merriment and music played on around them, while the men stood entrenched in their own private war of wills, as they always had been.

'Papa, there you are!' Rosa burst in between the men and clutched at her father's hand. 'Auntie Trice and I have been looking for you. Come try one of the apple tarts. You must be hungry after your winnings.' She tugged on his hand once more, jostling into Susanna's side.

Susanna released a nervous chuckle and smiled at Rosa. Her timing could not have been better.

'Sorry, my lady,' the wee lass offered.

'No apology needed. Apple tarts make me excited too,' Susanna added. Her relief over the young girl interrupting what could have been a horrid exchange made her limbs tingle.

'There are plenty. Perhaps you would all like some tarts?' She smiled up at each of them, awaiting their answer.

'I will be joining you,' Catriona quipped, rubbing her belly. 'I am famished.'

'I think we shall wait, miss,' Royce replied, smiling at the girl. His ire softening. 'We will be competing in the next event.'

'Will you be competing too, Papa?' she asked, looking up to him.

Rowan paused. 'I had thought to sit that one out, but I think a bit of a proper challenge might be in order.' He sent a meaningful glare to Susanna's brothers that could not be misread.

'So, you are doing the hammer throw?' Rosa squealed. 'Another victory to be sure.' She turned to Royce and Rolf.

'Not that I wish you to do poorly, sirs' she offered to them and shifted on her feet.

Royce chuckled and smiled at her. 'Of course not, wee lass. You must cheer for your papa.'

'But I do hope you come in second or third.'

Rolf suppressed a chuckle.

'Good luck,' she offered. 'May we go get some tarts now?' she asked.

'Aye,' Rowan replied. 'Seems the perfect time for some refreshment. 'tis a good thing, I have another lass cheering me on,' he offered, sending a heavy glance to Susanna, before turning away and disappearing into the crowd.

Blast.

He was angry with her. Did she blame him? She had done little to ease the waters between him and her brothers and had remained shocked in silence as the tension between them grew. Now they were all competing against each other in the hammer throw as some test of superiority and masculinity.

It was not exactly how she had hoped their initial meeting would go, but at least they had not come to blows. She cleared her throat and smoothed her skirts. But, who knew what would happen after the hammer throw? They might wrestle over the winnings.

'You say you wish to assess your options for a husband here and the first man you land on is Campbell?' Rolf asked.

'My thoughts exactly,' Royce growled in low tones, his gaze still following what she assumed was Rowan's movements in the distance. 'Care to explain, sister?' He crossed his arms against his chest.

Her cheeks heated. 'How dare you scrutinise me?' she

hissed, angry at being spoken to as a child rather than the grown woman she was. 'I am leaving all my options open. I believe you said I could pursue my own interests in a match, or have you changed your mind on that bit as well?' She mirrored him and crossed her arms against her bosom.

Rolf and Catriona watched the exchange between her and Royce in utter silence despite how much Susanna would have delighted in some sibling interference right about now. It seemed they remembered what she did: an angry Royce was not to be trifled with. No matter how softened and changed he had been by his accident on Lismore and by falling in love with Iona, he was still Royce. He had a temper, and his tongue could be sharp and spiteful, especially if he felt threatened. Based on his reaction to Rowan, their mutual disdain for each other hadn't wavered over the last decade.

Royce still hadn't answered her.

'So, have you changed your mind?' she asked again, not caring about what his reaction might be. She was too desperate to know the truth. The idea of an arranged marriage turned her stomach. A fake betrothal was much more to her liking.

'Nay,' he relented, the anger having abated from his voice. He exhaled and rubbed the back of his neck. 'But the idea of you considering every man will take some getting used to, especially the likes of Campbell.'

The knots in her stomach loosened and a rush of air filled her lungs. Catriona and Rolf seemed equally relieved.

'Then let us enjoy some refreshment before they have been devoured,' Catriona offered, tucking her arm around Susanna's elbow before leading her away. 'What are you up to, sister?' she asked in low tones as they wove through the crowd, greeting people as she awaited Susanna's answer.

Susanna had worked out her answer to this the night before once she deduced Catriona suspected her of something nefarious, which was an accurate account of her motives.

'Finding a husband,' she answered. She congratulated herself on how real and authentic the words sounded as they fell from her lips. Practicing in front of the looking glass had helped.

'Nothing more?'

'Nay. Nothing more. Although I cannot say I am thrilled about the idea of relinquishing some of my freedoms and attempting to find a man who can respect my mind as well as my wishes.'

Catriona chuckled. 'A tall order to be sure, but I have no doubt that if anyone can find one, you can. Just do not force it. Listen to your heart.' Her amber eyes set upon Susanna and her heart skittered.

Ach. How did one do that? 'It has been some time since I have listened to my heart in such matters,' she confessed.

'I know, but that does not mean you cannot begin now. Just look at me and Ewan. It took us both a good deal of time to believe we could love and trust one another because of our past and all the disappointments that accompanied it. But the risk was worth it. I cannot imagine being without him now. And soon we shall have our own family.'

The love in her sister's voice and gaze stole Susanna's breath and she paused. 'You make it sound so easy.'

'Easy?' Catriona scoffed. She let go of Susanna's arm and shook her head before calling back to her. 'Hardly. It is the most difficult thing in the world.'

Chapter Ten

Rowan ground his teeth as he approached the line for the hammer throw. Somehow, he'd been slated to go last. Perhaps because he had just won the stone put. Either way, he cursed himself for being drawn into participating in yet another event. His pride failed him more than once on past occasions, and he hoped this wouldn't serve as such a reminder again. He should have ceased while he was ahead with a victory. Despite it being merely late morn, he felt spent. So much socialising, small talk, and pretending to be agreeable wore him through. He didn't remember the Tournament being so tiresome. But he'd been younger and less battered and bruised then. Life hadn't yet had its way with him.

Unlike now.

He met Rosa's gaze across the field and remembered this was for her. Sure, he was fulfilling some ridiculous promise to Susanna, but by all accounts, Rosa's happiness in this weekend mattered most to him. He wanted her to remember it fondly. He also wanted her to be proud of him. He'd fallen short as her father many a day since Anna's death, and although he hoped she was too young to remember him falling apart and into the mad well of grief, he was no fool. She couldn't have escaped all of it. Replacing some of those horrid failings with these memories of him being a celebrated champion and respected laird would serve them both well for years to come.

'Campbell?' the older man assisting with the hammer throw called, bringing the present back into focus.

'Aye,' Rowan replied and took the heavy wooden handle from the older man. Rowan shifted it in his grip as he tested out the weight of it. It was heavier than he remembered. Yet another sign of his age. He cursed under his breath.

A small cheer of applause sounded, and he turned to greet the crowd with a wave. Although they cheered for him now, they would equally celebrate his demise. He was no fool as to the fickle nature of approval. His gaze searched the distance to see just where the furthest fabric marker rested fluttering in the swell of the breeze. The blue, green, and red Cameron tartan taunted him. Royce's throw was best, with Rolf's not far behind. Their success was an annoying complication to the situation.

Even now, both glared at him with hatred, at best disdain. He settled in a low wide stance, rocking back and forth from his heels to toes to gain traction in the moist grass that had become trodden by previous competitors. He completed two revolutions to gain speed before he set the hammer free with a wail of effort. To his relief, the hammer was gliding straight in the sky and hadn't hooked, which had impacted a handful of throwers before. It sailed past many of the markers before it dipped. He urged it on as the crowd fell into silence, watching its advance and anticipating where it might land. As the hammer hit, throwing up dirt and grass, before skidding to a stop, Rowan held his breath. It would be close. He couldn't tell where it had landed from this distance.

The lad carrying his grey and brown marker followed

the burly man in charge of the events as he jogged out
to the divot where the hammer had first hit the soil. He
stopped among the Cameron markers and studied the area.
He pointed to a spot and the lad tucked in the Campbell
fabric. It fluttered between the two Cameron markers.

Curses.

He was just shy of the win, but he'd bested one of the
Camerons. At least that would offer a bit of a sting to their
collective pride, which brought Rowan some temporary
satisfaction. The crowd cheered his throw despite it being
just short of a victory. Perhaps they favoured his unlikely
comeback after so many years. No doubt all the men and
women knew of his past difficulties after losing Anna.
Hell, he'd temporarily lost his title, the elders deeming
him incapable of ruling while he struggled with his grief.

He squared his shoulders. None of that mattered now.
He was laird. He was well. And he was here with Rosa…
who was now chatting with Susanna and Trice. His skin
prickled as he approached them. Seeing all of them together felt odd and uncomfortable, but he knew this would
be the first of many moments moving forward if he was
to uphold his end of their arrangement. He sucked in a
breath as he climbed the small slope, counted to five, and
released the air from his lungs slowly as he approached.
After all he had been through, this was a small challenge.

'Ladies,' he greeted with a nod.

'Papa!' Rosa turned and hugged his legs. 'You did well.
Second best!'

He ruffled her soft hair. 'Thank you, my sweet. Lady
Cameron's brother bested me this time.'

'Your brother won, my lady?' Rosa asked, craning her
head up and around to see Susanna properly.

'Aye. Laird Royce Cameron, my eldest brother won, and my youngest brother earned third.'

'What is it like to have two brothers? I miss mine.'

Rowan's heart ceased beating. Her words a crushing pressure upon him and his ears buzzed. Trice squeezed his hand, anchoring him back in the present. He squeezed her hand back, grateful for the small gesture to support him.

Susanna bent down next to Rosa. 'I have no doubt you miss him greatly. I bet he watches over you even now to keep you safe.'

'Aye. Just like Mama.' She smiled.

'Aye,' Susanna continued, and dropped her voice to a whisper. 'Having two brothers is much like being in this field. While it is quite nice to always have the company, sometimes you need a bit of time to yourself. I am lucky to have a sister too. She makes me laugh. You have met her. 'tis Lady Stewart.'

'Oh! She is quite nice, and she has beautiful eyes. Like amber.'

'Aye.'

'I hope to have a brother or sister again one day,' Rosa added, reaching over to fiddle with Susanna's cloak ribbon. It slid through his daughter's fingers before resting against Susanna's cloak again.

Susanna smiled. 'And you just might,' she replied. 'The future is full of secrets that we can only dream of.'

Her words stole Rowan's breath and reverberated through him, the hope in them igniting a seed of desire for a happy future.

The future is full of secrets that we can only dream of.

He stared at her. Did she really believe those words? He'd never thought her capable of such hope, and suddenly he saw her as a woman longing for more out of her life, much like he was. Had he misjudged her? Was she more than the manipulative, distant woman he had always perceived her to be after their relationship had ended?

She stood and met Rowan's gaze. 'My laird, I shall be off. Congratulations on your placement. I hope to see you and your family later this afternoon.'

'Aye,' he replied, his voice husky and low, with a bit of a crack at the end. Nothing else came to him. He just stared at her.

'Aye, my lady,' Trice replied, eyeing him suspiciously. 'We look forward to seeing you.'

'Bye, Lady Cameron!' Rosa called to her waving as she left.

Susanna headed off and turned to send one last wave to them.

'Have you been struck dumb, brother?' Trice asked, her brow furrowed.

'Nay,' he replied, clearing his throat as his gaze continued to follow Susanna's fluid movements across the field to where her brothers were. He was still foggy after her words, his mind ambling between memories of their past and present relationship, if one could even call it such. That misty idea of hope lingered about him, but he didn't trust his mind enough to hold onto it.

At least not yet.

She poked his arm and studied his face. Mirth filled her voice. 'Wait?' she asked, dropping her voice to an even lower whisper as she moved closer. 'Are you interested in her? Do you still fancy Susanna?' Her mouth gaped open, and that look—the look of giddiness she often had as a girl when she uncovered secrets of her younger brothers lit her eyes and features, making her look a decade younger. 'After all this time?' she asked, her words high pitched and eager for an answer. 'I never would have thought it.'

He frowned at her despite the bit of heat he felt entering his neck and cheeks.

'I am right.' She covered her mouth and chuckled without waiting for any answer from him. He realised now, not answering had been his fatal error. Omission equalled agreement to his sister.

Now what was he to do.

'She is pretty, Papa,' Rosa said giggling, adding to Trice's ridiculousness. 'And nice.'

His daughter's words yanked Rowan harshly to the present. While it might suit their plan in the long term, for hints of their 'renewed' romance to become whisperings among the crowds, Rowan needed to slow his sister's expectations and thoughts on the matter until they were ready to have such notions bandied about.

He rolled his eyes at both of them, eager to dismiss their enquiry. 'I do not fancy anyone but you, my little pitcher,' he replied reaching down and tickling her to help change the subject.

She squealed in delight, and he picked her up and popped her over his shoulders in one deft movement. He needed to enjoy this time with her. She was growing up far too quickly. Soon, she would be too grown to do such things.

She leaned down, wrapped her arms around his neck, and kissed his cheek. 'Thank you for bringing me, Papa. It is such fun here!'

He leaned his cheek against hers. 'Aye. And the weekend has only begun, my sweet.'

Chapter Eleven

Susanna tapped her slipper on the floor with impatience and sighed as the hands on the mantel clock of the study at Glenhaven Castle rested neatly together on the twelve as if in prayer. Perhaps it was a prayer for her patience. The chimes rang off, and with each passing echo, her frustration from waiting alone in a cold dusty study at midnight grew. Where was the man? She had sent a note to Rowan in his chambers a half hour ago and he'd still yet to arrive. At this rate, she would throttle him if she didn't freeze first. It was bad enough he'd said scarce more than a greeting to her at the dinner this eve. What was wrong with the man? He'd been attentive and almost doting this morn at the Tournament games, but then he'd all but disappeared.

She frowned. It was much like the way she remembered their relationship had been when they were teens: an awkward and infuriating dance of closeness and distance. Not viewing Rowan as a good enough match for her, Father had commanded her to end their involvement after Rowan had proposed, and she had agreed without complaint, frustrated by his moods and inconsistency. Soon after, she had met Jeremiah, whose warmth and constancy had filled her heart. Her chest tightened at the memory of his glorious smile and rogue dimple. After her father had sent Jeremiah away to punish him for daring an attachment with her and her for loving 'below her station,' and he had died in battle, she'd had little interest in marrying or pursuing attachments of any kind.

Her Father's forced engagement to Rowan's brother Brandon during his brief reign as laird two years ago was a ridiculous farce meant to punish her for refusing to take a husband. The fact that it would also sting Rowan had been an unexpected boon for her father. The farce of an engagement had been brief, but by aiding Brandon and his men with her own soldiers to help rescue Brandon's son and now wife, Fiona, from Audric's clutches, Susanna had gained her freedom from the betrothal *and* a favour that her father had never known about. It was the calling in of that same favour Rowan had inherited when he became laird once more that had brought her to this very moment.

And in this moment, she was alone, cold, and waiting in secret to strategize another scheme to escape marriage by crafting a pretend betrothal with her first love. In short, her love life was one complicated disaster after another and showed little hope of improvement.

Blast.

The second hand inched on towards the one and she stood, no longer able to sit and wait, and desperate to warm herself. She rubbed her hands together and blew on them. She roamed through the study with its books lining the walled cases as well as the additional standing bookcases lining the inner workings of the room. It was a maze of learning. Her fingertips trailed along the spines. She'd never been much of a reader although she didn't dislike it. The outdoors, weaponry, and strategy had always intrigued her and called to her far more strongly than inked letters on parchment. Poetry and literature really hadn't won her over. Evidently, the Stewarts were far more refined creatures than the Camerons, who were known more for actions rather than words. Shelves of literature, an unholy number of texts on botany, and a smattering of what she believed to be poets sat nestled in each case amongst other more mundane topics such as history, geography, and science. There wasn't even dust on them. They must *use* them… regularly. She lifted her brow in surprise.

Who had time for such reading?

A door creaked open, and she turned to see Rowan's sharp profile in shadow as he came into the room. She'd recognise those features anywhere: his strong nose and chin along with a full forehead. After he closed the door, she watched him study the darkness, evidently looking for her. She smiled and watched him.

'I know you are here,' he said. 'I can smell the scent of your perfume. Violets, if I remember.'

She pressed her lips together and gripped her skirts. How had he remembered such?

And more importantly, why did his remembering such make her heart skitter a bit in her chest?

'Aye,' she replied evenly, releasing the hitch in her breath.

He roamed through the bookcases that lined the middle of the room in search of her, and instead of revealing herself, she remained hidden, exulting in this small game.

'Why is it so dark and cold in here?' he asked, moving through the rows, his boots landing with a subdued hush.

'I didn't dare light a candle or ask for the fire to be lit. Surely, you understand.'

'Aye. Secrecy is essential to our ruse,' he replied.

'Care to tell me why it took you so long to arrive?'

'You failed to tell me *which* study. This is the third one I have been in.'

She smirked at the chuckle in his voice. 'I had forgotten. The Stewarts are readers to be sure.'

'This castle is also a bloody labyrinth.'

She laughed aloud at that, and then covered her mouth, lest she reveal herself.

He turned the row. 'Finally,' he said approaching her.

Her breath caught. In the darkness, his eyes sparkled with light, and she could see the playfulness in his gaze. His tunic was untucked and open at the neck, his hair mussed and unruly, begging to be touched, and his entire demeanour was relaxed.

But instead of saying any of this, she uttered. 'Why have you been ignoring me since this morn?'

He balked at her sharpness, his body suddenly tense. 'What are you talking about?' he asked, opening his palms to her.

'If we are to be believed to be rekindling something, we must be seen together.' She crossed her arms against her chest.

He stepped closer, his arms falling back to his sides. 'I know that, but it cannot be rushed, can it? While we want people to talk, we do not want them to 'talk' badly of either of us, especially you. Or have you forgotten how cruel and unrelenting idle gossip, especially among women, can be?'

She didn't answer. She well remembered. While he had a point, she didn't wish to concede it just yet. She shivered.

He looked at her, concern in his gaze. 'I did not bring a coat or I would give it to you.' He reached out and rubbed her arms from shoulder to elbow, the heat from his hands sent a flush of awareness through her like whiskey. 'You are freezing, Susanna. How long have you been in here?'

'A half hour,' she whispered, some of the irritation receding. The warmth and comfort of his touch was a delicious distraction.

'Then, let's be quick, so you can get back to your chambers and warmed.'

His kindness was distracting her. What had she been angry about again?

'And what of tomorrow?' she asked.

'Aye,' he answered, still rubbing her arms absently, his body closer to her now. The motion along her arms was hypnotic, and her limbs softened to him like clay warmed when it was held and worked. 'Perhaps a planned exchange when we break our fast? Then, a chance meeting again as the events come to close in the afternoon?'

She nodded.

The door to the study creaked open. Candlelight spilled into the room, casting dancing shadows on the floor. They both stilled. Rowan pulled her closer, an instinctive gesture of protection she didn't resist. Perhaps if they made themselves smaller, they might not be noticed.

Susanna's heart pounded in her chest and in her ears. If they were discovered, her reputation would be in tatters, their plan ruined—and then her brothers would kill Rowan and scatter his body parts along Loch Linnhe. She cringed.

Perhaps meeting here had been a poor idea.

Susanna could see the person more clearly now. She almost sighed aloud in relief. *Catriona.* Her blossoming figure and distinctive amber hair were unmistakable. Even if her sister discovered them, she would take such a discovery to the grave.

Catriona selected a book with care and headed back to the door. She paused and said quietly, 'While I know not what you are up to, Susanna, best you wait ten minutes before emerging. Ewan is up making me a kettle of tea for I cannot sleep.'

Rowan stiffened against Susanna.

She squeezed his arm. 'Do not worry,' she mouthed to him.

He scowled.

When the door finally closed again and they were left alone, Rowan frowned. 'Why should we not worry?'

'Because Catriona knows only I am here, not you as well. No doubt I need to wear less violet perfume. It is too distinctive,' she fretted.

'Or we should stop planning secret encounters that put our reputations at risk.'

'*Our* reputations?' she asked.

'Aye,' he replied.

'You are a man. You have no reputation to lose, especially after...' she began and then stopped realising her error too late.

'My what?' he asked gripping her arm.

She stared up at him.

'Go ahead. Do finish. My what? Bout with insanity?' he bit off angrily.

'Aye,' she answered.

'Well, anytime you wish to release me from this ridiculous ruse of yours, say the word. I would hate to damage your pristine reputation as cold and heartless.'

She yanked her arm free from his hold, his words a barb lancing her pride. 'And miss out on your quest for vengeance?'

'I could do so on my own.'

'Doubtful.' She took a step back, but he closed the space as he advanced on her again.

'You think me incapable?'

She said nothing and merely lifted her brow, uncertain as to why she continued to bait him. She could have denied it. She believed him capable. Otherwise, she wouldn't have dared to enlist him in her scheme, but she'd rather eat a volume of poetry than tell him such now.

'Incapable, eh?' he scoffed, moving closer, so close she could see the flutter of his dark lashes move against his skin and the bright blue of his irises catch the meagre light in the shadows. 'Like you,' he hissed. 'I am capable of cruelty and revenge. Do not test me. For I may rise to your challenge.'

He gazed at her lips, and she thought he would kiss her, but he didn't. He cursed under his breath and left the study, ignoring her sister's previous warning to wait.

Susanna leaned heavily against the bookcase, resting her forehead against the cool wood of the shelves. Why did it always go this way between them?

Hot and cold with nothing in between.

The woman was impossible. Infuriating. Irritating.

And he couldn't stop thinking about her and how close he had come to almost kissing her. Rowan ran a hand brusquely through his hair and cursed as he strove down the hallway with purpose.

Who did she think she was? Telling him he was unfit or incapable. It was she who had come to him begging for his help. He had a mind to search out her brothers and reveal her absurd plan. No doubt they would then owe him and my how the roles of debt would be reversed. He froze and turned on his heel with a smile.

That was exactly what he would do. He scanned the hallway with its many chambers and tried to remember exactly what rooms the brothers would be staying in. Candlelight danced along the floors and walls from the sconces lit at friendly intervals to aid the many guests in their travels. What he really needed was a map. Glenhaven was a labyrinth.

Frowning, he set his hands on his waist. It stood to reason that all the Camerons would be on the same hallway, would it not? And as family of Lady Stewart, they most likely had the nicest of quarters to stay in, which should be closest to Lady and Laird Stewart.

Now if only he knew where their chambers were... But he had no idea.

He smiled. They couldn't be far from the study they had just been in. Lady Stewart had popped in for a book. Surely, she would peruse the study closest to her own chambers so late at night and so heavy with child. He turned around and headed back down the hall where he had come from, made another turn, and then one more before he was on the hall with the study. He paused. By that logic, Susanna's room was also somewhere near the study. Why had she failed to tell him that before or met in her chambers?

Well, perhaps not *in* her chambers. That would be inappropriate.

He grumbled in irritation. Vexed by the whole situation. While he'd never asked outright, she could have offered him the information in case they needed to discuss any matters further. Although they had also just been arguing.

The large clock in the hallway chimed the half hour, and he continued with quiet, thoughtful steps, pausing along the doors to see if he could hear any noises that might give away who was in what room. It was a poor and rather risky strategy, but what other did he have? Three doors down, he heard what he thought was a knob turning and the hesitant opening of a door. He froze, scanned the hallway for a place to hide and scurried to a small alcove he spied across the corridor, most likely meant for servants to take a quick respite before continuing with their duties, and shoved himself into it. He held his breath and pushed himself a touch deeper into the space, wincing when the moulding of the small space dug into his back.

The door closed and a collection of footfalls echoed quietly down the hallway. Then, another door squeaked open and another voice joined in. He lifted his brow. The chances of him happening upon an evening rendezvous like this were odd. He couldn't help but be grateful for his good fortune. Whatever it was would provide him information on something and someone of import. Why else was there such a surreptitious meeting in play?

He could kiss Susanna now for making him so cross. He frowned. Nay, that was too far. He focused on the murmurings as they neared trying to distinguish who was talking.

'What is this about?' a man asked, his voice weary.

'Our sister.'

Rowan smiled. The second man was Royce. His brusque unyielding tone made his voice easy to distinguish.

'Catriona?'

'Nay,' he offered. 'Susanna.'

'Ah,' the other man said. 'Come to the study. This sounds

like it shall be longer than a hallway exchange, and my wife has finally fallen asleep.'

Laird Stewart! Now things were getting interesting. Why would Royce need to speak with his brother-in-law Ewan under the cover of darkness? Rowan's interest piqued, and gooseflesh rose along his skin.

'Aye,' Royce agreed. 'We have much to discuss with you and need your help.'

We?

Rolf must be with them, even though the man hadn't spoken a word during the exchange. Rowan pressed his palms flat to the wood of the nook he hid in, straining to hear, and leaned forward waiting for more. But the conversation had ended, and the men were walking away.

Their footfalls disappeared into nothingness as they moved further down the hall away from him, and then another door squeaked open and then closed softly. Most likely they had gone into the study he and Susanna had been hiding in but minutes ago. The irony of not being caught and now being so desperate to go back into the space he was so eager to leave not long ago was not lost on him.

He stilled. If Susanna hadn't left yet, she would now be trapped and forced to listen to her brothers and their plans for her. He pressed his lips together to prevent a chuckle. *Saints be.* He would pay good coin to watch her endure that exchange without saying a word.

Rowan waited. He *had* to know what they were talking about. This could be the break he needed to create an advantage over Susanna and the Camerons. He could almost taste the thrill of finally having the advantage over a clan known for having the upper hand on everyone else.

But it would be a risk. The only way to attempt to overhear anything would be to eavesdrop outside the door, in plain sight of anyone else who might be exiting their rooms or travelling the hallways. Surely, servants still moved about the large castle, tending to the needs of all the many guests here during the Tournament, especially this hallway, since it seemed he was correct in assuming the family chambers were here.

He could be one servant bell pull away from discovery. And if discovered, his rather precarious relationship with the Cameron brothers would be even more uncertain, if it didn't turn contentious. But the risk was well worth the payoff, wasn't it?

While Hugh would say it wasn't, Rowan was ready to gamble on his chances. He eased slowly from the alcove, eager to stretch his cramped back and bunched muscles from the tiny confines of the space. He stepped out into the hallway and his body sighed in relief. He smelled the air and scanned the long corridor from one end to the other listening for noise. Nothing. So he advanced slowly, rolling his feet from heel, ball, to toe as best as he could in his boots to lessen the sound of his movements. He passed one chamber door, then another, hearing little more than snoring.

Finally, he reached the door of the study. He settled on occupying the space on the opposite side of the door. That way if it opened suddenly, he would be facing their backsides rather than their faces and go unseen. Or at least he hoped that was how it might work.

Rowan pressed his ear to the wall, and soon he was able to decipher the men's words.

'So, you understand how challenging this situation is?' asked Royce.

'Aye,' Ewan answered, his voice weary.

'We know Susanna does not wish to marry, but she must. And while we have told her she has the option to choose her husband, if she does not settle on a man soon, we will choose for her. As with all things Susanna, it is proving…difficult.'

'And?' Ewan asked.

'We wish for you to ask Catriona what she knows about Susanna's plans or report to us on anything you may overhear between them. She has been odd as of late and prone to keeping her own secrets,' Rolf added in a lower tone.

Ewan scoffed. 'You wish for me to spy on my own wife and her sister and report back to you? Catriona is with child. I cannot cause her any further difficulty or strain. For the babe's sake and her own. Surely, this has crossed your mind?'

'Aye,' Royce answered, his voice hardening. 'We are her brothers and care for her well-being. Who Susanna chooses or does not choose may impact the clan's welfare as well as our own. Much hangs in the balance based on her choice.'

'Why? It is but one marriage.'

'There are rumours that other clans may be joining forces to overrun us to gain control of the Highlands before the British further their advance north,' Royce explained.

'Nay,' Ewan countered. 'Just idle gossip. I have heard no inkling of truth in those claims. Nor have any of my men.'

'Even so, we would be fools to ignore it,' Royce added.

'Are you calling me a fool?' Ewan countered.

'Nay,' Royce added in a softer tone. 'But we cannot afford to do so. Too much is at stake.'

Rowan stilled.

Violets.

He smelled violets. Glancing up, he saw Susanna watching him from her cracked chambers two rooms down from the study.

Curses.

'What are you doing?' she mouthed to him.

He scowled at her and wildly gestured for her to go back to her chambers with his hand.

She shook her head and popped her hands to her hips, returning his glare.

The talking ceased. 'Is there someone outside?' Rolf asked.

Blast.

Rowan moved away from the study door quickly, rushed into Susanna's chambers, and shut the door as quietly as he could. When she attempted to object, he covered her mouth with his hand, and pressed her against the wall behind her. 'Quiet,' he hissed near her ear. She stilled and they both waited, desperate to know if either of them had been or would be discovered. Rowan heard a door open and close, the hushed footfalls of boots in the hallway, more doors quietly opening and closing, and then…silence.

He sighed, his body relaxing. 'I will take away my hand but be quiet,' he whispered.

She nodded.

As soon as he removed her hand, she spatted out a series of hushed questions. 'What were you doing? And why were you shushing me away?'

'I was trying to overhear what your brothers were secretly meeting about with their brother-in-law at half past midnight,' he whispered. 'Then, you interrupted me.' His annoyance was returning with a vengeance. He stepped away from her and continued further into the room before he halted. 'Where is your maid?' he whispered, realising his mistake.

'Downstairs. There are not adjoining chambers in this room. You may speak freely, but quietly. I do not know how easily one can overhear conversations between rooms. But perhaps you know, since I caught *you* eavesdropping.' She crossed her arms against her chest and lifted a single eyebrow, her scorn over his actions evident.

'I did it for you,' he offered before moving deeper into the chambers. He'd leave out the part where he had been hoping to turn the tables on their arrangement and get the advantage on her family. She didn't need to know *that* bit.

She followed him into the room and headed to one of a pair of lush chairs in front of the hearth, where her evening fire still smouldered. Gesturing for him to sit opposite her, she settled in, tucking her legs beneath her, like she always did, looking like a contented cat having lapped up its fill of milk. She had removed her slippers, and his body reacted to the brief flash of her small, delicate pearly white bare feet before they disappeared under the folds of her dark dressing gown. She waited for him to begin.

He cleared his throat, moved the chair a bit closer to her, so they wouldn't have to speak too loudly, and settled into the soft cushions. The subtle fragrance of violets cocooned him, as if the room had absorbed her in the two days she had been here, and he began to relax. She ran her fingers over the dainty ribbon that held her long, woven plait of hair in place. How he wanted to pull the ribbon loose, set her bound hair free, and run his fingers through the long wavy tresses.

'Rowan?' she whispered, her brow furrowed.

Deuces.

He shook his head. *She* was making him addled. Or perhaps it was his need for touch that was making *him* addled. It had been some time since he had lain with a woman, well longer than *some time*, if he were being honest. He had not lain with a woman since Anna's death four years ago as he hadn't had many urges—until now—but he set aside that budding need and focused on a far more pressing matter…

'Rowan?' she hissed, this time with more urgency and annoyance.

'You are right,' he answered impatiently, rattling off the list of information he could surmise from his spying before she had interrupted him. 'First, your brothers have grave concerns about your well-being as well as their own and the clan's future. Second, I overheard them asking Ewan for help. They fear other clans are planning a combined attack upon them. Why they think this, I don't know. But they are trying to enlist him to spy upon your sister for information about your marriage plans. And—' he paused and took a breath before continuing'—they will marry you off if you do not select a match…and soon.'

She balked at the news and her lips parted as she stared upon him, but no words followed.

Perhaps he *could* have softened it a bit, but he wanted to be succinct and leave no room for doubt that something was afoot, as she suspected. She also had been harassing him for information, so he provided it.

Now that her eyes brightened with concern, he realised his error in his thinking. 'You wished to be wrong?' he asked, his tone softening.

She dropped her gaze from his and studied her hands, which worked the delicate lace edging her gown. 'Aye,' she answered quietly. 'I had hoped to be. They are all I have.

I do not wish to lose them. And the idea of being wed to a stranger…' her words trailed off.

Puzzled, he studied her. 'You mean despite the effort you have put in place to find the answers to their secrecy and to enlist a pretend fiancé, you deep down hoped none of it would be needed?'

She looked up at him and met his gaze. The desperation in her face matched the eve of their first meeting in the forge, and he felt as he did then: intrigued—and despite his past anger with her, he felt sorry for her. *This* was the young Susanna he had known all those years ago and cared for deeply, not the cold, detached woman she oft appeared to be to him now.

Before he could think too much upon it, he rose and knelt before her. Feeling like the young Rowan he had also once been before life had taken its hold on him and shaken out some of his hope, he grasped her hands gently in his own. The smooth, cool weight of her fingers was a contrast to the rough warmth of his own. They trembled slightly in his hold, and he squeezed them in reassurance. 'We will figure this out, you and I. I am far too deep within this intrigue to cease now,' he offered with a smile. 'Hell, Trice will have us engaged before the end of the Tournament tomorrow if we are not careful.'

She sniffed and shifted closer to him, not releasing his hands. 'And if something horrid does happen? If my brothers are killed, if I am married off to a man I do not know or like, if the clans are uniting to crush us beneath their feet, what then? Will you still help me?' Her gaze flicked up to his, the challenge in them evident and unflinching.

His stomach tightened into a knot.

Would he? Could he even promise such as laird of Clan Campbell and father to Rosa?

He squared his shoulders and risked the truth. 'If I can,' he replied.

She nodded and gave a small smile. 'At least you tell me the truth. You do not fill me with vapid platitudes and nonsense. Thank you.' She leaned forward and kissed his cheek.

The soft feathering of her warm lips against his skin and the heat and smell of her so close to him made him lean into her, turning his face just enough that his lips skimmed hers before she could fully move away.

Once their lips touched, they both stilled. He lifted a hand to cup her cheek, running his thumb along her cheekbone, eliciting a sigh from her lips. 'Kiss me,' she commanded, and for the first time this eve, he didn't question her words but gave in easily to her demand.

Still kneeling, he moved forward, holding his lips open near her own, letting the heat and desire build in him until he couldn't hold the dam of want any more. Then, he seized her mouth, letting his lips pull and linger upon her own until her mouth answered back with her own demands of him. Her palm slid up his tunic and neck before weaving into his hair. Small bursts of desire bubbled and popped beneath his skin, and he kissed her harder, deeper, claiming what he could of her in their kisses. She moved forward and her other hand slid down to untuck his tunic. While he registered the action in his mind, he didn't react but kept plundering her mouth. When her bare hand slid beneath the fabric and up his spine and back, he shuddered and pulled away.

'Susanna,' he murmured, resting his forehead against hers. 'I must go. We cannot. I should not.' His attempts at sentences and clarity were shattered somewhere along with his restraint.

'Aye,' she replied. 'I well know the limitations…' she replied between uneven breaths, 'of our arrangement. I just wanted to remember,' she finished before shifting away from him. She gently shoved him back and stood.

He sat on his haunches bewildered and confused by the sudden end to their embrace. What had just happened? He blinked back the cobwebs of lust and tried to focus on comprehending her words, but before he could rise, she was walking away from him.

Her robe slid to the floor in a liquid pool of fabric, revealing a sleeping gown so sheer that he could see the outline of her lush form in the meagre moonlight streaming in the partially open curtains. His throat dried.

She shook out her hair and let the ribbon fall to the floor before she continued walking, her body's gentle movements against the fabric arresting his attention. 'You can go,' she said coolly.

He balked. Had she just dismissed him as if he were a servant, and she was done with his services?

He cursed, rose, and tucked in his tunic.

'Christ, Susanna,' he muttered. 'You don't have to always pretend to be the cold-hearted minx everyone thinks you are and expects you to be. Remember, I knew you once or at least I thought I did.'

He closed the door behind him, perhaps a bit louder than he should have, leaving whatever illusions he had held about her being the young Susanna of his past shattered upon the floor.

Chapter Twelve

Susanna clanged the teacup on the saucer. Could one have a kiss hangover? That was sure what her pounding head, shattered nerves, and general irritation of this morn felt like. She had enjoyed their kiss last night more than she wished to admit and had wanted and needed to be fulfilled. Unfortunately, the kiss had left her wanting, which made her feel as she did now. When Rowan had ceased his attentions so abruptly, she'd felt rejected and angry, and had dismissed him. Now, she feared he might cast aside their plan altogether, and then where would she be, especially with the news he shared with her about what he overheard with her brothers.

She grumbled and rubbed her temple.

'Feeling unwell, sister?' Catriona asked as she entered the small family banquet room to break her fast.

Susanna cringed and attempted to reset her features before meeting her sister's gaze. As expected, Catriona studied her with a smirk and continued to the buffet where the morning meal was set out for the family. The guests were supposed to eat in the adjoining room, but Susanna felt she would be better able to volley the enquiries of her family rather than the rest of those attending the games, especially Rowan, so she'd sneaked into the smaller banquet room this morn.

'Merely tired,' Susanna answered, sitting up straighter in her chair and smoothing a few loose tendrils from her face.

'Aye. Not unexpected since you were up quite late.'

'Oh?' Rolf asked as he entered the room, having heard part of their exchange.

Curses.

Now she would have to answer to not one but two siblings. At least Royce was not here—yet.

'I had trouble sleeping, so I went to the study to select a book,' Susanna offered and then took a sip of her tea to hide the ridiculousness of her statement.

Rolf scoffed. 'You? The study? Gathering a book to read? Did you also find some fresh needlework that needed to be finished?' He laughed at his own joke and plunked some sausages and bread onto his plate.

Susanna rolled her eyes, trying not to rise to the bait despite the pounding of her head. 'That is why I gathered the book. To help bore me enough to fall asleep.'

Catriona sat across from her and lifted her brow. 'Did you sleep well after?' she enquired, a bit too sweetly for Susanna's taste. No doubt a further prodding for information from her younger sister would ensue later when they were alone.

At least her sister had not outed her to her brother. She mouthed 'thank you' to Catriona before biting into a chunk of bread with her favourite currant jam. As the sweet fruit hit her tongue, she sighed a bit and relaxed against the back of her chair. All she needed to do was take this day a bit at a time. She would make it through, and Rowan would keep to his word. She had to trust that he was more eager for revenge against Audric than punishing her for calling him weak.

'So, have you some contenders?' Rolf asked. He sat down

heavily, hitting his knee on the table, shaking the contents atop it. 'Sorry,' he added. 'It is lower than ours at home.'

Catriona chuckled. 'No worries, brother.' She set her gaze on Susanna.

Only then did Susanna realise he was talking to her. 'What?' she asked, confused by his enquiry.

'Contenders,' he said, cutting into his sausage. 'For a husband,' he finished and then bit into the hearty link.

Susanna's stomach dropped, her appetite evaporating with it. She set aside her bread. She shrugged her shoulders, trying to bide time. Names had to be mentioned based on the dire urgency Rowan mentioned to her from what he overheard last night.

But she couldn't lead with Rowan. That would be too obvious. But who else had she met? And why did she always forget everyone's names?

Well not everyone, just the people she had no interest in. She sighed and played with her napkin in her lap. 'Well,' she began and faltered. 'There was a man who finished third in the stone put.' Of course, his name escaped her, but he seemed a solid choice. Not too young, nor too old. 'And perhaps Laird Campbell.'

Rolf stopped chewing and swallowed, setting his knife and fork back on his plate. He assessed her, quietly. His eyes widened. 'You are serious? About Campbell?'

'What about Campbell?' Royce enquired, his tone was light, and he almost smiled as he entered the breakfast room, catching Susanna and everyone else in the room off guard. The three of them paused their conversation and watched him as he hummed, gathered a plate, and began to fill it.

Royce sat down, oblivious to their confusion, and asked.

'Where is Ewan this morn? I had hoped to see him before we set off today.'

'He is meeting with a few of his men and the servants to settle departure arrangements for everyone. I am sure you will be able to speak with him before you all head off for Loch's End,' Catriona answered. 'You are in a fine mood today,' she added.

'Aye,' he replied. 'Eager to be back home with Iona and the bairn on the way. But I am glad I came. There are many prospects here for you, sister.' His gaze settled on Susanna. 'Who have you settled upon?' He ate happily, and the knowing that she would send his good mood down the loch was unsettling.

'I have not selected *the one* yet, but there are many candidates as you mentioned. Rolf and I were just speaking of it.'

Royce swallowed and studied her, his gaze narrowing in on her. 'You were just speaking of Campbell. Are you telling me you are seriously considering the man, especially after all his—difficulties?' he added, dropping his voice, so as not to be heard outside the room.

'Aye. I am.' She paused, preparing to provide them the logic she had given Rowan early on that night in the forge that would help them agree to such a match. 'That is precisely why I am considering him. He can be handled quite easily, wouldn't you think? A man as fragile as that.'

Catriona stilled, the colour draining from her face. 'Susanna,' she whispered in disbelief. 'Surely, you would not take advantage of his past difficulties and use such weakness against him. You cannot be so cruel. He has a daughter. What of her?' She absently rubbed her swelled belly, an unconscious act of protection she probably didn't even recognise.

'Blimey,' Rolf muttered, shifting in his chair.

Royce moved the food quietly around his plate and they all sat in silence apart from the occasional scraping of a utensil across a plate, sip of tea, or squeak of a chair. Susanna's stomach curdled. Perhaps it was even too dark of a suggestion for Royce. She'd gone too far and played too risky of a hand in her game. She feared all was lost. Her pulse picked up speed and she wrung her napkin in her lap.

With his plate now empty, Royce sat back in his chair, wiped his mouth, and rested his napkin on the table. He lifted his gaze to her. 'This seems the best option for you at present?' he asked.

'Aye.'

'You would live with a marriage built on such deceit?'

'It would be not a marriage of love but of control, which you know I prefer. I could bend him to the whim of our clan and influence his decisions with ease to benefit our own interests.' The words sounded as cold and heartless as she had intended.

Catriona sucked in a breath. 'Sister,' she replied. 'Surely, you cannot be truly considering this.'

'Aye,' she countered. 'I am. I know I shall never marry for love. Father and Royce made sure of that,' she added, her words anchored in the hard steely resentment she still felt about what had happened with Jeremiah—*to* Jeremiah— because of them.

What may have been sympathy and regret flickered briefly in Royce's eyes before a muscle worked in his jaw. He held her stare. 'Then, if that is what you wish, I will support it. But I would encourage you to spend more time with him and with your thoughts about it before you officially choose such a course. Living a lie could be hard, even for someone such as you.'

His words cut her, deeply. Emotion tightened her throat, and she couldn't move. Catriona and Rolf watched her, waiting, while Royce pushed back from the table. 'Thank you for breakfast, sister. Brother, I shall see you on the field.'

He didn't acknowledge Susanna before he walked away, which was just as well. Any further words from him might have made her cry. *This* was the Royce she did not like. When they fought, they resorted to this role between them: he became like her father and she the spoiled daughter. And, as with every time it had happened before, there were no winners. And in the middle was Rolf—and now Catriona, since she had re-joined their family.

'He did not mean it,' Rolf offered, reaching his open hand across the table to her. The familiar refrain almost made her smile. This is what he always did. He tried to mend and soften whatever blows were made and tried to make her smile.

She reached across and took his hand and smiled back. 'And as you well know, he did, and that is all right, brother. Perhaps I deserved it.'

He squeezed her hand. 'Nay. That is just an old wound that never heals.'

Catriona set her hand atop theirs. 'But perhaps this could be the year it does.'

'Unless your future wee babe has the ability to unwind the past, I do not think such is possible,' Susanna teased.

Catriona shrugged. 'Perhaps not my bairn, but maybe Royce and Iona's. Seeing his wee babe in his arms next spring might change everything for him—and for you.'

'Let us hope you are right, sister,' Susanna offered, smiling upon her siblings.

Chapter Thirteen

Rowan rode through the open field and then back on the well-kept road leading up to the massive looming dark grey stone entity that was Loch's End. The trees were golden and mystical against the gothic style castle now that the first few days of November had arrived. The ethereal early morning light, dewy green grass, and crisp autumn air ignited his senses, making him even more alert and in tune with his surroundings than he already was. Even though the invitation to visit Loch's End so soon after the Tournament of Champions had surprised him, realising the invitation had come from Royce and his brother rather than Susanna had shocked him more. It had also set him on alert. High alert. So much so that Hugh had insisted on joining him for this visit, and Rowan had been grateful for the unsolicited offer. Something was off about the invitation, but Rowan didn't know what it was—yet.

His gaze scanned the horizon as the horses slowed to a canter, and he took in all the new sights and sounds of the Cameron estate. It had changed much since he visited many years ago. The Camerons didn't go around inviting just anyone into their lair, and usually there was a reason for doing so. This invitation had been vague, sudden, and without cause. Yet another reason Rowan's hackles were raised. The Camerons always had an underlying motivation for everything, and it was best to remember that.

'Seems we are not the only guests this morn,' Hugh said under his breath as they neared the barn. Rowan cut his eyes to where Hugh nodded and spied several stable boys hard at work brushing down horses that had just arrived and readying them for any future journeys. The various tartans and saddle types spoke to the variety of clansmen that had beat them to this gathering. His pulse increased at the sight of the red, navy, and green tartan on a dark stallion.

Devil's blood.

The MacDonalds.

His horse neighed and yanked on the reins to loosen Rowan's fierce grip.

'Easy, my laird,' Hugh offered. 'We don't know who it is yet.'

'I do,' he replied, his jaw tight. 'I can feel it in my bones. It's him. Audric's here.'

'Well, then, you best set to controlling your temper now. This could be a test. The Camerons may be setting you up to see just how capable or incapable you are as laird—and as their future brother-in-law.'

He scoffed. 'I don't plan to be one, so it is of no consequence.'

'Breaking your word already?' Hugh replied, patting his stallion's mane as he shifted on his hooves, eager to keep moving.

'Nay,' he replied. He'd never achieve his revenge if he messed up their scheme so early on. 'Perhaps I should be grateful for having spied his arrival now rather than in the foyer.'

'I know I am. I didn't have enough oats this morn to

hold you back from killing your mortal enemy.' Hugh stifled an exaggerated yawn and smirked.

Rowan clapped his trusted soldier and friend on the
shoulder. 'Point taken. I will not kill him…today.' He
shrugged. 'At least I do not plan to.'

'Just the words I hoped to hear, my laird.'

They continued, dismounted, and handed off their steeds
to the stable boys. Then, they headed to the main entrance,
climbing the large stone stairs two at a time. After being
greeted by several servants, who took their coats and
gloves, the men were escorted into a banquet hall, which
if memory served was where they held their large, crushing seasonal balls, one in summer and one closer to the fes-
tive season. As he scanned the room, he realised quickly
what the Cameron brothers had done, and he cursed under
his breath.

'Steady,' Hugh murmured, no doubt also realising what
the brothers had done.

They had created a 'husband market' for their sister
Susanna. Every man in the room was an eligible laird or
the father of one. And no doubt every man here was now
aware of it and in the same predicament Rowan was. Although insulted by being invited here under false pretences,
he couldn't show how he felt or merely leave. Otherwise,
he would be insulting the Camerons and have a target on
his back. And once you were in the crosshairs of the Camerons, there were few places to hide.

He shifted on his feet and commanded himself to hold
his open stance and position of power rather than crossing
his arms against his chest despite the annoyance he felt.

As always, the Camerons were scheming and had an
underlying motive for everything. They had seamlessly

created a situation in which they had the advantage. He fisted his hands by his side. He wondered if Susanna knew of what they had done and dared not warn him. His irritation with her intensified.

Until he saw her coming down the stairs. Dressed in a dark gown with her Cameron tartan draped gracefully across her torso and secured with a large brooch, she stole everyone's attention, including his. Her gaze took in her surroundings, her eyes widening and smile straining as she realised what he had: she was being made a fool.

While the men here were being offered up as some sort of husband market, she was also being shown off like a prize mare. The cords of her neck stood out as she sucked in a breath and released it. Rolf greeted her at the last stair and took her hand to help her down, whispering something in her ear. The tension in her face softened briefly before her gaze flicked over to Royce and tightened once more.

Evidently, she was just as surprised by this gathering as Rowan was, and he felt sorry for her. It offered a distraction as Royce began speaking.

'Thank you all for accepting my last-minute invitations, gentleman. My brother and I thought this the most efficient way for selecting a match for our sister, Susanna. We hope you enjoy your day on Loch's End. Please make yourself at home here and spend some time with our lovely sister. If you have need to discuss any matters with my brother or me, we will be available.' He then had the audacity to smile.

Saints be. The man had nerve. Rowan dared a glance at Susanna.

Colour rose in her neck, easing its way into the apples of her cheeks. Instead of making her look mottled and upset, the added colour made her more beautiful, and Rowan's attraction and feelings of the eve of the Tournament flickered and ignited in him once more. That had been the last time he'd seen her, and he realised he had—missed her. It was an altogether odd and unexpected feeling.

Her gaze met his and the utter agony in her face cut him to the quick. If he'd wondered if she'd had any inkling of what her brothers were planning, he had no doubt as to her ignorance of it now. Such embarrassment and anguish could not be manufactured, even in Susanna. She was capable of many things, but that emotional fabrication she was not. He thought about going to her, but the young Laird Macpherson made his way to her, unfettered by the circumstances of this gathering.

The lad had no idea what he was up against.

'Campbell,' a man called out across the room.

Every nerve and drop of blood in Rowan's body stopped and froze at the sound of Laird Audric MacDonald's voice. The room fell silent, all conversations coming to an abrupt halt as everyone's gazes rested on the two of them, despite the number of people in the room. The man had nerve calling out to him, but Audric always had nerve—and a flair for the brute drama of cruelty. In a moment, the past overtook Rowan.

The memory of Anna's death, the smell of blood, the sounds of her last exhale in his arms, and the hot rage of anger and grief he'd felt then flooded his senses. His pulse surged back at twice the pace of before. His hands rested on his leather waist belt. The old man wasn't far. His pale blue eyes, long white hair, and smirk of a smile were in this room, so close that Rowan could imagine killing him—finally. In a matter of seconds, Rowan could pull the blade from his belt, throw it, and watch it land in the brute's chest or neck.

His fingers twined around the cool worn handle easily, his mouth watering at the thought of such sweet bliss.

It would be so easy.

And it would feel so good.

Rowan could watch the old laird fall to his knees and know it was over. Finally, over.

For Anna.

For our son.

For their memories.

And the daily agony of guilt and grief he woke to each morn would cease.

His grip tightened, his breaths became shallow, and his hand slid further down the hilt, his index finger skimming the cool blade.

'Think of Rosa,' Hugh murmured low, resting his hand on Rowan's forearm.

Rowan blinked and came back to the present. Lifting his gaze, he found Susanna. Her features were tight and the soft blush of before was now darker and higher in her cheeks. The emotion in her bright blue eyes was unmistakable to anyone who knew her, and it held him transfixed. With a subtle shake of her head, some of the anger coursing through Rowan abated. She was warning him. This was a trap set by her bothers, and he'd not fall for it. Rowan breathed, counted down from five, and was able to take in his surroundings with more distance and clarity. His fingers tingled with awareness as his pulse slowed, and he could smell the subtle hints of horse, earth, men, and the remnants of a morning meal hovering in the air.

Emotion wasn't flooding his reason as it had been moments before. He took in the scene with fresh eyes. The gazes of everyone in the room were upon him and Audric as if *they* were the main attraction and event for the gathering this morn, not the announced meeting with Susanna and possible suitors to determine her future husband.

His stomach lurched.

Maybe they were. He gripped his sword anew. Anger washed over him again at the realisation that he was meant to be made a fool.

Was *this* Royce's plan all along? A way to bring him down amongst his peers and secure his hold over the clans in the Highlands while also finding a husband for Susanna. Rowan shifted on his feet and his mouth gaped open a measure before he clamped it shut and cursed under his breath.

Saints be.

He had not even considered Royce capable of such a diabolical plan. Perhaps Rowan was getting soft after being holed up in Argyll Castle and his forge the last four years since Anna's death. Either way, he had to find a way through this without losing his self-respect or standing with the clans, ruining his secret arrangement with Susanna, or ending up dead.

With Audric and the scene before him, it was a rather tall order.

But not insurmountable. He was known for his creative battle strategy. It was his greatest asset and never failed him. It was emotion that got him in trouble.

Rowan's gaze flitted back to Susanna, and she nodded to him as if she were following his logic and affirming that this *was* contrived, a test, and perhaps little more than a game to her brothers. He sent her a small smirk, and her eyes widened briefly.

Well, he would give them a show to remember.

And he would learn a few things for himself while he

was at it. He did still plan to have his revenge on Audric but it wouldn't be now.

Not yet.

Despite how he desired to taste the sweetness of such vengeance, it would have to wait for another day when not every leader in the Highlands was present.

Rowan took a heavy step forward towards Audric, and then another, the speed of his movements picking up slightly as he advanced. His hand rested on his weapon's belt, and he could hear the echo of Hugh following him close behind. Fellow lairds and their fathers parted to make way for their advance, some knew well not to interfere while others may have just been eager to see how the scene would play out. Everyone knew what Rowan had lost four years ago.

Everyone also knew that one day such vengeance against Audric would come due.

To his credit, the old man never moved as Rowan approached, not even a shift in his stance. Laird Audric MacDonald's gaze never wavered, and their intense glare between each other was locked in. Emotion tugged at Rowan, reminding him he could still take his vengeance now. He didn't need to wait. This moment could end the agony of grief and guilt that still weighed down his every step and every breath.

Think of Rosa.

Hugh's words from earlier echoed in Rowan's mind like a cadence and a motto with each step. Rowan stopped one boot length away from Audric, so close he could smell the man's stench from his ride here and what may have been dung on his boots.

'MacDonald,' Rowan replied loudly. 'Such a surprise to

see you here today. Are you looking to take a new bride?'
he said, sarcasm evident in his tone.

Audric laughed. 'Nay. I desire no further shackles for
this lifetime, but my son Devlin is in dire need of settling
down and taking roots.'

'Oh? I had no idea you had become…reacquainted.'
Rowan made an exaggerated effort to look behind and
around Audric for his son Devlin. 'Is he here?' he added.

Audric's lip lifted in what almost appeared to be a snarl
rather than an answer, and a quiver of pleasure rolled
through Rowan making his toes and fingertips tingle. He
had pricked a nerve, knowing fully Devlin was not here
and that he still had no interest in returning to his father's
fold at Clan MacDonald to be the next laird. Their falling out two years ago over the safety of Rowan's nephew,
William, who happened to also be Audric's grandson, had
never mended. In fact, Devlin had resided with his sister
Fiona, his brother-in-law and then laird of Campbell, Rowan's brother Brandon, and his nephew at Argyll Castle. He
had chosen to live on Campbell lands for some time before
setting out on his own as a soldier to find his own path
away from his abusive father and laird.

A fact everyone else in this room most likely also knew.
Rowan's barb had landed well, and he could not have been
happier to see Audric's anger bubbling up to the surface.

The room was stone silent. Rowan and Audric stared at
one another, and no one moved.

'Perhaps you gentlemen could continue your…er…dis-
cussion, at another time?' Royce said, breaking the extended silence. His loud baritone echoed amongst the
rafters. A hint of irritation clipped his words as he ap-

proached them, his boots echoed off the stone floors, matching his staccato tone.

His scheme had not worked. Not yet anyway.

Rowan almost smiled. Almost.

'Audric?' Royce added. 'Rolf and I would like to speak with you about Devlin and his...intentions. Join us in the study?'

'Aye,' Audric answered, not breaking his heavy stare with Rowan, 'Campbell and I will settle this at another time.'

'Aye,' Rowan replied, his tone menacing, 'we will.'

Audric followed Royce out of the room and into the study, where the door closed with a slam.

Susanna threaded through the crowd to Rowan, ignoring a few enquiries from some younger lads who seemed oblivious to her nature. He smirked as she approached him and offered her arm to him. 'Care for a walk in the gardens, my laird? I find I am in dire need of fresh air.'

He tucked her arm into his own and rested his hand firmly upon it.

'Shall I fetch your cloak, my lady?'

'Nay. I feel overheated and would appreciate the cool, sir.' A sight tremble escaped her lips on sir. Rowan squeezed her arm lightly.

Even for a woman with the steel nerves of Susanna, that exchange had proved a bit too much for her as it had for him.

Rowan nodded to Hugh before they departed, and his trusted soldier remained in the room, no doubt watching and taking in information as he saw it and heard it to report to Rowan later. Rowan and Susanna kept silent as they travelled through the crowd and headed to the main doors to the large, covered walkway leading to the gardens. Susanna's lady's maid and in this case chaperone, Tilly, fell in step behind them and followed at a respectable distance but was always within sight and sound of them, her gentle hum a reminder of her presence. He remembered Tilly from when he was a boy and smirked. She was a lax chaperone from what Rowan remembered, and he was grateful for it. He and Susanna had much to discuss, and Tilly could be trusted, no matter what she heard.

Rowan sucked in the cool, crisp air as it hit his face and almost lifted his cheeks to the sun like a child grateful for deliverance. And he was. He had faced down the man who had killed his wife and son and resisted the urge to slaughter him like an animal in a group of his peers. Three years ago, he might have stabbed the man right then and there in front of everyone and accepted his fate. Today, he had approached the situation with as clear of a head as he could and had not risen to the bait.

Rowan guided Susanna along the manicured path of stone and all the lush green shrubbery around it. Most of the flowers had died out long ago with autumn upon them and winter approaching. He stared out along the cool, still waters of the dark loch. His pulse slowed to the rhythmic sway of the material of Susanna's gown brushing against his legs and the shift of her body into his with each step forward.

'Anna would be proud of you,' she said quietly.

Rowan's steps faltered before he settled back in the steady cadence.

Are you?

The thought popped into his head unbidden, and he frowned. Why did he care whether Susanna was proud of him? He hadn't kept his cool for her—well, he had partly for her because of their agreement but mostly he'd done it for Rosa and the clan. He couldn't cause them further havoc. And it wasn't the right moment to take his revenge. His revenge would be a private rather than public act. He needed to kill the man alone.

Hell, he dreamed of it.

She stopped and faced him. 'I swear to you that I didn't know what they were up to this morn until I came down those stairs. When I realised why everyone was there and saw Audric and then you, I—' she paused'—I knew it was too late to do anything. And I was embarrassed.'

Rowan nodded. 'Aye. I know. Your surprise was evident.'

'Royce told me to dress nicely as we would be having company, and I was to greet them, but he said nothing of me being shown off like a filly at market.' She released Rowan's arm and rubbed her own absently, the colour rising high in her cheeks again. 'You would think after what happened to Catriona at the Grassmarket, he would have some awareness of what it looked like to everyone, but it seems not. What a fool,' she muttered, looking away and out along the meadow.

'If it is of any consolation, I think I was the main attraction today, not you,' he offered.

'You?' She faced him, narrowing her gaze.

'Aye. Imagine what a scene me killing the man that murdered my wife and son would be in front of all the most respected and powerful men of the area. And with such an event, he would have grounds as well as the opportunity, as would the other clan leaders, to make a move to challenge our reign over our people and perhaps conquer us all together and divide up the spoils.'

'And why would my brother do that? He has enough to contend with based on what you and I have both overheard in the last few weeks.'

He came closer and squeezed her shoulders. 'That is exactly it. It is because of his worries that he is being so extreme.'

Susanna shook her head. 'I don't follow your meaning.'

His hands dropped away in exasperation. Surely, she could see what he could, but perhaps the fact that Royce was her brother kept her from seeing him as the strategist Rowan always had.

'Your brother is not daft, Susanna. If he is worrying about maintaining his hold over the Highlands, what better way to do that than to absorb another clan with vast resources and land, such as my own. And if he is being threatened by another laird, he could offer them a shared portion of it as an olive branch to convert their relationship into a strong alliance.'

She stilled, her realisation of the danger of the situation settled in her now pale cheeks, the colour draining away as he spoke.

Rowan paced, walking away from her and staring far off into the loch. 'But why now?' he wondered aloud. 'If anything, I should be seen as far stronger to him than before. At the Tournament, I bested men far younger as well as those far wiser, and I have been seen by the masses as fit and capable. I am no longer the crumbling, grief-stricken man of years ago that was stripped of his title. It makes little sense.'

An unladylike curse yanked Rowan from his study of a pair of starlings chasing one another across the sky.

'It is my doing,' she said.

Rowan stilled, his blood chilling with Susanna's words. He turned slowly to find she was right behind him, close enough to touch. 'Your doing?' he asked.

'Aye,' she added with a sigh. 'Although I never imagined *this* would happen.'

'Explain,' he replied, resting his arms along his waist belt.

'I may have told my brothers of my interest in you as a husband too prematurely while we were at the Tournament. They wondered why I was spending any time with you at all, and I told them it was in an effort to help further our cause. I did not think they would react in such a way.'

'And?' he prodded, taking a step closer. Why this woman always had to swing between vexing him and driving him wild with desire, he didn't know. Minutes ago he'd wanted to kiss her, now—now he wasn't sure what he wanted except for answers.

'I told them you were weak and that I could control you because of your—past illness, and that I felt I could influence you to do as I and they might wish you to, much like we spoke of that first night in the forge. It was a way to make my interest and time spent with you at the Tournament believable. It was simply strategy to support our ruse, like we had agreed.' To her credit, her bright blue eyes held his and didn't drop away.

'And is that what you truly believe about me now?' he asked, his words sharp and menacing. Somehow before when she'd said it in the forge that night weeks ago, the idea of her perceiving him as weak had not bothered him, for he hadn't cared about her opinion or cared enough to challenge or correct her. But now, what she truly thought of him mattered, and he had to know the truth of it to move forward.

She didn't answer but sniffed and swallowed.

'Well, do you, Susanna? I have a right to know if you truly believe me to be the weak broken man that you told them I am. Is it part of the ruse or not?' he asked again, stepping closer to her, needing to know her answer more than he wished to admit. What she thought of him mattered. They were in this hellish agreement together, and he needed to know just how much of a fool he had been and whether she could be trusted at all. He loomed over her petite form, his pulse and breathing rate increasing as he waited. She shivered slightly, but Rowan didn't know if it was from the cold, from him, or both.

'I used to,' she answered, holding her gaze.

'Used to?' he countered, her honesty a surprise.

'Aye. When I first came to see you in the forge that night, I thought you were weaker and could be manipulated easily.'

'And now you do not?'

'Nay. I realised it is restraint, not the weakness I first believed, that I see in you now. And that—that is true power.'

He feared he might blow over with the first soft breeze. Whatever he believed she might say, he hadn't been prepared for those words. He turned away from her and walked off the garden path and into the lush meadow, needing the air and space to allow his body and nerves to settle. This was turning into a far different day than he expected.

And he didn't know if he wished to kiss Susanna or flee from her and the words she had spoken. While his gut told him it was the truth of how he felt, it brought up the array of guilt, shame, and pride he often felt when he thought of where he had been years ago after the death of Anna and his son and where he was now as a restored laird and father to Rosa.

He felt pinned in a vice, unable to wiggle free and unable to shed the past. Perhaps he was never meant to. If he forgot how lost he had become, it might happen again, and he never wished to return to that place of grief and madness ever.

A soft breeze blew, and he smelled a hint of violet in the air and smiled despite himself. The grass rustled next to him as Susanna approached.

'Tilly will be none too happy with you dragging that gown through the heavy dew this morn,' he said, still staring out at the loch. 'I was pleased to see you are still under her care.'

Susanna chuckled. 'She is oft displeased with me, so this shall be no different. And aye, I am lucky to have her.' She settled in quietly next to him, looking out. 'I meant what I said,' she said quietly. 'You are changed.'

He shifted on his feet, the discomfort growing in his gut. 'I am not, Susanna. I am the same man on the brink of madness.' He faced her, taking in the lovely full bloom of her in the wake of the soft light kissing along the edges of her face. Even after the strain of the morn, she was beautiful.

She stepped towards him, her heavy gown sliding over the tip of his boot. 'You do not seem so to me.' Her gaze raked over his face, and she studied him. 'I remember you then.'

His chest tightened under her expectations. 'You see what I show you.'

'Then what do you hide from me?' she asked.

He stared out and inhaled some steadying breaths through his nose. He focused on a large tree on the edge of the loch, leaning heavily over the water, struggling to hold its roots, much like him. 'Every day, I wake with the same rage in me. The anger has not passed or lessened. But each morn I greet and acknowledge that rage within me just as I acknowledge the hope and light and goodness of my daughter and the other blessings in my life. And each day, I choose that light over the anger, rage, and darkness, but it is always there. Close, ready to be set free, like a trapped wolf with its snapping jowls eying its prey before it has freed itself from its irons.'

Her hand wrapped around the clenched fist at his side, her fingers working to open his hand, each one sliding along his own slowly, until she wove her cool petite fingers through them. His breath caught at the intimate contact as if she had pressed her full body along his own and he shuddered but still dared not meet her gaze.

'When Jeremiah died, I retreated from everyone and let my rage soar. I cut down everything and everyone in my wake, and it felt…so good,' she began. 'I did not eat or sleep, but the anger and rage fuelled me until I was a shell of who I was and collapsed one day. I slept for days and then tried to live again. But it was so hard…' she paused. '…Pretending that the world was a place I wished to be in without him was a farce, so I focused on controlling everything and everyone else. I annihilated everyone in my path who would not bend to my will.'

Gooseflesh rose along his skin. How many of those thoughts had he also had? How many of those feelings had he also struggled with?

They were kindred spirits in their loss, and her vulnerability in sharing such with him surprised him as much as it unnerved him. Perhaps she had changed too. The Susanna of old had never been comfortable with speaking of her emotions. She hid them well much like she often hid within her cloak.

'I can honestly say,' she said turning to him, her eyes glistening with unshed tears as their gazes met, 'that if the man who slew Jeremiah on that battlefield had stood before me this morn, I would have cut him from throat to navel.' A tear slid down her cheek as her voice broke. 'The fact that you did not makes you a far better person than me. I want you to know that.'

Without thinking, he leaned closer, wiping away her tear, his thumb lingering along her soft, warm cheek. He kissed her gently on the other cheek and she trembled against him. 'Don't think I didn't imagine it,' he said with a chuckle. 'I just didn't wish to mess up your lovely carpets.'

She half choked on a sob as she laughed, and he felt a thrill in comforting her and in having her so close. It was a feeling he had not had in such a long time that he stilled, not sure whether he should trust it or not.

When she turned her lips to his and kissed him in a soft feathering whisper of a caress, he responded in kind, his mouth lingering over hers.

A cough sounded from behind them.

They both stilled and stepped back to create some semblance of distance between them. Rowan was startled to remember where he was after being forcefully yanked back to the present.

Devil's blood. He had forgotten they were in public. He risked a glance behind them expecting to see Tilly sending a chilling look of disapproval upon them both. Instantly, his shoulders dropped in relief when he saw only Hugh.

'Hugh,' Rowan said clearing his throat.

Susanna muttered under her breath and turned to face the

man as well. She smoothed her gown and set a forced smile to her lips. 'Are you enjoying the view from the gardens?' she asked loudly, so she could be heard by anyone else passing by.

Hugh pressed his lips together to smother a smirk. 'Aye, my lady. 'tis a fine view from here.'

Rowan frowned at him, fully aware of his friend's meaning since he had interrupted his kiss with Susanna.

Hugh cleared his throat. 'Shall we return, my laird?'

'Aye,' Rowan replied without hesitation 'I believe Lady Cameron and I have concluded our—erm—discussions for today, have we not?' *Curses.* He sounded like a dolt.

She set a glare on him in reply. 'I suppose so, my laird. For now.'

Rowan swallowed hard and heat rose along his throat. He offered his arm to guide her, and they began the small climb back up the sloping hillside.

'Have them ready the horses for us,' Rowan called to Hugh, a touch too loudly.

Hugh nodded. 'Already done. We can depart when you are ready.'

Of course, they were. Hugh often knew Rowan better than he knew himself and was able to anticipate many of his needs.

'You will leave without incident?' she asked under her breath as they walked.

'Aye. For now. When shall we meet next?'

'Here at the Holiday Ball, my laird. When your overt wooing is to truly begin. Although there may be whisperings of that beginning today,' she added, scanning the area around them.

'Aye. I blame myself. It was reckless to be out here alone with only your maid. Where did Tilly go?' he asked.

Susanna shrugged. 'I do not know.'

'We must be more careful. Otherwise, you may be found compromised and we may be truly stuck with one another,' he teased with a whisper as they reached the edge of the garden path again.

'There you are, my lady,' Tilly exclaimed. 'Mr. Hugh and I have been all about looking for ye.'

'I am fine, Tilly,' Susanna began, exasperated, leaving Rowan's jest unanswered.

As they walked away, a winkling of wonder stirred in Rowan's gut. Could Susanna have changed too?

He frowned and headed to the stables reflecting on what he'd admitted to her: she saw what he allowed her to see, and he hadn't really changed. Perhaps she did the same and only showed him the bits she had wanted to this morn and hadn't really changed either.

Or had she?

While he wanted to believe Susanna might truly care for him, he stilled as he remembered what she had said to him that first night in the forge: *'It is either you or my family, and as you well know, I will always choose them.'*

And he knew deep down that her words were true.

Chapter Fourteen

Susanna paced in her chambers.

'Ye will wear a hole in this very floor, my lady, if ye are not careful,' said Tilly, glancing up from where she was re-organising Susanna's wardrobe. That single grey eyebrow zeroed in on Susanna as Tilly shifted gowns about on their hangers.

'I can only hope so,' Susanna replied, making her steps louder. 'That way my brothers' prize mare will be injured and unable to be brought out to market again.'

'My lady,' said Tilly with an edge of sympathy and what may have been understanding in her voice, which set Susanna on edge. Kindness simply wouldn't do right now. Tilly set aside a lush goldenrod gown on Susanna's bed for her to consider.

'Throw it out,' Susanna sniped, desperate to cling to her anger to avoid the tears that might replace it. 'I despise yellow.'

Tilly sighed and patiently placed the gown on the tee-tering pile of rejected dresses on the bench seat near the large windows overlooking the meadows. 'Ye seem to de-spise them all today, my lady, but ye must wear something special for the upcoming Holiday Ball here at Loch's End, especially if ye hope to marry before the year is through.'

'Must I?' She cast a wicked smile at her maid. 'Perhaps I shall only wear a cloak with nothing beneath and shock them all. That will put an end to this marriage nonsense. Would it not?'

Her maid gasped and muttered something unintelligible under her breath before returning to the wardrobe. Susanna knew she was being a brat among other things, but she was so angry. Nothing would abate her anger until she could unleash it upon her brothers after the stunt they pulled this morn. And she couldn't do that until the last of their guests departed. Many of them lingered well into the afternoon, taking advantage of the time to meet with her brothers and offer terms for a possible union with her.

She wanted to scream and then retch all over the pile of glorious rainbow-coloured gowns Tilly had sorted through. Not only had her brothers treated her like livestock to be bartered over at a market rather than a person, they had set a trap that had almost ended in Rowan's humiliation as well.

She cursed. All because she had told them why she had set her attentions upon Rowan, in order to protect her own plan to discover their ridiculous secrets. *Ach*. It had all worked against her. Even in her exchange with Rowan today when she told him she believed he had changed, she'd revealed more than she'd wished to about losing Jeremiah, making herself vulnerable to him.

She shuddered. She had even cried. And she hated being vulnerable to anyone, even her family. To know she had revealed such feelings and intimacies with him of all people, especially after their past…

Blast.

She wrung her hands.

Then, he had been so—gentle with her. And his kiss had set her toes tingling, which made it worse. Then Hugh caught them kissing. She huffed in frustration and put her head in her hands. She was losing control of the situation. If her brothers would just tell her the truth, she could abandon her plan, create some distance between her and Rowan, and get back to her real life rather than this false one.

Rowan.

She touched her fingertips to her lips, remembering the tender touch of his own there, and the way their hands had fit together as sweetly as they had when they were young. All of it was making her addled and unfocused. She pulled the pins from her hair, letting her long locks fall free. Sighing in relief, she massaged her scalp. She could always think better when her hair wasn't bound. As she began pacing once more, Tilly released an exaggerated sigh, which Susanna ignored.

'Shall we speak of ye and Rowan?' she asked lightly.

'Oh, Tilly, please. I beg you. Nay.'

'Do not "Oh, Tilly" me, my lass. Ye are playing with fire, ye are, just like when ye were young. Ye two have always been, well, reckless with one another.'

Had they?

'What do you mean?' she asked, pausing her steps.

She shrugged and held up a lavender gown to Susanna.

Susanna made a fake retching noise in reply, and Tilly placed it on the discarded pile of gowns, rolled her eyes, and continued. 'What I mean is ye have an intense connection. Always have. Be careful. He is still recovering from losing his wife, is he not?'

'Aye.'

'And ye are still mourning yer Jeremiah, despite the time that has passed.'

'Aye. But I still do not understand?'

'Grief and loneliness can create a heady combination, especially when ye mix in the history of a past courtship. Do not get lost in it. That is all.'

Susanna scoffed and glanced away, her pulse picking up a bit of speed over her maid's warning. 'That is ridiculous, Tilly. You have nothing to worry over,' Susanna responded, perhaps too quickly and with too much certainty, as Tilly cut her a quizzical look.

'That, my dear, is *exactly* what I mean. Do not be so dismissive of it as a possibility. Be careful. I saw the way ye two were looking at each other.' She made a tsking sound and shook her head.

Before Susanna could counter Tilly's reply, the sounds of horses departing outside interrupted her, and she rushed to the window to look out. Three more men were leaving by horse. *Praise be.* While she didn't know if they were the last of their guests from this morn, she hoped they were. Heavy footfalls up the stairs and a loud knock at her chamber door confirmed they had been. If Royce thought he could give her a piece of his mind right now, he was mistaken. Susanna rushed to the door, ignoring Tilly's protests to wait.

Flinging the door open, Susanna saw Rolf standing with his fisted hand high in the air, preparing to knock again. His eyes were wide and pleading.

'I'm sorry,' he spat out softly before she could utter a sound, deflating her anger before she'd had a chance to expel it, much like her younger brother always did.

Her shoulders sagged, and she leaned on the door. 'Come in,' she replied.

Tilly nodded to them and departed through Susanna's chambers to leave them to their discussion.

Susanna and Rolf settled onto the large settee.

'For?' Susanna prompted, tucking her legs beneath her, and leaning her elbow on the back of the plush lavender fabric lining the couch. She refused to make this too easy for him. Not after all she'd been through today.

He stared back at her blankly, the strains of the day evident in his rumpled tunic and rather harried expression, both unusual for her carefree brother.

'You said you were sorry,' she explained. 'What are you sorry for? Treating me like I was a sheep at market? Not telling me you were planning to do so? Not having a backbone and standing up to our brother? Putting Rowan in a position where he might kill Audric and lose everything?'

Rolf squirmed with each question, his discomfort growing. Once she ceased her questions, he scrubbed a hand through his hair, ruffling it like he often did as a boy when he was thinking. Then he ran his hand down his face with a sigh. 'Everything?' he said almost like a question of his own rather than an answer to hers.

'Everything?' she mimicked him.

'Aye,' he replied with more certainty as he sat up straighter and faced her, setting his elbow on the back of the settee as well. 'You know what he is like, Susanna.'

She scoffed. 'Aye. And?'

'And despite how he *has* changed since Lismore and marrying Iona, he can still be this force—this immovable and oft unreasonable boulder one cannot persuade or shift about some things. This is one of them.'

She chuckled. 'Aye, I also know that. But this morn? Rolf, why did you not warn me? Not one single word from you. I was humiliated.' Tears heated the back of her eyes, despite herself, which angered her more. Why was she so emotional today?

Blast.

Her brother was her beacon of safety, that was why. His betrayal cut deeply. Far more deeply than Royce's.

He reached out and squeezed her forearm. 'I should have. I couldn't find the words to tell you, and I also hoped—' he let go of her arm and rubbed the back of his neck '—I had hoped Royce would come to his senses about the whole endeavour—and about Campbell. But since you put that idea in his head about Rowan being weak and conquerable, Royce can think of little else.'

'What?' she recoiled. 'This is somehow my fault?'

He shook his head. 'Nay. I am not saying that. But you said the words that triggered this plan of his.'

She waited.

He continued. 'He said today would serve multiple purposes. One, to see who wanted to be in a union with us by marrying you.' He continued counting on his fingers. 'Two, how well Campbell was by whether he would rise to the bait of Audric being here or not. And three, if he attacked Audric, we would know just how weak he was and could formulate a plan to overtake his clan with you as his bride.'

The words hung in the air. Rancid sounds and syllables she wished to open the window to let out. But she couldn't unhear them. Rowan had been right on all counts about what her brothers had done to her and him, and it pained her. Deeply.

'Why did you not stand up to him? Tell him what a fool-hardy plan this was?'

'As I explained, Susanna, you know Royce. He cannot back down once his hackles are up. And right now, with everything so…' he paused, searching for the right words, and then continued, '…delicate, he will listen to no one. I have tried.'

She clutched his hand in his lap. 'And what is this thing that makes me suddenly marrying so necessary and everything else so "delicate", as you say? Tell me, brother. I can help.'

He squeezed her hand and then pulled it away. 'Nay. You cannot. And I cannot tell you. You must trust us.'

'After today, you want for me to trust you both?' she scoffed. 'What happened to Royce no longer keeping secrets as he promised when he returned from Lismore? And about the two of us, you and me, *never* keeping secrets from each other, ever?'

'Susanna,' he replied, the agony evident in his tone and strained jaw. 'I know it is an unreasonable request, but we are in a precarious position, and caution is our best option over the coming months. The future of our family and the clan's future are at stake. We cannot afford a misstep.' He kissed her cheek, rose from his seat, and headed to the door.

'Brother, just tell me. You leaving me in the shadows of the situation may cause the very misstep you fear.' She pleaded with him one last time, the desperation making her voice high and almost shrill.

Although Rolf's steps briefly faltered, he didn't stop. He left the room. Susanna groaned in frustration, pounding the pillow on the settee until she was too weary to continue.

Chapter Fifteen

'You are late,' Rowan complained, emerging from behind his favourite pairing of trees in the rowan grove.

'And you are becoming predictable,' she countered, lowering her cloak hood, and swinging around the trunk of the tree just across from where he had hidden himself. Her hair was loose and swayed out around her in an arc. For a moment she seemed a young lass to him, sending a ripple of memory through him. The carefree action made him long for something else he didn't wish to name, so he batted it away.

'Because I continue to be irritated by having to wait for you?' he said, gesturing to the same boulder they had met at before to formulate their initial strategy, which needed some adjustments based on how the gathering at Loch's End had played out.

She made a face at him as she followed him. 'Nay. You disguised yourself behind the same pairing of trees. Why?'

He stiffened. Was he so predictable? Had he hidden behind the same trees each time they met here?

He cursed himself. Surely not. Today would be challenging on its own, but managing Susanna's snipes would make it even worse. He sent her a withering look to let her know he was not to be trifled with today.

'You are no fun, Rowan Campbell. It is a glorious morn, and I had a blissful ride here. What is there to grouse about so early?'

Evidently his withering look was not what it used to be. 'It is a glorious morn, but we have lost some of it because someone—' he replied.

She cut him off and lifted her palm. 'Because I was late. Blah, blah, blah. Let us begin, so we can get this meeting concluded.' She sat upon the boulder, settling herself too close to him.

He shifted away.

'I do not bite,' she teased.

Not yet.

He ignored her and unrolled the parchment. Together they placed rocks upon the corners to keep it flat. She leaned over it, reading the newest additions and findings to their scheme. Her hair slipped from underneath the hood of her dark cloak and over her shoulder, blocking his view. He reached his hand out to move it aside and found his fingertips lingering along the silken strands. Her gaze met his.

'Can you not tie back your hair? I cannot see,' he griped.

'My, you are in a mood today, my laird. I have never heard anyone so angry about my hair before.' She leaned back with a smirk and gathered her hair quickly, twisting it into a knot at the nape of her neck. The swift and graceful movements seized his attention, and he could not look away. Her hands fell, resting in her lap, and she studied him with concern. 'Something is wrong. What is it?'

'Nothing I wish to discuss with you,' he replied, his words sharper than he intended.

When she recoiled slightly, he softened. 'I did not sleep well,' he added in a lower voice and glanced back to the parchment, running a smooth palm over it. While a vast understatement, it was true.

It was just not the whole truth.

But she did not need to know it.

'Then I wish you better sleep this eve. For now, let us talk about our revised plan. What have you learned? Then I will share my own findings and see what we can piece together.'

'You share first,' he countered, unable to simply agree with her suggestion.

'I can do that,' she replied, watching him with caution. 'Seems whatever is plaguing my brothers has something to do with Royce's time on Lismore. I have heard them talking about someone named Webster. They have also traded a parcel of land to someone that also knew Webster.' She reached down her bodice, and Rowan could not help but follow her hand's movements, spying a flicker of creamy flesh and the rounded curve of a breast before she retrieved what lay hidden there. He swallowed hard and cleared his throat.

Susanna cut him a disapproving glance. 'It is the best hiding place. Do not judge.'

'Not judging. Just surprised.'

'Anna never hid anything in her bosom?' she enquired.

Why was she talking to him about this? They needed to focus. 'I've not time for this trifle. What did you learn?' he replied sharply.

She balked and shifted away from him. 'Your tone leaves something to be desired today. Shall I go, and we will meet another day? I have enough rebuke from Royce. I need not more from you.'

He closed his eyes, rubbed his brow, and sucked in a breath before opening his eyes and meeting her gaze. 'Nay. My apologies. Continue.'

She situated herself again on the boulder, and unfurled the small, rolled note on the parchment, holding it flat with her hand. 'The man's name is Chisholm. He selected a fine plot of land on the loch where one could easily dock. I made a small sketch of it here from memory. I spied it on my brother's desk before he could roll it back up. Seems suspicious, does it not? To give a man one does not know easy access to a port location such as that?'

'You made this from memory?' He leaned forward, impressed by the detail in her sketching.

She smiled. 'I mastered the art of reading upside down when I was a girl in my father's study, and I have a fine memory for visuals.'

'Good to know. I will be wary of what documents I have out if you ever darken my study door.' He smoothed his hand along the small parchment. The warmth from where it had been hidden sent a flush of desire through him, but he dashed it away. He had no time for such distractions today of all days.

'I believe the man may be planning a visit before the new year.'

'Oh?' he stilled. 'Why?'

She shrugged. 'I cannot say, but my brothers are nervous about the idea of him coming. Even Royce.'

Rowan leaned back, releasing the parchment, and it curled back up. 'Hugh said he overheard some of the other men discussing how the British are redistributing their soldiers along the Borderlands and that supply channels are being strained. Perhaps Royce wishes to get supplies from this man?'

'From Lismore? Not much is there, from what Iona has relayed to me.'

'What of neighbouring isles?'

'I cannot say, but I can find out. Iona is eager for a distraction these days with the bairn on the way making her so queasy.' She smiled. 'Royce is hoping for a son, of course, while I hope for a girl.'

A bairn. *A son.* Rowan's gut tightened. He ignored her comment, focusing on the task at hand. Only that would get him through the remaining hours of today. 'Anything else?'

'Nay,' she replied quietly. 'You?'

'The men have noticed Royce has spent time and manpower fortifying his border walls on all sides.'

'All?'

'Aye. As if he believes he has no allies and may be forced to defend his own lands alone. It is intriguing, is it not?'

'Aye. And frightening. Why would he think such? We have more alliances than anyone.'

'Makes you wonder what he believes would change that, does it not?'

'I cannot think of anything.'

Rowan sat silently. He had thought of one, but he could not say it. It was too reprehensible to utter aloud.

She leaned towards him. 'But you have thought of something. I can see it in your eyes. What is it?'

He shook his head. 'It is not possible.'

'What? Tell me. We are in this together, are we not?'

'That they have turned on us. All of us. And have secured favour with the British. Future protections in exchange for...' He couldn't finish the rest of it, but she would know what he meant.

She balked and leaned towards him. 'How dare you,' she hissed, her voice low and husky, her hands fisted. Her features flushed with anger, just as he expected they might. He would have been just as insulted.

Yet he wanted to tell her his thoughts. He didn't want to hide them from her.

He lifted his palms in supplication. 'I know, Susanna. I do not believe it either. But you asked what might cause your brothers to fear losing their alliances in the Highlands, and that is the only thing that came to mind.'

She sat back on the boulder and stared out into the grove. 'Despite all, I cannot believe either of them would manage any such arrangement. Ever.'

'I hope you are right, for there would be no turning back. Your clan would be outcasts if they pursued such a precarious route.'

'I know that. So would they. There must be another reason we cannot see yet. I cannot help but feel we are running out of time.'

'Why?'

'My gut, as illogical as it sounds for me to say it aloud.' She stared down her hands, studying the palms.

'I have made more than one decision based on instinct. And it has never failed me.' He watched her until she looked at him. 'Trust it.'

She lifted her brow and turned her body to fully face him. 'Then I shall do that now. What is wrong with you today? My gut tells me it is far more than you not sleeping well as you say.'

Deuces.

Why did she always turn him on himself? And in such an exquisite manner. It was irritating. He frowned at her, hoping it might quell her questioning. She merely lifted a brow in challenge. 'I have nowhere to be at present. Tell me. Some people say I can on occasion be a good listener.'

Did he dare?

They sat in companionable silence, neither of them pushing or prodding. Taking his own advice on trusting his gut, Rowan finally spoke.

'It is four years today…when I lost them. Anna and our son.'

He felt parched after such an admission, his mouth dry and his voice brittle as if the words had fought and crawled their way out of his throat against his will.

Perhaps they had.

She released a rather unladylike curse, and he couldn't help but chuckle.

'I am sorry, Rowan. I should have remembered before I sent you a note to meet today.'

He shook his head. 'Nay. There is no reason for you to remember. It is just a day to everyone else, but to me it is a day I can never forget. And the hours of each anniversary drag on painfully long.' He took a rock and scratched against the larger boulder. 'I merely pray to survive it each time it rolls back around.' The words felt easier now. He reminded himself that she understood his loss in her own way and that she would not judge him. Not about this, at least.

She set her hand around his own, which held the small rock. 'Truly. I am sorry. We can end our meeting. We can do this another time.'

'Nay,' he said, gripping her hand in his. 'We must make our plans for the Holiday Ball coming up at Loch's End so we can begin this pretend courtship of ours and prevent you having a horrid engagement to some other sot. I also wish to plan how I shall effectively end Audric. I have some ideas…many ideas.' He squeezed her hand and let go.

It almost felt like they were becoming friends, if nothing else, which was such an odd thing. Loss was binding them to one another in a way that their affection for each other in the past never had.

'Then let us discuss the Holiday Ball,' she said with a tone of resignation. 'I do despise such affairs, but I know this one is essential to our plan for this fake attachment of ours. How do you plan to woo me, my laird?'

'Dancing,' he said with a smile, setting the rock aside.

'Dancing?' she echoed. 'Is dancing not a normal part of the balls? How will this seem like you courting me?'

'You shall dance with no one else.' He gifted her another devilish smile.

She scoffed. 'No one else? How will that be possible?'

'I will continue to ask, and you will refuse anyone else who sets their attentions on you.'

'That would be rude.'

'Nay. That would be classic Susanna. Cold to those who mean nothing to her, fiercely loyal to those who do.'

'I see now what you are suggesting and where you are going with this, but how do I not offend any other suitors in the process? I do not wish to make more enemies for us to manage, and you lairds are a rather arrogant and delicate lot prone to having your pride pricked rather easily.' She lifted a brow at him and smirked.

'Simply show your interest in me first in a way that shall cast no doubt as to your intentions, so you will not appear to be misleading any other men with undue attentions that evening.'

'Again, how do I do that?'

'Shower *me* with your attention. It shall be easy.' He smiled at her, and she groaned.

'It will be difficult if you are so—arrogant.'

He ignored her complaint and continued. 'Oh, and you must wear a blue gown.'

She shifted and looked away. 'Can it not be another colour?'

'It could, but blue is the most stunning on you as it brings out your eyes.' He paused. 'Why can it not be blue? Do you dislike it? Now that I think on it, I cannot remember you wearing blue in quite some time.'

'It is because I choose not to.'

'Why?'

'It was Jeremiah's favourite colour on me. I have not worn it since he died,' she said softly. 'Everyone knows this. I am surprised you do not.'

'Perhaps I missed that part of our reacquaintance,' he muttered, unsure why she would believe he knew one whit about her fashion choices. 'But now that I do know this, you *must* wear blue. It will signal you have moved on. It will show everyone how serious you are about a betrothal. Your brothers and others will see the significance, and our ruse will be more than believable.' Excitement rushed through him.

'I do not know, Rowan.' Her voice was fragile now.

It was his turn to convince and support her as she just had for him. 'You can do this, Susanna. For your family, for your clan, and for yourself,' he added. 'It may even help you to heal and release some of your grief.'

She bit her lip and sat quietly. Too quietly for his liking. He moved closer to her. 'Think of all the other things you have done and survived. This will be a small thing once you commit to it.'

'Will it? It feels like a betrayal, even though it is only a dress colour.' She played with the ribbon of her cloak.

'Trice often tells me the only betrayal to those we have lost is to not live.'

Susanna narrowed her gaze at him.

Rowan shrugged. 'Some days I believe it. Other days it rings more of horse dung.'

She snorted. 'You, my laird, just said *dung* like you were five years old.'

'I did. And you laughed. I win.'

'Fine,' she relented. 'I will think upon your suggestion. Nothing more, mind you.'

He nodded. 'Fair. At the Holiday Ball, you may or may not wear blue, but you will commit to dancing with me?'

'Aye. As much as I can stand,' she agreed.

'Now, we must discuss Audric.' His body tightened instantly as he said the man's name. 'I have thought upon my revenge after we unearth this secret of yours.'

'And?'

'You will secure me an invitation to visit you at Loch's End a suitable time after the Holiday Ball, when our official "attachment" has begun. I will visit while he is there, and he will simply…vanish.'

'Vanish?' she asked. 'You have lost me. One cannot vanish a laird.'

'Nay. But I can drug him, bring him back to Argyll Castle, and have some time with him before he is dispatched from this world.'

'Your family approves?'

'They will not know.'

She shook her head. 'Aye. They will know. They are not daft.'

'In the forge I can. No one is allowed in when I work late at night. It is my sanctuary and has all the tools I may need to serve my purposes.'

'And that would give you peace?' she asked with a raised brow.

'Peace? Nay. I am merely trying to stop the agony of my grief and grant some justice to my wife and son. Peace is a dream I gave up long ago.'

'Killing him in such a way will not haunt you?'

'Not more than my memories of that day.'

'You have never told me all of it,' she replied, a question in her voice.

He studied her. Perhaps if he told her all, she would have a better understanding of why Audric's death was necessary. It was a risk to share such with her, but she had just shared with him more about Jeremiah. Perhaps she could understand. Perhaps he could dare trust her in this budding friendship of theirs.

'The attack was sudden.' He began settling into the scene in his mind. 'One moment, Anna and I were asleep. The next, guards were shouting, maids were screaming, and the clash of weapons filled the night air.' He took a breath as his pulse increased. 'They had stormed the castle from within, breaching our walls using a hidden tunnel that only the family knew about, or so we thought. Brandon had secreted Fiona in through that very tunnel to continue their affair once her father, Audric, had forbidden it to continue, but we didn't know that. Fiona's maid had overheard the exchange. As you may have expected, that maid told Audric to earn his favour.'

Susanna sucked in a breath. 'I had heard bits of this as rumour, but I didn't know if any of it was true.'

He nodded. 'As with most gossip, there are some parts that are true.' He paused. 'Once the walls were breached, the castle was swarming with MacDonald soldiers, and we all took up arms to protect our home and those we loved. Even my Anna.' He smiled at the memory of her fierceness. 'She never wavered in her efforts. While I went off to gather Rosa and ensure our daughter's safety, she stayed in our chamber, sword in hand, to protect our wee son.

'I fought my way to Rosa one soldier at a time and reached her as a MacDonald soldier had just breached her door. I was able to rescue her and her maid in time, but when I returned to gather Anna...' His voice broke.

Susanna reached out and took his hand. 'You do not have to continue if you do not wish to.'

'Nay. You need to understand. I *need* you to understand,' he replied, the urgency to finish driving him on. 'Audric was at the doorway of our chamber when I reached it. His sword was bloodied and drawn, and Anna had crumpled to the floor behind him, with our son in her arms.'

His chest tightened, his pulse raged, and the smell of the death and bloodshed of that day seized him, turning his stomach. Sickness threatened.

'I attacked him,' Rowan added. 'A rage fuelled me, but when I heard Anna call out to me, I shoved him off and rushed to her. As I cradled her and our son in my arms, I knew it was too late and that she had little time left. Our son—' he shuddered '—was already gone from this world. Anna left me soon after to join him.'

'And Audric?' she asked.

'Little did I know it, but he had remained at the door,

watching her die in my arms. When I cried out in agony, he said that now I would know and understand sons would pay for the sins of their fathers—always.'

Susanna stilled, her mouth dropping open. 'I... I cannot fathom it. What did he even mean?'

'That my son's death and my suffering from losing him as well as Anna and so many others that day was revenge for what my father, grandfathers, and great-grandfathers before me had exacted on his clan in the Glencoe Massacre decades before.'

'And so you will continue that cycle of revenge and kill him?'

'Aye. I will,'

'But, Rowan,' she began.

He gripped her forearm. 'Nay. We had an agreement, Susanna. You know this was part of it. Do not act as if this was not what I had in mind. If you try to back out, I swear I will—'

She yanked her arm out of his hold. 'Do not be so dramatic,' she countered. 'I just want you to think upon the risks if you are caught, that is all. You have a daughter and clan counting on you. What you do impacts them all. And killing him will not bring your family back.'

'I know well my role in this,' he scowled, refusing to address the rest of her statement. He stood abruptly, rolled up his parchment, and tucked it in his waist belt. 'See to it that you do not forget yours.'

He'd had enough of this meeting and Susanna scrutinising him and his decisions. She couldn't know what he'd been through. Not really. No one could. Why she didn't have more of an understanding after all he had just shared with her, he didn't know. Why had he even tried to make her understand?

He left her, headed off through the hillside, and kicked at the ground in frustration, sending up a tuft of grass and a loose stone. It didn't matter if she understood or not. He just needed her to help him take out his revenge on Audric. Nothing else mattered.

As he started down through the grove, glancing up at the position of the sun, he cursed. It wasn't even midday. Several more hours remained before this horrid day would be through.

Chapter Sixteen

'Stop yer fidgeting,' Tilly instructed and swatted at Susanna's hands as she adjusted her gown for the one hundredth time.

'I am not so sure, Tilly. I do not think it suits me, and the bodice is far too tight.' Music and merriment echoed up into Susanna's chambers, but she could not get herself excited about this year's Holiday Ball. The more she looked about her room, the more perfect it seemed. 'I could just stay here for the evening.'

'Nay. The gown fits ye as it should and isn't hanging off ye like the other ones ye have. Ye look glorious. The blue was a fine idea. Ye will be the belle of the ball.'

Susanna rolled her eyes and sagged forward. While she wasn't normally prone to such insecurity, tonight her nerves fluttered and bubbled, and every flaw she had stared back at her from the standing mirror. Her bound-up hair was too limp, her breasts too small, her waist too narrow, and her skin too pale. And while the gown was a gorgeous sapphire blue, she did not do it justice. She feared it may well look better on its hanger than upon her. Even if she was trying to appear ready for marriage and a future engagement, who would want her? She was older and not the typical lass lairds were eager to bind themselves to.

As Rowan and her brothers were quick to point out, she could be a tad stubborn, difficult, wilful—and now she just looked, well, odd.

'I do not think I should go,' Susanna said quietly.

Tilly paused and took her hand. 'I know the significance of ye wearing this dress colour this eve, wee girl. And I am so proud of ye for trying to move on, to heal, to live yer life. Jeremiah would have wanted this for ye. We all do.'

Jeremiah.

She stared back in the mirror and almost smiled. He would have loved this dress. He would have teased her to no end about how much he'd wish to get it off her, and she would have laughed. He would have joined in with that deep, throaty laughter of his, and she would have felt like the most beautiful woman in the world.

Which was the opposite of how she felt now. Her heart sank. 'I do not think I can do it.'

Tilly crossed her arms against her chest. 'And what shall I tell him, then, when ye do not show?'

'Who?'

'Ye know exactly who. Laird Campbell. I am no fool.' She began folding the other shifts Susanna had not selected for the eve and set them aside. 'While I am not sure what ye are about, I know ye are up to something together. And I saw ye in the garden that morn.' She slid her gaze to Susanna and then went about her folding.

Susanna began to utter a rebuttal, but Tilly put her hand on hers. 'I do not need to know the details of anything. I just want ye to remember that ye will be disappointing people if ye don't go. Yer brothers will be there. Lady Cameron is there, no doubt longing for more familiar faces at her first ball as grand as this. Yer sister and her new husband will be there, and Laird Campbell—as well as any other suitors. If ye do not go, there will also be talk. Most likely ugly talk. Ye know how some of those ladies can be.' She went and put the shifts away in her wardrobe, leaving Susanna with her reflection.

And her conscience.

'You win, Tilly. You have persuaded me, but I will not have any fun. You cannot make me enjoy it.' She blew out a breath, popped her hands to her hips, and pulled back her shoulders. She could do this.

She was wrong. She could *not* do this. Susanna stood at the top of the large staircase that led down to the main entrance of Loch's End. Her brothers flanked each side of the doors, greeting the guests at the expansive and ornately decorated entryway as they arrived. Her sister Catriona and sister-in-law Iona stood beside them, exactly where she should be—instead of hovering behind the large wooden railing at the top of the stairs, hoping no one would see her.

She sucked in a breath. *Rowan.*

He walked through the door and greeted Royce as coolly and calmly as if the man had not set him up for absolute ruin weeks ago. They were almost a matched pair standing hand in hand. They were similar in height and stature, with Royce perhaps a hair taller and more muscular. But Rowan had an underlying ferocity and emotional intensity her brother lacked. He also seemed to have developed far more patience. He cut an impressive figure with his dark fitted coat, Campbell plaid and kilt, and crisp tunic. A shining silver brooch winked at her from his shoulder, and she wondered if he had made it himself.

His gaze clicked up as he neared the staircase. When he

saw her, he stilled, stopped cold as if he had been arrested by the sight of her. She flushed and bit her lower lip, fighting the urge to wring her hands.

Why had she allowed Tilly to talk her into this?

Rowan's heated stare softened, and he smiled up at her. 'Good evening, my lady. You look enchanting this evening.'

Enchanting?

Her throat dried, her heart picking up speed. She clutched the railing for dear life.

Her family looked up towards her, and soon all their gazes were locked on her. Iona clapped her hands together, turning to Royce. 'I told you she would come, and she is perfection.'

Royce kissed his wife's cheek. 'Aye. But not as perfect as you.'

She batted his shoulder. 'You say that because you must and I am carrying your child, but I love to hear it anyway.' Then she kissed him back.

'Join us, sister,' Rolf called out to her, waving her down the stairs encouragingly.

Susanna faltered. Uncertainty weighed down her feet. It was one thing to be greeted warmly by her family and Rowan, who were charged with approving of her. It was quite another to wade into the swamp of lairds and ladies below. They would smell her fear and be primed to devour her. Perhaps it was not too late to cry off and disappear into her chambers with a megrim. To her surprise, Rowan started up the stairs to her, his gaze full of appreciation—and what looked to be desire. Surely not. Everything she did irritated him, and he plagued her. Only their bargain held them together, and even that was precarious.

'My lady,' he said, offering his arm. 'Smile,' he whispered when his back was to everyone else. 'I am here,' he added. His blue eyes were strong and steady, and held the world. 'You are not alone.' Susanna's heart squeezed in gratitude as she slid her arm through his and finally smiled. If he could play his part as the doting suitor, then she could settle into her role as a woman eager to secure a powerful match this eve.

She lifted her chin, pulled back her shoulders, and nodded to him.

'There we are,' he murmured. He turned, leading her down the stairs. 'May I have the first dance?' he asked her, loud enough for her family and most everyone in the nearby room to hear.

'Aye, my laird,' replied, pleased there was no tremble in her voice.

Susanna smiled at her family as he guided her past them. To her vast relief, her brothers held their tongues and did not chastise her for not greeting guests as they arrived or challenge Rowan for stealing her away with such brazenness. As they entered the thick of the crowd, he cooed in her ear, low and husky. 'Keep smiling,' he encouraged her. 'We are nearly there.'

Fine music echoed in from the outer ballroom. Susanna swallowed back the acid rising in her throat as the overt stares began. Men and women alike gaped at her as she walked past, and she forced herself to meet every gaze and acknowledge them with a nod.

Enchanting, she reminded herself. *Be enchanting.*

Soon they were on the dance floor. He guided her along with an unexpected grace, their feet gliding along to one of her favourite reels. She smiled. 'I had forgotten you were so skilled, my laird.'

He lifted his brow in challenge.

'On the dance floor,' she added, a mock frown on her lips.

'I believe there is much about me—and us—that you have forgotten,' he said, his words heavy with meaning.

She didn't answer, but allowed herself to relax in his hold, some of the space between them disappearing as she did so.

'All eyes are upon you,' he whispered close to her ear. 'Just as we had hoped. No one can be in doubt of your intention to secure a husband now. Not with the way you look tonight.'

'Am I enchanting?' she teased, using his earlier words against him.

'Aye,' he said, his voice dropping lower. 'You look beautiful. Every lady here wishes that she were you or that she could kill you and steal that gown from your bones. Every man here not related to you wants to ravish you.'

Her breath caught in her throat.

Even you?

But she would not ask it, for either answer would strike terror through her. To be desired by Rowan would be just as dangerous as being repelled by her.

'And we are happy about this because…?' she asked.

'You will be the talk of the ball, whether good or bad, and no one will be unaware of your intention to marry and my intentions towards you, no matter how false.'

'Which suits part of our plan perfectly, but what of getting more information? Of discovering what my brothers fear?'

Rowan pulled back from her, his smile falling into a bit of a scowl. 'We will have to do what we both despise: socialise.'

Dread prickled along her skin.

'I know,' he said with a sigh.

'Did you not tell me when we met last that it was essential we dance together all eve? To show our affections for one another and to make our engagement later believable?'

'Aye,' he replied, looking over her shoulder as he spun her out and then back to him with an ease and delicacy that surprised her. 'But Hugh reminded me of the flaw in such a plan.'

'Flaw?'

'Staying together would limit the amount of information we could gather. Splitting up, mixing with the other guests here, will allow us to linger, eavesdrop, and whatever else seems reasonable. Then we can share what we have learned and hopefully have some more meaningful information to piece together than what scant information we have gathered as of now.'

Drat.

She couldn't fault the logic behind his words, but mingling? It was akin to driving thistles under her fingernails.

'All night?' she asked, her voice forlorn.

He chuckled. 'Nay. That would be more than anyone could bear.' He squeezed her hand and ran his thumb along her own. 'One hour. Then we gather again. Perhaps at the refreshment table? Or out of doors for fresh air?'

'Definitely out of doors, but not too far within the gardens. There must be nothing unseemly,' she added in a hushed tone. She hoped he would remember what had happened during their last foray into 'gathering fresh air.' He'd nearly kissed the life out of her, and they were lucky not to have been seen by anyone but Hugh and Tilly. Such risks they could not take now.

He smirked. 'Understood.' The reel came to an end, and they separated and joined in the crowd's applause. As the next jovial chords began, Rowan bowed and took his leave. 'Have fun,' he murmured, 'and be nice.' Young Laird Macpherson swooped in, almost knocking into Rowan in his hasty and haphazard approach to Susanna.

'My lady,' Laird Macpherson said, his gaze raking over her face and then down to her bosom in a rather indelicate fashion that told of a man undisciplined by youth. 'You look beautiful this eve.'

'Thank you, my laird. Are you enjoying yourself?' she asked, intrigued by his confidence. He was wide-eyed with floppy chestnut hair. He also had an easy smile, and the promise of a nice stature once he grew into his body. He was much like a sloppy puppy eager in his approval and devotion, but uncertain as to how to show such affections.

'Aye. And I would enjoy myself even more if you would join me. This reel is one of my favourites. May I?' he asked, extending his open palm to her in invitation.

Susanna watched Rowan walking away and being approached by a young lass who happened to 'drop' her handkerchief just as he walked by. He paused, picked it up, and returned it to her, unable to escape the woman's attentions. Susanna valiantly did not roll her eyes and set her gaze back on Macpherson, his face open and expectant…hopeful. She remembered what such young hope and desire felt like. His smile widened.

This was part of their game, and she and Rowan both had to play it if they were to uncover the secrets that threatened her family *and* keep them safe *and* prevent her from being forced into a marriage with someone like this young colt. Susanna slid her arm around Macpherson's, pleased to feel the slight flex of his muscle beneath, and smiled. 'Aye. Of course, my laird.' Playing with him for a bit might be fun, but then she remembered Rowan had *also* commanded her to be nice. She quirked her lips and sighed.

Blast.

It would be a trying hour.

Chapter Seventeen

'Well, that hour was horrendous. Is there no easier way?' Susanna pouted at Rowan and bent her head down as she readjusted her bodice, pulling it back up slightly. A long wavy tress fell from its pins and skimmed along her creamy skin.

She was an utter vision in blue, especially in this mix of soft moonlight and the tender flames of the torches lighting the garden path outside where they stood. Although Rowan hadn't known Jeremiah well, he was a wise man. Susanna was bewitching this eve, and their plan of making her appear a ready and willing participant in securing a husband had been a success. People could talk of little else, and every man in that room had trouble taking their eyes off her.

And *he* needed to stand guard, lest he act on his body's endless awareness of her beauty this eve. Their attachment was a ruse, nothing more.

Rowan watched her and frowned, distracted by the continued tugging and tucking on her bodice and sleeves. 'What are you doing?' he asked.

'Moving my gown back to its rightful location.'

Had it been in the wrong location? He flushed, suddenly determining her insinuation. 'Susanna, when I said be fun and kind, I did not intend for you to—' He gestured towards her bosom but said no more.

'Do not be a dolt,' she replied, blowing the hair out of her vision as she continued to struggle with the gown's material. 'If you did not already know, gowns as heavy as this pull down as the evening goes on, especially with all the dancing. And despite how I might wish it, I am not as—ample—up top as others, so it is even more prone to slide and stretch.'

He stared at her. What was she talking about? She was perfection. And her breasts, from what he could remember and see of them now, were just the right size to cup in his palm, which was ideal for him. For any man, really. His throat dried.

He scowled at himself. He *was* being a dolt. He needed to refocus his efforts, or he would have an entirely different problem at hand. Even now his body throbbed in all the right places in response to just this conversation and his mind's suggestive imaginings.

She paused. 'What? Why are you making that horrid face at me? Just because I do not have huge breasts does not make me a beast.'

He shook his head. *Devil's blood.* 'What? I am not—' he began and then stopped. He ran his hand through his hair in frustration. He couldn't even recall what they were supposed to be talking about.

He sighed and closed his eyes, willing some of the blood to flow back to his brain so he could have a coherent thought. After counting down from ten, he looked back up.

She was scrutinising him and had her hands on her hips. 'Please tell me you learned something to make the last hour worth such agony?'

The familiar sound of Tilly's humming nearby reminded him that they needed to drop their voices a touch to not be overheard. He edged closer to Susanna, tilting his head so she would follow his lead and come nearer as well. They hovered together at the edge of a tall hedge, and Rowan realised his error as soon as the familiar hint of violets arrested his senses.

His body kicked up a small revolt again, and he shifted on his feet.

Not now.

He forced himself into warrior mode, setting his emotions and body on shutdown with his mind alert, or at least he really tried to. His body was too far attuned to her to pretend she was not there, her bosom rising and falling within his gaze as she breathed.

Deuces.

He clutched the hedge, letting the prick of a broken limb in his palm focus his energy elsewhere as much as possible. 'Lady Menzies was quite talkative.'

'I noted she was quite a close talker,' Susanna added, lifting a brow at him.

'Aye. But nothing to be worried about. She was adamant that any attachment we formed would be temporary and for pleasure alone.' He smirked.

Susanna frowned. 'And? Did you agree to such an attachment?'

He sighed. 'How could I when I have you as my betrothed, beloved?' His sarcasm hit its mark, and Susanna pinched his side. Hard.

'Ow,' he groused. She'd always known exactly where to pinch him so it hurt the most. He rubbed the spot. 'Lady Menzies made a friendly and adult offer of companionship that I might have agreed to if I knew I wouldn't end up dead. Lady Menzies's affairs are short-lived. Word has it Laird Menzies is quite a jealous man who adores his wife.'

Susanna chuckled, her breath a whisper along his cheek. 'Aye. I have heard he believes they bewitch her. He does not believe she is the pursuer. Poor sod.'

Poor sod indeed. Rowan was starting to feel quite bewitched himself. He blinked away his desire. 'She also told me your brothers have been in talks with her husband about securing his fortifications along the border he shares with the MacDonalds.'

'Hmm.' She stilled, staring off in the distance. 'The young colt Macpherson told me the same. He was trying to show me that my brothers approve of him, since they have been working hand in hand to get portions of the border walls re-established.'

'Did he provide a reason?'

'Nay. I think he was busy investigating my too-small bosom,' she countered, glaring at him.

'I never said—' he started, but she cut him off with a raise of her hand.

'Too late,' she said.

'Uh,' he replied, vexed by her persistence on the matter. 'What else?'

'I intercepted a note from Royce's study earlier today. Just let me remove this rock,' she muttered, tugging her slipper off to shake the stone out. Tipping slightly, she clutched his shoulder, and he steadied her by holding her waist. The smooth, firm feel of her beneath his hold, along with the unexpected view down her bodice of the slight curve of her breast and its darkened nipple, threatened to bring him to his knees.

Focus.

'Got it,' she said in triumph before replacing her shoe. Then she pulled a note from her bosom. Unfolding it, she handed it to him. 'Here is the note from my brother's desk. It means little to me, but perhaps it will mean more to you.' The parchment was warm to his touch, another reminder of where it had been...nestled. This was going to be a very long night. Shaking off his distraction, he studied it. When he realised what it was, his desire buckled.

'This is a battle plan,' he said.

Her eyes widened, and she peered over his shoulder. 'It does not look like one.'

'Well, it is. I am certain of it.'

'Why would my brothers be drawing up a battle plan? Do they think they will be attacked? Or are they planning to attack?'

'I cannot tell. To be honest, what is here would serve both purposes. It is focused on protecting the castle from outside as well as within. As if it would be done in two phases if need be.'

It was a worst-case scenario if the outer fortifications fell, and they were forced to fight inside for their lives and for those they loved. The sight of it chilled him to his bones. The attack on his family at Argyll Castle four years ago had been too similar. The MacDonalds had used the secret entrance to their castle to try to overrun his soldiers by surprise and they'd almost succeeded.

Susanna's hand closed around his own and the parchment. 'You are trembling. Rowan, can you hear me?'

When he turned to Susanna, he saw her face overlapping Anna's, and he blinked rapidly to dismiss the horror of his memories. What if Susanna died as Anna did? He thrust the thought away. 'We need to know what this is about. Now,' Rowan said. 'Waiting may not be an option.'

'We cannot simply barge in and ask,' Susanna replied. 'They do not know I took this from them in the study. We will reveal ourselves if we do so.'

'Would you rather reveal yourself or be dead?'

She balked, her hand falling away from his own.

'There is no need to be dramatic or cruel.'

'I am being neither. I am reacting to what I see on this page.' Rowan stared at her and saw his own agony and fear reflected in her eyes. He cursed himself. Losing his temper or his reason wouldn't help them.

And they were at a ball. What could he do right this moment?

Nothing.

He tamped back his emotion and handed her the paper. 'You need to return this to Royce's study immediately. Your brothers will be alarmed if they find it missing. Once you have done that, you can tell me more of what you have discovered, and I will do the same. Although I cannot imagine it holds more significance than this.'

She watched him with scepticism. 'I will return the paper. Then you will explain to me what this—' she drew an exaggerated circle around him to emphasise her point before continuing '—reaction was all about. It cannot just have been from that paper. It is only ink and tree pulp.'

He gestured for her to go without agreeing to her terms. He didn't need to explain himself to anyone. And she'd never understand. Not completely.

The night had cooled since they had first stepped out, and even Rowan felt chilled as they wove back through the winding paths of the garden to the castle. Tilly still trailed behind them. The woman had the patience of a saint and ought to be canonised.

'My jacket?' he offered, beginning to shrug it off.

'Nay. It will only lead to more questions from my brothers. I would rather remain chilled.'

As they crossed the threshold of the doorway and into the warmer ballroom, Royce called out. 'Sister. I was wondering where you had been off to. I'd like a word.'

'Royce,' Rowan offered in greeting.

'Campbell,' Royce replied with a nod and a scathing glare of disdain that could not be missed.

'My laird, thank you for the walk. Aye, brother, what do you need?' she asked as he led her away.

To their keen luck, he appeared to be taking her to the study. Rowan frowned. Or he was taking her there because he had already discovered the paper was missing and believed she might have it?

Either way, she would be interrogated. Either about why she was with him or why she had taken the map. Rowan did not envy her in the slightest. He spied the refreshments table, gathered up a full glass of wine, and threw it back with fervour. He reached for another.

'Campbell.'

Devil's blood. He set the wine back on the table. He'd suddenly lost his taste for drink.

The sound of Laird Audric MacDonald's voice did that to a man, especially him.

How had Rowan not seen him here already? Doing a quick visual sweep of the area behind the man yielded nothing other than the watchful gaze of Rolf from far across the room.

There was something he was missing of great importance regarding the Cameron brothers and this plan of theirs. Why was Audric always around? Were they forming an alliance? One to unseat him as laird? Rowan's gut churned with unease. Even the Camerons would not be so desperate, would they? Audric couldn't be trusted. No alliance with him was true. If anything, it would leave them more exposed as they would have their guard down and believe he could be trusted.

'Something on your mind, lad?' he asked with an arrogant smirk. 'Seems we never settled that discussion from before.'

'Oh? And here I thought we had no need to communicate further.' Rowan's spine tightened, and he stepped forward, an instinctive move to show the old man he held no power over him.

'Perhaps not yet, but in future we may need to renegotiate our boundary walls. I have some old maps that say you are encroaching on what is mine. But I will let Devlin bring up such matters with you. I am far too old to care.' He took a long draw from his tankard.

Rowan released a low, hearty laugh before his lips fell into a tight scowl. Narrowing his gaze and baring his teeth, he said, 'Do not attempt to provoke me, Audric. You will regret it. I have special plans for you, and one day you will know what they are. You should fear them. For they will be slow, lingering, and full of agony—for you.'

'Oh? After all this time?' Audric said with a shake of his head. 'I doubt it. You are not man enough, Campbell. You could not save your family then, and I doubt you shall be able to save your new lass now.' His gaze cut to Royce's study and then back to him. 'Oh? You do not know?' He chuckled and covered his mouth to recover. 'Then I can hardly wait for you to find out.'

Rowan grabbed the old man by the tunic, lifting his feet from the floor just slightly. 'Do not test me. I can end you. Here. Now. Gutting you may ruin these lovely floors of theirs for a time, but it would be worth it.' His voice shook, and his body vibrated with rage.

'Gentlemen,' Rolf intervened, placing a firm palm on each of their chests. 'This is a celebration, not a battlefield. If you must—settle your differences elsewhere. Do not make me remove you by force.' His voice was firm with an edge that caught Rowan's attention. Rolf was usually the most subdued of the siblings, but Rowan recognised the familiar steely Cameron resolve in the man's tone. Cameron soldiers were also closing ranks around them as quietly and swiftly as one could manage at a ball. Rowan caught their subtle movements in his peripheral vision.

Cursing, he released Audric roughly and stepped back. He had fallen into MacDonald's trap. All gazes were upon them, and the dancing had stopped. Evidently, the possible bloodbath between them was far more interesting than continuing into the next reel even though the musicians still played.

'Royce wishes to speak with you, my laird,' Rolf offered.

Rowan looked up, but realised the younger Cameron was speaking to Audric, not him.

'One day, we will settle what is between us,' Audric offered. 'But I suppose it shall not be today?' He released a dramatic sigh as if disappointed.

Steady. Think of Rosa.

Rowan said nothing but glared at the man as he left, watching him disappear down the corridor, passing several rooms before being guided into the study. There in the darkened shadows just beyond that chamber, Rowan's gaze met Susanna's unexpectedly, and a surge of relief, desire, and longing crushed him. She mouthed to him and pointed to the other end of the hallway indicating that he should meet her there. He wove through the crowd as the dancing picked back up. Some people still stared he passed, which was no surprise, but some of their words were. He gritted his teeth and ignored them, focusing on the task at hand: getting away from Audric and to Susanna. Somehow in all of this, she had become a beacon of safety for him. The irony was not lost on him.

His world had been turned on end, all because of Susanna Cameron's late-night visit to his forge. She walked down the hallway ahead of him, and he followed at a discreet distance. He rounded a corner and paused, staring at an empty hallway. Where had she gone?

A hallway door creaked open, and she waved to him. *Deuces*. They would be trapped in another room together. He shook his head. He was out of patience, among other things. She waved him on again, her eyes pleading this time. Something was wrong. Against his better judgement, he tucked himself into the room, which turned out to be a small alcove beneath the stairs.

'Could we not have met in a larger space?' Rowan complained. 'This is not even meant for one person, let alone two.' The smell, heat, and feel of her was consuming him, and with his defences already worn down after yet another encounter with Audric, his body was surging, responding with speed to his desire for her this eve.

He pushed his body as far against the wall of the small room as he could, attempting to create distance between their bodies. He failed. She was still touching him, and his body could not be fooled otherwise. 'Shh,' she countered, pressing a finger to his lips. 'Listen.'

Rowan fell silent, and her hand dropped away. 'We are out of time,' she said breathlessly. 'My brothers have decided upon a match for me already. One that they say it is imperative I agree to. They say I may no longer choose.'

'And?' he asked.

'Of course, I refused. But now they plan on ignoring my desires and forcing me into it anyway.'

'Why? What has created such urgency?'

'I do not know. That is why we are in here. They will not tell me who I am to marry, but that it has been decided.'

He stared at her quizzically.

She glanced away and fiddled with her gown sleeves. 'You can hear quite well from this vantage point.'

He smirked. 'Their study, you mean?' he whispered.

'Aye.'

'Is this how you have gained some of your information?'

'Aye.'

He nodded. 'I am impressed. Have you tried every chamber along this hall?' he asked, anticipating her answer.

'Aye, I have.' she said.

'I cannot fault your strategy. 'tis a fine one.' He smiled at her. Only Susanna would have tried every room near the study for the best advantage to eavesdrop.

She smirked back at him. 'And now we shall discern who they plan to shackle me to. Or at least to make the attempt.' She leaned her ear against the wall closest to the study, which caused her to be pressed side to side with him. When she shifted to get closer, he slid his arm around her waist to make it more comfortable for her, and she smiled.

'That is better,' she whispered.

Perhaps for her, but not for him. His body shifted into a higher gear of alertness. She smelled of violets, wine, and something sweet. The warmth of her pressed alongside him felt like a drug, making his muscles relax against her own.

Then he could hear the murmurings of voices, and he pressed his ear to the wall and closed his eyes. Although it was hard to discern the voices at first due to the music from the ball, finally Rowan could hear some of what was said, but not all. He concentrated and slowed his breathing, and soon it became easier.

'I have spoken to my son,' Audric said. 'He is not yet enthusiastic about the plan, but with the proper incentives, I know he can be persuaded to come around to my position on things.'

'And what additional incentives would be necessary?' Royce countered, an edge of annoyance in his voice.

Audric made a dramatic pause. 'Some additional land, perhaps an extension of our shared border wall, and a promise of a yearly payment of resources.'

'What *specifics* might that include, my laird?' Rolf added, his voice low.

'Hmm… I venture one hundred acres and a ten per cent share of your yield of goods for trade would suffice.'

Rolf cursed.

Royce took longer to respond. 'We will half that request. Fifty acres and five per cent of our yield of goods while our sister lives. If anything happens to her under your son's care or your own during her marriage, our arrangement will end.'

Rowan stiffened, his chest tingling, and met Susanna's gaze. Her eyes were wide and wild with disbelief. He had not imagined the words or their intention. Her brothers meant to marry her off to Devlin, and she would be the daughter-in-law to the devil himself, Audric MacDonald. Well, he'd not allow it. He clutched her hand, and she held it fiercely as they continued to listen to the exchange.

'Then we are agreed,' Audric replied, the sound of a chair scraping. 'Draw up the agreement. If it is sound, we will announce the arrangement. I want them married by the end of the year.' Audric paused and added, 'Be sure that sister of yours is in line. Any disobedience will not be tolerated.'

'And you, my laird,' Royce called out, his boots resonating on the floor. 'Your disobedience or your son's will also not be tolerated, and our sister will be well cared for. If not, you will answer to us—personally.'

Chapter Eighteen

Susanna clutched Rowan's hand. She shook her head and stared at him. A scream and a sob duelled at the base of her throat, and tears of rage rather than sadness threatened. How could they do such? Her own brothers trading her off to the MacDonalds? What could she have done to elicit such a punishment, and what did they fear so much that they would risk her life and well-being to secure an alliance with him?

She stared ahead but saw nothing but a blurry figure. Her ears buzzed, and she struggled to hear anything at all. Rowan cupped her face with his hands and pulled her close to his ear, murmuring to her. She could not decipher the words, but the feel of him brought her back from the fear and disbelief threatening to devour her from within. Her family was her world, and yet they were ready to sacrifice her? Why?

A shaky hiccup sounded in her throat, and Rowan's cheek pressed against her own.

'Breathe,' he murmured, his warm breath skimming her cheek. She sucked in one trembling breath and then another. She gripped his wrists, clinging for solid ground and safety. She felt like she was floating, and blackness edged in on her narrowing vision.

'Aye,' his voice cooed. 'Good. One more.'

Another shaky breath in and out, and the blackness ringing her vision began to recede.

'You are safe, Suze. I won't let anything happen to you. You will not marry into that family. And he will never—' he growled '—touch you. I swear it. I will die first.'

She believed him.

Suddenly, she was that young lass Susanna in the rowan grove all those years ago. Her father had reprimanded her and made her feel like she was less than nothing for standing up for herself. Rowan had made her feel safe, protected, and beautiful. Just like he did now, when she felt her world as she knew it was splintering in two.

Perhaps he was still the boy in the grove who loved her.

She crushed her mouth to his and kissed him fiercely, desperate to find out. He stilled under her touch at first, and then his hands fell away from her cheeks. She let go of his wrists and wove her fingers through the hair at the nape of his neck before plundering his mouth again with a heated kiss, her teeth tugging at his lip. His hesitation was palpable, but she knew the moment his dam of uncertainty broke. He groaned, took control of their kiss, and squeezed her waist, pulling her body flush with his, even closer than they already were in the confined space. And she felt alive, so alive, for the first time—since Jeremiah.

She answered his demands and tucked herself into the folds of his body, her legs twining with his as his lips trailed along her neck. She gasped, and she felt his lips curve into a smile along her throat.

'I still remember,' he murmured. Confidence laced his words.

She smirked. 'Well, I remember too,' she whispered,

sliding her hand under his plaid and between his legs, feeling the full length of him harden and shudder against her. She stroked him with the base of her palm before closing her hand around him.

'Deuces,' he said through gritted teeth. 'Aye. You do.'

While they had never fully consummated their love affair when they were young, they had always been passionate with one another. It seemed time had not changed their bodies' memories of one another or their mutual attraction. If anything, it had become more intense. They were adults who knew how to make each other's body sing under their touch.

'Susanna,' he murmured, pulling his lips away after some effort. 'We are in little more than a closet. There are hundreds of people on the other side of this door.'

'And?' she replied. 'I can be quiet,' she teased, running her fingertips over his length once more.

He shuddered, and the muscle in his jaw tightened as he gripped her wrist to cease her movements. 'I do not wish to take advantage,' he whispered, his tone serious and concerned. 'You have had a shock and—we are not truly betrothed. We are pretending, remember?'

'Aye,' she replied, wondering deep down if really *they* were the ones lying to themselves. What she felt now didn't seem like they were pretending. It seemed real, true, and she didn't want it to stop, no matter the words he spoke, no matter where they were.

No matter if it was to be only this once.

'Aye?' he asked, his brow furrowed, not knowing what she meant.

'Aye,' she replied, her voice low and husky. She freed her hand from his and held his gaze as she lifted the heavy fabric of her skirts. Then she slid her bare leg slowly over the rough wool of his kilt, until it coiled around his bare thigh and calf. The flesh-on-flesh contact made his eyes close, and he rested his head back against the wall, his Adam's apple bobbing as he swallowed.

'Susanna,' he murmured, his voice a low growl of satisfaction.

'Aye, my laird?' she replied, leaning against his chest, allowing her bodice to gape open. The air hit her flesh, making her skin pebble with anticipation.

His hooded gaze met hers, the desire evident in his eyes. He gifted her a sultry smile and leaned forward, his lips barely touching her neck, sending trills of sensation all throughout her body. Lazily his lips travelled along her collarbone and then drifted down her chest. He seized her breast in his mouth. His lips worked her nipple until it was so sensitive that the skim of his teeth against it almost made her cry out in pleasure. She bit her lip instead and moved restlessly against him.

'Not yet,' he murmured, holding her waist gently, his scruff scraping along her breast.

Why was the most impatient man ever being so patient? She shifted against him, the ache for him increasing.

Not used to waiting for anything she desired, she reached beneath his kilt and took hold of him, revelling in the power she felt as he stilled and cursed against her chest.

She smiled as he tugged up her skirts, having broken his resolve to tarry.

He lifted his head and met her gaze as he positioned himself. Then, with one swift and certain movement, he was inside her.

Rowan held Susanna's waist tighter and roughly seized

her mouth with his lips. What other choice did he have to quiet their lovemaking and hide them from the ladies and lairds on the other side of these walls?

Her lips clashed against his and were as soft and warm as he remembered. Her form was as toned and muscular as when she was a young lass on the cusp of womanhood, but now—now he could feel the fullness of her hips and breasts against him as she pulled him closer. His body tightened and surged with need, a base and hungry need he scarce allowed himself to feel any more as he slid in and out of her warm body. Her urgent response fuelled his desire even more. *Saints be.* He was cresting soon, and so was she, by the tight feel of her core around him. And they were in a bloody closet.

Imagine what would have happened if they weren't confined by space, time, and a castle full of people. She gasped in his mouth and shuddered as she climaxed. Soon he did the same, clinging to her.

They leaned heavily against each other, holding one another upright as best they could.

'My laird,' she murmured with inflection, her voice relaxed and purring with contentment.

'Aye, my lady,' he panted out. 'I agree.'

He slid down the wall with Susanna alongside him, until they rested in a tangled mesh of limbs, flesh, and fabric.

'I do not think I can stand,' she chuckled.

'Then let us sit,' he murmured in her ear, relishing this sweetness in her that he knew he would never have again, for he'd never let this happen again. Despite the fact that it had been more beautiful than he'd thought possible. After Anna had died, he never believed he'd feel anything close to such a connection again, but he had—with her.

It sent his heart pounding and his mind into confusion, but he closed his eyes as she leaned her head into the crook of his neck and sighed.

All of that would matter later.

But for now, all that mattered was this, the sound of her soft breaths, the feeling of her gentle heartbeat against his chest, and this quiet contentment.

Chapter Nineteen

Everything around her was warm and lush, her body as languid and relaxed as a summer loch, and she eased her eyes open. It was dark, and her limbs were heavy with sleep. She shifted and stilled. Someone was holding her; she eased back, trying not to panic.

Rowan?

Rowan.

She cringed and clutched her forehead with a curse as a flood of memories came back to her. They had been hiding in this small closet to eavesdrop when they'd heard of Audric and her brothers' plan to marry her off to Devlin. She and Rowan had kissed, and then— She curled her toes in her shoes and smiled. She tried to feel some sense of shame about it, especially with it happening in a closet, of all places, but she couldn't. What had happened between them had been lovely. More lovely than she ever thought she would feel with a man after losing Jeremiah. She could not begrudge what she and Rowan had shared so freely and without expectation with one another. It was as if a chapter that had been left undone between them for so long had been written—and written quite well.

'Where has she disappeared to?' Royce asked, his voice drawing Susanna from her daydreams to wakefulness.

Without the music and noise from the crowd of the ball, it was quite easy to hear the conversation.

'Perhaps she has deduced your plans and run from here. I couldn't blame her. There must be a better solution, brother. *She. Is. Our. Sister.* And that family—Audric—I have been patient and gone along with your schemes, but *this*—it is too much.' Rolf cursed, and Susanna's mouth gaped open. She had never heard him use such language before. Her younger brother was angry. Very angry.

She shifted her ear closer to the wall, and Rowan stretched his arm across her waist, gripping her hip. The possessive yet gentle action made her smile. Her pulse increased, her body remembering the pleasure his touch had brought her hours before. Her leg cramped, and she flinched, stretching it as best she could so she wouldn't cry out. The movement jarred Rowan. His eyes opened into small slits, and he squinted. Then they widened once and then twice before he opened his mouth to speak.

She pressed a fingertip to his lips and shook her head, pointing to the study next door that the closet wall shared. He frowned but closed his mouth, leaning back against the wall again. 'It is the only plan I can think of that can protect them both. And I cannot sacrifice one for the other.' Royce's voice wavered.

'He may never know, and then this will never be a problem. We may be making it more of a problem than it might ever be.'

'You think no one on that island will ever speak of it? I never should have gone there. It is my fault, and I know that. I was stubborn and arrogant to believe that I deserved to know the truth. That I knew better than Father. They knew it was best to let it rest and stay hidden, but I was determined to uncover it. And to think, originally, I was relieved to have discovered the truth. And now—now it plagues me to think one day, all will know, and our clan's livelihood and our family's lives will be at stake.'

Rowan's body shifted, his features alert and his brow raised.

Susanna held her breath, reached for his hand, and held it, desperate to know what her brothers said next. This could be it. This could be all that she had been waiting to find out.

'Who would benefit from telling him?' Rolf asked, his voice dropping low.

'Chisholm,' Royce's answered.

Rolf sighed. 'We have already dealt with him. He is pleased with his arrangement.'

'And when he wants more? Or one of his family members discovers the secret and wishes to make a deal with Audric instead?' Royce asked.

Blast.

Susanna squeezed Rowan's hand. Audric was part of this secret? No wonder her brothers had been appeasing him and willing to marry her off to his son, whether Devlin wished to marry her or not. But what could he have on her family? They didn't deal with the MacDonalds unless necessary, one of the few of her father's rules she agreed with.

Rowan's scowl deepened, and his grip around her hand tightened. He pressed his ear closer to the panelling. Susanna nibbled her lip and waited.

'No one will know that Catriona is his daughter unless we tell them,' Rolf said, his voice almost inaudible.

'How many times have I told you never to speak of it

in this house?' Royce growled, slamming down his fist to the table and rattling the contents on it.

'I cannot talk to you when you are like this,' Rolf argued.

'Like what?' he countered, his anger building.

'Like Father. You are obsessed and making aggressive decisions based on fear and the need to outmanoeuvre them, whoever they might be, before they make the first move against you. I am going to bed. Hopefully, when I wake tomorrow, Susanna will have returned. I cannot bear to think she is gone for good, and that we have lost yet another sister. Wasn't losing Catriona for almost a decade enough of a price to pay for our father's fear?'

'Perhaps he knew what was best for all of us.'

Rolf scoffed. 'You cannot mean that. The life she lived. What she was subjected to? She is still our flesh and blood, even if it is only half. Do you not care?'

'We have much to lose, Rolf,' Royce said in a quieter tone. 'If Susanna is bound to them by an alliance of marriage, if something does come out, he will be unable to strike out against us.'

'And Susanna? What of the cost to her?' Rolf's voice broke.

'She is strong. She can—'

'Nay, brother. It is a betrayal she will not survive. Nor will I.'

The door of the study slammed shut, sending a vibration through the wall and against their ears.

Susanna stared blankly ahead.

Catriona was Audric's daughter?

How was that even possible? Susanna had watched her mother carry her youngest sister and saw her moments after she had given birth to her. And if Father knew—what had happened to Mother? Had something horrendous happened to her? Or had she chosen to be with a man as cruel as Audric and shamed her husband?

None of it made sense.

Susanna's mind fought the information, and she sat dumbfounded. They had to be wrong. It all had to be untrue. It was madness. Utter madness.

Rowan's touch along her cheek startled her, and she flinched, gripping his hand. Their gazes locked. In his eyes, there was sympathy and—something else she couldn't name. He pulled her into his arms. She knew she should, but she did not resist his comfort. She leaned into his embrace, buried her head in his rumpled tunic, and wept.

Rowan's mind raced as he held Susanna. His hand smoothed over her hair, and he murmured words of comfort to her as loudly as he dared. They were still hiding in a closet, after all. The absurdity of being in such a situation and hearing the news she had long desired, but it being as horrible as it was, made it almost unfathomable. He couldn't imagine her thoughts and feelings right now. Part of him felt conflicted with the sympathy he felt for her and her family's position if what they heard was indeed true. The other part of him felt a cool, calm peace. As if this was supposed to happen, especially after their evening together. They had risked vulnerability with one another, and now he and Susanna could face this new chaos together. They had a common enemy now, and they could strike Audric down. The Camerons and Campbells could join forces and end Audric for good. It would be in both of their best interests, and it would end this farce of her having to marry Devlin. He smirked. While he now found he liked Devlin, the lad was no match for Susanna. She would raze him to the ground. What she needed was a man like him.

He stilled. Did he need a woman like her?

Part of him believed he did. She challenged him, pushed him, and spoke her mind. She was strong, intelligent, and unholy beautiful. He played with the end of a wavy tress, running it between his fingers. Who said this fake betrothal plan of theirs couldn't become a real one? But could he trust her? His hand stilled, resting along the smooth nape of her neck. Trust? Of that, he wasn't so sure. She was a Cameron, and her family had always been her priority. She had not been shy about reminding him of it. He didn't know if that could ever change. And he couldn't bind himself to a woman who didn't put her family first, Rosa included. The wee girl deserved the world.

By the time Susanna's tears had subsided, and she gave a last sniffle into his sleeve, the house was quiet, achingly so. 'Perhaps we should try to sneak out while we can?' he offered.

Susanna lifted her head. Her eyes were bright and glassy and her nose a bit puffy, but she was gorgeous. If anything, seeing her so vulnerable and soft made his heart ache. 'Aye,' she replied with a bit of a croak, and began untangling herself from him as they both struggled to stand after being in such a cramped position for hours.

He gained his footing first and winced as his left foot tingled. He rolled his ankle. 'My foot fell asleep,' he murmured.

She chuckled. 'And I have lost half of my hair pins.'

He studied her half up, half down hair and nodded. 'Aye.

And your—' he began, gesturing to her bodice, which was far too low and awkwardly twisted to one side. She began tugging and twisting it until she had it close to where it was when he first saw her this eve at the top of the staircase. That moment seemed a lifetime ago. As if they had gone into a cave in that closet and emerged a year later. He felt like a different man and her a different woman. And perhaps after all that had happened between them and all that they had learned in those hours, they were.

He gripped the doorknob and turned it slowly before peeking out into the hallway. It was dark but for the flicker of a sconce lit in the hallway. He stepped out and waved her on to follow. She squeezed his arm and shook her head. 'Follow me,' she whispered.

He rolled his eyes at her need to lead but pressed himself back against the wall until she exited.

'My exact steps,' she added. 'This floor creaks.'

So perhaps there *was* a reason for her to lead. Such things like floor creaks he wouldn't know, and every squeak or groan would echo in this silence. He closed the door, released the knob, and fell in step behind her, matching her stride for stride despite how much shorter hers was than his. They made it down the hallway without incident and turned a corner. Voices sounded from the outer room, and Susanna flattened herself to the wall. Rowan followed suit, holding his breath so he could listen.

Fortunately, the young lasses, most likely maids, were too far away to distinguish, which meant Susanna and Rowan could continue. Soon they were out the back door and into the chilly night air of the garden. Rowan took a deep breath. Being able to move freely and take in some air after being cramped for hours in such a small space was bliss. Susanna stood beside him with a similar smile of relief.

'What an evening,' she said, shaking her head.

'Aye. There is much to take in.'

'Perhaps too much,' she replied, rubbing her forehead. 'My mind races, but my thoughts are incoherent. I do not know what I think about anything now.'

'Much has happened. That is expected.' He fisted his hand by his side. It was the most neutral answer he could give. He needed to give her time, despite how eager he was to discuss their plans to end Audric. His mouth watered in anticipation.

'I will leave you to your thoughts and to rest. It has been a trying evening,' he said, risking a small kiss to her cheek, revelling in the sweet smell of violets that still clung to her skin. 'When you are ready to move forward, send word.' He squeezed her hand briefly before letting go.

'Move forward?' she asked, tilting her head, her eyes glittering in the moonlight.

He stilled. 'With killing Audric,' he whispered.

She shook her head. 'We cannot move forward with that now. Our plans must change. To kill him would put my sister and family in danger.'

Was she addled? 'Nay. To allow him to *live* would put you in danger. Did we not hear the same words?' He moved closer to her, his blood pulsing through his body, disbelief roaring through him. 'And we had an agreement. Do you plan to go back on your word now? Now that we are so many weeks into this plan?' He stood over her.

She squared her shoulders and met his gaze. 'You will force me into nothing. You were repaying a debt to *me* by helping me unearth this secret, and so we have.'

'And your betrothal to Devlin? You will just marry him to appease your brothers and to keep your clan safe by insuring such an alliance?' Outrage caused his volume to increase.

She gripped his forearm. 'Lower your voice, my laird. I will do what I must do to protect my family. I will contact you when I have decided on my next course of action, not before.'

He stepped closer, his disbelief rising like bile in his gut. 'And what happened between us this eve? Did that mean nothing?'

She dropped her hand from his and studied him, as if calculating her next words with care. 'I believe it served both of our—needs in that moment. It does not have to *mean* anything.'

He scoffed. This was the Susanna he knew. The one he warned himself about. Perhaps he had only imagined this woman as having feelings and care for someone other than herself and her beloved family. 'And just when I thought you had changed. You are just the same cold and calculating Cameron you have always been.'

Her face hardened. 'And you are still the emotional, impulsive man you have always been. Just spouting off words and doing things without thought of the consequences to others.'

'Then I shall take my leave of you and our agreement, but know this. I will have my justice as you promised, with or without your blessing.'

'Even if it ruins us?' she challenged him, her gaze pleading.

'Aye,' he growled. 'Even if it burns you bloody Camerons to the ground.'

Chapter Twenty

Susanna watched Rowan stalk away, his rigid and angry gait a harsh end to their evening together. She scarcely knew what had happened. This eve was a blur of emotion and crushing fatigue and confusion weighed her down. As he disappeared through the garden, her body felt heavy. She hadn't wanted it to end this way between them, but perhaps it was meant to. This was what always happened between them, wasn't it? They were fire and ice. Heat and passion followed by distance and discord. Why could they never find the middle ground and fight alongside one another rather than with each other?

It didn't matter.

She had far greater matters to tend to now that she knew what her brothers had been keeping from her and what their worries were. If this was just about Catriona, why had they not brought her into their circle and allowed her to help her sister? Susanna would ask them that very question—tomorrow. For now, she was too tired to do much other than wearily climb the stairs, shrug out of her gown, and crawl into her bed. She made her way through the castle, skilfully avoiding all of the squeaks and creaks as she went in case her brothers or others were up. She opened her chamber door, entered the room, and closed the door. She relaxed against it with a sigh and took a deep breath. The smell of musk and shave cream stilled her.

She was not alone.

'Although I am beyond relieved you are back, where in hell's name did you disappear to for hours?' A candle flickered to life near the settee, casting shadows on her younger brother's face.

Rolf.

Her body sagged forward in relief followed swiftly by outrage. 'You are a fine one to lecture me upon anything. Perhaps I merely wished to have some brief moments of joy before you and Royce barter me off to Audric and his son like livestock to keep your secret safe.'

His eyes widened and she smiled, enjoying being one step ahead after feeling behind in their game of secrecy for so long. She plucked off her shoes and tossed them on the rug. She joined him on the settee and rubbed her toes, almost sighing aloud at the relief of being back in her own room and off her feet.

His rebuttal died on his lips as he scrutinised her. 'We will discuss how you know any of that in a moment. What happened to you? You look...' He was kind enough not to finish the sentence.

She held up her palm. 'Do not change the subject at hand. I am fine, except for this business with Catriona being Audric's daughter, you both lying to us about it, and making me feel a fool looking for a husband when you already had other plans for me.'

'We never intended—' he began.

'What did you intend, then? Beyond the lying and deception?' She leaned her head back and pulled the remaining pins from her hair, letting them fall haphazardly to the floor.

He said nothing, so she lifted her head. 'Although I do appreciate that you at least stood up for me. Tried to reason with Royce because you feared I might perish in the clutches of Audric and his son.'

'How do you know all of this?' he sputtered.

'Eavesdropping,' she said smiling sweetly at him. 'I am quite good at it.'

'Why am I not surprised?' His tone reeked of exasperation.

'You are annoyed because I learned the truth you were hiding from me?' she snapped back.

'Aye. Who else knows?'

She pressed her lips together.

'Susanna,' he said, his voice low with warning.

'Campbell,' she replied, lifting her chin a notch.

'How?'

'We found out together.'

'You were both eavesdropping?'

'Aye.'

Her brother scrutinised her once more. 'Did he do this to you?' he asked, pointing to her rumpled gown and mussed hair.

'Only because I asked him to,' she replied with a wink.

Rolf cringed, his face souring. 'You are my sister. Not only should you never tell me such things, but it is a disrespect to you.'

'And you are a virgin, I suppose? My chaste brother, Rolf?'

He blushed, the colour rising high in cheeks. 'That is different,' he muttered.

'Because you are a man?' She laughed. 'We are adults. I am beholden to no one yet, so I may make my own choices.'

He clutched her hand. 'Susanna, this is no game. It is serious. All of it.'

She squeezed his hand. 'I know that. And I wish to speak to you and Royce tomorrow. You *will* include me in your plans moving forward.'

'I will ask him,' Rolf replied, letting go of her hand.

'You misunderstand me. It is not a request, brother. I *will* be joining you.'

After a long bath and even longer sleep, the next morn, Susanna dressed and went to Royce's study.

Royce's frown told her Rolf had briefed him on last night's events. All of them, by the depth of his scowl. Susanna sent Rolf an accusing glare, and he just shrugged back. So much for not revealing everything to her brothers.

'Sit,' Royce commanded.

Susanna closed the door and settled in across from him and next to Rolf. It felt as if she were a wee girl being brought to Father's study for a punishment. She was in no mood for it.

'Have you summoned me to apologise?' she asked, crossing her legs and sitting up taller in her chair.

'Susanna,' Rolf warned under his breath.

She ignored him. She was weary—of everything. The secrets, the aloneness, and the dread of whatever might happen next that she couldn't control. Speaking her mind was well overdue with her eldest brother and laird.

Royce leaned his head forward. 'Excuse me?' he said, pretending to have not heard her.

'You heard me. I am waiting.'

Rolf sighed. Susanna glanced over to see him shaking his head and then rubbing his temple. 'Cease,' he murmured.

'I will not,' she answered aloud. 'I am bone weary of doing your will, doing Father's will, and trying to be compliant. What has it served me? You are to marry me off after making me promises that you would do nothing of the sort. And then to keep me and Catriona out of learning the truth of who her real father is? I can still hardly believe it. If I had not heard you say it aloud from this room, I wouldn't.'

Royce rested his arms on the desk, interlacing his fingers. 'And how did you happen to be in a position to be eavesdropping?'

'That is of no matter.'

'It is of great matter,' he mocked her.

She sat with her mouth clamped shut.

He waited her out for some time before giving up. 'And what do you plan to do with such information?' he finally asked.

'I have thought upon it, and I think we should tell her. If she knows, she can be mindful and take care, and Ewan must also know. He cannot protect her properly otherwise.'

'We will protect her, without either of them knowing.'

Susanna scoffed. 'Even you cannot be so arrogant, Royce, as to believe that you and you alone can protect them.'

When he did not reply, she continued. 'They have a babe on the way. You cannot leave them in the dark about such an important matter. What if Audric discovers the truth and retaliates?' She gripped the chair. 'If roles were reversed, you would want to know so you could protect Iona and your bairn, would you not?'

He leaned back in his chair. Her words had landed where she had hoped they would: on his heart. Iona and his bairn were the most important part of his life. Finding her and building his own family with her had changed him.

Or at least, Susanna thought it had.

'I am not trying to put them in greater danger, but in less,' he finally replied.

'Telling them *is* a way to protect them. The only way, as far as I can see. Especially if you fear the truth may reach Audric and his clan in ways you may not suspect.' She pressed her nail into her fingertip, finally asking the other question she wished to know the answer to. 'Do you understand how such a thing happened? I cannot imagine Mother would have...' She dropped her gaze.

'We have not been able to unearth how, but we have guesses. I wish to think upon none of them.' His voice was low and subdued, a mirror of what she felt.

'And Father? Did he know?'

'Aye. It was why he left her there, according to Webster. She is the woman I went in search of on Lismore, although before I met her, I believed her to be a man.'

'Left her there? What are you talking about, brother?' Susanna's pulse increased, and she moved forward in her chair, glancing at Rolf.

The sadness in Rolf's gaze told her it was true, and Susanna's stomach made a sickening flip. He reached out and took her hand in his own. 'It seems,' Rolf began, 'that Father knew she was on Lismore for quite some time. He paid Webster. She was charged with caring for Catriona, but as we all know, that *care* was less than ideal.'

Susanna's eyes welled, and her throat tightened. She swallowed back the agony of such a thought. 'He left her? He left his daughter on a strange island alone? Left us all to grieve her? How could anyone...?' she began, but a sob escaped her, and tears fell down her cheeks.

Rolf clutched her hands tightly.

'I fear I may be sick,' she murmured, leaning forward.

Rolf let go of her hand, rose from his chair, and rubbed her back as she grasped her knees. Susanna tried to still the churning in her stomach and the sickness roiling there.

'He believed he was protecting us all in the best way he could.' Royce's voice was distant and stoic, as if he did not believe his own words.

'There had to be a better way,' she muttered, lifting her face. She wiped back her tears with her sleeve. 'All that happened to her and us could have been prevented.'

'Aye. It could have,' Rolf added quietly. 'But it cannot be unwound now. And telling her. It will break her heart.'

'Has her heart not already been broken?' Susanna asked quietly. 'Isn't building a future on truth important for us and for her family? Now more than ever?'

'But we still do not know all of the truth,' Royce countered. 'We do not know what happened between Audric and our mother, why Father did what he did, and if we really know all the impacts revealing such a truth will bring about, especially with the Highlands being in such a delicate state politically. It could bring us and the MacDonalds or even more clans into a war.'

'Over Catriona?'

'Possibly. But most likely, it will be over the deception,' Royce added. 'Audric is a vindictive man. His only children, Fiona and Devlin, have all but abandoned him for the Campbells. He may try to convince Catriona to come to his clan—or worse, exact retribution.'

'How?' she asked.

'By stealing his grandchild once he or she is born,' Rolf added quietly.

'A child for a child,' she murmured, a tremor in her voice as she shivered. 'Is that what you fear?'

'Aye,' Royce replied, his voice heavy and cryptic. 'To my very bones.'

'Then why are you doing things to bring him closer to us? This sham of an engagement to Devlin? Giving him more land and resources? I do not follow your logic, brother.'

'If we have an alliance of marriage with us *before* he discovers the truth, he will be less likely to retaliate.'

'Less likely?' she asked.

'With Audric, there is no hundred per cent certainty of anything. He has little left to lose, and he is aging.' Royce stood from his chair and paced.

'There must be another solution,' she replied.

'Killing him would only make matters worse,' Royce added.

'What if someone else killed him?' she said quietly.

Rolf and Royce stared at her.

'Laird Campbell. You know he wishes to take revenge on him. You have all but set up the conflict with these gatherings of yours, which have included invitations to them both. You know how close they have come to attacking one another.'

'Nay, Susanna. That was not our intention, not really. To create discord between them was a way to further our cause and alliance to get Audric to trust us, nothing more. We cannot kill him. At least not yet. I believe he holds part of the answers. We cannot kill him, nor can anyone else, until we have those answers.'

'That might be a problem,' she added and blew out a breath.

'Why?'

'Because I already promised Rowan I would help him kill the man.'

Chapter Twenty-One

Rowan wiped sweat from his brow and then continued shaping the heated metal with his forging hammer. Finally, it was softening and turning into something other than a hunk of—well—nothing. The reverberation through his arm as he fashioned the metal on the anvil eased some of the tension coiled tightly in his body. Over the last few days, he'd found himself working extra hours in the forge. His obsession with killing Audric was consuming him, and memories of his tryst with Susanna were a close second. Between the spirals of rage and desire, he was wrecked and could focus on nothing but the physical labour that might bring both of those thoughts to an end—even if it was only temporary.

He had to find a way to exact his revenge on Audric and banish his mind from further thoughts and hopes about Susanna. She had made her choice, her family, and he had made his, exacting his justice for his wife and son. There was no middle ground. He could wait no longer. Audric had to die. Justice was far overdue.

'Late hours, even for you,' Hugh said as he entered the forge, letting the barn door slide closed behind him.

Rowan looked up. He had no idea what day it was, let alone what time. He did not answer his friend. 'I need no lecture from you,' he muttered, grabbing tongs to flip the metal slab on the anvil.

'Well, you need something, my laird. The soldiers are talking, and your family is worried about you, especially Trice. She has mentioned calling back Brandon early from his trip up north with Fiona and wee William. Daniel agrees with her.'

'As usual, Trice frets with no cause, and her husband Daniel is too soft with her. There is no need to bring back my baby brother and his family from their travels.'

'Oh, no?' Hugh crossed his arms against his chest. 'When was the last time you ate? Or spent some extended time with your daughter?'

He set aside the tongs. 'This morn.'

Hugh pressed his lips together and shook his head. 'Nay. You have not eaten this morn, and Rosa has not seen you since the day prior.'

'Are you following me? You have no other pressing matters to attend to than my eating habits?' He glowered at Hugh.

'You are my prime duty, as you well know, with Brandon away. So is your welfare, my laird. And aye, I am concerned. You are losing your way.'

'You have no right to speak to me in such a manner.' He tugged off his leather apron and threw it on the large workbench.

'As your friend, I believe it is a requirement. As your most trusted soldier, it is my duty to ensure you are able and willing to lead our clan. Both demand I speak the truth to you.' He approached, his gaze softening, and he rested his hands on his waist belt. 'What happened the night of the Holiday Ball at Loch's End last week? When you returned, you were a different man.'

'What didn't happen?' he spat out as he ran a hand through his hair.

Hugh waited in silence.

Rowan continued, knowing full well that Hugh would wait in silence for days for him to speak. It was one of his friend's most admirable and irritating qualities. 'Susanna and I discovered her brother's secrets, and we also—' He did not finish, hoping Hugh would deduce his meaning.

Hugh's brow lifted in surprise. He nodded, a smirk flashing briefly before his features returned to their usual neutral position. 'Well, that is an interesting, but not unexpected, turn of events. And it explains your—current state.'

'Which is what?' he challenged.

'You are not yourself. Since this ruse with Susanna began two months ago, you have been partly energised but also distracted, bent on this revenge against Audric. Now that you two have...reunited—' he paused, choosing his words with care '—and discovered whatever it is that set you off course a week ago, you are—'

'I am what?' he asked, closing in on Hugh, daring him to speak his mind.

'Obsessed, irritable, and distracted. It is an odd combination. While it is similar to how you were after Anna's death, it is somehow different.' He said the words with objectivity rather than censure, and it yanked out the foundation of Rowan's temper.

Mostly because he knew it was the truth.

While Rowan didn't feel the same grief and rage he felt when Anna and their son died, he felt an agony of disappointment over not having Susanna's help to exact his revenge on Audric as he'd planned, but also an anger at himself for being vulnerable with Susanna and for believing she might have changed. He'd thought maybe, just maybe, when they had made love and been hidden in that closet for hours, that they were being given some new chance and beginning with one another. That she could walk alongside him on this path to healing from the past by helping him kill Audric, but also that she might choose to be a part of his future.

He cursed and sat down on the bench with a hard thud, scrubbing his hand through his rather dirty hair, and was aware of his own stench. He needed a bath. Perhaps Hugh was right.

'I was a fool,' he said.

Hugh sat down next to him on the bench. 'About?'

'Everything relating to Susanna, and I hate myself for it. Much like I did when we were teens and I believed she cared for me, for us. All she cares about is her family and keeping the Camerons as the most powerful clan in the Highlands. There is nothing else in her heart.'

Hugh's silence egged him on.

'She has gone back on our agreement. She will *not* assist me with killing Audric and finally getting the justice Anna and our son deserve, because it no longer suits her plans,' Rowan continued.

'While I still do not wish for you to kill Audric for a variety of reasons, I am curious to know why the Camerons now wish to protect him. Seems out of character even for them. Although I did find it curious that he has been invited to Loch's End more than once recently.'

'I shall share this with you as long as you agree to tell no one. Not even your horse.'

Hugh scoffed. 'It shall not leave my lips, although you know even if I told Clover, she would tell no one. She is a horse.'

Rowan lifted a brow at him, and Hugh relented. 'Fine,' he muttered. 'I will tell no one, not even Clover.'

Rowan inched closer to him, dropping his voice further. 'You know Susanna's long-lost younger sister, Violet, who we now know as Catriona?'

'Aye.'

'Well, evidently she is actually Audric's daughter. She is really their half sister.'

Hugh's mouth fell open in shock, and he sat a full minute in silence as he took in Rowan's words. 'I do not understand,' he finally offered. 'How could that be? And why?'

'We had the same questions. None of which we have answers for. I can only relay that Susanna's brothers fear that Audric or someone else in his clan will learn of this information and retaliate.'

'But wouldn't they *want* to kill Audric then? Would that not provide greater protection for them? I do not follow their reasoning.'

Rowan shrugged. 'Nor do I. There must be more to the situation than I understand. Susanna said she did not wish to kill him because it would put them in more danger.' He scrubbed a hand down his face. 'The brothers have arranged for Susanna to marry Devlin and provide a dowry of land and resources to the MacDonalds upon their union. None of it makes any sense to me at all.'

'While I have come to believe Devlin is a good man, to marry your sister into that family by choice?' he shook his head. 'You're right, there must be more to the story,' Hugh added. 'Something that puts them in grave danger, since they are making such extreme choices.'

'Which is why I am so frustrated and irritated. I cannot reason it out in my mind, and I am crushed by the outcome of it all.'

'Have you not just asked Susanna what else she has found out?'

'Nay. I cannot bring myself to do so.'

'Because of your pride?'

'That is part of it,' Rowan answered truthfully. 'She has rejected me, after all.'

'And the rest of it?' Hugh met his gaze.

Rowan sighed. 'Because I do not trust myself around her. I cannot make good decisions. My emotions rule me in her presence, which we both know leads to nothing good.' He looked down at his palms, rubbing the dark smudges of coal into the lines there, wishing they held some answers for him.

'So, your plan is to work yourself into exhaustion by hiding in here and hammering out your anger and frustration?' Hugh asked.

'That was the gist of it,' Rowan answered, almost smiling at Hugh's deduction and its accuracy.

'And your plan now?'

'To meet with Susanna and figure out what the hell is going on.'

'Might I suggest a bath first?'

He sniffed himself and coughed. 'Aye. I will bathe, take a meal, and see my daughter. Then I will see to Susanna.'

'I will have the horses readied and travel with you.'

'Aye. Give me three hours, and we can depart.'

'When Tilly told me you were here at Loch's End, I did not believe her at first.'

Rowan's body tensed at the sound of Susanna's voice as

she entered the parlour, where she had kept him waiting for almost a full hour. During that period, he'd had much time to think about and much practice in mulling over his words and what he wished to say. Perhaps too much time. When she came in and dared sit right next to him on the small settee, her gown pressing in against his trews, her violet scent assaulting his senses, every well-planned-out sentence and remark fell into a black abyss.

'I do not give up so easily on the idea of us,' he said. 'And I will collect on my arrangement with you.'

Her blue eyes assessed him, cool, icy, and without emotion. A flash of their coupling in the alcove in this very hallway flashed through his mind. Could she be so unaffected? Was only he thinking of that intimate memory between them now? His body hummed at her proximity and the memory of what they had shared. He picked up her wrist gently. A rapid pulse thrummed under his thumb. He caressed it in smooth circles.

'So, you are not as unaffected as you seem. At least I know you are human,' he said before setting her hand in the folds of her gown and releasing it.

She glared at him. 'What would you prefer I do, my laird? Swoon at your feet? I am not the type, as you well know.'

'I do.' He sat back in the settee. The anger that flashed back up in her abated his own.

'And?' she asked, sitting up straighter.

'And nothing.'

'Then why are you here?' she asked, her irritation growing, which pleased him.

He stretched out his arm on the back of the settee behind her, allowing his fingers to play with the end of her plait that rested there. He toyed with the silken strands. He could play the game as well as she. 'To ensure my part of the agreement of our bargain is fulfilled. I assume you have enlightened your brothers as to our farce and your part of the agreement. That you have promised your help in Audric's death.' He ceased moving and set his full attention on her response.

She shifted, her vexation reflected in her stiff, brittle movements. She leaned closer and dropped her voice. 'I have told them of our arrangement, and they forbid my further involvement in it. Causing Audric's demise may well cause our own, and I cannot have that.'

'You cannot have that?' he scoffed. 'And what of me? What of your promises to me? Of what I want? Of what I need?' Emotion edged into his voice.

'I am asking you to set that aside until we can see another solution, Rowan. For the sake of my family and clan, I ask you to be patient.'

'Until when? Until you are wed to his son? Until he kills more innocent people on a whim? Until when exactly?' he challenged her.

'Killing him will not bring them back,' she said quietly. 'So much time has passed that a bit longer will not matter. And it could protect my sister and her family. They have a bairn on the way. You know that.'

'A bit longer will not matter, you say?' he scoffed. 'You cannot understand. I thought you could that day when you spoke of Jeremiah with such affection and vulnerability, but you cannot. You are a woman.'

She recoiled, her anger piqued. 'I cannot understand your pride because I am a woman? I think I can. I do.'

Something roared deep within him, fracturing the reserve and patience he had been fiercely clinging to. His voice dropped so low that he almost did not recognise it. 'Nay. You cannot. It was my sworn duty, my vow as a man, father, and husband, to protect my wife and my son. My child. I failed in that. I failed utterly. They died because *I—I* could not protect them.' He stood, pointing to his chest. 'That was no one else's job but mine. That failure is a cross I bear every day. It rests so heavily upon my chest that some days I cannot breathe. Some days I do not wish to live. It is Rosa that brings me back to now. She helps me live. And as of late, if I am honest with myself, you did too.'

Chapter Twenty-Two

Susanna could only gape up at him. She gripped the soft fabric of the settee, frozen at the sight of Rowan, Laird of Campbell, standing before her, confessing his grief and at the same time his unexpected devotion to her. *Her*. After all these years, could he truly care for her or grow to love her? Could she trust what might be blossoming between them?

Did she dare?

She tried to clear her throat, but it was scratchy and dry as if she had swallowed a tuft of wool, and no words would come to her. At least none that made sense. Her heart screamed to get up, go to him, and hug him. To physically *show* him that she did care for him. But her mind commanded her to stay still, to not reveal her feelings, to keep them close at hand, lest she be hurt. In case his words now were untrue and in case he did not respond well to what words did finally come to her.

'It does not matter now,' she said.

He shook his head. 'What does not matter now?'

'How you feel or how I feel. I have agreed to marry Devlin and to assist my brothers in their plan to protect my sister and the clan. I can no longer help you with Audric. If anything, I must try to protect him—from you.'

He stalked to her and pulled her up beside him, holding her by the elbows. His gaze was intent. 'You will betray me?'

She settled into his hold, having missed his touch far more than she wished to admit even to herself. 'If that is what I must do to protect my family.'

'After all I risked for you to uphold my end of our agreement? After all we shared with one another these past weeks? Did it mean nothing?'

It meant more than nothing, but it didn't mean everything. He wanted all of her and all from her, and she couldn't give him that. Her family would always be a part of her, an incredibly important part, and she couldn't give them up. She wouldn't.

Not even for him.

Not even for the sweetness that he had awakened in her. Not even for the promise of something more.

'And what of you? Could you give up your vengeance? And let go of the past? For me?' she challenged him. Rowan could never give up his vengeance, his need to avenge his wife and son, and his grief over the past. He held on to his grief tightly. He was possessive of his loss.

He loosened his hold on her, uncertain how to continue. 'I cannot merely forget the past. It is a part of who I am. Anna, my son...'

'I am asking you to face the past, not forget it.' She gripped his tunic, the heat from him a reminder of what his flesh felt like on her own. Her body buzzed.

'I do face it. Every. Single. Day. It is what I think of the first and last moments of each day. How dare you suggest I do not face it?'

'Then why can you not say his name?' she whispered, knowing well she was treading on very dangerous ground.

'Whose name?' he asked, confused.

'Your son's. When we speak of him and your wife, you always call her by name, but never your son, as if you cannot bear it…'

He tried to pull away and wrapped his hands around her own to loosen her grip on his tunic, but she held on tightly. 'Do not speak to me of him…' His voice wavered.

'Rowan,' she whispered.

But he looked away and closed his eyes.

'What was his name? I do not even know it,' she murmured. 'Honour his memory,' she pleaded. 'Say his name aloud when you speak of him.'

With an anguished growl, Rowan pulled himself away from her hold, and she staggered back. 'I will say his name,' he began, his breathing laboured and his voice harsh, 'when I have avenged his death, and I deserve to say it. I will do that on my own, no matter the consequences to you or anyone. I have waited for my justice long enough. So have they. I will wait no longer. Best you prepare for the outcome, whatever it might be.'

He held her gaze for a moment before turning sharply on his heel, exiting the room, and slamming the parlour door behind him. Although he was not the broken, bedraggled man of two years ago, overcome by grief and floundering his way back to reality, he was losing himself. Guilt wriggled its way in, and she remembered that night in the forge. She knew what she'd promised him by offering to assist him in his revenge against Audric. She'd known well the pit of grief she might drive him back into by offering her help to fulfil his wishes—and the obsession to fulfil that wish that would follow once their farce had begun. Grief was a delicate tether. She knew that more than anyone.

And she had thrust him down into the well of sorrow, severing that tether in two, and offering him no way out. She remembered his words from that night in the forge:

'For revenge against Audric, I can and will do anything. I will hold you to your promise, Susanna. Nothing will stand in my way of finally ending him. Not even you.'

A shiver went up her spine, making her hands tingle. She had awakened the grief in Rowan all right, just when her family was most in danger, without even knowing it, and now there was no stopping him. The ripples of damage from what he would do were unfathomable. She had not felt so helpless since she lost Jeremiah. But she would not wallow in her grief as she'd done then. She would try to make things right somehow.

She rushed from the parlour and out to the barn in hopes of stopping Rowan and interceding. He was riding off along the road, his back to her. Hugh intercepted her.

'You must leave him be,' Hugh commanded, his features tight and his hold upon her arms even tighter.

'I cannot,' she argued.

'You must. He will not listen to reason. Not now.'

'Hugh, if he follows through with his plan...' she pleaded.

'There is nothing that you can do, but I will try to reason with him before he destroys himself and his future. Now go,' he said, releasing her. 'I need to be not far behind him.'

She nodded and watched him jump onto his mount and gallop off in pursuit of Rowan, kicking up dirt behind him. All Susanna could do was watch and hope somehow both of their clans wouldn't be left in a smouldering pile of ruin. And blame herself. She had set all of this in motion, had she not? Perhaps some secrets were better left alone. Nothing good had come from unearthing this one, nor from Royce's uncovering of the truth of why Father had written about Lismore in his journals.

She stood staring dumbly after Rowan and Hugh, noting the stillness that followed. A cold, wet nose hit her palm, followed by a slobbery kiss, yanking her back to the present. She looked down to see Jack, Iona's beloved hound, smiling up at her with his joyful eyes and wagging tail.

'I could not help but overhear,' Iona offered as she approached her from the meadows. 'I was walking with Jack.'

Susanna turned, relieved to see her sister-in-law, and greeted her with a warm hug. 'You have divine timing. I am glad you are here. May I join you? I have no wish to go back inside and face the interrogation from my brothers.'

Iona smiled and hooked her arm through Susanna's. 'As long as you do not mind the extra company Royce has assigned me,' she whispered, nodding to the soldier following at a distance. 'We are always up for company on our walks, are we not, Jack?'

The pup barked and snapped his jowls in the air before dashing down the drive, only to circle back and join them moments later, falling in step beside Iona. His devotion to her was unmatched, except for Royce, of course.

'Love is a precarious creature,' Iona offered. 'Royce and I had a similar sparring before we finally relented to one another. Neither of us wished to yield too much for fear of losing ourselves in one another. If I was to guess, I believe that is what you and Laird Campbell are doing now.' She smirked at her.

'How did you…?' Susanna asked, heat easing up her neck and cheeks.

'You have been happier and softer since he has been

around.' Iona chuckled. 'That is a fine marker for love, is it not?'

'I do not know if it is or could be love or not,' she began, savouring the cool air and sweet smell of the trees and the breeze despite the crispness of winter fast approaching. 'We knew each other when we were young. And after losing Jeremiah, I do not know if I can fully love again.'

Iona listened quietly and offered a soft smile of encouragement.

'And it is of no matter now anyway,' Susanna added. 'Royce has selected my match for *the good of the clan.*' Her last words weighed heavily on her. As much as she was willing to marry Devlin for the sake of the clan's future, it did not mean she wanted to. Especially now that she knew her feelings for Rowan were like his own for her. They might have had something, but now—it did not matter. There was no way forward for them, especially with him hell-bent on killing Audric.

Far too much was at stake, and their affections for each other were of little consequence.

Weren't they?

'Do not dismiss it all so quickly. Royce's mind can be changed. But he must be open to hearing your words. Allow him some time.'

'You know him well.' Susanna laughed.

'With each day, I discover more about him. It shall be the same for you and Rowan, I think—with time.'

Susanna sighed. 'That is the thing. We do not have that luxury, and we are at odds over an issue that is of great importance to both of us.'

'And you are both stubborn and will not yield?'

'Aye.'

'It was the same with Royce and me, and look at us now. Married and with a babe on the way. Why can it not be the same for you and Rowan?' she asked with a hopeful smile.

'While I hear your words, I just do not believe it possible for us. 'tis best I let go of such hope. It will only lead to disappointment. And we have far greater issues weighing on us at present.'

'Oh?' Iona stopped and faced her.

Susanna blanched. Why had she said that? 'Nothing to worry you over,' she added a bit too late.

'For all of your cunning, you do not lie well,' Iona said with a smirk. 'Now, tell me what these great issues are, or I shall march us into Royce's study and wrest it from him anyway.' She crossed her arms against her chest.

'Then we are off to your husband's study, I fear.' She reached out and took Iona's hand in her own. 'Follow me. I dare not utter a word of it to you, especially out here. And especially without Royce knowing first.'

Chapter Twenty-Three

'If you wish to aid me in my endeavour, then stay. If not—' Rowan shot Hugh a glare '—leave. I have plans to make.' Rowan yanked open a drawer of maps, riffled through them to find the one he needed, and spread it out on the table in his study.

Hugh handed him one large ledger and then another in silence to help Rowan anchor the map and keep it from rolling in on itself. Each time, his knowing gaze chipped away at Rowan's resolve.

'And what would you have me do?' he answered Hugh's unspoken question.

Hugh shrugged. 'I have not said a word.'

'You are speaking with your silence, as usual. It is infuriating. Especially when I have my revenge to plan out and wish to enjoy it.' He slammed the drawer closed.

Hugh shut the door to the chamber quietly and sat on one of the bench seats, leaning forward and resting his elbows on his knees, linking his hands together. 'And what of Rosa? And the clan?'

Each question jabbed into Rowan's resolve, leaving him pained and uncertain. He sat across from Hugh. 'And what of Rosa and the clan if I *don't* do this? How can I be a father and laird if I let Audric go unpunished for his brutality? If I waste even more time than I already have waiting for the perfect opportunity for justice?'

'What if it is not your justice to impart? Have you thought of that?'

Rowan balked. 'How could it not be? He murdered my wife and my son, and countless other men and women died that day because of him and his unwarranted attack upon us. Do you not remember?'

Hugh lifted his brow in challenge, his jaw tight. 'You know well I remember. You were not the only one to lose someone that day. Do not insult me with such questions, my laird.'

'Aye. That was not fair of me. I know you remember. You fought by my side.'

Hugh's posture relaxed.

'But whose claim for justice is it, then? And how can I ever be released of this agony, this crushing shame,' he said, his throat tightening with emotion, 'if I do not finally kill him?'

'Trust me. That agony will never leave you, no matter what you do,' Hugh offered. 'It has never left me despite how I believed it would if I killed enough British soldiers. It is within you, and you must make peace with it, or it will consume you. Until recently, I thought you had come to peace with it.'

Rowan shook his head. 'Perhaps I have pretended well. Too well. I can say what I know you all wish to hear from me. And the discipline and structure I have set upon myself have helped to keep the hounds of present in charge, but recently, I feel the other wolf within me rising back up, begging to be heard. Begging to exact its wishes to wipe Audric from this earth, pressing the other, more rational part of me back. I can taste it. My mouth waters for such revenge.' He fisted his hands and let his eyes close. His heart pounded in his ears. 'I fear the wolf may win this time.'

'Not if you focus on the present. On Rosa. On the future. On your family.'

Rowan sucked in air through his nose and exhaled out his mouth, counting as he went, until his pulse slowed and he could think more clearly. He opened his eyes. Hugh stared upon him with empathy.

'Before my gran died, she told me a story that I'll share with you.' Hugh shifted on the bench, and his features relaxed, as they always did when he spoke of his family.

Rowan nodded to encourage him to continue.

'It was about an old man, beaten down by age as well as time. He was kind, helpful, and never turned his back on anyone in need. One day a younger man, lost and uncertain, clutching a small bag, came upon his hut. The old man offered him food, water, and shelter, and the younger man was grateful, but all the while he would not set down his bag. Not anywhere. Always he was holding it, watching over it, and protecting it as if it were gold. The old man was curious and asked him of its contents. The young man, suspicious of the old man despite his generosity, hid the bag behind him, telling him it was none of his concern.

'The next day the old man provided the younger man directions as to how he could reach his destination, but he warned him that some of the mountain passes were dangerous, and he would have to use both hands to help navigate them.

'The younger man ignored the man's warnings, intent on holding on to his prized possession rather than putting it in a satchel upon his back or leaving it behind all together.'

'Let me guess,' Rowan interrupted. 'He perished because he wouldn't let go of whatever he was holding on to.'

Hugh smiled. 'Aye.'

'And your message for me in this is to let it go?'

'As overly simple as it sounds, aye, that is my message to you,' Hugh replied. 'You cannot hold on to two worlds so tightly. One hand cannot cling to the past while the other clutches for the future.'

'Your gran laid all of this upon you as a lad?'

'It was an odd tale to tell a boy so young, but she knew what hatred was in my heart after I lost my parents and sister in that attack from the British. Perhaps she knew I needed to hear it to survive. I held on to my rage tightly for a long time. It wasn't until I let loose of it that I started to live.'

'You make it seem so simple.' Rowan shook his head.

'It is one of the most difficult things I have ever done.'

'Such encouragement,' Rowan scoffed, rubbing the back of his neck.

'But you are strong enough. You have come out of this grief and rage before. You have been on the precipice of sanity and come back from making decisions that could have ended badly for you and your family. Think of the rescue of Fiona and wee William two years ago. You could have let them perish so you could have your revenge against Audric, but you chose to save them instead. You pushed through that rage and put them first. You chose the present over the past. Hope over revenge. You can do it again. And you can choose your future. You can choose to be a strong leader, to be a good father, and to be the laird you want to be. Who do you want to be to your daughter, to your son, to Anna? Make the present you want, Rowan.

Do not be enslaved by the past. Let go of it.' He clapped Rowan on the back and rose. 'I will leave you to decide.'

'You sure know how to lay a burden on a man, Hugh.'

'It is not a burden to be able to choose. Think of all of those who can't, my laird. Those whose choices were made for them or those who no longer have voices to share in this world. We are two of the lucky ones. Do not forget that.'

Hugh's final words before he walked away landed hard. Rowan's gut tightened with the knowledge that his friend was right. He was alive, he still had choices to make, and he could choose to live a life without this deep-seated desire for revenge. But how? How did he let it go? How did he just move on, step fully into the present, and seek out life as hungrily as he used to before he lost so much? He gripped his neck and groaned.

Saints be.

He didn't know.

But maybe that was what he was meant to find out. While he didn't know *how* to do it, he knew where he needed to start. He pulled himself up and began the walk he needed to take. The one he had put off for too long. He needed to see his son: Keir. Setting one foot in front of the other, he climbed across the meadow to the site of Anna's and Keir's graves. It was a glorious afternoon for such a walk. The sun was high in the bright blue sky, and the crisp breeze of late autumn rustled the leaves that remained. Next August, the ridge would be awash with shades of lilac, lavender, and deep purple as the heather took over the mountainside.

Anna would have loved it. It was one of the many reasons he had chosen this spot for her and their son. Even though it wasn't nestled next to the other family plots, he knew she would have approved. He smiled when he saw how well-tended the plots were. The slate stones were clear of debris and overgrowth, and small trinkets rested upon the stones.

Trice.

His heart tugged in gratitude. It had to be her tending them with such care. He stilled when he saw a tiny wooden horse atop Keir's gravestone. Rowan knelt to pick it up, and a swell of emotion overcame him as he turned it in his fingers. He had whittled this very horse for Rosa last month, and she had cherished it so. To know she had brought it here and gifted it to her baby brother stole his breath. Trice was doing what he should have been doing: bringing Rosa here to see her mother and brother when she asked.

Why hadn't he been the one to do such?

It ought to have been him.

He cursed.

Sucking in a breath, Rowan realised for the first time how selfish and oblivious he had been to everything and everyone but his own grief. Even now, when he thought he had been getting better, he was still stuck. Rosa had lost her mother and brother, yet she charged fiercely through the world with joy. She had not been waylaid by such grief. She had not even wanted to bother her father with a request to see her mother and brother at their graves.

Rowan had been holding on to his grief and loss for so long that he had not even seen what his daughter was going through. He had not been there for her. Not really. He had not been there for his family or his clan as he should have been.

He pressed one palm on Anna's gravestone while resting the other on Keir's, the smooth, cool stone beneath his flesh soothing. 'I am so sorry, Anna,' Rowan whispered. 'I have failed you even when I thought I was better. I should have been here. Seen you. Brought our daughter. Visited our son. Visited—Keir.' His son's name came out in a tremble. He had not said Keir's name aloud since the day of his death. It sounded foreign and yet precious on Rowan's lips, so he said it aloud again, and again, and again, until the knot of grief in him loosened a whisper.

He felt along his neck, clutching the lopsided and rather ugly-looking brooch he had fashioned for Anna all those years ago to make something special for her. The one that she had worn without fail every day after he had gifted it to her despite its appearance, and that he had worn on a cord of leather ever since the day she died. 'I know, my love,' he whispered with a small smile as his eyes welled. 'It is time. Past time.' He pulled a blade from his waist belt and cut the leather cord around his neck. He pressed a kiss to the brooch and placed it gently on Anna's gravestone.

'Keir, I promise to be a better man,' he said, running a palm over the smooth stone. 'To be the father and laird that you would have been proud of. Starting today. This moment. I promise you.'

How long Rowan knelt before them, praying, talking to them, and listening to the wind, he couldn't say, but dusk was beginning to turn over day to night when he began his walk back to the castle. And while he wasn't cured and he wasn't whole quite yet, he felt lighter. He opened both of his hands as he walked, letting go of the fierce anger of the past while welcoming in the sweet hope of the present.

Chapter Twenty-Four

Susanna paced the parlour at Loch's End, her gaze sweeping from the mantel clock to the window overlooking the front drive and back to the mirror on the opposite wall. The last two weeks had been a fretful whirl of worry and frustration for Susanna. Not only had she mulled over the conversation she had had with Rowan a thousand times and found her replies wanting and at fault each time, she had no idea how to mend what she had done. While she had a right to ask him to choose her and the present, she had no right to ask him to let go of the love in his heart for Anna or his son. One could never let go of those in their heart.

But she'd been angry at him for not giving in to her demands of putting off his revenge in order to protect her family. If she were honest with herself, she was also hurt because whether she wished to admit it or not, she was beginning to fall in love with him, just as Iona suspected. She had begun to long for him and for a future she dared not hope or dream of. At the first sign of trouble, she had bolted like a wild horse and retreated, unable to drum up her courage to ask for another chance with him.

But it was of no matter now, was it?

She would marry Devlin to enhance their standing with Audric and the MacDonalds, and today they would be telling Catriona the truth about her parentage and unfurl all the secrets they had been keeping from her. Susanna's stomach curdled.

Susanna had been dreading this day since the afternoon she and Iona had walked into Royce's study and her brother had shared the truth of what was truly happening with his wife. With each day, the dread had grown, building on itself day in and day out.

A carriage came to a halt outside the large windows. Soon Catriona's sweet, joyful voice echoed as she walked through the entryway of the Loch's End, followed by her husband Ewan's low baritone. Rolf greeted them, and Susanna thought she might be ill. As much as she had demanded Catriona be told what her brothers had discovered about her disappearance to Lismore and her true lineage, now that the moment to tell her was here, Susanna wanted to run to the stables, hop on Midnight, and flee from Loch's End at a gallop.

As their footfalls signalled their approach, she stood up and clutched her hands behind her, forcing a smile. Royce emerged from his study down the hallway and greeted them warmly before following them into the parlour, where Susanna stood, waiting with a full spread of tea and offerings to tempt them. Not that anyone would feel like eating after the news was shared.

'Sister.' Susanna rushed to her Catriona and wrapped her a tight, warm hug.

Catriona tensed for a moment before she settled into it. 'What a warm greeting,' she murmured, hugging her back. She pulled away and clutched Susanna's forearms. 'Is everything well? You seem—not yourself. Tired.' Catriona's gaze assessed Susanna's face, and heat eased up from Susanna's chest. Her heart raced.

'I have not been sleeping well, but it will pass. Do not concern yourself,' she rushed out. 'You look well.' And they did. She was glowing, and so was Ewan. She clung to that and shoved away the knowledge that their news would most likely shatter some of that glow.

'Join us. Would you like some refreshment after your journey?'

Catriona and Ewan's gazes met briefly before they sat together on one of the settees. Ewan clutched Catriona's hand in his own. Whether it was out of instinct or doting over his wife's present state didn't matter. Susanna was grateful for his support. His being here would soften the blow to Catriona. Or at least, Susanna hoped it would. Royce closed the door after they and Rolf had settled in and chose a seat across from all of them.

'Thank you for coming to see us this morn,' Royce began. A muscle ticked in his jaw. 'We need to speak with you, share some news. It may be upsetting, but we all felt it was necessary to tell you, especially Susanna.'

'Are you unwell?' Catriona asked, leaning forward with concern.

'Nay,' Susanna replied quickly. 'I am well. We all are.'

Catriona settled into the cushions, releasing a sigh of relief.

'It is about my trip to Lismore,' Royce began, leaning back in his seat further, 'and you.'

'Me?'

'Aye. You were the reason for my trip last June to Lismore. I was reading Father's journals, and there was a reference to Lismore, someone named Webster, and you. I also found odd accounting in the ledgers, so as a means to discover the truth, Athol and I went there without telling anyone. I had tried to keep such knowledge to myself and Rolf for I didn't wish to hurt you by what we discovered.'

'And now?' Ewan asked, his brow raised questioningly.

'Circumstances have changed. We feel we must tell you what we discovered as well as what we still do not know so you can take precautions if need be and protect yourselves.'

'What do you mean precautions?' Catriona asked, clutching her abdomen instinctively.

Ewan rested his hand on her knee. 'Let us hear them out.'

She nodded to him and refocused her attentions on Royce. Susanna squirmed in her seat, the anxiety building. Rolf leaned forward, resting his elbows on his knees.

'Father…' Royce began and released a breath, staring down at his boots briefly before he lifted his head and continued. 'He knew you were on Lismore. He left you there on purpose under the care of others.'

She balked. 'He knowingly left me there? And under whose care?'

Ewan tightened his hold on her and awaited the answer.

'Aye. He did. He sent money to a woman named Webster and her family to care for you.'

She gasped. 'Webster? I remember her. I worked for her family. They were not horrid, but they were not kind. I don't remember them ever caring for me, though.'

'Why would your father—hell, why would any father do such to their child?' Ewan asked, anger brewing in his tone.

Royce faltered, and Susanna stepped in. 'While on Lismore, Royce found out the reason,' Susanna replied. 'Laird Cameron was not your father.'

Ewan scoffed. 'You must be joking? If Laird Cameron was not her father, who was?'

Catriona stared at them all, wide-eyed and confused.

'Laird Audric MacDonald,' Royce said.

Silence fell over everyone.

Ewan scanned their faces, staring around the room. He paled. 'You are serious? This is no joke?'

'We would never do anything so cruel, especially after we have just got you back into our lives after all this time,' Rolf added with a weak smile that faded away. He looked upon Catriona with soft eyes. 'I am sorry, sister. I cannot imagine what a shock this must be.'

'It is beyond a shock,' she sputtered out. 'How long have you known?' Her gaze landed on Susanna.

'Only two weeks, sister. Once I found out, I begged them to tell you the truth. I wanted you to know in case—'

'In case of what?' Ewan asked, his posture rigid.

'There is a chance Audric or someone within his clan may discover this and take measures against us or you.'

'Curses. Just say what you think may happen. All this vagueness is wearing. What do you think the man capable of?' Ewan asked, exasperated and angry. 'I cannot protect my wife and child without an understanding of everything. If you do not wish to say it with everyone present, then let us meet separately. But I will not have you withholding information from me, Royce. I will know everything to its finest detail. This is my wife's and child's well-being we are speaking of!'

Catriona squeezed Ewan's forearm, and he faced her, lifting a hand to caress her cheek. 'You will be safe,' he said. 'I swear it.'

'I know,' she replied, pressing a hand over his own. But

there was no mistaking the tremble in her voice. It made Susanna's stomach churn.

Susanna clutched the arm on the settee for courage. Before she lost her nerve, she spat out what Royce and Rolf had tiptoed around.

'What we fear is that Audric will be angry and driven to retaliation.' Her words were rushed and breathless, but she continued. 'And that he will take your child, once he or she is born, as his own.'

Ewan and Catriona stared at her, seemingly shocked into silence. Susanna felt the glare from Royce upon her back, but she ignored it. She had had her fill of secrets and the dangers that accompanied them. Her sister would know everything she did, no matter how Royce and Rolf felt about it.

'Saints be,' Ewan muttered, running a hand through his hair before grabbing the back of his neck.

Catriona's features hardened. 'I dare him to try. I will cut him to the bone if he does.'

Susanna couldn't help but smirk at her sister's gumption. 'He will have to go through all of us, sister, to get to you and your bairn. Even if he tries, he will be felled by all of us first, so that shall not happen.'

'She is right,' Ewan added, turning to his wife once more. 'There is an army of protectors for you here and at Glenhaven.'

'Is there any chance all of this information is wrong?' she asked. 'That I am not his daughter?'

'I have found and read more of Father's journals since I returned from Lismore,' Royce answered. 'I also thought about how your colouring is far closer to that of his other children, Devlin and Fiona, than ours. It seems irrefutable, as much as it sickens me to say it.'

'Aye. They are fair of hair and eye colour as I am. Funny how I never thought upon how different my colouring is from your own. Did Mother know about Father leaving me on Lismore?' Catriona asked quietly.

'We cannot say for certain as of yet,' Rolf replied. 'But we are still looking.'

'I would like to think she didn't,' Susanna added.

'So would I,' said Royce. 'It is hard enough to accept what Father did.'

'It is hard enough to think upon how I came to be here, then, if I am not my father's child.' She worried her hands in her lap, unable to meet anyone's gaze. 'Did Audric force himself upon our mother? Or did she choose such an affair? Or was this something else entirely we do not understand?'

'Catriona,' Ewan said quietly. 'Please do not think upon such things. It will only upset you and the babe.'

She shook her head at him and looked at everyone. 'It may seem odd, but I feel I must know myself before I can bring this child into the world. You will tell me when you discover the truth. No matter night or day, I want you to send word to me. I must know.'

'Of course,' Royce began. 'If it is that important—'

'Nay, brother,' she interrupted him. 'Do not patronise me. I have had enough uncertainty in my life. I will not accept more.'

The upset and desperation in her sister's voice was Susanna's undoing. She'd been such a fool. She had commanded Rowan to let go of his vengeance as if such a thing would be so easy, railing at him for holding on to the past. Yet after one conversation with Catriona about the danger she and her babe were in, she wanted to kill Audric Mac-Donald herself.

'I must step out for a moment,' Susanna said, quickly forcing a smile and exiting the room before the sob of anger, frustration, and sadness gathering in her throat escaped. The last thing she wished to do was upset her sister further. After closing the parlour door as softly as she could, she dashed out the entryway of the castle, hugging her arms to her body and half falling down the large stairs outside the front door. At the bottom, she collided with Iona, who steadied her with a firm grip on her upper arm.

'Susanna? What has happened?' Iona asked, her eyes searching for an answer.

Blast.

Just when Susanna thought she had escaped and wouldn't make a scene in front of her family. 'I just—' she stammered, fighting off the sob valiantly before it finally burst free. 'I just needed some air,' she choked out.

'Come with me,' Iona murmured, wrapping her arm around Susanna's shoulders and guiding her back down the walkway from Loch's End. 'Jack and I were thinking about extending our walk this morn, so join us, won't you?' Jack barked in the background and gave chase to a bird that dared settle in the grass nearby.

Susanna cried against her sister-in-law's shoulder as they walked down the rolling walkway and past the gardens, allowing herself to be guided along without question, weeping as she walked. What a sight she must have been. For the first time in a long time, she didn't have enough energy to care what anyone else who happened by them might think. She had had enough of pretending to be strong. She had had enough of a great deal many things.

The afternoon sky was grey, the kind of grey that signalled the end of autumn and the onset of winter. Fewer animals were out in search of food, and the leaves on the trees hardly moved. The air was warm but hinted at a chill this eve, and the smell of animals hit her nose. Glancing forward, she saw they were at the old barn that Iona and Royce were converting into a healing centre of sorts.

'I was going to save this as a surprise for you,' Iona said, her voice whimsical and full of mischief, 'but I think now is the perfect time.'

'What are you talking about?' Susanna sniffed, wiping her eyes with the bell of her sleeve.

Iona tugged her closer. 'Follow me and find out.'

'But I am in no mood for—' Susanna countered.

Iona ignored her and kept talking. 'Wait here. I will bring her to you.'

'Bring her?' Susanna countered, continuing to wipe her tear-stained cheeks, intrigued, and concerned for what might happen next.

The barn door opened and then squeaked closed. Unable to wait, Susanna went inside. She gasped. What she saw was incredible. The old barn had been transformed into a true sanctuary. And within the large pens, fashioned from old wood and wires, she saw animals. All in various stages of recovery.

Logan, one of the youngest of the stable boys, rushed up to them, holding a bird gently in his hands. 'Lady Iona! Lady Susanna!' he called, 'I believe he is ready to fly!'

Iona clapped her hands together. 'What perfect timing! We shall set our sweet friend free, and then you can show Lady Susanna Little Midnight.' She winked at the boy.

Logan laughed at their shared secret. 'Aye, my lady.' He rushed ahead and out of the barn. Susanna followed them, getting caught up in their joy, despite her mood. Soon they were out of doors, standing in a small half circle. Susanna saw the bird clearly in the full light and gasped. 'Is this not the peregrine falcon you found along the shore?' she asked the young boy.

'Aye, he is. Had an injured wing a few months ago, but look at him now.'

'No doubt due to your care, Logan.' Susanna smiled, and the boy beamed with pride.

'And Lady Iona's. She taught me how to help him heal and grow stronger.'

'Now is the hardest part, Logan,' Iona said, bending down close to the bird, and running a finger over the shiny feathers along the falcon's back. 'You must help him remember he is strong enough to fly on his own. Set him down on the ground, and then we will wait.'

'How long?' Logan asked, doing exactly as Iona told him too.

'As long as it takes,' Iona replied. 'He must be confident and trust in himself to take that first step, even though he doesn't know if he can fly or not.'

Susanna shivered as she stared down upon the beautiful falcon that took a step here and there, stretching out its wings, wobbling and with hesitation, only to close them again. No doubt the bird was as uncertain as she as to its next steps. Minutes ticked by, and falcon grew more confident. It flapped its wings in succession a few times and hopped along. Then in one swift movement, he turned his head back to them briefly, stretched out its wings to as full as she'd ever seen, and flapped them once and then twice, lifting him off the ground in one glorious motion. Before Susanna could take another breath, he was in the air, moving away from them, rising higher and higher until he was above the treetops.

'Do you think he will ever come back?' Logan asked quietly, wiping his nose with his sleeve with a sniff. 'I'll miss him.'

Iona bent down and kissed his head before ruffling his hair. 'I think he'll be back one day, but if not, every time you see a falcon in the sky, you can know you made a difference for him. You helped him fly again, even when he thought he couldn't.'

Susanna's eyes welled. 'That was beautiful,' she whispered.

Iona squeezed her in a side hug. 'I think she is ready for her surprise, Logan. Don't you?'

'Aye,' he replied and hustled back into the barn. 'I shall ready her.'

'We will be in shortly,' she replied. After he had left them, she faced Susanna. 'Now, tell me what has you so upset. I have never seen you thus.'

Susanna sighed. 'We met with Catriona and Ewan.'

'I knew of the meeting today. But this seems like something more, if I can speak so frankly with you.'

Susanna nodded. She shouldn't have been surprised by Iona deducing such. The woman had instincts and intuition far beyond what most people possessed. 'It is far more. I am lost. The more I try to control things, and help protect my family, the more out of control things have become, and the more defeated I feel.'

'What do you mean?'

'I was so desperate to determine what the secret was that my brothers were keeping from me and Catriona, and why they were so desperate to have me married and protected, that I created my own plan to unearth them—with Laird Campbell.'

Iona watched her silently, and Susanna continued, emotion tightening her throat once more. 'I called in a favour he owed me and made him pretend to be my fiancé to keep Devlin and the others away—and in return, I promised him I would help him kill Audric, so he could finally have his vengeance against him for the loss of his wife and son.'

Iona gasped.

'Do not worry.' Susanna clutched her hand. 'I have told him I would no longer assist him with his plans, for Catriona's sake. But now that we have learned the secret, things are far worse. Our family is in danger, I am at odds with my brothers for my lying to them, and Rowan…hates me. And I cannot say I blame him. I have made a fine mess of things.'

'Why do you say that?' Iona asked.

'I was wrong,' Susanna murmured. 'I commanded Rowan to let go of his vengeance as if such a thing would be so easy. I railed at him for holding on to the past, and yet after one conversation with Catriona about the danger she and her babe are in because of the man and his past actions with my mother, I want to kill Audric myself. I feel like such a fool. And worst of all—' she continued, her voice shaking '—I miss Rowan terribly, and it is too late. I have ruined any hope of a future between us.'

'You must let go and stop trying to control everything,' Iona replied, squeezing Susanna's hand. 'I learned the same lesson not so long ago. I worked so hard to create a safe world for myself that I was not living. And the illusion I had constructed wasn't real. Not really. I'll wager you are doing much the same. Let go and live your life in the present for you and no one else.'

'How?'

Logan emerged from the barn, cradling a small rucksack with great care, and Iona nodded. 'One step at a time, and I would recommend she be your first one.'

'She?' Susanna stared as the rucksack squirmed in Logan's hold.

'This is Little Midnight,' Logan said, smiling. 'Found her weak and hungry and all alone. She was the runt, I think, but she has spirit.' He held out the satchel to Susanna.

'We hoped you might help care for her and keep her as your own if you like. She was dark just like your horse, so we named her Little Midnight.' Iona gestured towards the small mewling kitten. The wee cat was so dark that Susanna could hardly see her face until the kitten turned to her and opened her bright blue eyes.

'She is a beauty,' Susanna cooed, running her finger over the small pink nose. The kitten tentatively licked Susanna's finger with its scratchy tongue.

'Will you keep her, my lady?' Logan smiled.

'Only if you will help me. Teach me how to care for her properly.'

'I can do that.'

'Then I shall do my best,' Susanna replied with a smile, cuddling the soft bundle close to her chest.

'And that, sister, shall be exactly enough,' said Iona.

Chapter Twenty-Five

Rowan sat in the grass, setting his knife to work on the newest creation he had decided upon for wee Rosa. She played along the hillside with Poppy, her new wolfhound, gifted to her from Catriona and Ewan from the Stewarts' newest litter. Rosa's laughter and joy travelled down to him, and Rowan paused, looking up to wave at her. She tossed a stick but instead of chasing it Poppy barked and ran after her until she stumbled into a rolling ball of fur, sending Rosa into another fit of giggles. Rowan smiled, grateful for his daughter and for this beautiful autumn day, a warm one for this time of year. He was also beyond grateful for this new trajectory he had set his life upon since he'd spoken with Hugh. Spending time with his daughter was now an essential and joyous part of Rowan's day, and he cherished his adventures with her over the last two weeks.

After each day was spent and he'd continued to let go of his anguished hold on the past, his grief, and his quest for vengeance against Audric, a part of Rowan that had not been quiet in some time was now at peace, and a new part of him had awakened. Finally, the wolf within him was at bay—for good. His time in the forge had lessened as he sought to make his amends and peace in other ways. He visited Anna's and Keir's graves regularly, spoke to them, and spoke to Rosa about them. He'd brought his love for them back into the light, and with it he had brought part of himself back into the light as well.

He couldn't help but also think of Susanna as he worked. He had forced her hand by accusing her of putting the needs of her family ahead of his own, when he had done the very same by placing his vengeance for his own family ahead of the current safety of her own. He knew the safety of Catriona and her bairn mattered more now, as his Anna and Keir were already lost. Nothing could be done to bring them back, but Catriona and her bairn could still be protected, and setting aside his grief to help was the right thing to do.

He just wished he hadn't lost Susanna in the process of realising his own folly. Now he had lost her twice. Both times because he had allowed his emotion and impulsiveness to rule him without restraint.

'What are you making me, Papa?' Rosa asked, rushing down the hill towards him, rescuing him from his brooding.

Rowan hid the blade and wood behind his back with one arm while he caught her in his other and hugged her to his side.

'It is a secret,' he teased, pressing a kiss to her cheek.

'I love you,' she said softly. 'I am glad you are happy now.' She gazed into his eyes and patted his cheek with her wee soft hand before kissing it. She laughed and scrunched up her face. 'Your cheeks are scratchy again, Papa.'

'Aye.' He laughed, making a note to shave later.

Poppy rushed down to them and barked, dropping a stick in front of Rosa's feet.

'I'll be back,' she told him. She picked up the stick, threw it, and ran up the hill after Poppy.

Rowan watched her and smiled, knowing just what his new creation would be. His blade slid into the soft wood and continued making a tiny copy of Poppy, whom his daughter adored. He was so engrossed in his work that he didn't hear his sister Trice until her shadow blocked his sunlight. Shading his eyes, he gazed up at her.

'You two look like you are having a fine afternoon with one another,' she said, smiling down at him.

'Join me,' Rowan said, patting the grass next to him. 'I'd like to speak with you.'

His sister bit her lower lip, her uncertainty evident.

'Please, Trice,' he said softer. He wanted to make amends, and now seemed as good of a time as any.

She hesitated a beat more but relented and sat down next to him. For a moment, he was transported back to when they were children sitting upon this same meadow, playing side by side. A deep longing for such simplicity overcame him, and he sighed. While the simplicity of youth might well be over, he still had much joy to embrace. He knew that now. He had more ahead of him than behind him.

He plucked two blades of grass and wound them into a small budded flower, or at least, he attempted to. He laughed and gave it to her. 'Sorry it is not nearly as good as the ones I used to make. For you, Trice.'

She took it from him, twirled it in her fingertips, and smiled. 'How many hours did we spend along this hillside, you, Brandon, and I?'

'Too many for Father's liking, I am sure.' Rowan set aside his blade and twig and leaned back on his hands as he watched Rosa. He took a moment to gather his nerve and began the speech he had been practicing in his mind over the last week. It was long overdue.

'I am sorry, Trice,' he began and met her gaze.

She furrowed her brow and pulled her long plait around her shoulder, running her fingers over the end. 'What for?'

He smiled at her sister's sweet, nervous gesture. 'For not being here since Anna and Keir died. For not being a good brother, or laird, or father to Rosa.'

Her fingertips stilled.

'You took up all the duties I was too lost or sick to remember to do. Or too grief-stricken to think about doing— especially how you cared for Rosa. Talking to her about her mother and brother when I couldn't. Taking her to their graves when I could not bear to do so. It is more than anyone should have had to do. Yet you did all those things and more without complaint.'

'Brother,' she began, but he interrupted her.

'Please let me finish,' he said. 'Otherwise, I may lose my courage.'

She pressed her lips together and nodded, her eyes shining with unshed tears.

He swallowed hard and continued. 'I was so lost in grief and vengeance that I could not move forward. Even when I thought I was better and functioning in my day-to-day life these last two years, I really wasn't. I've been in a fog. I was not *here*. Not really. But I want to be now.'

'I have seen the change in you these last two weeks.'

'You have?' he asked, encouraged.

'Aye. Even Rosa has spoken to me of it. She is pleased to have her father back. Each afternoon she rushes in to tell me of her daily adventures with you, as you both call them.'

His chest tightened. 'Then I am finally doing something right. And our time together is healing me too. I have decided I will no longer seek vengeance against Audric. I have decided he will have his due, in his own time, but it does not have to be by my hands. I will not ruin us or our clan's future by taking measures to do so myself. It is not worth it.'

'I thought as much,' she said quietly.

'How did you know?' he asked, studying her.

'It was the brooch on her grave. When I saw it there, it stole my breath.' Trice pressed a hand to her chest. 'I had hoped you had finally let it go, but now I know I was right. I am happy for you. You have a life and future waiting for you to claim.'

'Aye,' he said. 'You are right. I do. Now, if only I knew how to do such. I fear I have allowed my desire for revenge to ruin some of those chances.'

'What do you mean?'

He stared into her searching eyes, so similar to his own. Should he tell her all he had been up to? Did he dare? He sucked in a breath and charged ahead, leaving nothing hidden between them.

'You may have noticed my distractions over the last two months,' said Rowan.

'Aye, Trice replied. 'You have been a bit secretive, and all this business with the Camerons, especially Susanna, had the villagers talking and me wondering.'

'Well, that was a ruse, or at least, it started out that way.'

'A ruse? I do not follow,' she replied, shaking her head.

'I was pretending to be her betrothed in exchange for her help in killing Audric.'

'Rowan!' Trice chided him.

'I know,' Rowan replied. 'It was ridiculous—and you need not worry, the intrigue is over. But along the way, I thought what used to be between Susanna and I long ago was rekindled. I thought maybe we had been given a second chance, that we could have even had a future together.'

'What changed?' she asked.

'She chose her family over me. I was angry that she went back on her promise to help me kill Audric so she could protect them.'

'Was it for a good reason?' said Trice.

'Aye, even though I do not wish to admit it,' Rowan answered.

'And now?'

'What do you mean?'

'If you no longer feel this desire for revenge, then why not take a chance and see if any of it was real?' Trice asked. 'Approach her again without this scheme between you. Offer her the you of now and an opportunity for a future. Leave the past behind and see what happens.'

'I am not so certain,' he replied, watching Rosa.

'What *is* certain? Nothing. And I have always thought you two were a match. A volatile match, to be sure, but a match just the same.'

Rowan laughed. 'I suppose we always were a bit intense, but perhaps now that we are older, we could learn to temper those emotions.'

'You will never know if you don't try, brother. Go to her. Offer her the man you are now. She would be a fool to refuse you, and while Susanna Cameron is many things, she is no fool.' Trice set the grass flower Rowan had made behind her ear.

''Tis no longer so simple,' he replied. 'Her brothers have promised her to Devlin in some misguided belief that it will provide them protection and security in their relations with Audric, which I know is a farce. The old man and his clan are not to be trusted. Despite how much I have come to respect Devlin after all he has done for Fiona, Brandon, and wee William, the very idea of her marrying him makes my stomach turn.'

'Then do something. I've never known you to accept any outcome you have not liked. Why start now?' she said with a smirk.

Rowan nodded. 'You make a fine point. Perhaps I will send word to her this eve when we return.'

'You can be quite persuasive when you set your charm to it. So be charming, brother.'

'I will try, but my charm is a bit rusty from lack of use,' Rowan quipped.

'Until then, you best get busy with that new creation of yours,' Trice added, hugging him before rising to leave. 'As of now, it looks—like a twig.'

'I have only just started, sister. It will be something beautiful. It just takes time and patience.'

'All beautiful things do, my brother.' She winked and left him to his work.

Chapter Twenty-Six

'Enjoy your nap, little one,' Susanna cooed, running her fingers gently over the kitten's smooth belly, which was now swollen with milk. The sweet girl yawned and purred before her eyes drifted closed.

'How is Little Midnight?' Iona asked as she entered the barn.

'I have decided to shorten her name to Dorcha, which means *dark*. I think it suits her. Little Midnight was far too long a name for the wee girl. And to answer your question, she is well and off to sleep after her morning feeding.'

'I see you are quite taken with her. Each day you are up earlier and earlier to see her.' Iona beamed as she began her check upon the animals and gathered their food and hay.

Susanna rolled her eyes but did not refute her sister-in-law. 'I adore her. I only hope I will be able to bring her with me.'

Iona scoffed, pausing her movements. 'You mean you plan to go through with this sham of a marriage to Devlin?'

Susanna shrugged. 'What choice do I have? I cannot refuse and put Catriona or the clan in such danger.'

'And what if it doesn't even work? Audric plays by his own rules from what I know of him. How will you feel about sacrificing your happiness if it served no purpose?'

'And how will I live with myself if something happens to Catriona or the clan?' She stared upon the steady rise and fall of Dorcha's belly. A tiny snore escaped the kitten.

Such contentment Susanna envied.

Iona shook her head. 'You are doing it again.'

'Doing what?'

'Trying to control the uncontrollable and trying to create ultimate safety and security when no one can be guaranteed such. Did nothing we spoke of before set in?'

Susanna frowned. 'I know what you said, but I cannot just let things happen.'

Iona chuckled. 'Nay, you *could* do that.'

'I cannot be so reckless.'

'Could you be in the middle?' Iona asked. 'Could you care for yourself and live the life *you* want while still caring for your family?'

'Maybe,' Susanna answered.

'Maybe?' Iona asked, crossing her arms across her chest.

'Aye.'

'Then do that,' Iona replied. 'That is what I mean. Not all is so black and white.'

'And if I want what I cannot have?' she asked, pressing a kiss to Dorcha's head.

Iona's face softened. 'Then at least you will know that you tried.'

'I hate it when you are right,' Susanna muttered.

Iona laughed and began cleaning out the next pen. 'So does Royce.'

'My lady,' Lunn called as he came in the barn. 'A messenger just delivered this for you. Asked me to pass this along to you with haste.'

Iona and Susanna stilled, bracing for bad news.

'Who was the messenger?' Susanna asked.

'No one known to me, although he wore a Campbell plaid.' Lunn approached Susanna and held out the sealed letter for her. At the sight of the maroon seal and the Campbell crest pressed into it, Susanna's pulse increased. She and Rowan had not had any communication since the afternoon in the parlour where she told him she would no longer honour their original arrangement to have his revenge upon Audric.

When Susanna didn't take the letter, Iona stepped up. 'Thank you, Lunn. I will see she reads it.'

'Thank you, my lady,' he said and left as quickly as he arrived.

'Susanna?' Iona asked.

'I cannot read it,' Susanna stammered. 'We have not spoken since our last disagreement, and I do not wish to know if he hates me.'

'But not reading it will not change the contents of the letter,' Iona stated. 'Wouldn't you rather know where you two stand with one another?'

'Not if it is bad,' Susanna replied, setting Dorcha back into her small pen, tucking her deeper into the folds of the old plaid she wrapped her in.

Iona gifted her a knowing look.

'Fine,' Susanna said, taking the letter from her. She broke the seal and held her breath as she read.

Suze,
If it is not too late, I must speak with you. I have been a fool.
    Meet me in the rowan grove tomorrow morn.
    Hoping not all is lost,
Ro

In the bottom fold of the letter was a pressed and dried bluebell. Where he had found one to send to her, she didn't know. They bloomed in the spring, not the autumn. But they were her favourite. The fact that he still remembered made her heart swell with hope.

'I must see Royce,' Susanna said. 'Where is he?'

'His study, I think. What did the letter say?' Iona asked.

'That there is still hope. I can still choose my future, so I must go.' She rushed to Iona, hugged her tightly, and then ran from the barn, across the meadow, and into the entrance of Loch's End. She had to speak with Royce before her engagement was sealed by ink and deed. She slid across the stone floor and into his study. He looked up from his ledger with wide eyes.

'Sister?'

'I do not wish to marry Devlin. I want to marry Rowan. I love him, and I believe he loves me. And for the first time since I lost Jeremiah, I want to follow my heart rather than my fear.' Her words were rushed and scrambled, and her breaths afterwards were ragged and uneven. She stared, waiting for his answer.

To her horror, he said nothing at first. Finally he said, 'Sit.'

'I cannot sit. I am not waiting for your approval or your answer, brother. I just wanted to tell you before I went to him.'

He leaned back in his chair and studied her. Then, surprisingly, he did the unthinkable. He smiled.

'Then go to him, sister,' he said softly. 'I will not stand in your way.'

Her eyes welled. 'I do not understand. I thought you

would be angry or forbid me to go. Why are you agreeing? Me not marrying Devlin may lead to a horrible outcome.'

'And so might marrying him. Even if you do, Audric may attack us for another reason altogether.'

'Then why did you go along with the plan for me to do so?' she asked.

'Because you agreed to it so readily, I thought you did not care, Susanna. When I spoke to Iona, she told me otherwise. Seems we still have work to do on not keeping secrets from one another despite the promise I made you months ago.'

'I only agreed to please you and because I hoped it might keep Catriona and our family safe,' she added, feeling weak in her knees.

'Nothing can guarantee that,' he replied.

'I know. I am just figuring that part out,' she said. 'And realising that I can dare hope for happiness again.'

'Go to him,' he commanded. 'You will only have regrets otherwise.'

'Aye, brother.' She rushed to him and hugged him. 'I will. At once.'

He hugged her back. 'And I will see to undoing this engagement of yours.'

Susanna pulled back and met Royce's gaze. 'Thank you,' she whispered.

'You can thank me by being happy, sister,' he replied. 'That is all any of us want and require of you.'

'I will. But now I must go.'

She fled the castle with haste and headed to the stables to have Midnight saddled.

Lunn stood outside the barn with Midnight, waiting for her. She slowed and stood before him. 'Are you ready, my lady?' he asked.

'I am. But how did you know I would need Midnight?' she asked.

'The messenger who brought the note told me. And Cynric and I have seen the way you look at Laird Campbell, my lady. We know how lonely you have been without Jeremiah.' He cleared his throat. 'We want you to be happy. So would he.'

'You two have been the best of friends and champions to me. I—I—' she stammered, unable to finish.

'I know, my lady,' he said, pressing the reins into her hands. 'And it is okay to move on. To be happy.'

She nodded and accepted his help as she mounted, settling into Midnight's familiar saddle.

'Cynric will ride with you, my lady,' Lunn said with a smile. 'He is just beyond the bend.'

'Thank you,' she said and started a fierce gallop. If she hurried, she could make it by nightfall, and she knew exactly where she could find Rowan, the man she loved. She just hoped it wasn't too late.

Chapter Twenty-Seven

Rowan studied his newest creation with wonder. His thumb caressed the smooth metal and its fine chiselled carvings as they reflected in the flickering torches in his makeshift forge. Had his hands finally made something of such beauty? The brooch was perfect and had come out even better than he believed possible. Susanna would love it.

If she comes tomorrow.

He set the small oval brooch in the square of plaid, wrapped it carefully, and tucked it in the leather satchel on his waist belt.

She will come.

Knowing Susanna as he did, he assumed her curiosity would bring her to the grove in the morn to hear him out, if nothing else. Whether she would agree to give him a chance—*them* a chance—he didn't know. She might very well be engaged to Devlin or on her way to marry him already. He cast the worry aside. No good would come from such thoughts.

The barn door opened and slid closed behind him.

'I am finishing up, Hugh. There is no need for you to chase me out,' Rowan said with good humour.

'I could not wait until the morn.'

Rowan froze.

Susanna.

'Oh, no?' he replied, still facing away, so he could gain his bearings. 'Why not?'

'The bluebell. I didn't know you remembered.'

'There are many things I cannot forget about you, Susanna, despite how much time has passed.' He exhaled and faced her. The sight of her almost brought him to his knees. Colour was high in her cheeks, and her eyes were the brightest of blues, catching the light in the forge. She wore her signature dark cloak, and it was pulled high over her hair.

He came to her, his heart pounding in his chest. 'Cool night for a ride,' he said, stopping just shy of too close. He reached out his hand, and it trembled along her own. 'I hope you didn't catch a chill.'

'Nay,' she replied, stepping closer to him and twining her fingers around his. 'We travelled quickly. I was eager to hear what you had to say.'

He met her gaze and faltered briefly before he began in earnest. 'I have been a fool. I was so caught up in the past and in my need for vengeance that I couldn't see you in the future that was right before my eyes.' He paused and continued. 'I couldn't see anyone, not even my daughter. And you were right. I needed to grieve for my son. I needed to say his name aloud, speak of him, and celebrate him, but I couldn't do that until I let him go. And I couldn't do that until I released my vengeance and my anger and my grief.'

Susanna took his hands in hers and held them. Her eyes beckoned him to continue.

'His name was Keir. We named him that because his features were so dark. He had black hair, wavy like his mother's, and dark brown eyes like the bark of a tree. He had a glorious smile and the mightiest laugh. He could make everyone laugh with his antics. I could not bear to remember all of those things about him, so I clung to my vengeance and my hatred. It was so much easier than remembering him and all I lost that day.'

Tears streamed down Susanna's cheeks, and Rowan wiped them away.

'Thank you for demanding I remember him, because it's what he deserved and what Anna deserved,' he said with a sniff. 'And you helped me realise I had to move on. So did Trice. I know that when I thought of moving on, I saw you alongside me. I was a fool to let you go and to let you push me away. I want you in my life if you will have me.'

For long seconds, Susanna stood and stared at him as if he were a strange creature she had never seen before, and perhaps he was. He was standing here, heart in hand, pledging his affection for her and begging her to spend her life with him and to choose him over her family.

Her answer was a crushing kiss to his lips, and he responded in kind with equal parts affection and gratitude. She slid her arms around his neck as he pulled her closer and wrapped his arms around her waist.

'So, is that a yes?' He asked after their kiss ended.

'It is a yes a thousand times over, my laird.'

'You are not pledged to Devlin? And your brother will not punish you for your decision?'

'Nay,' she answered with a coy smile on her lips. 'He was the one who told me to come.'

'You Camerons are always up to something,' he replied. 'But for once, I find I like your surprises. Which reminds me, I have a surprise for you.' Rowan opened the satchel on his waist belt and pulled out the small tartan cloth holding the brooch he had just made. 'While it is no fancy ring or gem to show you my affection, I crafted it with my own hands for you. To show you my pledge and promise for the future and to us.'

Susanna gently accepted the plaid and opened it slowly. A smile bloomed on her lips. 'You have made this? For me?'

He nodded. 'It is a rowan tree. To symbolise where our relationship began and where it was renewed. I find there is always hope and promise in the rowan grove, don't you?'

'Aye. I do. Just as I find hope and promise in you.'

Epilogue

❦

'**W**ho would have imagined this a year ago?' Susanna asked, her head resting in Rowan's lap as she stared up at the cold winter afternoon sky.

Rowan leaned over, blocking her view of the clear blue sky above, but the sight of him made her heart flutter. He skimmed a finger along her hairline. 'Who would have imagined this two months ago?' he teased. 'But I am pleased by such a surprise.'

'As am I,' she murmured, reaching up and running her hand through his lush dark hair before cupping his cheek. Rosa played at the base of the meadow below them with Poppy and a very daring Dorcha. The young girl's laughter coiled into the air, making Susanna smile. Rowan's daughter had carved her way into Susanna's heart since their engagement. She could hardly wait to care for her and try to be the kind of mother the wee girl deserved.

Susanna's siblings were excited for her match and her newfound release from their expectations. Rolf seemed the most pleased by her choice and more determined than ever to resolve the situation with Catriona on his own, despite Royce's objections. Susanna could not fault her younger brother's dogged determination. She secretly hoped he would find the key to unlocking the mystery of Catriona's conception and bring all the messy intrigue to an end so everything could go back to normal. Even Devlin had sided with the decision to end their engagement, pleased with the idea of halting such a match to thwart his father's plans.

'In a few days, we will be wed,' Rowan said, staring off into the distance, his fingers flitting along her scalp. The light skimming touch sent her senses reeling, and her mind drifted to memories of a far different kind. 'Are you ready to be Lady Campbell?' he asked, lifting his brow.

'More than ready,' she replied. 'Although—' she paused and frowned, toying with the edge of his plaid '—I do think the Cameron plaid suits my colouring better.'

He rested his warm hands along her waist and leaned closer, his voice husky and full of promises she could not wait for him to keep. 'Do you need convincing otherwise, my lady?'

'Aye,' she replied, her body humming as his hands slid down her torso.

His lips hovered over her own until she ached for them. He kissed her and lingered before pulling away slowly, his eyes hooded with desire. 'I look forward to the challenge.'

'As do I, my laird.'

* * * * *

A NOTE TO ALL READERS

From October releases Mills & Boon will be making some changes to the series formats and pricing.

What will be different about the series books?

In response to recent reader feedback, we are increasing the size of our paperbacks to bigger books with better quality paper, making for a better reading experience.

What will be the new price of Mills & Boon?

Over the past four years we have seen significant increases in the cost of producing our books. As a result, in order to continue to provide customers with a quality reading experience, the price of our books will increase to RRP $10.99 for Modern singles and RRP $19.99 for 2-in-1s from Medical, Intrigue, Romantic Suspense, Historical and Western.

For futher information regarding format changes and pricing, please visit our website millsandboon.com.au.

HISTORICAL

Your romantic escape to the past.

Available Next Month

A Marriage To Shock Society Joanna Johnson
The Scandalous Widow Elizabeth Rolls

The Viscount's Christmas Bride Bronwyn Scott
One Night With The Duchess Maggie Weston

BRAND NEW RELEASE!

A hot-shot pilot's homecoming takes an unexpected detour into an off-limits romance.

When an Air Force pilot returns to his Texas hometown with the task of passing along a Dear Jane message to his best friends ex, the tables are turned and she asks him for a favour…to be her fake fiancé in order to secure her future. But neither expects the red-hot attraction between them!

Don't miss this next installment in the Cowboy Brothers in Arms series.

In stores and online October 2024.

MILLS & BOON

millsandboon.com.au

Keep reading for an excerpt of a new title
from the Medical series,
REBEL DOCTOR'S BOSTON REUNION
by Amy Ruttan

CHAPTER ONE

IT'S SO SHINY!

Which was probably not the correct thing to think silently, but Madison was ecstatic. She was squealing inside and it was hard to contain her giddiness and remain professional in front of her new colleague. The lab she had been given for the next year was bigger than anything she had ever worked in. All the equipment was brand-new and state-of-the-art.

It even had that fresh, unused smell. Like a new car.

Only better.

The best thing? Her name, Dr. Madison Sullivan, was listed as the lead doctor on the outside of the lab. The last lab she'd worked in she hadn't been the lead researcher. Now she had a sparkling new lab and was an oncologist at a great research hospital.

It was a dream come true.

"What do you think?" asked Dr. Frank Crespo, head of the board of directors, following her discreetly. He was not a medical doctor, but he believed so much in her research that he had reached out and offered her this position at Green Hill Hospital in Boston.

"It's amazing," Madison gushed. "When can I start?"

Dr. Crespo chuckled. "Now, but I want to take you to the oncology wing so that you can meet the rest of the staff and of course, our department head, Dr. Antonio Rodriguez."

"Right." Madison hoped that Dr. Crespo didn't hear the hesitation in her voice, because she was very familiar with Dr. Antonio Rodriguez.

Very.

Familiar.

She and Tony, as he'd liked to be called, had been residents together out in California years ago. They'd constantly butted heads and just didn't see eye to eye on how things should be done. However, when they did agree, things were explosively good.

Hot.

Electric.

The sex had been phenomenal. No one ever had come close to the absolute magnetic pull that Tony seemed to have on her.

If they weren't arguing about something, they were in bed together.

The times they did get along, they worked like an unstoppable team. The problem was Tony was too rigid and took too long to take a chance. He was always questioning her. It felt like he didn't believe in her. He didn't trust her judgment and it hurt.

Too much. And that's why she'd ended it when their residency was over. How could she think of settling down with someone who didn't believe in her abilities?

Not that he ever asked her or talked about a future. And she hadn't asked him about his plans either. Tony had always been so closed off with his emotions.

Just like her father.

It had hurt to let Tony go. In the end it was for the best. Career came before love, marriage or the baby carriage as the old song went. She'd accepted a job in Minnesota and he went back to his home in Boston.

She was a bit worried that she would be working with Tony again and that he'd be her boss. Tony was head of oncology, but she was hopeful that enough time had passed that they could work together. Green Hills Hospital, or GHH, was one of the best on the Eastern Seaboard for cancer and research. This was about saving people's lives by working to cure cancer.

She couldn't save her mother, but she could save someone else's loved one. A brief stab of sadness moved through her as her mind wandered to the memory of her mom. Her mother was her whole reason to pursue this medical field.

This new job at GHH was the next step in her journey. She just needed a good place to work, to research and to publish some more papers on her research into CRISPR-Cas9, an exciting new genome editing technology. When she got some more articles published, she was going to apply to work at one of the most world-renowned cancer research facilities in Europe and hopefully with her idol, Dr. Mathieu LeBret, a Nobel laureate and brilliant physician. He rarely took others under his wing, but she was hoping to be the next one. The research facility and Dr. LeBret had made it clear that she needed more credentials. At GHH she'd get what she needed.

She was so close to that reality and she wasn't going to let a decade-old heartache get in the way of that.

Not at all.

Nothing tied her down and nothing would stop her from making her dreams become reality.

"Well, I'll take you down to the oncology wing. It's just down the hall, not far from your lab." Dr. Crespo opened the door and extended his arm. "Dr. Rodriguez will be eager to meet you."

Sure.

The Tony she had once known barely showed any emotion. She seriously doubted the inflexible Tony had changed that much.

Madison reluctantly left her bright, shiny new lab. Dr. Crespo shut the door and they walked side by side down the winding hall that led out into a beautiful atrium which had a gorgeous garden in full bloom.

"This is our cancer garden. Patients, caregivers and even staff can find respite here. We also have memory plants and trees," Dr. Crespo pointed out.

"How lovely."

And it was. It gave a sense of peace in the sterility of the hospital, a place for those hurting to find solace.

He nodded. "Ah, there is the man in question. Dr. Rodriguez!"

Madison's heart skipped a beat and her stomach dropped to the soles of her expensive heels as Tony turned around from where he'd been standing in the atrium. It was like time had stood still for him, save for a few grays in the midst of his ebony hair at his temples. There were an extra couple of lines on his face, but he was exactly the same as she remembered. Stoic expression, muscular physique which seemed to be perpetually held stiff as a board. No smile on his face. He was just so serious.

His dark eyes fixed on her and a jolt of electricity coursed through her.

Her body was reacting the exact same way it always did when she saw him.

And she could recall, vividly, how his hands

had felt on her body, the taste of his kisses, every sensation he aroused in her. His broody exterior barely expressed any emotion, but he showed her through every soft touch, every tender caress how he wanted her. She melted for him every time. It was all flooding back to her in that moment as she stood there staring at him.

Dr. Crespo was blissfully unaware, and for that she was glad. She was annoyed that even after a decade she was still like a moth to Tony's flame.

Tony ripped away his gaze and smiled half-heartedly to Dr. Crespo.

"Dr. Rodriguez, I would like to introduce you to Dr. Madison Sullivan. Dr. Sullivan, this is our chief of oncology, Dr. Antonio Rodriguez."

Tony's eyes narrowed and the fake smile grew wider, but there was no warmth in his gaze. She wasn't surprised he was being polite, but it shocked her how it bit at her. This was the way he was. Nothing had changed, so it shouldn't smart like it did. She was over him.

Are you?

He held out his hand, as if it were perfunctory. "It's a pleasure to see you again, Dr. Sullivan."

Her hand slipped into his and she was hoping that she wasn't trembling. "Indeed, Dr. Rodriguez. A pleasure."

Tony pulled his hand back quickly and she nervously tucked back a strand of hair behind her ear.

She was suddenly very hot and she could feel her cheeks burning.

She always flushed when she was angry or sad or happy. Whatever emotion she felt showed up in her cheeks. It was frustratingly hard to keep a poker face.

"You two know each other?" Dr. Crespo aske, in amazement.

"I did mention that," Tony replied stiffly. "We were residents together. We learned under Dr. Pammi out in California."

"I must've forgotten. Dr. Pammi is an excellent oncologist. Well, this is great then," Dr. Crespo exclaimed, clapping his hands together.

Madison swallowed the lump in her throat. "Yes. Great. It is nice having a professional acquaintance in a new place."

Tony didn't say anything but just nodded.

Curtly.

Big surprise. Not.

"I'm going to continue to show Dr. Sullivan around. Perhaps after lunch you can show her the oncology wing?" Dr. Crespo asked.

Tony's eyes widened briefly. "Sure."

Honestly, she thought he was going to say no.

He's a professional.

And that she remembered all too well. He did take risks, but only those that were well thought out. Tony liked to play it safe and he was a rule follower. Never made a scene, but defended himself when he was sure he was right. Whereas she'd always been a bit of an emotional, exuberant student. She and Tony had clashed so much. And if she made a mistake he'd point it out, which annoyed her.

Greatly.

She went on a path toward oncology research, and he threw his life into the surgical side of cancer treatment. They both attacked the dreaded disease using different approaches.

She'd been foolish to fall in love with him, but being with him had been such a rush. At the time, he made her feel alive and not so alone. It was refreshing after spending a very lonely adolescence taking care of herself and her grieving father.

She was a fool to have those little inklings of romantic feelings for him still. They weren't good together. Leaving him had been agonizing, but it was the right thing to do at the time.

She thought back to one of their characteristic interactions in residency.

"Why did you say that to Dr. Pammi? What were you thinking?" Tony lambasted her.

"Uh, I was thinking about all the research that I did! And how I was right in the end. It worked."

"It was risky," Tony grumbled, crossing his arms.

"And it worked," she stated, staring up at him. *"Is this why you dragged me into an on-call room? To yell at me for getting something right?"*

Tony sighed. "You just have to be careful. This is a highly competitive program."

"So?" she asked, shrugging. "I'm here to play and win. Don't worry about me. I'm strong."

Tony smiled at her gently and then ran his fingers over her face. "I know, but you're hardheaded too. You didn't have to call Blair a butthole."

Madison sniggered and slipped her hand over his. "But Blair is a butthole."

Tony rolled his eyes and then pulled her into his arms. "You drive me crazy sometimes. You know that?"

"Ditto."

She snuggled into him.

She felt safe with him. Especially in those few scattered moments he let his guard down. This was the Tony she loved.

"Could you meet me at the main desk in oncology in two hours, Dr. Sullivan?" Tony asked, interrupting the memory that came rushing back.

"Sure," she said, nervously. "Two hours. Yes."

"Good. Well, enjoy the rest of your tour at GHH." Tony nodded at Dr. Crespo and quickly walked away in the opposite direction.

Madison watched him striding down the hall, his hands in the pockets of his white lab coat, his back ramrod straight and other people getting out of his way as he moved down the hall like he owned the place.

That hadn't changed.

Tony always had that air of confidence. It's what she was first drawn to. It was clear he still affected her the same way.

Working with him again was going to be harder than she thought.

Tony had been completely off track all day and he knew the reason. It was because Madison was starting today. When he first saw the memo come through from the board of directors he thought about saying something, anything, to keep her from coming here, but that wasn't very big of him.It was petty he prided himself on being professional.

Madison was a talented oncologist and researcher; it would be completely foolish to deny GHH that expertise and talent because he still had feelings for her after ten years. Try as he might, no one had ever held a candle to her.

And he had tried to move on after she left him. Only, he couldn't.

He wanted to marry, settle down and have a normal life, something he'd never had growing up. Tony wanted roots. Except he fell in love with Madison, a wanderer.

Part of him hoped he could change her, but he'd been wrong and she'd left. For so long he'd wondered what had happened. He was sure it was him. He was too set in his ways. He had a path in his mind and nothing was going to deter him from that.

And nothing had.

The number-one complaint he always got from his exes was that he worked too much. It was true. Work never let him down.

Except that one time…

He'd forgotten that Madison was going to be starting today of all days. It was the anniversary of the day he lost his best friend. The one life he couldn't save. The one time he decided to take a risk, act like Madison always did, and it hadn't paid off.

Jordan died.

Even though it wasn't Tony's fault, it still ate away at him. He was reminded of Jordan every time he went to see his godson—Jordan's son, Miguel—who wasn't so young anymore. On the anniversary of Jordan's death, he always went to the garden and spent some time there thinking about his friend and replaying what he should've done over and over.

Not that it did any good, but it was a habit. He'd just plain forgotten Madison was starting and that he would have to show her around. Today was the day that she was walking back into his life.

Not back into your life. Remember?

And he had to keep reminding himself of that.

When they had been together, it hadn't been good for either one of them. It led to too much heartache, for both of them, and he knew first-hand what heartache looked like.

He'd seen the devastation in Jordan's widow's eyes and then he'd seen that absolutely soul-crushing and heart-shattering pain when his father eventually left his mother. His father had gambled away her future and then left them in ruin.

Trust was hard for Tony. That was also part of his problem. He just didn't fully trust Madison. She'd left him before and she was so willing to try anything. She was a wandering soul and he wasn't. He was settled here and he wasn't going to put himself through a tumultuous relationship with someone who was going to leave him again.

So no, she wasn't walking back into his life. And today was not a good day. He was struggling to compartmentalize everything, but he was a professional so he just had to suck it up and make it work. He wasn't going to be, as Madison used to call difficult people, a butthole in front of the board of directors.

A smile tugged at the corner of his lips as he thought of her calling many obnoxious fellow residents buttholes. Usually under her breath, but he always heard it. Except himshe never called him that.

When he saw her there with Dr. Crespo, it made his heart stand still, because it was as if time hadn't touched her. It was like the last time he saw her.

The only difference was, there were no tears of anguish and anger in her gray eyes. Her pink lips were as luscious as he remembered. Her blond hair was tied back in a ponytail, the same way it always was, with that tiny wavy strand that would always escape and frame her face. Her cheeks were flushed with a subtle pink and he had no doubt that her skin felt smooth and silky.

He briefly wondered if she used the same coconut shampoo. She always smelled like summer. She exuded sunshine and warmth, especially during the hardest times of their residency. She always cheered everyone up. And she always looked so darn cute in her light blue scrubs and neon sneakers.

Except she wasn't in her resident scrubs and trainers. She was professionally dressed in a white blouse and a tight pencil skirt with black heels that showed off her shapely legs. He recalled the way her legs would wrap around his hips. With aching clarity, he could still feel her skin under his hands.

How soft she was.

How good it felt to be buried inside her.

His blood heated and he scrubbed a hand over his face. He had to stop thinking about her like that. She was not his. Not anymore. It was going to take a lot of strength, but he could make this work. He had to make this work.